ADVANCE PRAISE

"A harrowing, international coming-of-age story, *Juventud* is unforgettable, erotic, and suspenseful. I was willing to follow the protagonist Mercedes anywhere; into the Cali nightclubs, to her shooting lessons, into bed with her lovers, and to the dangerous activist meetings and rallies that mark a point-of-no-return in her adolescence. This novel is part political thriller, part love story. It kept me up at night and that's the highest praise."

—PATRICIA HENLEY, National Book Award finalist and author of *Hummingbird House* and *In the River Sweet*

"Vanessa Blakeslee's remarkable debut novel takes us inside Colombia through the eyes of Mercedes, a privileged half-Colombian girl who leaves the safety of Papi's hacienda to embark on a life touched by disappointment and splendid achievement. Her story echoes the conflicts of our twenty-first century's transnational, uneasy global culture."

—XU XI, author of *Habit of a Foreign Sky*

A NOVEL

JUVENTUD

VANESSA BLAKESLEE

CURBSIDE SPLENDOR

CURBSIDE SPLENDOR PUBLISHING

Published by Curbside Splendor Publishing, Inc., Chicago, Illinois in 2015.

First Edition

Library of Congress Control Number: 2015939308

ISBN 978-1-94-043058-4
Edited by Gretchen Kalwinski
Designed by Alban Fischer

Manufactured in the United States of America.

www.curbsidesplendor.com

For my parents

"What matters in life is not what happens to you but what you remember and how you remember it."

—GABRIEL GARCIA MÁRQUEZ,
Living to Tell the Tale

"There is no one so ugly he does not have beauty within him—no one so weak he does not have a great strength, and no one so poor he is not endowed with richness … Each person is of invaluable worth."

—MOTHER ANTONIA BRENNER,
founder of the Eudist Servants of the Eleventh Hour

PART ONE

CHAPTER ONE

For years I kept my only photo of us propped against my bedroom mirror, until I lost it—the fading print unframed, each crease memorized. The shot is a poor one: we're outside at night, during a street festival, the lighting dim. I'm leaning back underneath a crumbling Spanish archway, one foot up against the wall. My long, thick hair drapes over my shoulders, mouth open as if the photographer caught me by surprise. But Manuel gazes confidently into the camera, chin lifted, eyes wide. First love—was that what drew us together, and nothing more? How have I spent the last fifteen years punishing the wrong man?

On the cusp of the millennium, 1999, we appear smooth-faced and young. Manuel was twenty-one then, and I was fifteen. My American friends are always shocked at the early age Colombians start dating. At thirteen, girls start going to clubs, having sex if they have a serious boyfriend—their novios five years older, maybe more. In a country so overwhelmingly Catholic, parents give permission because many couples marry after high school.

Or at least that was the way things happened then.

This is how I remember my last five months in Santiago de Cali. Along with most of the upper-class, I moved through my daily routine largely unaffected by the troubles: one in five residents out of work and unemployment rising, the streets jammed with listless young men, the guerillas and the government still at war after four decades, one- to two- million Colombians displaced from their villages by the bloodbaths. That January, peace talks had been suspended between the FARC, the dominant rebel army, and our president, Andrés Pastrana Arango. In February, government officials met with Garcia, high-ranking leader of the other revolutionary force, the ELN—lesser in number than the FARC but no less determined to one day topple the government, to win back Colombia from the ruling elite, and install a Marxist Socialist regime. The government was purportedly extending the olive branch to the rebels, claiming to give them a legitimate political stake and control of land—for the revolutionaries and rural poor to unite in driving off the narco-traffickers. The radio programs mentioned little about the paramilitaries, however, and I wouldn't find out until months later how also in January, these unofficial branches of Colombia's armed forces had carried out a series of civilian massacres—the main reason for the violent backlash both guerilla armies would unleash in the months ahead. All I knew then was that the year had barely begun, and all sides had failed to agree on dates and a location for a political convention to push the peace process forward.

Otherwise, the disparity outside my windows didn't faze me much. I was still mourning the loss of my first crush, whom I'd met at a Valentine's dance and whose parents had swiftly enrolled him at a military school in the United States a few weeks later, after the FARC captured and assassinated three indigenous-rights activists, all American. That was my luck, I thought, almost sixteen and still no boyfriend. Like any teenage girl, I yearned to fall in love. Beyond that, I had few desires. I had never traveled outside of Latin America; my father, whom I called Papi, owned a satellite TV but we watched few channels. I never imagined living anywhere but Colombia, if not Cali, where the mist hovered along the dense jungle of the mountainsides like the smoke from my father's cigars, and the salsa pulsated from the clubs at night.

The day I first saw Manuel, I had just completed my first dreadful term at Hebrew school. We took classes in Hebrew language and religion in addition to English, and those subjects bored me. But my father insisted I enroll since the school had the most rigorous education available, more so than the Catholic Schools or the British School. My mother had been

Jewish so the school accepted me in January, even though my grades were average. Two months had passed since then, and Colombia was celebrating Semana Santa. That year, Holy Week coincided with Passover. My school celebrated the end of the term with a Seder meal at midday for students and families, and my father demanded that I participate even though he refused to attend. He listed his usual reasons for staying on the hacienda: the work of a farmer did not stop during holidays and so on. He forever avoided discussing the true reason: he distrusted organized religion. But in his eyes I needed to make a better effort to know my teachers and the other students—more of an effort, perhaps, because I was not a practicing Jewish girl but enrolled solely for academics. The description of the Seder also bored me, and the prospect of dressing in my drab uniform even though classes were on holiday put me in a sour mood. As soon as I was done with the reading, hand-washing, and nibbling of bitter foods on my plate, I fled.

I headed off alone, since I still hadn't befriended any students. This was, in part, a silent rebellion against my father for removing me from my previous high school in la Ciudad Jardín, where Ana and Gracia, the closest girls I could count as friends, attended. The Hebrew school was located off the Plaza de Cayzedo downtown, in the historic district. I had told our driver I would meet him on the main street across the square. I walked slowly, enjoying the dry April afternoon. A crowd spilled out of the great Catedral de San Pedro, and the bells tolled three o'clock. Incense permeated the air, a scent faintly like burnt sugarcane mixed with the gritty Cali fumes of car exhaust. I stopped, curious. Old women and men, children, teenagers, bowed their heads and made the sign of the cross. An eerie stillness crept over the square. I made a sign of the cross, too, just because it seemed right, then remembered and felt strange for doing so in my Hebrew uniform. I didn't believe in religion, but nevertheless Catholicism surrounded me; only in that respect had I ever felt like an outsider in my homeland.

From a side street, a procession appeared of a half-dozen young men, bare-chested, hoisting a chipped, plaster Jesus statue shoulder high. I pressed among the bystanders for a better view. Three more young men followed, carrying a rugged cross made of twisted tree limbs. A throng of pilgrims surrounded the last trio, whose grave faces captivated me, especially the one with the lightly tanned face, delicate features, and head of thick dark hair. He caught my hand as he passed by, and I gasped; just as quickly, he released me. Only after he was a dozen strides ahead, his back to the throng, did I step away, leaving me to wonder if I had imagined the encounter. I knew I hadn't, but someone rubbed my elbow—an old man grinned up at me, eyes yellow and teeth missing, and said, "Knows what he likes when he sees it. Me too," and slid his hand along my waist. I wrestled out of his grasp and hurried off. "No shame in it," the old man said, trailing after me, and spat on the cobblestones. "Think you're too good! Juventud."

Youth, he muttered. But at that moment, I felt suddenly older. Halfway across the square, I spun around. The young man and tail end of the cross slipped inside the tall cathedral doors. Cali teemed with two million people. I wasn't likely to see him again.

In the driver's seat, Fidel snoozed with his *El País* and lotto tickets strewn across his lap, the handle of his 9mm just visible beneath the newspaper. I rapped on the bulletproof glass to wake him, and minutes later, we were passing the open buses on the autopista toward home. Fidel, whom I guessed to be in his early thirties, had only been with us a few months. Atop the dash he had affixed a plastic Virgin Mary statue that bobbed as we struck potholes, and below, a sticker of a sexy girl in a bikini—a contradiction I caught myself smirking at more than once. We hadn't spoken much beyond small talk about the weather and Cali's often-gridlocked traffic. Unlike Medellín and Bogotá, Cali's infrastructure was terrible: detours, gravel roads, and broken pavement proliferated, even in the city's center. Sometimes the commute to and from my school took over an hour.

Today the holiday had cleared the highway of traffic. We wound our way through outlying towns. The latest reggaeton hit belted from the radio, and Fidel drummed the wheel.

"Have you ever been in love?" I asked.

He glanced at me in the rearview mirror, grinning. "Why? You have a boyfriend now, princess?" Princesa was the nickname of Papi's workers for me.

I shook my head and stared out the window. "I just wondered if you believed in love."

"Why are you asking me? Your father is the one to ask."

We'd stopped at a light. A few teenage boys and older men with creased faces held up bunches of peppers for sale, sleeves of cheap sunglasses and watches. Papi didn't have a serious novia; he never did. Occasionally he had parties at the farm and invited our neighbors, hacienda owners, and sometimes a woman would stay the night in his room. But in the morning her high heels clicked faintly out the door, followed by an engine's rumble. Such women remained elusive, absent from our daily life.

Seas of sugarcane rushed past on either side, the valley speckled with the bamboo lean-tos and rubbish heaps of the poor. A pregnant woman draped laundry over tree branches, a toddler balanced on one hip.

Or did Fidel mean something about Papi and my mother? She had left when I was less than two, and where she was now Papi said he could only guess. The phone had never rung with her voice on the other end, and no letter had ever arrived for me in her handwriting. The simple life was too empty for her, Papi would say, stirring his tinto for a beat too long. She needed ideas, unusual personalities, and expeditions. I knew little else about her.

We sped around a bend. Fidel slammed on the brakes and we lurched, tires shrieking. A half-dozen Jeeps and canvas-topped trucks surrounded a city bus. We skidded to a stop just short of a Jeep's rear. A camouflaged figure leaped out, pointed and shouted at us; pock-marked and thick-browed, he was no more than a teenager. Fidel flicked off the music and snatched the 9mm onto his lap. The dozen bandidos on foot pointed automatic rifles at the bus. Passengers spilled out and lined up with their hands behind their heads, the small children wailing. An old woman stumbled from the bus into the gravel, her dress askew, lumpy thighs and swollen veins exposed. A bandido yanked her to standing.

"Get down," Fidel hissed. He palmed the steering wheel and shifted gears; our car jerked to the left. Then he punched the gas. We surged forward and swung around the hijacked bus, into the blind curve of the other lane. I crouched forward into the back of his seat like the crash position on airplane emergency cards, silently choking down the stench of burnt rubber. *Oh, God*, I thought, hoping for what or whom to save us? So this was how life could just end, one instant chatting about boyfriends over the beats of reggaetón, and then the next, smashed or shot? I recalled T.S. Eliot's "The Hollow Men:" *This is the way the world ends / Not with a bang but a whimper.*

"Pigs. Robbing on Semana Santa. You can get up now, Mercedes."

But I stayed hunched, rubbing my sweaty palms in my skirt folds. We heard about hijackings and robberies but I had only witnessed one, a long time ago: a checkpoint where Papi had paid off the armed men with American dollars. Colombians who had the means avoided rural routes and traveled cross-country by domestic airlines. If Fidel had not acted so quickly, would I have been dragged from the car, forced into a Jeep—and then what? At last the tires crunched gravel. We had turned onto the road that led up to the gate of our hacienda.

On either side, Papi's sugarcane crop arose like two pale green walls bordering the road home. Rubber-booted workers fanned across the fields and hopped in and out of pickups. Fidel beeped at Luis, Papi's main jefe, as we zipped past, who touched his hat brim from astride his Paso Fino. March and April brought an end to the dry season; the workers were draining the soil to prepare for the next crop. Our hacienda was situated in the Valle de Cauca at the foothills of the Andes, where on the steep hillsides we grew coffee, and on the warm valley slopes, raised alpacas and horses. Thousands of acres of cane not being enough for Papi, he became irritable when idle. He and his half dozen jefes, men whom I had known ever since I could remember, ran the farm and oversaw the workers who labored in our fields or rented small plots of land from us.

Our jefes lived in a guesthouse near the stable, all middle-aged but unmarried—uncles and protectors, even if they weren't our blood. I imagined myself riding next to them one day, running the farm with Papi. Most had lost their families to either the Fuerzas Armadas Revolucionarias de Colombia, better known as the FARC, or the Ejército de Liberación Nacional, the ELN—if not the guerillas, then the bloodiness of the drug cartels. In the evenings they gathered outside to smoke cigars and drink rum or beer, and their laughter drifted to my bedroom window. Our land, aglow in the sunset, stretched empty and vast.

The car approached the driveway, Fidel waved to the guard, who then pressed the button that opened the gate at a sloth's speed, and a minute later, the gate closed, the roadside robbery shut out. I climbed the slope, past the paddock and up the stone steps, inhaling the scents of fresh tamales and horses. The breeze carried the manure stench up the hill, despite the wide lawn that separated the house from the stable, which stood just inside the gate. Right behind the house, the mountainside arose abruptly, bare stretches of trails visible here and there in the dense tropical brush. Opposite, the foothills tumbled to flatness, the cane carpeting the valley for miles.

Papi sat in his chair, a stack of glossy brochures and forms next to his ashtray. He'd tucked his cotton pants into his high rubber boots, an ankle resting on the opposite knee, his shirt unbuttoned halfway down his brown chest. Gitano music rollicked from the stereo. With one hand he clutched the purple bandanna he usually tied around his head, and he pinched a cigar between his fingers with the other. Shaka and Zulu, our young Rhodesian ridgebacks, squeezed next to his chair to be petted, and our adopted strays, Cocoa and the three-legged Angel, clamored for attention between the giant haunches of the purebreds. I threw down my school bag; Papi sprang to his feet. But I didn't move; my legs had become like fence posts.

"What happened?" Papi asked, advancing. "Was the Seder so terrible?"

Fidel stepped inside, hung the keys on the hook. "We passed a bus hijacking."

"Who was it? Guerillas?" Papi pulled me close and rubbed my back.

Fidel shrugged. As Papi hugged me, I eyed the materials by his chair. School brochures in English. Papi told me to change into some comfortable clothes and then we could talk. "Take your time," he said. "I want to discuss some things with Fidel, and you're upset. I'll tell Inez to fix you a snack." He waved me upstairs and addressed Fidel. It would do no good to protest.

We lived in a split-level ranch house, Spanish-style, with the bedrooms upstairs. Downstairs we had an open kitchen—Papi disliked the closed kitchens common in Latin American households with servants and preferred the American style, with barstools at an open counter and the living room adjoined. Tile floors extended throughout both levels of the house, adorned here and there with Moroccan carpets. Inez and the maids slept in small bedrooms on the other end of the kitchen, near the laundry. My room had a window seat overlooking the front courtyard and the valley, and Papi's had a small balcony that did the same. When he was back from the fields, he spent most of his time downstairs with the glass doors of the living room thrown open. Although our leather couches displayed few pillows and the maids scrubbed the floors until they gleamed, our house always felt warm, like home.

The only exception to this was the lack of photographs. Whenever I visited the homes of schoolmates, pictures abounded—snapshots of celebrations, beach trips to Cartagena, black-and-whites of grandparents from years past. But Papi kept none on display, except for the portrait of my mother beside his bed.

As I changed out of the brown-and-yellow Hebrew school uniform and into jeans and a cotton blouse, he and Fidel lobbed heated words back and forth—not an argument between them, I could tell, but about something or someone. Probably the latest guerilla uprising.

I passed Papi's bedroom, the door ajar, and paused, then crept inside and lifted the frame with my mother's face. She had such pale skin; I had gotten my sprinkling of freckles from her. Some might not consider her pretty, but I did. Paula—was she still alive, and would I ever meet her? Around holidays and my birthday, I had bugged Papi about how we might find out where she was. "Once you're eighteen, you can go look for her all you want," he said. "But she's fragile, I doubt she could handle the guilt. Probably best to forget it."

From below, the conversation lulled. Wistfully, I returned the frame to the nightstand and headed downstairs. Fidel left, shutting the front door behind him, but not without giving me a little wave.

Papi patted the seat next to him. I slumped into a cushioned armchair; the ridgebacks stirred. They squeezed out the gap in the sliding-glass door and bolted down the lawn. The mutts, Cocoa and Angel, planted themselves at Papi's feet. The laziest of our plantation dogs, they were his round-bellied favorites. Angel licked the side of his boot like a devoted mistress.

"What is this about?" I asked, gesturing toward the brochures.

He nodded over my shoulder to the valley. "What happened today with the bus," he said, and drew on his cigar. "Things are only going to get worse. I want you to finish high school in the United States. Then go to university. Not stay here and get kidnapped."

I said nothing. Leaving—no. Wasn't danger just a part of life? Six years before, Pablo Escobar had been killed in Medellín and the Cali Cartel, headed by the Rodriguez Orejuela brothers, rose to dominate and supply most of the world's cocaine. Some fathers dealt cocaine; my father earned his living from commodities, and shipping. Those who could afford to lived behind gates and hired drivers.

"Fidel has a gun," I said. "You and the jefes have them, too. We have the biggest gate. All those guards at school—who's going to kidnap me?"

"Girls your age shouldn't be worrying about who is protecting them with a gun. You have other things to think about."

Inez entered with a tray of tea and English biscuits, my usual after-school snack. Papi poured a cup, sifted through the brochures, and talked about the American boarding schools. To be accepted I would need to speak and write English at a far greater level than I did. How could he even think of shipping me off? I nibbled at a biscuit, but it turned to sawdust in my mouth, and I tossed it aside. I rubbed my temples. "I want to be a flight attendant," I whispered, staring at my lap. "Like Tía Leo."

Papi gathered the brochures and sat down on the hassock before me. "The education abroad is much better," he said. "You could start next year. January, maybe even sooner. Then attend one of the American universities."

"I can go to the university here." I poured a cup of tea, frowning.

"You're missing the point. I don't want you to get stuck in Colombia for the rest of your life. It's not safe." He glanced around as if someone even now might be listening. In the outdoor courtyard our two parrots in the big cage squawked as a maintenance worker fixed our fountain that had been broken since Christmas. Papi said, "You can blame me, okay?"

"Blame you? I don't want to leave you. Or anything." I reached down and fed Cocoa the remainder of my biscuit.

"I should have sent you a few years ago. In a way, it would have been easier for both of us." He drank his tea and smoked in between sips, the haze hanging around his head. "All I'm asking is that you trust me on this. I'm prepared to do whatever it takes, mi preciosa. I'm glad to take care of the costs."

"Couldn't something just as easily happen to me there? And look, you wouldn't even be around," I said. "Don't they have crazies committing murders all the time in the United States?"

"There are no guarantees, it's true. But as a rule their problems with violence are not like here, like what happened today."

"How can you be so sure? I could live here for years and be fine."

"Mercedes, do you really want to find out what happens when you aren't lucky enough to get away?"

Gitano music ripped through the silence between us, the voices bellowing and hands clapping to the staccato beat. "No," I said.

"Believe me, this isn't an easy decision for me, either." He got up slowly, as if his slight paunch were already too much for his forty-six-year-old knees. "Boarding school; I didn't even know that existed at your age. I hope I'm not turning you into a spoiled brat."

I lifted a brochure. *Sacred Heart*, it read, and the one beneath read *Country Day*. Teens in crisp polo shirts beamed in front of brick dorms. "I'll pick a cheap one," I said, dropping them back onto the pile. "Even though I hate the idea."

Papi went for a cookie then, and I slapped his hand. "No, you're getting too fat," I told him. He pointed to his belly and made a quizzical, innocent face. I chucked a cookie at him; it bounced off his chest, and Cocoa snatched it greedily.

Fidel drove me to Ana's the following night for her Easter party. As we approached the Cali exits, I thought again of the bold young man outside the cathedral. Who was he? If I went there again, might I have a chance at running into him? The brightly-lit mansion towered three stories, the homes on either side dark and silent—their gates locked and inhabitants likely on holiday to beach towns, Cartagena or Santa Marta. Cars lined Ana's driveway, the guard perched in his booth in front of her father's Land Rover and her mother's Volvo, munching chips and jabbering on his cell phone. To my surprise, Ana opened the door instead of the maid. "Chica, you look beautiful!" she gushed, holding her wine glass aside as she leaned forward to peck my cheek. A moment later, I choked on perfume as her mother, aunts, and housekeeper hugged me so hard, I slipped a little on the marble floor. Before dinner, they had all attended the biggest mass of the year, Holy Saturday. Their cheerful faces reflected back from photos as Ana and I climbed the steps, the stairway so crammed with frames, not an inch had been spared—more than a few of Ana in a sash and crown from the many beauty pageants she had competed in.

Upstairs and before a wide-screen TV, sound system, and giant painting of the Virgin Mary, Gracia, Ana's cousin, rehearsed flamenco. Both had the straight, dark hair of many colombianas and which I envied, but Gracia was taller than Ana, and lithe; her strong limbs gracefully sliced the air. At six she'd discovered her passion for folkloric dance and flamenco, and the year before the Mirador, an exclusive restaurant, had hired her—the youngest dancer ever to perform there, and where she now danced several nights a week. Unlike Ana, who loved to lie on the beach, spend afternoons at the mall and salon; Papi thought her lazy and indulged.

Yet Ana, despite her penchant for luxury, ducked into church after school to light candles and pray, and spent weekends volunteering at clothing drives for orphans. Once, after I had waited on the sidewalk for her to finish her devotions, I asked her what she prayed about. "I pray for my problems, but mostly I pray for the world," she said. "For everyone in Colombia to find love and peace." Everyone? I asked, even the drug traffickers, the paras and guerillas? She just stared at me and said, "God lives in everyone, even the worst." I had marveled at her remark, and how those we thought we knew, whom we shared gossip with over ice cream and churros, we hardly knew the depths of.

I shared my encounter the day before in the square, how nothing had happened, a mere moment—yet it had been something. Did they think I had a chance of meeting him again?

"Why didn't you go after him, Mercedes?" Gracia asked. She threw a pillow at me. "You're crazy to have passed up the chance. Now he's gone."

Someone set off a firecracker in the yard. The cathedral ceiling echoed with the laughter and outbursts of Ana's siblings greeting their friends.

"Once you have a boyfriend, your father will forget all about this boarding school idea," Ana said. "Trust me, he wouldn't know what to do with himself on that farm without his princess around, and his grandchildren one day. Your own estate, just down the road. I can't wait for all of that to happen to me," she added.

We headed downstairs.

Beneath the fireplace, Ana's boyfriend, Carlos, stocky and round-faced, sat in one of the intricately carved rocking chairs plucking a guitar. A few minutes later, Ana flicked the lights. Gracia entered in a blood-red flamenco dress, her novio Esteban in black pants and a tight-fitting T-shirt. Several inches taller than Gracia, he stood erect and confident; he drew attention from not just women, but men, too.

"Come in," Ana called to those lingering, and that's when I saw him: the *joven* from the cathedral was making his way across the room. Only instead of shouldering a cross, he carried a guitar case and was grinning. He claimed his place beside Carlos, a few seats from me; his forearms and neck glistened. Party-goers crowded inside, abandoned their drinks on windowsills; in the rush, a chubby girl knocked one over and yelped, the drink staining her jeans. The guitarists' voices and the fast rhythm of their guitars in unison broke across the chatter; the dancers' swift movements and clicking heels blurred. The cross-bearer's eyes shut tight as he sang, his voice, rich and clear, swelled with an ardent longing that eclipsed the words—would he remember me? Gracia stamped to the flamenco beat, her face as stiff and solemn as a saint, eyes blazing, chest heaving. The maid came by with a tray of Perrier and I snatched one, drank it gratefully.

Afterward, the room buzzed. I stood and my legs shook. Guests mobbed the performers; a pair of older girls cornered the guitarists, laughing and flipping their hair as they thanked them. I grabbed Ana's arm, my lips to her ear, and told her I needed to talk to her right now. She ushered me into the kitchen. The door swung shut behind us.

There the mood was oddly quiet, even somber. The two maids were washing cocktail glasses and listening to someone on the radio preach about Christ and the resurrection. I told Ana the guitarist was the young man from the cathedral. "Isn't that weird, that he's here? So he and Carlos must know each other well, right?"

"But don't you know who that is?" Ana played with her necklace; a gift from her parents, its emerald studs glittered. Her status as a city dweller seemed to give her an edge over me, and I was forever trying to catch up to the knowledgeable sophistication her social skills bestowed upon her. His name was Manuel, and he was the older brother of Carlos by two years, she told me. "He's really involved with the Catholic youth group my brother and I go to sometimes—very popular. Girls chase after him like crazy. He'll talk your ear off about social justice if you let him."

"Will you introduce us?"

She rolled her eyes at me as if to say, *of course*. "Manuel, he's a good one.

Passionate, too. If you can handle that." She pushed open the door to the dining room, eager to rejoin her guests.

What had she meant by that? It almost sounded like a warning, or a challenge. But a moment later, I was standing outside in the shadowed yard, the streetlights shining across Manuel's face, his eyes once again locked on mine.

Right after Ana introduced us, she slipped off to flirt and left Manuel and me alone. The mountains made dark silhouettes by the city lights and the moon. Some friends casually kicked a fútbol among them. Their cigarette smoke cut through the heady sweetness of the tree blossoms and their banter boomed and fell.

"I saw you yesterday," I said. "In the square."

He studied me, shifted his stance. "Jeans are a much better look for you, Mercedes Martinez." A car revved on the main street, bass beats vibrating, then shrieked off. I had never kissed anyone before, and while we stood there, unmoving, it was all I could think about. I didn't want to move unless it was to touch him, to kiss that small mouth of his, place my hands on the back of his neck and draw him toward me.

"Strange I haven't met you before, since it seems like we know the same people," he said finally. "And then to see one another, two days in a row. During Holy Week, no less." I felt him taking in my white skin and smattering of freckles. Might he easily dismiss me for lacking the right attributes? Ana was sitting next to Carlos on the steps, playing with the hair above his ear. I envied her and Gracia, and the other girls I knew, their curvy hips and creamy skin without a blemish. My features stuck out next to theirs. I had a nose that I considered stubby, and thick, curly brown hair that I needed a flat iron to straighten.

One of Ana's brothers lifted a girl in horseplay; as he set her down, both gave us a sidelong glance. I asked Manuel if he'd like to go for a walk. We nodded at the guard and headed down the street.

"Are you a dancer? One of Gracia's friends?" he asked.

"Flamenco, no—I wish. I've known Gracia since grade school."

"Can you sing?"

"Sing?" I echoed. "No, I sing like a dying parakeet sounds."

He laughed a little, lightly touched my back. "I'm sure you're not as bad as that. So how do you know Ana then? From church? I've never seen you there."

"I've never been to church. Ana's parents know my father."

"Never?" He shoved his hands in his pockets. "I see."

Manuel was twenty-one. He had just finished two years at a trade school and was now building cabinets for his father's furniture business. I asked about his family. "My parents are good middle-class people," he replied, "and very religious." An older brother, Emilio, planned on entering the seminary in September to become a priest. Carlos, the youngest brother, had just started attending university to study engineering. Manuel lived with them on the outskirts of la Ciudad Jardín in a neighborhood I'd never been to, but had heard was decent. Then he asked where I lived, and about my parents. When I mentioned Papi and our hacienda, his expression changed. He pretended to study me, finger to chin, eyes squinting comically—like the ways Papi teased.

"Hmm," he said. "You don't appear dangerous. I guess you might be worth the risk."

"What are you talking about?" I trailed my hand along the low-lying branches of a tree we passed, the petals like newborn skin.

"Your father is Diego Martinez, right?" His expression was one of disbelief. "There are stories about your father that aren't too nice."

We walked briskly. "What stories?" I flicked a blossom I'd picked at the V of his shirt, and he caught it. "My father runs a big farm. Is he not a good businessman?"

"You haven't heard stories about his days in the cartel?"

I slowed my pace. I said, "People like to invent stories, I guess. Because the truth is boring."

"But it's somewhat foolish to imagine that it's all purely false, don't you think? If the people saying such things were actually there?"

"Foolish?"

"Easy, simple. And yes, foolish."

"That's crazy, okay?" I stopped and faced him. "My father is completely obsessed with my school progress. He's generous to his workers, our house staff, everyone." What was he talking about and why was he asking so many questions about my father, and not me? Was this what Ana had meant? We'd reached the small square and Ana's church. A wreath of white lilies adorned the entrance, and a gust of wind blew a lone sheet of newspaper against it. I blinked back tears.

Manuel touched my shoulder. "I'm sorry. That was silly of me, to bring that up. Of course people talk. I'd much rather hear about what it's like for you, growing up on such a big farm." His thumb traced my collarbone; I shivered. "What you're doing in downtown Cali, hanging around holy processions."

"I don't usually," I said, and laughed. "I guess I had better watch out."

"You should," he said. Then he pulled me toward him and kissed me. I clung to him hard; his hands ran down my body. His mouth tasted faintly of lime and soda water, his stubble grazing my face. I opened my eyes, caught my breath. Candles burned at window shrines. Somewhere in the valley gunshots rang out.

"I'm sorry, I just had to do that," he said. We both laughed. Then he said, "You know, you're very well-spoken for being fifteen."

"Oh, really?" This time I drew him toward me, the hair at the nape of his neck as fine and slippery as corn silk.

"I had better get your number before I leave," he said. "We might be testing our luck if we count on running into each other again."

He removed a little notebook and pen from the back of his jeans pocket. Rather peculiar. When I asked him why he carried those, he replied that he wrote his own lyrics, including some of the songs he had performed with Carlos.

At Ana's he helped Carlos load the guitars into a Honda. Manuel led me to his motorcycle, handed me a CD before he mounted the bike. "Something to keep you company until we see each other again," he said. I told him where my school was, suggested we meet up the next afternoon. Underneath his helmet the corners of his eyes lifted up. The air swept my face, the moto's roar crackled in my ears, and a moment later he rounded the block, out of sight.

The festivities over, I joined Ana's family for a late meal of lechona. Ana's father stood over the roast pig, his carving hurried and erratic; he apologized, laughing, as vegetables and rice spilled out of the belly and onto the tablecloth. Foisting a slice of pork onto my plate, he asked if I had any plans yet for my future. I talked about working for Taca like my Tía Leo and avoided mention of the boarding school idea, which Ana's parents would no doubt praise. My response drew a few chuckles and raised eyebrows, and her father said only, "Well, that would be a nice way to see the world, wouldn't it?" Then the conversation shifted to their emerald mines in the Andes; Taca Airlines evidently did not rank highly on their list of occupational goals.

Fidel and I drove home in silence, the radio off. Under the stars, the remaining sugarcane left to be harvested swirled with the breeze. I rolled down the window, stuck out my arm, and spread my fingers. In the city or on the autopista, we could never lower our windows and locked the car as soon as we shut the doors; Gracia's mother had been carjacked outside the Cali courthouse several years before. We rounded the curve where the bandidos had held up the bus. Now that side of the road was bare, with no trace of what had happened but my memory of it.

I raised the window, took out the case holding the plain disc Manuel had given me, and rested it on my knee. "Sucursal del cielo" he'd titled it in black marker—in English, "Branch of Heaven."

On the porch Papi played cards with the men, their weekend tradition for as long as I could remember. Cash piled up in the table's center: mostly American dollars, peso notes in higher amounts, plus some coins strewn on top. Sometimes visitors were invited to join, or Fidel, but not often—he probably didn't earn enough. I guessed they had eaten a typical Colombian meal for their Easter dinner, sancocho or another soup of potatoes and rib meat, nothing fancy. The cigar smoke stung my eyes, but I leaned down and kissed Papi on the cheek anyway. He asked if I'd had a good time. Guillermo's cards buckled in his thick fingers as he broodily studied them. Vincente muttered something to the horse trainer, who was absently stroking his day-old stubble; the two erupted in laughter. At the far end, Luis slapped the table's edge and swore. He was the ignorant, sloppily-dressed main jefe of the cane fields, and almost never quiet.

"Is it okay if I have a friend over for dinner this week?" I asked Papi.

"Sure. Who's the friend?" He fanned the cards onto the table. Luis groaned.

"Oh, someone I just met at Ana's. From her church."

"Talk with Inez, decide which night. Hey, did you take a look at those brochures?"

"Not yet, but I will. I promise."

Luis and two others laid out their cards with drawn faces. Papi reached up, tugged the end of my ponytail, and wished me a good-night. As I turned to leave, he swept the pile of money toward him.

Scalp tingling, I slid the glass door shut on their noise. I wished Inez a happy Easter and asked if she'd seen her family. She stood on a stepstool to scrub at the sink; by age twelve, I'd surpassed her by a few inches, her short height not unusual for those descended from indigenous blood. Papi had hired her before my mother's arrival. When I was younger and she got angry with me for letting the dogs run in just after she had polished the floors, she used to remind me that I would not have survived without her. I never heard Papi say a sharp word to Inez as he sometimes did to the maids when they didn't do something right; he had raised me to mind her as much as him.

I sat at the counter facing her and said, "So, I think I'm going to have a friend over for dinner soon, and I want you to make something really good. Maybe get some fresh fish from the market? Or maybe a pasta dish, something Italian?"

Her mouth curled up as she whisked a towel over a platter. "Something special? Who's the boy?"

"I didn't say it was a boy! Look, I haven't told Papi, just said it was a friend. Which is true. So please don't say anything." I grabbed the tail end of the towel.

"Okay, no problem. But do you really want to start a romance when you're going to be leaving?" She eyed me, resuming her place on the stepstool, blew a strand of hair off her lips. "I'd be happy to stick to parties with my friends if I were you. How was Easter dinner at Ana's? Did they serve lamb or the roast pork?"

"Pork." I swiveled idly on my stool. Luis stood giving out another round of beers, but Papi waved him off. My father's expression had dimmed somewhat. Bottles clinked, followed by muffled laughter. I said, "I wish we had a big family to celebrate holidays with, sometimes. Do you remember holidays when Papi's parents and brothers were still alive?"

Inez shook her head. "That was before my time," she said, staring down at her dishes.

"They farmed coffee, didn't they? Before the market collapsed?"

"Coffee, yes. They were good Catholics, his parents. Hardworking, honest. Everyone said so. How they each must have suffered in the end—it wasn't right. Only God knows."

"You mean they had cancer or something? Was he not there with them, when they died?"

"Cancer, no—they were both strong as mules, your grandparents. They could have lived to be a hundred." Steam billowed from the sprayer; her face a grave mask, flushed pink along her high cheekbones. She set down the sprayer and squared her stance toward me. "You know, your father and aunt have kept this from you long enough. I'll tell you, but you mustn't let them know how you found out, okay?" I clutched the countertop and nodded, waiting for her to begin.

"Your grandparents," she said, chin lifted, "they were gunned down by guerillas."

A web of cracks split across the mosaic tiles that she rested the platter against, and the counter chilled my arms. "Why didn't Papi ever tell me?" I asked.

"Too painful, perhaps. And you knowing may lead to other questions."

"About my mother?"

She squeezed her sponge, hesitated before she spoke. "Your mother, yes. This farm did not have all the comforts it has now. When she arrived, you know—the house was just a few bare rooms. I didn't think she would stay, even with my help."

"Because she was rich? From Miami?"

Loose hairs clung to her damp cheeks as Inez shook her head. She raised her suds-covered hands. "You think your mother could kill a chicken?" she asked, and mimed snapping one's neck in the air. "No, not if her life depended on it, and all we had running around here was chickens and goats. So she left. Your Papi let her go. He had to. She had a nervous breakdown."

I ran a towel over a pot. A breakdown, how did that happen? How *did* you kill a chicken? I was half-American; did this mean I wasn't worthy of Colombia, wasn't tough enough? That I might, too, end up broken one day? "But if he loved her," I said, "why why couldn't he have lived with her in America? Don't they have ranches there?"

Her face remained as smooth as a plate; she peeked over my shoulder at the men. "If I know one thing in my life, it's that your father is a good man. But I also know a few other things." She dragged another pot into the sink, dipped her sponge in soap and scrubbed. After a few moments, she paused and brushed a moist rope of hair behind her ear. "Your father cannot go to the United States," she said calmly. Then blasted scalding water over the pot.

CHAPTER TWO

Several days later, Manuel met me on the side street by my school. I had asked Fidel to pick me up two hours past the usual time. Thus began our ritual. Manuel and I would roam the historic district, buying a flavored ice or another street snack to eat on the steps of the Museo de Arte Colonial. When Manuel's shirts were always dusty with sawdust and wood-shavings, and he smelled like freshly cut lumber and the faint grease of tools. I wore my horrendous school uniform with the baggy vest and the skirt that hung to the knees.

On the main street we passed a tall building, a Taca Airlines office inside the lower mall. The metal detectors beeped incessantly; a businessman sprang open his briefcase before a guard and lost his grip. Papers flew, and both men fumbled to retrieve them. A Taca ticket agent rummaged over her purse, swiftly adjusted her navy skirt and white blouse, and changed from street flats into heels. I hung back, peering through the glass at the posters of the Panama Canal and Machu Picchu. When Manuel joked about me booking a trip, I told him about my dream of becoming a flight attendant, asked if he thought that was silly.

"You'd look cute in the uniform," he said.

We were holding hands and he drew me gently away from the glass and kissed me. Lady shoppers and businessmen in suits streamed by. My body flushed; where could we go? Since the party I had been picturing us together, out with our friends at street festivals and nightclubs, but also alone. I wanted more than just kisses and sweet touches; I wanted to be naked with him, to sit on the edge of a bed somewhere and pull him toward me in the dark.

His hand grazed my side. He hooked a finger in the waistband of my skirt. We continued walking. I bought an arepa in front of the museum, and we sat down on the steps. Below, a man dressed in a scruffy poncho and cowboy hat called after the passersby. He toted a plaster donkey that he placed on the sidewalk, gesturing for people to sit on its back and get their picture taken. But the business professionals, vagrants, and pedestrians breezed past with barely a glance. By the time the vendor handed Manuel his corncake, the Juan Valdez imitator was sitting on the poor plaster donkey like a Colombian Jesus with no place to go. Finally, a gringo couple shoved a few American dollars in the man's palm, and the woman struck a pose with the prop.

Did I appear American to other Colombians? To Manuel? Or would he be shocked if I told him about my mother—not only that she was American, but Jewish? What difference did it make? Yet I felt sure that it would. I blew on my arepa before taking a bite of its sweetness.

The streets teemed with vagrants, dozens of young men Manuel's age with a hunger in their eyes and a shiftless manner. Families, too, perched on corners with signs that read *Ayuda, somos desplazados*—Help, we are displaced. A grubby child wandered up and gawked at me eating the arepa. He stared like our dogs, waiting for a scrap of meat at mealtimes; I shrank away. Manuel got up and returned with something sugary-smelling inside a wax paper. The boy squatted next to us and choked down the steaming plantains from the greasy folds; he didn't take his eyes off of us.

Manuel asked him where he had come from, before Cali. "My village," the boy said, between licking his fingers. "We all left."

"Your whole village—why?"

"A pipe blew up." The boy raised his arms above him in a circle, his eyes wide. "Big. The kind the oil runs through. All the buildings, smashed. Like this." He crushed the corner of the wax paper.

Manuel frowned. "Guerillas," he said, and handed the boy a napkin. "Right?"

The boy nodded vigorously, plantain juice bathing his chin.

Soon after, I climbed into the car, breathless and tousled. The locks sounded. Fidel eyed me in the mirror. "No bags?" he said.

"What?" I said, taken aback.

"From shopping?"

"Oh, with Ana," I said quickly. "She had an errand, not me."

He scoffed as we jutted into the traffic. "I have never seen a girl go shopping and come back empty-handed."

I didn't answer but knew that I'd been caught in a lie. I prayed that he said nothing to Papi. We scooted around a city bus, its tailpipe billowing a black cloud of diesel fumes. The handgun jutted out from beneath his daily paper.

When we turned onto the road for home, I saw the remaining cane had been cut, the landscape oddly bare, like the first sight of a shorn alpaca. At our gate, two dozen men in faded clothing loitered, pacing. A small gang of children lingered to jab sticks and stones in the mud. The jefe Luis pranced on horseback among the mob. He and several field hands yelled for the desplazados to let us through, to leave; Fidel blasted the horn and inched the car ahead. Vincente thumbed the pistol in his holster.

"What do they want?" I asked, the window cool against my forehead. The sunken eyes of one of the displaced stared back at me. I thought him old at first, then realized he was much younger—his cheeks so thin that the jaw line jutted out.

"Work, what do you think?" Fidel said. "But we have nothing for them now." The gate opened, and we zipped through.

That afternoon Papi's brow was creased with worry, even after I approached his chair from behind and hugged him hello. In one hand, he crushed his purple bandanna. The living room sat silent, the stereo dark. "What's wrong?" I asked, alarmed at his lack of attention.

"Did you see all the poor outside the gate? Because of the guerillas, they become my problem. They want land to farm, and I can't give it to them. Not even to rent."

"Don't we have a lot of land?" I stepped over to the window.

"There's not enough to go around, princesa." He jumped up from his seat, pulled his hair with one hand, and paced. Shaka, the ridgeback, approached him with a ball and whined.

But Papi kept his cigar between his fingertips, and Shaka slumped into her place by his chair.

I fetched Manuel's album, said, "Listen to this, and tell me what you think." The guitars and voices soared. Papi strolled to the great windows. A breeze cut through the smoke. I doubted he was listening until he said, "Pretty good, this. Who is it?"

"This is who I'd like to have over for dinner one night soon. He played at Ana's party. We've been hanging out. I want you to meet him."

"You like this boy?" Angel, the three-legged mutt, hopped over. Papi rubbed her head. "A boyfriend—are you sure you're ready for that?"

"Why not? As long as we like each other." I spun the globe, my eyes following the pale golden peninsula of Florida sticking out into the Caribbean green. I hugged Shaka, avoiding the prickly ridge along her spine. Underneath me she felt warm, solid. "Will you come and visit me at boarding school?" I asked.

His calloused hands petted the mutt. "You'll come back for vacations. You know I can't leave the farm for that long." Then he reached over and mussed my hair. His cigar sprouted from his wide-lipped grin.

The evening began politely enough. Having spent nearly every afternoon with Manuel for more than a week, his meeting my father felt like a necessary formality and inevitable next step. We sat in the living room, Manuel and Papi discussing Andrés Segovia and other famous guitarists. Papi shoved Manuel's album into the player, and I reclined, listening. "A rare talent you've got," Papi said. He nodded and pointed at Manuel with the CD case. "You'd better pursue it."

Manuel stood squarely, scratched his head. "That's a great compliment, coming from such a classical aficionado as you, sir. I certainly intend to." He and I exchanged a heartened look.

Luis rapped at the sliding door. Papi invited him to eat with us, and I shuffled the CDs in the rack to hide my grimace. When Vincente and Guillermo, who oversaw the coffee farm, horses, and alpaca station, joined us for meals, they spoke little. When they did, the conversation revolved around livestock and the weather. They kept to themselves and their quarters, away from our house. But Luis left his shirt open in the fields with his hairy stomach bulging over his pants. Tonight Papi ordered wine to be brought up from the cellar. Both their tongues would be loose. Worse, Inez plunked down sopa de guineo—pork, potato and guineo infused with the savory smells of cilantro and onion, which I liked. But hardly the exotic dish I'd hoped for. Maybe this was her way of voicing disapproval over a boy; by her brisk demeanor as she served, I couldn't tell. Surely my mother would not have let me down.

Luis rambled for most of dinner about the guerrillas in the southern mountain passes. They were running more peasants from villages—extended families, their whole lives, from pots and pans to sacks of rice, strapped to the backs of donkeys, begging for work. "But I don't have the time to deal with it," he said. "Eventually, it gets easier to turn them away." He addressed Papi, ignoring Manuel and me.

"Easier?" Manuel asked. "What happens to them?"

Luis took a gulp of wine and shrugged. "If I give jobs to ten men, there're ten more behind them, and a dozen more down the road besides, on and on. They can't read or write, can't get better jobs in the cities, so they beg out here. Am I Mother Teresa?"

I pushed at the steaming guineo on my plate. The boy who had scarfed down the plantains had told the same story of carnage in the south.

"That's the trouble with the poor," Papi said. He removed two cigars from the humidor, handed one to Luis. The lid clapped shut. "The poor breed more poor, while the rich feed them."

"True," Luis said, and lit the cigars.

"It's become more desperate recently, no doubt." Manuel petted the mutts under the table. "Maybe even the dogs are affected." He cracked a grin. Papi and Luis chuckled, eyes dancing over their cigars as they puffed. Manuel said, "We all must choose where we place our energies, sooner than later. Understand we're contributing to the good. If we're not, well—"

"Contribute to the good, exactly," Papi interrupted. "Each man must do as he sees fit." He reached in the humidor, offered Manuel a cigar.

"No thanks." Manuel waved him off. "I don't know that contributions can, or should be, so narrowly defined. The individual tends to underestimate his influence."

"How so? You know, it's not often we have a bright young mind as our guest."

"Oh, I don't know that you want to hear all the intricacies of my stance. A rather heavy subject for such a lovely night, don't you think? Manuel patted my arm.

"Nonsense. This is a welcoming home. I'm eager to hear your thoughts—what young people are up to these days, I have no idea." Papi sat back, cross-legged, and waited.

"Well," Manuel said, and straightened his shoulders. "I believe the lines between good and evil are clear. And for all its flaws, the Church is trying to do it right."

"Really?" Papi said, sounding genuinely surprised. "Please, go on."

"Now, I know what you may be thinking. Are the churches in Europe filled with gold, much of it robbed from this part of the world? Has the Vatican harbored child molesters? Sadly, yes. But that is precisely the point. Evil springs up anywhere it can, if you're not on guard. A soul divided ends up turning black."

"You really think the lines are that clear?" Papi said, and tugged over his finished plate. "Watch." He picked up a knife, drew a line through the mound of rice on the edge. "In reality, some grains fall to one side, some to the other."

"Yes, but we aren't grains of rice," Manuel said. "We have a conscience. A choice."

"Pretty young for all this, aren't you?" Luis asked with a grunt.

"I admire your ideals." Papi pushed the plate aside, amusement flickering in his eyes. "And I am—that is, we are," he glanced at Luis, who gave a curt nod, "—men who prefer only to deal in reality. But I'm afraid the reality is more difficult. Is there a war between good and evil? Of course, anywhere you go. Only in some places the choices are limited, and the battles bloodier. Like Colombia. Those who have the means must leave while they can. Go somewhere less chaotic where they can make a difference. For their own good and this country's future." He called for Inez to bring coffee.

"Then why don't you leave, if it's that simple?" Manuel asked.

The end of Papi's cigar blazed sunset-orange. "I have obligations," he said, gesturing toward the window and fields beyond. "For Mercedes, it's different. She's going overseas to finish school, maybe as soon as August.

My idea of social justice is running this farm, providing jobs. If I were to leave, I would never come back."

"Neither would Mercedes."

"She can choose to come back whenever she likes, later on—if things stabilize."

Finally, I cut in. "You speak as if I'm not here," I said, my voice louder than I expected. "This is my home, too. What if I don't want to leave?" Inez set down a tray and poured us each tiny cups of tinto. I spilled some sugar as I dumped it in my cup, the espresso black and scalding.

"I'm afraid that doesn't matter, princesa. You're fifteen. If something happened to you, I'd lose my mind." Papi breathed heavily, nostrils flaring. "Though with your ingratitude, I sometimes wonder why I bother." He glanced from me to Manuel. "What do you think, eh?"

"I want the best future for Mercedes, if she wants it, of course," Manuel said.

"That's good. He's a bright boy, gets the point," Papi said. "The sooner, the better."

Scowling, I shrank in my seat, skin prickling at the tenor of their conversation. Why was I being discussed so abstractly? And why was Papi being so callous?

"Well, the obvious thing to do is leave," Manuel said, stirring his *tinto*. "It's easy. Colombia is full of men who make messes like children and refuse to clean up, just walk away without acknowledging their contribution. But I guess you don't know any of these men, Diego?" He tapped his spoon on the cup's edge before setting it down.

Luis dropped his cigar in the ashtray. Papi's mouth twisted. "Just what are you accusing me of?" he said, his voice even, restrained. "Did you come here for my daughter or just to insult me?"

"Not at all," Manuel said. He blanched. "I'm just bringing up the point that many play both sides."

Papi raised his cigar and brought it a few inches away from Manuel's face. "May I offer you something?"

"Whatever you like," Manuel said quietly. "As you said, this is your home." He lifted his cup, drank.

Papi spoke so softly I could barely hear him. "Where's your fucking farm, eh? What do you know about having forty, fifty, a hundred workers and their families dependent on you?"

"Nothing, sir. I only meant—"

"What's that?" Papi cried. "Please, shut your mouth and save your dignity. The only thing I can't stand more than a witch-hunt is a lie."

Manuel finished his tinto in one gulp and stood up. "It's excellent coffee. I've got a long ride, I'd best be going, sir. Thank you very much." He breezed out without shaking hands.

Trembling, I jumped up and darted after him.

Manuel had parked his motorcycle just inside the gate at the end of the steep driveway. At the foot of the mountain, the shadowy bodies of the alpacas shone pale in the moonlight. A few raised their heads at our approach. "I guess I won't be back here any time soon," he said. He started up the bike, and it chugged and huffed like an irritated boar between us. "Which is fine. The less I see of your father, the better."

"We can still see one another," I said, grabbing his arm. "In Cali."

He peered over my shoulder at the house. "Pay attention to the little things more, Mercedes. There's a lot about your father that you don't realize. You're too close to see it."

"Why do you say that? You don't have proof."

He drew me closer and into a long kiss. "You know Ana's church, La Maria, in the Ciudad Jardín? Sunday evenings, after mass, my brother Emilio leads a meeting. It's up to you, of course. But he has become somewhat of an expert on cartel and guerilla connections. If it's proof you want, he may have it. Goodnight." The guard opened the gate. The bike's lone headlight flew down the deserted road, as if Manuel couldn't wait to put a great distance between him and the hacienda. I swallowed hard, my mouth bitter.

When I entered, I overheard Luis. "You smell something?" he doubled over with laughter, chest heaving. "It reeks of self-righteousness in here."

Papi laughed more like a gentleman, as if he had a tickle in his throat, his elbow on the table and cigar thrust forward. "I should hire him to work a day in the cane fields with all his poor pals," he said to Luis. "Rich city boy wouldn't last a day."

"He's not some rich city boy, okay?" I interrupted. "He works hard. He's smart."

"If he's so smart, why isn't he at university?" Papi asked. "Not too smart, if you ask me."

"And he's dedicated to the Church, you know what that means," Luis said, nudging Papi. A fresh glass of wine sloshed in the jefe's hand. His eyes blazed red and he grinned too widely, like a clown. "Cooking, cleaning, and popping out babies, one right after another," he said to me. "You think I'm kidding, huh? Man, what an exciting life. I'm jealous."

"His brother's going to become a priest, so maybe he'll decide to become a man of the cloth," Papi said, and raised his eyebrows. If he was serious or facetious, I couldn't tell. "You never know."

"Better him than us." Luis elbowed Papi again.

"I like priests," Papi replied. "I haven't ruled out the priesthood yet, myself."

Luis snorted with laughter. "Only if he's still a virgin," he said. "Or else you can forget that. Is church boy still a virgin, Mercedes?" He thumped the table. The sugar bowl and glasses shook.

"Luis—that's enough." Papi pushed his chair away and wandered to the door, gazing over the moonlit valley. Luis's laughter died. He hung his head, caught his breath. I ran upstairs.

One afternoon a couple of days later, Fidel held up the rosary I'd presented him, bought from a Catholic store downtown. He looped it over the rearview mirror. "Thank you," he said. "I don't go to church like I should."

I sat tall in the back, kneading my skirt, chin raised. "I have a lot of after school activities coming up." I searched for his gaze in the mirror. "You might have to wait for me."

His eyes met mine and held them. "Whatever you say, princesa." He slid on his sunglasses—Ray-Bans, brand new. Expensive for a driver. Then he cranked up the radio and drove, the long red beads slapping the dash whenever we hit a pothole.

I arrived home to find Papi in the living room, his hair neatly combed. A slight, pale woman, distinctly un-Colombian, was seated next to him. Inez chopped and puttered about the stove, chicken simmering. The mutts, Angel and Cocoa, trotted up to sniff my legs, their nails scratching the tile. "This is my daughter, Mercedes." Papi arose, his touch light on my shoulder; his dress boots squeaked. The gringa beamed at the both of us, stood, and clutched her hands in front of her gray skirt. School applications covered the coffee table, forms and pens strewn on top. "Mercedes, this is Sister Rosemary. She teaches at the mission."

She extended her palm, and we exchanged *con mucho gustos*. The poor attended the mission schools, so why was she here? Papi loathed the Church, after his divorce.

"I hope you get along," Papi said. "From now on Sister Rosemary's going to help you with your English and to prepare your applications, for two hours every day after school."

I glared at him, anger expanding in my chest like smoke. "Two hours a day?" I said. "No thanks. It's too much. " I pleaded that I'd study extra on my own and ask the teachers if I could stay after school. My voice sounded shrill and strained, unlike myself. I ditched my school bag and stood there, arms folded.

Angel scratched and gnawed at a leg sore; in the courtyard, the ridgebacks and Cocoa tumbled and yapped in play. "Why don't you go ahead and prepare?" Papi said to the nun. He instructed her where to find the office—at the top of the stairs between his bedroom and mine.

Papi then turned to me, motioned for me to sit. He peeled the purple bandanna from his head and balled it in his fist. "You really think I don't know what's going on? That I don't know you've been running around with that boy? You haven't even bothered with the forms."

"I went shopping with Ana this week. Ask Fidel. He'll show you the gift I bought him."

He raised a hand. "Don't cross me, hija."

I drew a pillow onto my lap and picked at its fringed trim.

He sifted through the applications, held up a form. "These are complicated," he said. "They must be filled out correctly, and my written English is not perfect. Besides, you have to pass a language exam. So I asked around. Our neighbors recommended the nun."

He clenched and unclenched the bandanna. His expression was one of sadness. Why did he act as if this was the only hope for me? If Colombia was so dangerous, why hadn't we already left? Didn't he understand that I was bound to break out—pursue my own ambitions, however I chose? That if I went to the United States, I would somehow seek out my mother, her family? I could not see myself at boarding school and ignoring the possibility that she might be a few cities or states away. The dog whined in her throat. Finally he said, "Three days a week, then. But you had better be here at exactly four o'clock on those days, with your nose in those books. Monday, Wednesday, Friday." He struck his finger to his knee as he named the days. Then handed me the bandanna and told me to dry my face and get upstairs. Tears wet my stiff yellow blouse. My brown vest gaped.

Sunday afternoon the house hummed and creaked, deserted but for the spinning fans and parrots in the courtyard cage. Papi and the men had gone to a horse auction, and the maids had the day off. I left and caught the bus on the valley road. Every time we creaked to a halt, I swallowed and tried to squelch the nausea brought on by the diesel fumes, cow manure, and fear. We passed where the bandidos had set up their roadblock, and I raked my sweaty palms over my thighs. My friends and I were forbidden to even ride the city buses in Cali's center because armed bandits hijacked those, too, despite the police. But today the only presence blocking the road was a herd of cows. The driver honked, the cows trotted to the side of the road, and I exhaled in relief.

Manuel met me at the bus stop, on the corner of La Maria church where we had first kissed. He steered me across a courtyard with well-manicured rosebushes and into a smaller makeshift outbuilding—no more than a frame constructed of two-by-fours with plastic sheeting for sides and a roof and a few dozen folding chairs arranged in a semicircle. Young people streamed in after us. He refused to tell me what the meeting would be about, just said, "You'll see," and nodded toward the front. A young man dressed in a collared blue shirt and jeans stood there, hands on hips. He surveyed the assembly similar to the way Papi observed our alpacas from the fence. "My brother, Emilio," Manuel said.

But for subtle differences, I might have guessed they were twins: Emilio stood a few inches taller and broader than Manuel, whose build remained slight, more boyish. Yet they had the same soft black hair, the same delicate jaw line and cheekbones, the same eyes.

Emilio called the room to attention. Bodies squeezed together; a faint odor of perspiration and cologne filled my nostrils. Carlos took the last chair by the entrance, and Ana slid onto his lap. Those gathered fell quiet.

The meeting turned out to be an open forum on how the Catholic Church advocated that the local community might peacefully defend itself against the two dominant rebel groups, the ELN and the FARC. Since January, attacks and kidnappings on the Church and civilians had sharply arisen across Colombia, but especially in the Andes region—incidents like the bus hijacking, as one young man brought up in a quivering voice, toying with his ponytail as he stood above the crowd. "How is turning the other cheek going to faze these so-called revolutionaries?" he said. Emilio reminded everyone that it wasn't just the leftist guerillas who terrorized civilians, but the paramilitaries who infiltrated villages controlled by the ELN or the FARC, then rounded up and assassinated anyone deemed "sympathetic" to the guerillas' cause. Despite the fixation of the politicians and media on the guerillas, the paras were responsible for a majority of the violence and horrific civilian massacres. "Sympathizers" included pharmacists who filled prescriptions for guerilla leaders, doctors who treated them, even bus drivers who had provided transport—ordinary citizens just doing their jobs who faced torture or death at the hands of the paras if they didn't comply.

I had listened to enough of Fidel's radio broadcasts to know both factions caused most of Colombia's unrest. But I had never paid much attention to exactly what occurred in which province or town—now I wondered why I hadn't. Had I believed our military and the paras a lesser evil, if such a thing even exists? Emilio was correct—the media focused mainly on the threats posed by the guerillas. "The private armies of the Autodefensas only protect the wealthy," Emilio was saying. "Some of you may even know those who fund the AUC. But we must stand against them as well as the guerillas." Military patrols had cut through our hacienda on their way into the mountains, and Papi invited them to stay for dinner, spend the night. The soldiers who had shown up last year—hadn't Fidel been one of them? He'd been in uniform when he asked Papi for a job after returning from their mission; Papi even addressed him as Captain. Had the troops been military or paramilitary, and what had been the lettering on their uniforms? Was Fidel, with his Virgin Mary figurine on the dashboard, capable of slitting a bus driver's throat for giving a guerilla a ride? Maybe Papi had just been polite in housing them—or they didn't give him a choice. Emilio said the Colombian army and paramilitaries were one and the same, that the paras simply carried out the dirty work of human rights abuses that the army wanted "taken care of" but didn't want to be responsible for.

Manuel leapt up. "How much longer will it be before the Church toughens its stance against both insurgencies?" he asked. "Archbishop Duarte states that it is his personal duty to take on the risks himself in trying to protect his people. Why don't the rest of us do the same—isn't it our right?" But his words only met a silent room, with heavy looks exchanged over clasped hands and the creak of chairs. No one agreed with or challenged him, not even Emilio.

After the meeting's close, Emilio walked toward us. The two brothers exchanged a quick embrace. "What're you doing up there, Professor? Trying to put the audience to sleep?" Manuel said, brushing his brother's shoulder in a playful jab. Emilio, grinning, shook his head and clicked his teeth. "You just better stick to building cabinets." Their easy way with each other made me yearn for a sibling. Manuel introduced us, and when Emilio's lips brushed my cheek my stomach flipped. I hoped Emilio had not felt anything.

Emilio ushered us over to a table and folding chairs in the corner, away from the young people chatting in clusters—a small relief. Dampness chafed my underarms. Ana waved, exiting the tent behind Carlos. Manuel disappeared and returned a moment later, handing us each a cup of lukewarm water; I managed a few tiny sips, the water too chlorinated for my taste. A street lamp lit the worn face of the courtyard Virgin, her robe and feet hidden by roses, in full bloom and deepest red. "So tell me what it is you do again," I said to Emilio. "Besides studying to be priest. Since you don't build cabinets."

"Cabinets, no," Emilio said. He and Manuel exchanged small smiles, and Manuel chuckled in his throat. "Only one of us is handy with a saw, I'm afraid. Hmm, what to call my current duties? A peacekeeper, of sorts?"

"More like a go-between," Manuel said, adjusting his seat. "Right? A liaison."

"That's it." Emilio nodded, sipped some water. "I'm a representative for the diocese between the guerilla leaders and the government. So I have access to diocese records going way back. The Church is rather excellent at keeping records. Among other things." He rolled the cup, light now, in his slender fingers; his hands lacked the musculature of Manuel's.

"What does that have to do with anything?" I asked.

Emilio removed a folder and legal pad from a backpack, placed a document before me. Even in the dull light, the seal glimmered; an ink smudge marked the tail end of a signature. He said, "I don't suppose you know that your father, Diego Martinez, was formally excommunicated in the early nineties? Or what might have led to that?"

I lifted my cup and let the water touch my lips but didn't drink. "His divorce," I said. "He says the parish priest won't even look at him if they run into each other—that he crosses the street."

"Divorce? That's what he told you?" Emilio's remark sounded more a statement than a question. "According to church records, he and your mother were married in 1982, divorced the following year, and he received an annulment a few months after that. He had to be in good standing at the time to get an annulment."

"What does that mean? He got into an argument with the priest or something?"

Manuel leaned forward on his elbows and lowered his voice. "The Church mandates excommunication for a variety of things." He closed his hand over mine and squeezed, the coarse warmth of his palm jarred me ,but I didn't pull back. "In the case of your father, for very specific reasons. It was the eyewitness testimony of a former cartel operative that turned him in."

"Cartel?" I said. "That's impossible." Somewhere in the middle of the tent a cell phone rang. The young man with the ponytail answered it, talking excitedly. His group rocked with laughter. "If you're going to make accusations like that, you'd better have proof."

The brothers exchanged knowing looks. Manuel nodded toward the manila folder, and Emilio withdrew a stapled packet. "This is the testimony of a dear friend, Father Juan. Only much later in his life did he find the Church. Before that, he was a subordinate in the drug war until after the collapse of the Medellín cartel. This is far too long for you to read tonight," Emilio said, and tucked the packet back inside the folder. He folded his hands on top. "I'll just tell you his story."

Emilio was seventeen when he heard Father Juan speak at a youth retreat, a soft-spoken man, broad and graying, with a rosary cinched to his cargo pants. Once, when Emilio had gone to visit an impoverished village the priest was ministering to in the southern Andes, they'd gone to swim at a waterfall, removed their clothes. A knotted patchwork of bullet wounds scarred the priest's shoulder. What had happened for this man, in mid-life, to repent and work to rescue those most at risk to join the guerillas? Father Juan removed his glasses, and as he rubbed them with the end of his shirt, he stared at the peasant teenagers diving and shouting. "Some are born with black hearts—do you believe that?" the priest asked. "Well, I don't. The heart is the most neglected aspect of humanity, and the most critical. How it grows, whether it hardens with greed and fear or expands with love, depends on how we each are taught to feed it. When it turns black, the only way to reclaim it is through pain."

Even the three bullets hadn't been enough to stop him, back when he was known as Juan Perez. That wasn't what drove him inside a village church in the Andes one night, where he crawled up to the altar on his knees and prostrated on his belly, begging God for peace and salvation or else he'd get back in his car and, alone on his way to Medellín, drive himself off the next cliff. Escobar's empire was collapsing. The heads of the Cali cartel, the Rodriguez Orejuela brothers and their subordinates, including Juan Perez and Diego Martinez, had given themselves the name Los Pepes and arranged the murders—"as clean as possible" they had agreed upon meeting. Then one of Escobar's traffickers received the bloody head of an alpaca on a platter, with a note threatening that he would be "the first of his herd to go to the slaughter." Two days later he went missing.

Juan Perez hadn't known about the hit. He suspected Diego had carried it out because he raised alpacas on his plantation. When he confronted Diego and asked what they had done with the trafficker, if he had used him to find out some crucial information, Diego told Juan he could find him in the alpaca pasture and do the questioning himself. Instead, Juan found the man's body disemboweled, dumped behind the alpaca shed. Vultures circled and picked at the bloated corpse. The stench was rancid from ten feet away.

That was what had driven Juan from Cali that night, into the chapel, never to return to the cartel.

"From Father Juan, I saw just how important it is to stay connected to the youth—not just the peasants who are drawn by the guerillas, but those who think that joining the paras will keep their families' lands safe," Emilio said, voice husky. He cleared his throat. "Around that time your father abruptly ceased cartel activity, which is why we suspect he had a falling out. That's why, even though his businesses have been legitimate for over a decade, we think he pays people off to keep quiet. Or receives illegal payments himself for the same reason. To which organization, we're not sure. Silence commands a hefty price."

"No one knows for sure," Manuel added. He cupped the back of my neck gently; his hand felt cold. "We're trying to find evidence that proves the current connection. Your father has been a person of interest to the Colombian and American authorities, and to activist groups, for a long time."

"But this isn't just some rumor," I said. My stomach had become granite. "Father Juan's not some employee, upset because my father fired him. And you're telling me he's still involved somehow—Diego?" How desperately I wanted it not to be true. His name on my tongue, those three syllables I wasn't used to uttering. Another name, another life.

Men with automatic rifles had once stood watch from towers across our property and patrolled at night. The ninjas, I'd called them—stone-faced young men, their snug black T-shirts and camouflaged pants showing off trim physiques. I had darted behind the fountain whenever they crossed the courtyard in jaunty strides, throwing the caps of their Coca-Colas onto the stonework. Their Adam's apples jutted toward the sky as they tipped the bottles upward and guzzled. Their shoulders rippled beneath the rifles strapped to their backs. After the cartels, the violence had waned for a time. The posts they'd occupied had long since gone deserted, my ninjas happily forgotten, and Papi allowed both displaced and tenants to dismantle the towers for firewood and building materials. A guard still kept watch twenty-four hours, in the small room over the main gate, roughly a hundred meters from the main house—a fixture at the large haciendas. "It's a big farm, you know," I said quietly.

"He provides a lot of jobs, it's true," Emilio said. "We're convinced that individually, he's not a threat—not anymore. But he still contributes to the larger problem of doling out payoffs for protection. And that's a very big deal."

A gust lifted the tent flap, the light bulbs swaying overhead. We were the only three left. I clung to Manuel's shoulder as we arose. Speckles, gray and white, dotted the Virgin's face in the streetlight; the water streamed in its silvery arc, but I couldn't hear it. Dizzy, I collapsed into Manuel. He led me to a bench, waved his brother away.

"What do I do now?" I cried softly. "What do I do?"

Manuel didn't speak, just stroked my hair. His eyes had momentarily lost their liveliness; I could tell he felt sorry for me. The pungent fragrance of roses mixed with the odor of cooked meat from a street cart, and my stomach turned. Children milled around the cart, eating chorizo on a stick. "I can't have girls sleep over, but in this case my parents would let you stay with us," he said, and after a pause, "Do you want to go back?"

I wanted to see his house, meet his parents—but like this? I shook my head. The lights of the bus flashed at the crest of the hill.

"Look, you're not taking the bus. Hop on my bike."

"If Papi sees you—"

"So what?"

He removed his jacket and I wriggled into the sleeves. The leather was warm, the rest of me numb.

Moments later, we whipped down the autopista. I had never ridden a moto before, and as I clung to Manuel, his T-shirt billowing white in the moonlight, I thought: this is what it means to be free, to never die. We were going fast, but I wanted it. The world revealed itself in a new way, more alive. Low overhead, a passenger jet roared in ascent from the nearby Cali airport, heading north out of the valley. What power airplanes possessed, to remove people from one place, to deliver them into a new life. No doubt it was headed for another country, perhaps even the U.S. One day soon I might board one of those flights, either on my way to study in an oddly named state of snow, or to work in a uniform, dress shoes, and pantyhose, wheeling a suitcase.

We swooped down the exit ramp, through the outlying towns that led to the hacienda. The one- and two-story pulperías and shops loomed like gravestones, their fronts shuttered, graffiti splashed over the corrugated metal. Inside a well-lit market, men and boys played pool, the music pulsating through me. I shivered, my legs cold; Manuel must have been freezing in his thin shirt. A skinny, filthy man warbled and staggered along the crumbling sidewalk, one of Cali's many crack heads. The street reeked of trash and old rainwater. We turned at the zapateria where Papi and the hired men had their boots and holsters made. Tonight no boots or belts hung outside on display, but the small shop stared back, shadowed and asleep.

Cali lay beneath us as we hugged the winding hillside, the city ablaze like the candles lit by parishioners. We passed the turn where the bus had been robbed, but I felt safe. Then we descended down a side road spotted with boxy middle-class homes, the cars squeezed in short driveways behind locked gates, one after another like rows of prison cells. The scent of earth and cows replaced the city stench, and then the flat road to the plantation, muddy from the recent rains, with Papi's fields stretching out on either side as far as one could see to the tree line of the jungle and the slopes where the coffee grew wild. At last the hacienda came into view.

Manuel dropped me off a few dozen meters away. I pushed the button on my keychain to open the gate, the barbed wire on top glinting in the moonlight. On the concrete walls the wire was partially hidden by the purple bougainvillea that grew over the top, but here and there the metal still shone. One of the ridgebacks, Zulu, jumped to her feet and growled low as I passed until I called her name and reached to pet her. The stereo glowed on the mantle, the dinner dishes dried in the rack. I shut the door behind me, but inside appeared different, altered: Papi was watching a news bulletin and drinking beer from a sweating bottle, both unusual activities for him. As soon as I walked in, he muted the TV and bolted to his feet.

"Sorry I'm late," I said.

"Where have you been all evening, eh?" He clamped a hand on my shoulder, steered me to the couch, and sat us both down. Before I could wriggle aside, I caught his scent and cologne, and trembled.

The Papi you know is different than the man Emilio talked about, I told myself, breathing long and slow. *Right now it's just you and Papi.*

"I went to church," I finally said. After the long ride home I had figured that Manuel's idea to tell the truth—or at least the part I was able to tell—was better than a lie. I said, "I took the bus because I was afraid to tell you."

"To church?" He brushed his palms on his jeans and stood up. "That's one thing. Taking the bus is another. What the hell were you thinking?"

"I'm sorry."

"*Sorry* works nicely until you're dead. Then it's harder to say."

"I hear you, Papi!"

He bumped the coffee table, knocking a magazine to the floor. He didn't bother to pick it up. "Listen, with this boy business, I don't want any sneaking around. From now on, we must be honest with one another. That's all I ask, okay? Now which church was it?"

"You didn't need to worry. I was in the nice part of town."

"Which church?"

"La Maria, where Ana goes."

He set down the beer hard, drew back and began to rub his temple—then shot forward and swatted the bottle, knocking it to the floor. Beer trickled out as it rolled, hollow against the tile. The dogs scattered from their places, skirting the spilled contents. "Very disappointing," he muttered, and then more loudly, "Never are you to go there again, is that clear?"

I cringed. Was this the parish that had excommunicated him years ago? "The service went fine," I mumbled. "I don't understand."

"What don't you understand? Are you stupid or something? It's trouble," he screeched, voice cracking in fury. The veins on his neck bulged like barbed wire. "You might as well forget applying to those fancy schools—they won't want you. Tell me, have I raised an idiot? Eh?"

No, that's you, I thought and bit my knuckle, mind racing. I didn't know yet what I was going to do. I couldn't tell anyone what I had found out; I could not see myself telling Ana or Gracia. Nor could I run away to Cali or anywhere else, to get lost in a barrio with prostitutes, drug addicts, and the displaced; I would be killed. I had no money, no bank account that I knew of—he gave me an allowance every week to buy arepas after school, more if I was going to a street fair or shopping. "Do you know nothing?" he cried. I remained frozen, afraid to stay for what other awful things he might say. Afraid to go.

Finally he stopped. He knelt on one knee at the coffee table between us, removed his tobacco pouch and papers from his shirt pocket. "The school deadlines are the end of this month," he said, and jerkily began to roll a cigarette. "You don't realize, mi hija, but some people would think nothing of kidnapping or killing you. And I can't protect you forever. So leave, or it will only be a matter of time." He spilled some leaves and swore—"Imbécil!"

"Imbécil?" I said at last, rising. "You raised me. And I do realize it. Protect me—you think I have no idea what goes on around here?"

He crushed the cigarette between his lips, snapping the filter, cursed, and rerolled it. The embers flared. Smoke, leafy and sweet, trailed me up the steps.

CHAPTER THREE

The next morning, Papi had been up for an hour when I stowed my book bag in the back of the car. He, Luis, and some farmhands faced the just-risen sun with Papi's back to me. The courtyard fountain sloshed, drowning out their talk. Fidel sat on its lip, dazed, and flicked the ash of his cigarette. When I said, "Let's go," he looked up in surprise and irritation and pitched the butt onto the stone pavement. Papi's voice boomed as he headed for the house, chiding me for skipping breakfast. When I told him I'd grab an arepa outside school, he said, "You eat too many of those greasy things. Get inside."

Sulking, I followed. At the dining table we sat in silence. The smell of coffee, eggs, and warm bread trailed Inez as she set our plates in front of us, and Papi his tinto. "Eat up," he said, digging into his gallo pinto. "You'll need a lot of energy if you're going to wear that frown."

"How do you expect me to feel, after last night?" I asked.

"I'm sorry for blowing up," he said. "Finish those applications, and you can go to all the masses you want. I used to be quite devout at your age."

"I don't believe you."

"If I still talked to family, I would tell you to ask them."

I chewed slowly, the beans and rice flavorful but lukewarm. Other than Tía Leo, Papi didn't speak to relatives—because of his divorce, he'd claimed. "Divorce isn't such a big deal," I said. "Gracia's parents are Catholic, and they're divorced. Why would anyone hold that against you?"

"It wasn't just the divorce. I brought a lot on myself, especially after your mother left, but I never turned my back on family." He scraped the last of the beans and rice from his plate with quick, harsh strokes. "I crawled to them on my belly, but they turned their backs to me. Tell me, what choice does that leave?" Someone opened the front door—Luis. He announced that an alpaca had gone missing, a young one. A field hand was searching for it.

"Couldn't have gone far," Papi said. He shoved his chair away, tied his bandanna around his head, and groped his shirt for his sunglasses. When I was little, I had liked this look of his and used to call him a pirate until he chased me around the house.

"I'm sure he'll find it soon enough," Luis said, fist on hip. "No use you wasting your morning digging through brush."

Papi breezed past him. "Morning light is best. Won't be the first time."

Now I wondered: had Papi's brothers been killed along with my grandparents or suffered a different brutal fate, and were our other relatives alive or not? Surely we must have aunts, uncles, cousins somewhere? Our land included his parents' old property, and he rented their cement-block house to a tenant farmer's family. Minutes later, Fidel and I wound along the narrow country roads and past the plots of such farmers, their houses little more than shacks. Once, when riding along in his pickup, Papi had told me how he had thought his family wanted for little until he was twenty-one. That spring he spent two months in Bogotá with an older cousin, ate at fine restaurants and attended the theatre for the first time, danced at clubs with beautiful women. When he returned, everywhere in the countryside there seemed no escape from poverty. That day we'd driven for three minutes before we finished passing the displaced. "Los miserables de Dios," he muttered even as he waved, speakers booming Rachmaninov.

Late that afternoon, in the muggy upstairs office of our house, I combed through a Spanish-English dictionary. My elbow pressed upon the pile of applications. Papi had filled out some of the information—his careful block handwriting scrawled across the boxes at the top—and Sister Rosemary ticked off and completed the rest. Twenty minutes remained for the session, but we had not even finished two forms. "You'll need to write a lot faster and not make so many mistakes if you're going to take regular subjects in English," she said. Her pale eyebrows rose.

"If it's so easy for you, why don't you write it?" I slouched, dropping the pen. "Isn't my father paying you?"

Jaw set, she thrust the pen back at me. "For tutoring, yes. Not baby-sitting."

My face burned through to my scalp. I snatched the pen. "The questions in the boxes—I don't even know how to answer some of these."

She lifted a form, glancing over it. "Which ones?"

"Like this one: *Describe your participation in clubs, leadership roles, or volunteer organizations.*"

"Straightforward enough, don't you think?" She replaced the form before me, folded her hands in front of her.

I hesitated, then wrote, *La Maria Juventud Para Justicia Social.* After a pause, I added: *Secretary & Event Organizer.* What did they know? It certainly sounded impressive.

The nun looked over what I'd written and frowned. "La Maria Juventud? Is this true?"

"Sure," I said. "I'm very involved. Why do you care?"

Her lips made a thin line. She shrugged, then nodded at the form. "Please, finish."

Papi poked his face in the doorway at six o'clock and asked if she would join us for dinner, then about my progress. She showed him the incomplete forms, and he pouted, stroking his stubbly chin. "I want all eight of these in the mail, Federal Express, by Monday," he said.

Could I miss the deadlines on purpose? What if the forms weren't ready, and I had to wait another six months to apply again? I wanted to be with Manuel, not in my father's swivel chair, an oversized dictionary in front of me, next to a woman who had never been in love. "But aren't there admission tests?" I asked. "I'm not ready at all. Won't I miss those deadlines?"

"Mercedes has a boyfriend now," Papi said. "She's somewhat distracted." He smirked and reminded me of Luis. "We must convince her that going to one of these schools will be the biggest adventure of her life. She will never look back." Then he left, humming a tune.

Shades of pink blanketed the sky as Sister Rosemary organized the forms and gathered her things. I wasn't sure how I felt about her. She didn't seem cold, exactly, just somewhat removed. She was an outsider, so perhaps it was part of her gringa personality. North Americans had different ways, and I guessed my mother had them, too. I might never know.

"Do you ever wish you had stayed home, and not come to Colombia?" I asked.

She wound an indigo shawl around her shoulders; it appeared a deep purple in the dying sunlight. "I miss my family, it's true," she said, tucking the fringed ends underneath her arms. "But with God, I have learned to accept it. I wanted to see the world, know myself. Sometimes the only way to see your life clearly is to leave it."

The mood at dinner couldn't have been more unlike the disaster of Manuel's visit the week before. Papi sat tall as he ate, joked, and steered clear of topics like the Church and the poor. In Miami, he boasted, the city streets smelled like exhaust but not trash. Every middle-class family had two cars so that six people didn't cram into a single one the size of a shoebox. The homeless pushed carts and begged underneath the highway ramps, but you didn't see nearly as many of them, certainly not so many women and children.

Sister Rosemary disagreed, however. She pointed out that America had just as many faults as Colombia, and if the problems didn't seem so glaring it was because Americans were not fighting the same types of wars inside their borders. But the wars were still there—over lack of health care, drug addiction, the environment. When I lived in America, I constantly felt like I was wearing a beautiful coat, she said, shiny and well-tailored on the outside, but inside the lining was ripped and the coat was not so warm.

Here, neighbor helped neighbor. The zapateria owner stopped by the mission every week, fixed belts and resoled shoes for the desplazados, for free. Once she had helped lead a peace rally downtown when a dozen youth from a cosmetology school arrived, turning heads with their outrageous dye-jobs and stylish jeans. They fanned out into the worst streets, combs, capes, and scissors in arm, to give free shampoos and haircuts; when asked, they said wasn't that a surefire thing to lift the spirit, and needed by everyone? If more Americans saw firsthand the horrors here of dead bodies in ditches and the number of people who barely had beans and rice to eat, there would be riots, she said. But most Americans did not see it, so they did not care.

Papi nodded, his face as grave as when he had set off to find the alpaca earlier.

She had not only finished college but earned a higher theology degree in Chicago, one of the northern cities. I didn't know any Colombian woman who was so educated and not a doctor or a lawyer. "I wish I could have had the opportunity to study in the United States," Papi said, giving his mouth a quick pat with his napkin. "But I made my choices, and at a certain point it is too late."

"But why couldn't you?" I asked.

"Most people in this country cannot afford tutors to get them into American schools," he said. "I had to make money, so I worked in the commodities business, and then decided I wanted to farm. And I met your mother."

I blew on my steaming ajiaco. If he had married my mother, wouldn't he have become an American citizen then, able to come and go freely to that country, and stay? Perhaps they hadn't gotten married, and she had me illegitimately. Was that why his family turned their backs, being such devout Catholics? But then the Church here had the records of the marriage and annulment; Emilio had shown me. So Papi and Paula must have gotten married here. And with a half-American daughter, why wasn't he a dual citizen?

"Why did you leave the States then, if it was so great?" I asked.

He sopped up his soup with a piece of bread. "America has many good opportunities for some businesses but not for others. I wasn't happy there until I met your mother. By then I had decided I wanted to farm in Colombia, near my family. The simple life."

This was the best answer I was going to get out of him: vagueness and half-truths. "Well, then you should understand why I don't want to leave home," I said.

"I understand perfectly why you don't want to leave," he said. "You just don't understand why you must go."

Sister Rosemary asked him something about the coffee trade, and the conversation moved on; I wished she had not been there, and I might have pressed him further. If I searched his drawers and files, maybe I could find some answers about his business affairs with the farm and elsewhere. Even though, I realized, the answers I wanted were probably not located on paper.

Someone thumped the glass door, opened it a crack. Luis stomped the mud off his boots, entered, and removed his hat when he saw company. "Pardon me," he said. "But I think you should turn on the news."

We rarely watched television during mealtimes. Papi believed it corrupted the soul. But this time he hunted for the remote and flicked on the big screen. The Colombian news was broadcasting coverage of an airplane on a dirt strip, followed by headshots of wanted guerilla leaders. The large print at the bottom read: "ELN hijacks domestic Avianca flight and takes 46 hostages."

Sister Rosemary made a sound in her throat. Papi and Luis stood a few feet from the TV, their arms crossed and legs spread wide. Five men dressed in business suits had boarded a turboprop from Bucaramanga that morning, bound for Bogotá. But once in the air, the men pulled handguns and forced the plane to land on a remote airstrip where they met ELN guerillas who whisked away the hostages. They abandoned the plane in the jungle.

"Pretty brilliant, huh?" Luis said to Papi. He wore a wide grin but shook his head slowly as he watched the screen. "Do you know what this is going to do to the country?"

"Fools," Papi said. "This will come back at them tenfold." He shook his head, too, but as he returned to the table his arms remained tightly crossed, his eyebrows furrowed into a single barbed wire. He paced by his chair, and when his gaze fell on me, he pointed to the screen. "What did I tell you, about the troubles getting worse? How happy do you think those flight attendants are right now, marching through the jungle with guns at their backs?"

"I could work an international route. I wouldn't be scared to fly to other countries."

"And you don't think that's next?" Papi asked, his voice sharpening. "These guerillas will hijack Delta Airlines if they think it will win them more ransom money."

Sister Rosemary looked from Papi to me in puzzlement; I had never mentioned my desire to be a flight attendant to her. I stared into my empty soup bowl. Inez skirted around us, clearing dinnerware. Luis remained in front of the TV, but had twisted his head around to listen. Why wouldn't he leave? The nun pushed back her chair and stood, hugging herself. She had shrunken from the woman who had been talking and laughing moments ago.

Papi apologized to her for yelling, wiped his brow with the bandanna. The rains drummed, gushing out the gutters. He asked Luis to drive her back to the mission. She squeezed my shoulder good-bye, leaned in close and pressed a card into my hand. "My number, direct, in case you need me," she whispered in my ear, smoothing my hair as she withdrew. Lavender, I smelled, and the faintest trace of sunscreen. I nodded, brushed the back of my hand along the fringed tail of her shawl as she hovered at the door, awaiting Luis to jog up with the umbrella.

Once the two of us were alone Papi grasped the back of a chair, leaned forward. "Maybe I should have insisted your mother raise you. Then we wouldn't be facing this separation now. I know you're afraid. But this problem we face, there's no escaping it."

I asked what had happened earlier with the young alpaca, lost on the mountainside. He had hacked through the brush for two hours before he found the creature, he said, but the little thing had slid down a slope and broken both its hind legs. He'd had to shoot it on the spot. I told him I was sorry before I hugged him good-night. I imagined the flight attendants in their snug skirts—stumbling up the jungle paths, heels sinking in the mud, faces smacked with insects and heat. Were the guerillas the same men in fatigues and machine guns as the ones who'd stopped the bus, spray-painted *ELN PRESENTE* across the back? *Don't move*, they'd barked, voices muffled behind black knit masks. They had sounded much more frightening than Papi at his worst, yelling at me for sneaking off.

When I called Tía Leo later that night, Jacki answered. I had long admired my cousin—she surfed as well as any boy, and belly danced. Since her father had died, however, she was helping her mother more: managing tenants, selling off land. They'd heard about the hijacking and were worried for us. I told her it was just Colombian craziness but that Papi was determined to send me away to school, adding, "That's why I want to talk to your mom."

"That poor cabin crew," Jacki said. "Did I tell you I might be working for Taca? Mami got me the interview. I just got the call back." Four hundred girls had applied for six spots, she said, and now she was in the final group of twenty-four. I asked why the job was so competitive. She said among other skills you had to speak excellent English.

Jacki prattled on, but her news distracted me. Of course, an airline like Taca would require employees, especially flight attendants, to speak Spanish and English—no problem for my cousin since she was half-American, raised with a father from Arizona. Hard to believe Taca wouldn't hire her, with her thin, athletic build, gringa features, and knowledge of both cultures. Did she find me a peculiar cousin, half-American, but with a foreigner's choppy grasp of English? In what ways might I be different, had my mother stayed? Would I be more worldly and poised? Outspoken? Would she have hovered over my studies and agreed with Papi that I go away to boarding school? She might have enrolled me in dance classes, or stayed up late with me, watching American TV rather than the telenovelas Inez and the maids blasted in the laundry room, that I knew by heart. I'd met few Americans, had seen even fewer in Cali. What did it mean to be an American? Why wonder, when Paula had fled this valley of armed teenagers at roadblocks and most other gringos did the same? The only exception being diplomats and special forces.

My aunt picked up. When I asked how she was, she said, "Ah, well, I knew this year wouldn't be easy. So many bills. Now I'm managing a few rentals owned by Californians—that's keeping us afloat. If only I'd taken some business courses or something years ago, and not left everything to your uncle. The tenants and taxes—I had no idea. And you?"

I asked if she'd persuade my father to let me stay with her and finish school. She remained quiet for a few moments. "I will," she said, "but only if you promise to take seriously the benefits of an education in the United States. Look at Pilar." Jacki had disregarded obtaining her degree there like her older sister. But now Pilar lived in LA, had a career she loved in television production, and earned a salary unheard of by Costa Rican standards. By the way my aunt spoke, Pilar might be helping them financially. Tía Leo doubted my father would listen. "He can be such a stubborn goat," she said. Her tone, sorrowful and frustrated, penetrated the phone.

"Is that what caused difficulty with the family?" I asked. "With your parents?"

"No," she said. "He betrayed them about something, and they turned their backs. Everyone did, even me for a while. Only after what happened to them"—emotion caught in her throat—"did he and I reconcile."

"You know, Papi has never told me the story. About your parents."

"It's a long story. But I prefer not to tell it over the phone."

A beat of silence hung between us. "Well, I'd like to know something," I said.

My aunt's dogs barked; she yelled for them to be quiet. She said, "Okay, then. Diego had betrayed them twice with promises. The third time he asked our parents for forgiveness, they didn't give it. They may have welcomed him back, in time, but I think the hurt was too much for them. And the shame of his deeds upon the family—can you imagine? He might have proven himself otherwise, reconciled, but no. Too late. His heart hardened. Then the guerillas came through."

"ELN or FARC?"

"FARC," she replied. "They were kidnapped, taken into the mountains. They died there." Her voice quivered. "After this happened, Diego believed he had brought it on them. When they died, neither had forgiven the other. So your father never forgave himself. I don't know that he ever will."

"Other relatives?" I asked. "In Colombia?"

"Panama and here," she said. "Many left in the eighties and early nineties. Our Martinez cousins, your great aunt and uncle, even abandoned property they couldn't sell in time. Then after what happened to our parents, the remaining relatives fled. Between the guerillas and the cartels—it was a bloodbath. Only your father stayed."

I thanked her and told her I wished we might talk more. "Come to Costa Rica, daughter," she said. Hija—she often called me that, even though I was not her own.

I explained how I was in love. She laughed. "Ah, I see now why you're not leaving. You must visit, yes," she said, "but I also meant for school." Then she informed me of how many gringos, Americans and Canadians but also Europeans and British, had recently relocated to Costa Rica, and how many good private schools had cropped up there. "If you went to American high school here, you wouldn't be so far away, and you would get the education your father wants. Should I mention this to him?"

I told her yes. At least Costa Rica felt familiar, and I would be close to Tía Leo and Jacki. I might even live with them, visit Cali on weekends. Hardly thrilling but a viable compromise. She promised to call Papi soon, and we hung up.

For a long time I remained at my window seat, legs drawn. My grandparents' bodies—had they ever been recovered? She hadn't mentioned the deaths of their two brothers—had they crossed Papi and ended up behind the alpacas' shed? Fatigues-clad youth marched the faceless figures of the grandparents I had never met—forced them to their weakened knees in a half-lit thicket, then pressed guns to the backs of their gray heads. Shots cracked, and the malnourished bodies tumbled down, lost forever in the impenetrable brush.

Papi and Luis had been right. The morning radio commentators talked about how the hijacking—only the third in Colombia's history—had already paralyzed the country. Since the ELN and the FARC had never before targeted domestic air travel, flying had long been deemed the safest way to avoid roadblocks and kidnappings on rural routes. I didn't even know what the Valle de Cauca beyond our plantation looked like—several times a year, I flew with Papi to Bogotá or to Barranquilla if he had business there. For years, Ana's family had kept a beach house on the Caribbean, in Santa Marta, and flew there on weekends. But I couldn't imagine that they would risk a trip after this. Colombians who needed to travel could now only trust the international airports with high security, or private aircraft.

One afternoon Fidel dropped me off at Ana's house. I'd told Papi that I needed to see her to plan a surprise party. This was partly true; I was helping Ana with her ideas to celebrate Carlos's birthday, but over the phone. Instead I met Manuel in front of the church on his moto. The walk would have taken us forty minutes at most. He drove fast. We darted around patches of missing pavement, wandering mutts. His street lacked the trimmed hedges and guard booths of Ana's. I hopped off the bike unsteady, Manuel's arm smooth and solid.

I had pictured it differently, leisurely, that he would first lead me through his father's furniture shop as he did later—the circular saws pointing out like crocodile teeth, the half-built bedframes and dressers in varieties of woods, the aroma heavy with grease and varnish. His parents' house stood next door, and I heard the splashing of water, a woman scolding a dog. But instead he grabbed me by the hand outside the shop and led me up an outdoor staircase to an apartment. "I share this with my brothers," he said as he opened the door.

He escorted me through the main room. On the center wall surrounding a great crucifix hung several acoustic guitars, and above the tattered couch, a poster of the singer Shakira: lips parted, back arched, blond mane flowing over her halter top. We passed a desk strewn with papers, a Bible, mostly theological books from what I could tell at a glance, but I saw a few dog-eared volumes by Garcia Márquez, our national hero, as well as Karl Marx, a name that meant nothing to me at the time, other than sounding flat and foreign. We moved on to the far room. Three twin beds filled most of the space, nightstands and short dressers cramped in between. Bars encased the louvered glass. A fan oscillated, thick with dust. The apartment radiated heat.

Heat drew us together; I had but a glance around the room, the unmade beds. I was vaguely aware of the one behind me as Manuel guided my face to his. I had thought that I wanted to talk, but I didn't. Words interfered. I unbuttoned my clothes, fingers shaking, but left my underwear on, he did the same, and I groped for the bed, traced the muscles of his abdomen. Might someone walk in—Carlos, his parents? I felt almost as I had in the churchyard or in the driveway with the gate creeping shut behind me—cut off from everything, losing and discovering myself at once. He stood naked between my opened knees, and I pressed my thighs against him.

We lay together for what seemed like hours, but couldn't have been since we didn't have much time. So many mysteries unraveled that I had thought would take months to navigate once I did have a lover: his lips brushing to the back of my knee, my lower back, my thrusting against his hand, yanking down my underwear. Nakedness. We stopped just short of the act itself. But I guessed by the sure way he touched me and where, that he had done this many times, and probably—although I didn't want to think of it—with more than one girl.

Finally we broke apart from one another and half-dressed but then lay back again, lazy in the afternoon heat. Traffic honked and thundered below. We began talking, about nothing at first—each declaring the other's unique flaws and perfections to one another. "Where did you get this scar?" I asked, thumbing his knee. A spider bite when he was eleven, he said. He flipped me over, pinched me through the sheet. "You've got the most beautiful ass, you know that?" Face burning, I spun away and thrust my cheek to the pillow, laughing. I asked about his music, if he had hopes for his talent. Carlos had booked a recording studio for June, and then who knew? Maybe they would become a world famous guitar duo, maybe not.

"What do you want?" I asked, tracing his eyebrow with my middle finger. He said, "Right now? You," and tickled my side, but after a moment he stopped and grew serious. I propped up, chin in my palm, and studied him.

"I suppose I want to live a similar life as Emilio's, just not as a priest, obviously." A smile once again broke over his face, and he motioned to us pressed together and half-clothed. "Be a great Catholic leader, a saint. Perhaps that's not possible without being a priest."

"I'm sure it is. But what exactly do you want to do?"

"Free people from evil. Expose those who feed the system. Bring peace. We're organizing a rally this Sunday, me and Emilio? You should come, if you can."

"I can see you now, the singing missionary of the mountains," I said, grinning. "Riding your donkey up into the villages, strumming your guitar." I took my chance and tickled him back near his navel, so that he reeled onto his side to stop me.

"But it's true, you know?" he said, laughing. "And you know what's strange? I actually feel connected somewhat to the ELN, despite the terrible things they do. Do you know their history?" And he told me how the ELN, unlike the FARC, which had four times the number of members or twenty thousand throughout Colombia, had been founded on sound principles, but those principles had been corrupted over the course of our decades-long civil war. The ELN had been started by former priests, Manuel Pérez and Camillo Torres. My Manuel was more interested in Torres, who had cast aside his priest's robes to lead his band of guerillas against the army and was killed in battle in 1966. Pérez was a thug, according to

Manuel, but history may have been different had Torres survived and went on to become leader. Pérez had succumbed to hepatitis B last year, it was rumored—this Emilio had found out as a negotiator—and the ELN was now headed by someone named Gambino. But the organization lacked a visionary who might lead them into the future.

"So you're going to become a guerilla?" I said, rolling my eyes. "This will really go over well with my father."

He shoved a pillow into my face, said, "That's the last thing I'm going to be." I pushed it away; he grabbed my wrist and we wrestled for a minute. But then he dropped his hold and lifted my chin toward him. "Guerillas kill people, Mercedes. There's nothing romantic about them." I told him the story of my ride home with Fidel and the bus then. He said I was never to take the bus again, he would have never let me come on the night of the church meeting had I first told him about what I had witnessed. We fell silent. The fan's breeze stirred my hair and cooled my neck and face; tiny bumps appeared on my arms. He asked me what I wanted. Maybe to live on our farm, have a family, I told him, if I couldn't work and travel as a flight attendant. "But right now I want to find out about Papi, as much as I can," I said.

"I know you want to know the truth, but please be careful." He hesitated, then asked, "If you find out anything that strikes you as odd, will you be sure to tell me?"

I nodded and said okay, still giddy. But something in his demeanor—a pointedness and preoccupation—stirred my stomach. We talked so easily. He liked me, liked my body—was I glimpsing another intention? Whatever the alarm, I squelched it, asked something else. Did Manuel think we should keep up the ruse about me going to Ana's house on my free days after school? He didn't like lying, but he didn't think it wise for Papi to think we were seeing each other more than on weekends for now, and I agreed, especially with the recent hijacking. Then he urged me up; the time was getting away from us.

CHAPTER FOUR

Afternoons for the next couple of weeks, Manuel and Emilio organized the rally, making signs, printing leaflets and calls to action. Emilio designed T-shirts to raise money for La Maria Juventud. I had never attended a demonstration of any kind before, and couldn't imagine what I would do. Wave signs? Shout into a megaphone? What would I shout? The rally would take place in front of the Catedral de San Pedro where Manuel and I first met. When I pressed him about the possibility of violence breaking out, he assured me that police presence would be heavy and the authorities would fly helicopters overhead. Still, I felt uneasy.

Sister Rosemary and I finished the forms. I had made mistakes, but she praised my efforts. "Always do your best, have a positive attitude, and even the most difficult task will become easier," she said. I winced at these empty words but said nothing, wishing that she would talk to me like an adult. She promised I would never regret learning a second language and quoted to me a saying I liked: "Another language, another soul." I would take the EFL exam in June. It would be challenging, she said. We couldn't prepare enough.

She explained that the beatitudes, or corporal works of mercy—to feed the hungry, shelter the homeless, visit the imprisoned—were not so much orders from Jesus but declarations of how a person filled with the spirit of God lives, their actions. She wrote down several verses for me:

Matthew 5:3-10 and James 2:15-17. A Catholic who took Holy Orders chose to serve these calls, and others, with total dedication. She had been working at the mission for nine years—she was thirty-eight, although by her small-boned frame I had guessed younger. As for the ELN and their roots, they had traditionally recruited members who believed in Liberation Theology, a branch of Roman Catholicism that combined Marxist and Christian teaching. "I have no doubt that goodness lives with evil inside those men, as it does with all of us," she said. "I believe much of what they advocate is just—for peace, for an end to government corruption. For the paramilitary atrocities to stop. And I can understand their criticism of the elite. The gap between the rich and poor is dire. But violence is never the way."

Later on, I combed the house for a Bible in vain. Papi was getting ready to go out with neighbors to a jazz café on Avenida Sexta in Cali. He rarely socialized beyond the farm; a couple of times a month he accepted invitations to join acquaintances at restaurants or for a night of salsa. I knocked on his door. "A Bible?" he asked. "Why do you want that?" He stood stiffly in jeans, buttoning the cuffs to his shirt, white, the collar embroidered, the doorway ensconced by his cologne. I wondered if he had a date. Maybe if he acquired a girlfriend, he would forget about me and Manuel.

"I need to look something up," I said. "For school."

"I don't think I have one," he said. "Ask Inez."

I left in search of her. Wouldn't my grandparents have owned a family Bible? But then, we had no crucifixes or pictures of the Virgin Mary, no signs of religion anywhere, unlike Ana's house or Manuel's apartment. Papi didn't wear a cross like so many other men. I wondered if he'd purged the house of everything holy.

Inez showed me where to find the verses in the New Testament. First I came upon the verse by James: "If a brother or sister has nothing to wear and has no food for the day, and one of you says to them, 'Go in peace, keep warm, and eat well,' but you do not give them the necessities of the body, what good is it? So also faith of itself, if it does not have works, is dead.' But I had difficulty with the beatitudes. According to them, the poor and weak were supposed to inherit the land and the kingdom of heaven. Prosperity might happen for those like Manuel who had the resources to work and bring about results, but how was change supposed to occur for those who didn't—the hungry and homeless? What about the guerillas who considered themselves Catholic—did this mean they thought their attempts were for ultimate good, and they just didn't see how taking hostages and threatening the government made things worse?

Sister Rosemary had said that good and evil lived inside each of us—Manuel, Ana, even me. What was that evil inside me? Inside Papi? If the heart could turn black so easily, depending on what you fed it, could that happen to me? Because I wasn't sure I could tend to mine on my own. Maybe none of us could, and that was why we were doomed. Or maybe there were places where evil took root more swiftly, and others where that same evil would be strangled, starved out. Suppose I stayed, and evaded getting abducted or killed. What would my life be like, in this place where fear permeated the everyday and exploded—while shopping for groceries, strolling through a park? Might I be harmed even if I tried to modestly do right—become lesser somehow?—when what I really craved was resilience, courage. Stability. If I found Paula, could she offer me that? What alternate life awaited me in the United States? I paged through my passport, blank except for the stamps from Costa Rica. I could always come back.

Not long after dawn, someone opened Papi's door and whispered—a woman's voice I didn't recognize—followed by footsteps on the stairs and the click of the front door. I drifted back to sleep. When I crept downstairs mid-morning, music flooded the sound system, an album by the famous guitarist Pepe Romero. It was surprising, since Papi never listened to music in the mornings, only at the close of the day. Even the dogs acted aware. They tugged over an old toy in the living room and glanced up expectantly every time one of the maids passed by.

Papi, still damp from his shower and dressed in boots and faded work jeans, read his newspaper as he ate breakfast. The front page depicted the Avianca turboprop in grainy color, headshots of the ELN leaders alongside, "Gambino" named in the caption.

"I want to go with you this morning," I said, referring to the property rounds he conducted on Saturdays.

"Oh?" He regarded me over his paper. "Why is this?"

"Can't I come?" I had accompanied him before, but rarely—perhaps three times a year at most, to see how the fields changed with the growth cycles of the sugarcane.

He folded his paper and set it aside. "You had better change. It's been muddy."

We climbed into his splattered pickup and headed out, turning left on the road toward the cane fields. A minute later we veered off-road. Our land seemed to go on forever; I liked this feeling which was more akin to stewardship than ownership—that everything as far as I could see was our responsibility and, in turn, sustained us, from the chicken in our soup to the aguardiente, better known as guaro, a grain alcohol made from sugarcane and a fixture at parties on the haciendas. As we headed farther away from the main road and over deep tire tracks, we passed our many field workers and wagons pulled by tractors and horses. I asked what the workers were doing—hadn't we just drained these fields? Even though Papi had explained the intricacies of farming sugarcane dozens of times, I always forgot. Left to itself, sugarcane matured about once a year, but big operations like ours managed multiple growing cycles. Currently we yielded three main harvests, he said, but the way he and Luis decided to rotate the fields depended on several factors. In one field workers were replanting; they dropped pairs of cut stalks into furrows, and these would grow shoots in several weeks. Then we passed another set of fields, void of workers, where only short green shoots pointed up from the ground; Papi called these ratoons and said that these grew naturally after a field's first harvest. A field only needed replanting every three harvests. And we passed yet a third set of fields that swarmed with workers and plows; these peasants were planting sweet corn. When I asked why we did this, he said that this set of cane fields had been harvested late, so Luis had decided to plant a different crop in its place—fallow planting, it was called.

"Displaced farmers?" I asked. Papi always referred to our field employees as workers, not campesinos.

He gripped the wheel with one hand and adjusted the bandanna on his forehead with the other, eyes darting on the road ahead, watching for potholes. "Yes," he said. "I gave those fields to some of the displaced who have been fleeing through here. But only for a few months, until those fields are ready to grow cane again."

We rolled along in silence, my heart hurting as if struck by the stones the tires kicked up. This was the Papi I had loved all my life: the father who had taken me for rides on his saddle, laughed at the way the dogs backed up against his chair, demanding to be stroked, even the Papi of stern remarks who wanted me to go to the best schools. "Did sugarcane bring you to Florida?" I asked.

"I worked for a rum factory at first. That's how I learned about sugar. Why is that important?"

"I'm your daughter," I replied, tight-lipped. "Don't I have a right to know?"

He said, "Family business is no one else's. I don't know that you understand."

"Of course I do. But will you stop talking to me like I'm an employee? Please."

The truck lurched into a pothole; we bobbed in our seats. "If I tell you," he began, "that puts things in jeopardy. I signed on to certain arrangements. You must swear not to tell anyone." His black eyes bore into mine. He let go of the gear shift and held out his hand. For a second I didn't realize he meant for me to grasp it. Scratches etched his fingers, his callouses scraping my palm.

"I won't. I promise." I cast him a sidelong glance. "You didn't get rich in Miami working for the rum company, or the sugar refinery. Did you?"

He shook his head, his mouth taut as a rope. "Sugarcane, no. Cocaine is what I shipped."

Another pickup approached, tires spewing mud. The faded blue seemed to take forever to reach us, Vincente at the wheel. He raised a wiry arm in greeting as he rolled by, but I remained still. "How?" I asked. "Why?"

"I was young, chasing dollars and women. The money was easy. But mostly I wanted to come back and buy land." Here Papi opened his hands toward the surrounding fields. "I wanted to give my parents who had broken their backs all their lives a nice house."

"When were you going to tell me?"

"I hoped you would never ask. But all of that is far behind me now, I want you to know."

I shook my head. "You've been lying to me my whole life. Why should I believe you?"

His eyes flitted and his grip on the wheel tightened. "How was I supposed to make you, a little girl, understand? Maybe I shouldn't have told you now. I thought you might be old enough."

A breeze blew in through the half-opened window and raindrops stung my cheeks. "I won't say anything," I said.

We drove on, the mud thickening as the lane sloped down at the bottom of the fields. He turned off, and we headed toward a cluster of trees; I had never been to this part of our property before. "I want you to see something," he said.

Matted, skinny dogs descended upon the truck, barking. He slowed to a crawl. Several dozen shanties built out of scrap metal, bamboo, and cardboard leaned among the trees. Laundry hung on lines between branches. Women squatted in the murky shallows of a creek, washing clothes. A child of five or six, bare below the waist, crouched behind a fallen branch as he defecated; he hugged himself and ducked down as we rumbled past. The air smelled of burnt garbage, and trash littered the ground everywhere: metal cans, scraps of paper and plastic containers, a torn canvas shoe. A few men sat around on crates or logs, or even in the dirt. Most of them didn't move as we crept by, but some advanced at a clip, extended their hands and called out, "Jefe, tiene más trabajo, jefe?" One had droopy eyes and a scar down his face that made my stomach curl. He said, "Boss, your truck is dirty. Let me wash it for you!"

Papi spoke to them through his half-open window, shook his head, and waved. "Why aren't you in the fields, planting?" he shouted at them. The oldest among them muttered a reply, something about other jobs at the main house. "No, no—what do you know how to plant, other than coca? You, tell me the crops you've grown." He pointed from one man to the next, and each shook his head no. "The men in the pickups can tell you where to get the seeds, yuca and corn. Okay? Next time I drive through, don't let me see grown men lounging around like housecats." Then he touched the gas and we charged up the slope on the other side of the trees, out of the settlement.

From there we passed the cement-block houses and smaller plots of land, one after another, of our tenant farmers. I had seen their homes before; these simple dwellings were a vast improvement from the shacks we had just passed. Chickens clucked in the yards, dogs lunged and circled on their chains. A few children tottered and chased one another, barefoot in shorts and shirts. Several mothers bent over hoes in small gardens, most of the others alongside husbands in their plots. Two women carrying a hamper between them waved as we rolled past. At one property, Papi pulled off and jumped out, leaving me in the cab.

Talking to the tenants, he bent down to plug his fingers in their garden plot and poke the toddler in his belly; the child let out a delighted squeal. Papi accepted an envelope from the farmer and briefly checked the contents before the couple led him over to their cottage, where a set of shiny pipes ran up the outer wall and inside. I imagined my father exchanging suitcases of money on the boat docks of Barranquilla, or over sacks of cocaine amassed inside a warehouse, surrounded by men with handguns—images I had gleaned from TV and movies. Something told me these depictions weren't quite accurate. Could there be other groups beside the ELN and the FARC, or the Autodefensas, the AUC paramilitary army, and why did he maintain ties when he seemed strained just talking about it? Had the ELN been to blame for his parents' murders?

He returned. We left the row of tenant plots behind and cut back across the fields. I tried to picture myself as thirty years old, driving a pickup, discussing the harvest cycles with the jefes and collecting rent. But I couldn't.

"You're quiet," Papi said. "What you saw down there must have shocked you."

"No, the coca."

"I had thought you might have figured it out. But I wasn't a kingpin or anything. I tried to stop as soon as I could, but once you're in—it's difficult, almost impossible. Please, keep this quiet."

Haciendas dotted the cleared foothills—how many had been built with blood money? Behind our house, past the coffee shrubs where the alpaca had gone missing, might Papi allow peasant farmers to grow coca? The alpacas dozed underneath a tree in a great heap, the valley too hot for them. Their eyes remained slits as they slept, forever on the lookout for predators; the breeze carried their musty scent. The broken one he'd had to shoot—what had they done with it? I only hoped they'd given it to one of the men begging for work, for his wife to roast over a fire and not the vultures to eat.

"Why did you show me the displaced?" I cried.

The truck stopped. The gate inched open. "Because, my daughter," he said, "that is how close the poor are to us, and why we must provide for them in small ways. Otherwise, if thousands continue to pour out of the hills with the guerillas, squatters will take over. That's what happened in Nicaragua. The guerillas and the poor drove the people like us out, seized plantations, and let the lands go to filth and ruin. Even more suffered and starved. Then *we* will be the displaced, and Colombia will descend into even more of a bloodbath."

"Is that what happened to your parents?"

He shot me a sharp glance, and his face flushed red. "Who told you that?"

The engine revved as we clambered from gravel onto the stone pavers. One of the alpacas popped up her head, ears twitching. "Nobody, I was just wondering," I said. We zipped through and the gate shut swiftly behind us.

Papi opened the door but his hands dropped to his lap, and he leaned back in the seat. "Not because of land." He sifted the keys in his palm, stared at the fields. "Someday I may tell you." The dogs hurdled down the stone steps, jumped and crowded the truck. He greeted them, smiling and calling their names like children on his way to the house.

In Ana's upstairs living room with the Virgin Mary eying us from the wall, we cranked up Gracia's dance music, sipped Fanta (a treat, as Papi did not allow soda), and talked about our boyfriends. It was late Sunday morning. The rally was set to take place that afternoon. With Ana's parents at morning mass and no one but the maids downstairs, we were able to speak freely. Ana had made reservations for Carlos's birthday at the Mirador. Afterward, we might all go out to a club; she was thinking of booking a room at the Intercontinental and buying, for herself, some sexy lingerie. She stared at her lap as she said this, but a slight smile played across her lips.

"What happened to his present?" I asked, prodding her rib.

She shrank away, feigning protest. "He wants sex. What else do I get? Colored condoms?"

I laughed but Gracia wrinkled her nose. "Those are awful," she said. "Use the pill."

"I thought you didn't want to be having sex with Carlos," I said. "Are you sure you want to stay the night with him somewhere?"

Ana waved at me, brief and dismissive. "Oh, it's fine. He's into me." She giggled and sipped her Fanta, then asked how things were going with Manuel.

Grinning, I told them he knew what he was doing, and it was better than I had ever imagined. "But he insists sex is a sin, that he won't," I said.

"Are you kidding?" Gracia said. "I give you a month at the most. Just be sure you use something, or else."

A beat of silence hung in the air. We all knew what she meant. Only two options existed for a pregnant teenage girl in Colombia—either to drop out of school and life, marry her novio, and give birth to the first in a long line of babies, or seek out one of the illegal abortion doctors.

"So our sexy guitarist Manuel is hard to get," Ana said. "That means he lives his faith."

"Oh, please," Gracia said, rolling her eyes. She set down her soda can; it scraped the glass. "There's nothing more beautiful than sharing that experience with someone you love," she said to me. "And you don't have to be married. The Church is wrong."

"Manuel won't agree," Ana said, her chin tensed. She toyed with her soda tab. "If you take the pill, don't tell him. Just have him pull out and believe that works."

At noon, Ana handed each of us a T-shirt printed with the titles of a dozen groups with names like La Maria Juventud Para Justicia Social, some affiliated with Catholic Churches, others with Cali universities. Across the front, the words LIBERTAD and COLOMBIA blazed in bold black lettering, a Colombian flag in the backdrop. Then the three of us piled into the family's Land Rover and the driver whisked us off to the Plaza de Cayzedo. I was expecting something larger than the youth group meeting, but more formal: Manuel and Emilio each leading the demonstrators in a few rounds of chants, and then everyone would disperse. We would have the rest of the day to ourselves.

When the armored Land Rover trailed behind the edges of the gathering three blocks away, the size of the crowd astonished me. A group of young men hoisted a large banner overhead: VIVA LA PAZ, and on the other side, COLOMBIA SOY YO. A pair of older women frantically waved miniature Colombian flags in yellow, blue, and red, their arms linked around each other's waists. A father paraded a toddler on his shoulders.

Just beyond the thousands of demonstrators, a white tent and stage had been erected next to the cathedral steps. TV cameras formed a horseshoe in front; an anchorwoman fluffed her hair in front of a hand mirror. I had never seen the square so filled with people.

We moved through the crowd and up the cathedral steps. On the portable stage Carlos adjusted sound equipment. His pudgy middle poking out the flag on his T-shirt's front. He grabbed each of our hands and pulled us up; below, the city police pressed back at the crowd's edge. The square swelled, alive with whistles and chants. Our spot seemed ideal, until I looked up. Atop a roof a sniper in black uniform crouched, the stage and its speakers an easy target for someone with a rifle or a bomb. And where was Manuel?

He emerged from the mobbed cathedral steps moments later and bounded onto the stage. He didn't say hello at first, just took my hands and squeezed them. Singing broke out over the rising chants and claps, and electricity charged the air. We stood there for a moment, staring at each other and swaying. "I'm so glad you're here," he said, and added, "I'm nervous. Only just a little." He tilted his head toward the crowd, grinning. He let go of my hands and quickly brushed his palms on the sides of his jeans.

I cupped his shoulder. "You'll be great." He paced a few steps, scratching his head, then bent over and lifted his guitar from the case. He checked the strings. I told him I had driven the property with my father the day before and visited the encampment of desplazados. But I stopped short. I couldn't bring myself to divulge further.

"Did you?" he remarked, rising. "You're brave." He drew me to him and kissed my head. His scent mixed with the factory odor of the new T-shirt. When he stepped back, he smoothed my hair and said, "I'm so in love with you, Mercedes."

When Emilio stepped up to the mike and thanked those who had assembled, Manuel let go my hand and stood alongside his brother. The multitude quieted to a murmur.

"Today is independence day," Emilio said. "I want to invite you all to celebrate this day in the spirit of freedom—freedom from fear and violence. Think about each moment, and how we can make ourselves more and more free in that way."

The ponytailed young man from the social justice meeting spoke, halting but convicted, from notecards. He turned out to be the leader of the Universidad del Valle peace organization. Then a priest, obese and commanding, led a prayer for Colombia and other nations that suffered atrocities. I had rarely thought about the world outside before, but now I pictured countries like ours, in Africa and Asia, with jungles, refugees, guns. I recalled the eyes of our desplazados and tried to guess at the numbers of people who lived that way on our planet: so many Colombias, countries I couldn't name, worlds without end. On stage the same light shone in Manuel's eyes as when he lay back in bed with me, talking of his dreams, telling me that he loved me.

I had thought that Manuel would speak to this gathering like he did at the youth group, but after the speeches concluded, Emilio led the demonstrators in a chant. "LIBERTAD! LIBERTAD!" we cried in unison. From the back of the stage, Ana, Gracia, and I pumped our fists in the air, the flags fluttering in the breeze. Manuel said, "This is a song we want to play for anyone who worries," and the whistles and cries died down. Manuel and Carlos began playing, voices soaring in harmony; the loudspeakers crackled. Thousands sang along. Ana wiped a tear from my cheek; I hadn't even realized it was there.

Afterward, Manuel approached with his guitar case, rubbed the back of his head, and stretched. I liked his forearms, muscular from maneuvering furniture. Ana caught my eye, her brow raised; time to leave. "Will I see you tonight?" I asked him.

"Sorry," he said. "But I've got to stay and clean up, and I'm exhausted." He touched my chin. "Soon. I want to hear what happened with your father."

I nodded, disappointed. I had hoped that we could at least meet in Ana's neighborhood for a walk before Fidel came to pick me up and the busy school week started. At the far end of the square a few groups lingered, carrying on their chants for peace. Manuel kissed me good-bye, our fingers entwined. Someone called out for him. Was this how things would always be with us, his causes always tearing him away? At last I climbed down from the stage with Ana and Gracia, the two of them jabbering and me silent. As we crossed the square I marveled at how quickly its everyday filthiness had returned, with the magical efficiency of a circus that had performed, dismantled, and left town. Nothing remained on the ground but some abandoned cardboard signs, a trampled miniature Colombian flag, and trash.

CHAPTER FIVE

One afternoon following the rally, I stepped out of school to find Papi on the sidewalk. In the crook of his windbreaker he cradled the bulky folder of applications; he approached me at a clip. Several letter-sized white envelopes fell out, hitting the toe of his oxford. He squatted and gathered them, careful not to let his crisp slacks brush the gritty sidewalk. "What are you doing here?" I asked. My stomach somersaulted even though Manuel and I hadn't arranged to meet.

He waved the letters. "Sister Rosemary contacted your teachers to write you letters of recommendation for the schools. I needed to pick them up. We can mail everything right now." He'd squeezed his pickup onto the side street. I climbed in and as we shut both doors, the locks sounded. How odd to see him out of his rubber boots during the day. The outline of his gun bulged from beneath his pant leg; when he left the hacienda he wore it on his ankle.

He locked his gun in the glove box before we went through the metal detectors and inside the lower mall. At the shipping counter, I wrote the schools' addresses on large envelopes and matched up the application materials for each—all neatly divided and paper-clipped together by Sister Rosemary. Papi paid, and the clerk dropped the packages into a huge plastic chute—my future falling out of sight.

Since the hijacking, Fidel had become glued to talk radio. One day the news reported that the ELN had released nine of the frailest hostages from the Avianca flight, including a baby and elderly captives. Experts were saying the ELN had only done this because of a promise they had made the previous July to stop kidnapping the weak. The guerillas had also released a nun, an American, and a Colombian congressman. Then the announcer mentioned the massive peace rally, organized and led mostly by young people as a response to the hijacking. "Turn that up," I said.

Fidel's fingers hovered over the dial. "You went to that rally the other day, right?"

"So what if I did?"

"Juventud," he said. "Must be fun." His tone sounded mocking. He raised the volume just barely, but the report had concluded.

The car glided into Ana's neighborhood, the mansions like great marble prisons behind their high gates. At Ana's the curtains were drawn, the house deserted and asleep at siesta. "It's a peaceful group," I said, and clutched the door handle, ready to jump out.

"Doesn't matter," he replied. "It's the narrow-minded extremists I'd be worried about." The news broadcast rattled off updates on bandido activity outside the city, routes to avoid.

I lifted my chin. "I refuse to live in fear," I said, a quip of Manuel's.

He flicked off the radio and twisted around to face me, the rosary beads dangling from the mirror, red as blood. He said, "That's not what I'm talking about. Things quickly get out of control, even the best-intended messages of peace. Strong words bring about a strong response, sometimes."

"Isn't that the idea?"

His face softened as he glanced over me. "Just be careful, princesa. You know who your father is." Then he unlocked the doors, and I sprang onto the sidewalk.

The car coasted away and turned the corner. I paced until Manuel roared up on his moto a minute later, no helmet, to my irritation and dismay—I was coming to learn that he often left it behind when dashing around, preoccupied. But I said nothing, just smiled and swung onto the back. Soon we were weaving in and out of traffic, and the brief yet eternal afternoon hours stretched ahead.

The apartment appeared much the same as on my first visit, dim and stuffy. Beats drifted low from the stereo, the singers' voices faint. I started for the bedroom, but Manuel drew me back and shook his head—Emilio was home, napping. In the half-lit hallway we clung together, kissing; he steered us over to the sagging couch. I slid my hands to his stomach, the soft cotton of his T-shirt a contrast to the firm muscles underneath, sliding farther, until he pulled back and regarded me with a playful smile. He started telling me that he found me so mature for my years, so beautiful. "But I've never met another girl like you," he said. "You're bold. And I'm honored that you want me to be your first. But right now, with what the Church is facing—I can't just forgo my beliefs and pretend it doesn't matter. Do you understand?"

I told him yes even though I didn't and kissed him again. His hips and the hardness underneath his jeans pressed against me, his hands running up and down my body as if they couldn't get enough. He reached underneath my skirt and felt me.

"How is your brother going to take vows as a priest?" I kissed his neck, inhaling his scent. Cedar and musk. "Is he crazy?"

"No, not crazy. He just has extraordinary faith—from his habits, mostly. The first hour of every day he prays and studies. Some thought of the saints as crazy, you know?"

How easily he forgot that I wasn't Catholic. I wasn't even sure if I'd been baptized. I said, "Lucky you're not up for the priesthood." Grinning, I gripped him through the crotch of his jeans. "I'm afraid you wouldn't make it."

"I wouldn't?" he said, laughing. "Let's just say it's not my calling."

"But your brother is so attractive. You both are. Girls must have chased him."

"Oh, they did. But he made up his mind for good, last year. I think they've left him alone since then." He drew me close and kissed me again, slow and sweet. Then he said, "You never told me what happened the other day with your father. What did he tell you?"

"Nothing you don't already know," I answered, my tone mischievous.

"Tell me," he said. He tickled my ribs and I snickered but drew back, slightly annoyed at the shift to conversation and the frustration we had worked up together. I guided his hand beneath my underwear. "I'll tell you later," I whispered into his ear.

He gave me what I wanted then, or at least the most we could accomplish, and I had my first sweet release of pleasure in that shadowed apartment on the sunken couch, with his brother, asleep in the next room. Only Emilio might not have been asleep because a few minutes after we had finished, he shuffled out, squinting. We were sitting up then, hands to ourselves but disheveled. Emilio muttered a hello and sank into his desk chair. He rubbed the sleep out of his eyes, picked up one notepad, then another. Manuel raised an eyebrow and shot me a half-smirk as if to say, *that was close.* I sat up with my skirt smoothed over my knees, but I liked the idea that Emilio might know what had just happened, and was possibly tempted by our exploits.

"What you showed me at the meeting was a start," I said. "Do either of you know anyone else I can talk to? What about the priest you mentioned, Father Juan?"

Emilio frowned. He tore off a sheet of notes, crumpled them in the trash. "That won't be easy," he said. "He spends most of his time in the mountains, remember? Trying to catch village boys before they get recruited by the FARC and ELN."

"But which group would have an interest in kidnapping me? That's what Papi's most worried about. I'll look for information—I just have to make sure nobody's around."

"Watch yourself," Manuel said, and picked up his guitar. "Diego's not a stupid man."

"Well, what do you suggest?" I laughed. "That I interview him? Set up a tape recorder?"

"Not at all." Manuel adjusted the strap, tugged the strings. "Because if you ask too many questions, he might wonder if you have other aims against him—to expose him."

"Expose him?" I asked, and caught the laugh in my throat. "What good would that do?"

"Because the world needs transparency," Emilio cut in. "The end of lies will be the end of this fallen world, and the beginning of the new Earth." His fingers tapped the rigid, dark cover of a book I assumed to be the Bible.

"Look, I just need to know the truth for my own sake," I said. "Until then I can't even think of inheriting the hacienda one day." To Emilio, I asked, "Why is it so important to you? About my father?"

He sneered, as if my question was both absurd and juvenile. "To you I'm just the leader of La Maria Juventud. I don't think you realize what being an activist requires. Let's just leave it at that for now, okay?" He swiveled in the chair, knees wide, a pencil playing between his fingers. Part of me disliked his haughtiness, but when he regarded me I felt that twinge again. An attraction.

"And I should be looking out for what, exactly?" I asked, a hint of sarcasm in my tone.

"Changes of routine, unannounced trips somewhere, visitors." Emilio let the last word hang in the air like a question.

I told them about the woman's voice outside Papi's bedroom door, the light steps on the stairs. "Doubtful," Emilio said. "Way to go, Diego. Getting lucky on his hot date."

I winced. Good thing I hadn't disclosed Papi's confession. Emilio hunched over his notebooks, Manuel tinkered with a new song. I told him how captivated I was by the set he and Carlos had played at the rally. "Really?" he said. He'd been composing lately, he told me, and sometimes he had to leave his work in the shop to jot them down, the calls for peace, justice, and togetherness more fervent—and the most joyful, exhausting experience he'd ever had. I longed to tell him what he had told me at the rally: that I loved him in return. But Emilio sat there, scrawling away amidst Karl Marx and Thomas à Kempis, stabbing notecards onto a bulletin board.

At our next meeting, I asked Sister Rosemary about baptism, and sins that couldn't be forgiven. If I had been baptized, I was sort of halfway there, she told me with a laugh, but I hadn't been fully inducted into the Church out of my own free will, another sacrament altogether. The baptism should be relatively easy to find out. There were two types of sins—small or venial sins, such as missing church or lustful thoughts, and mortal sins, like killing, stealing, and adultery. But when I asked her about excommunication, she cocked her head and eyed me suspiciously.

"Excommunication?" she asked. "For that you must do something, or many things, which cut yourself off from God, and in turn the community no longer allows you to belong. You cannot go to mass and receive the Eucharist. Perhaps you have heard mention of this in the news, that the archbishop has threatened the guerillas with excommunication?"

I hadn't but nodded anyway—not off to a good start, I thought, in the venial sin department. "So to be excommunicated, a person would have to commit mortal sins?"

"Not only many mortal sins, but also not show remorse for them. There's a big difference between a repentant sinner and one who refuses or keeps committing the same sins—insincerity, if you will." She leaned forward and placed her hand lightly on my forearm. "These questions—what's troubling you?"

Papi's voice boomed from the doorway. "I thought you were supposed to be speaking English," he said, his tone upbeat, joking. "Isn't that what I'm paying for?" He wore a two-day beard and his pants were streaked with dirt. This was unusual, as he liked casual clothes but also had a penchant for appearing neat.

"Indeed, sir," she said, and jumped of her seat. "Mercedes just needed some clarifications." She gathered our materials. Papi blocked my attempt to brush past.

"What are you bugging the nun about, eh?" He reached over to pinch my cheek but I ducked.

"Nothing," I said, smiling. "Just questions about American schools."

"You've been seeing this boy every weekend," he said, stepping back into the hall. "I hope you're not in love with him." He sounded bemused, facetious. I pictured him in the alpaca field, the sun in his eyes and his work shirt splattered, a gun in one hand and a body pooling blood at his feet.

Downstairs reeked of bandeja paisa, and I grimaced. Although I loved chicharrón, the greasy combination of fried pork and dirty rice gave me a stomachache. Inez bustled about, her long braid swinging across her back. I asked about my baptism, if she recalled it.

"Of course," she said. She sliced an avocado; her fingers wielded the knife deftly.

"How could I forget? Your mother didn't want anything to do with it. She was Jewish, you know. But your father insisted."

That night I found a verse in the Bible borrowed from Inez: Revelation, Chapter 21. "Behold, I make all things new...They are accomplished. I am the Alpha and Omega, the beginning and the end." I read further about the second coming of Jesus but recoiled at the idea of God as a great external power whom we were to rely on to rescue our bloody mess, showing up to judge humanity one day. If we were to be rescued we needed to do it ourselves, the same way Manuel and Emilio had worked to create the peace rally; I didn't see anyone coming to save us. A final judgment would only be useful if it meant all of us examining ourselves, seeing how we'd done and how we might do better—more of a final observation. But then what was final with God? I liked the line about God being the Alpha and Omega, the beginning and the end. Perhaps because of the poetry, I read it over and over again.

I met Gracia at La Iglesia de San Francisco, near the municipal theatre and her dance studio. She showed up in tight black exercise pants, her backpack slung over one shoulder, listening to her battered old Walkman half tucked away, wires disappearing beneath the bag's zipper. She was either crazy or fearless or both, and somehow the thieves hadn't ripped the headphones from her ears yet. I scolded her; she stuffed it and the earphones away and zipped up her bag, laughing. Then she exclaimed that she had news. "I might be going to the dance academy in Bogotá next term," she said, her words rushing out almost on top of one another.

I asked her what she was talking about; she had mentioned nothing of this until now. The possibility of my going to school in America had sparked her to investigate the Bogotá dance academies, she said, where the teachers hailed from Spain, Argentina, even the U.S. Her parents enthusiastically approved. She didn't want to get her hopes up, but she had just mailed the applications and audition tapes. She added, "I haven't told Ana yet, so don't say anything."

"What about Esteban? Aren't you in love with him?"

She grew quiet. "I am," she said. "He could move there with me, I suppose."

"Don't you want to marry him?"

She laughed. "I don't know if I want to marry anyone. They all end in unhappiness anyway, like my parents. But this opportunity I just can't pass up." She explained how recruiters from international dance companies visited the Bogotá academies, searching for new talent.

"Who knows where it will lead?" she said. "I'm not going to dance at that restaurant forever." We walked for a moment in silence, skirting the rubble of the crumbling sidewalk. I was taken aback not only by her news, but that she had told me before Ana. This marked the first time she confided in me outside the company of her cousin, and I couldn't help but feel pleased at this turn in our friendship. And of course, I bemoaned that we would miss her.

"Oh, you'll probably be in California or somewhere else, a thousand miles away by then," she said. She asked about the American schools. I told her the applications had been mailed, although my aunt had introduced the idea about finishing school in Costa Rica. "The lesser of two evils, I suppose," she said. "But other than Manuel, why don't you want to get out of here?"

"Live in the cold, where it snows? And have to speak English everywhere I go? No."

"Maybe I just think differently because of dance," she said. "A dancer has to be able to move around—and I mean both ways, with her body and with travel, if she wants to perform for great audiences and become famous."

"Is that what you want?"

"What artist doesn't?" she said. "We sacrifice too much for anything less."

We crossed the plaza near the theatre, the farmacia just beyond. An old man in a tatty suit crouched on a crate with a large, mysterious box and microphone, singing into a karaoke machine he must have lugged around with him from corner to corner. A plastic container sat near his feet, a few coins at the bottom. He had a harelip and missing teeth, not one of the uprooted peasants but a desplazado of another sort. Into which category did he fall, sinner or saint? Who were we to ever judge another when we could not know a single experience of anyone, let alone all the experiences that shape a life?

"Do you think Ana will marry Carlos?" I asked.

Gracia frowned. "I'm worried for her," she said. "For instance, with the birth control." We crossed the street, Gracia charging ahead in her espadrilles. "I'm afraid she won't use anything or something will go wrong with those flimsy condoms. I can just see it."

We entered the store, the shelves behind the counter crammed with medications. Many could be bought without a doctor's prescription. Gracia fished inside her bag, produced a thin pastel box, and gestured for the clerk to assist us. He asked how many we'd like. Gracia and I exchanged glances and burst out laughing. "Three," she told him. To me she said, "That should have you covered for a few months." I paid for the supply out of my Christmas money, about thirty U.S. dollars.

On the sidewalk I opened one of the boxes and peeked inside. "Good luck," Gracia said. "And if Manuel doesn't come to his senses and forget this idea of sexual sin, then I suggest he enter the priesthood like his brother."

At home, bedroom door latched, I read the pill package three times. I couldn't take them for another two weeks, which felt as far away as Christmas, and so stuck the pack in my purse pocket where the maids or Inez weren't likely to stumble across them. I didn't mention the pills to Manuel during our phone call that night, either. Instead I asked him if Emilio could obtain more solid information. "I know my brother can come off as arrogant sometimes," Manuel said, "but I promise he's not bluffing. He has all sorts of connections with political groups, government. I know how important finding out the truth is to you. It would be for me, too."

Moments after we hung up the phone rang again, and I expected to hear his voice. He likely had forgotten to mention something, or to tell me again that he loved me, which he had not said since the rally.

But whoever spoke sounded gruff and robotic, hardly human. "If you want to keep your nice life on the hacienda, Mercedes Martinez, you better stop hanging out with La Maria Juventud." He stopped then, breathing raggedly—the armed guerillas of my nightmares suddenly transfigured, real. The alien, electronically altered voice somehow reminded me of the man with the karaoke machine from earlier, but this was someone who knew about me. The blood rushed in my ears. I saw myself standing on the edge of a jungle precipice, *the Alpha and the Omega, the beginning and the end.*

"You can tell your lover boys Manuel and Emilio they're going to die," he said, and clicked off.

The phone was a brick in my hand. My breath jolted—I needed to move, to walk. The caller had known me—did I know him? Might he have been one of the jefes, or even Fidel, disguised, delivering the threats at my father's demand? I roamed downstairs into the darkened living room and lowered onto the tile, the coolness rising to the bottoms of my feet as I leaned back against Papi's chair. I yearned for the dogs, their furry muzzles and solid warmth; they slept on an old mattress on his balcony. I remained as the terrorist had wanted me: paralyzed by fear, and alone. Until a chain jingled, and Angel slowly hopped down the stairs on her three legs, climbed into my lap. Calmer now, I crawled into bed.

But I slipped in and out of sleep, only to awaken in a sweat. I saw myself ripped out of a crowd, hauled into the back of a camouflaged Jeep, beaten with a rifle butt in an encampment shrouded with leaves. In some dreams I was abducted alone; in others Manuel and I were together, sometimes Emilio as well, jostled by masked men. The guerillas swept their guns in our direction, as if spraying hoses, yelling, and I heard again the voice on the phone. My dreams possessed the sensory sharpness of visions: the sweaty stink of the guerillas' body odor, mixed with damp earth and the smoke of campfires, the snaps and swishes of the jungle.

In one I was marched to a drop-off to be killed. I could see across and down to the next mountain slope. It appeared bottomless. Even in the dream I realized this was a view I had experienced as a child: on a visit to Costa Rica we had once taken a zip-line rainforest tour. Nowhere else did such giant, ancient, exquisite trees exist. I wept with shock that this was the simple, final end, but also with joy at sight of the trees, each as magnificent and breathtaking as a view of Earth from space.

The guerilla told me to look ahead, to not turn around. I felt the barrel of his gun press into the back of my skull.

In none of my dreams did anyone come for us.

CHAPTER SIX

By late morning on Saturday Papi had returned from his rounds. I went searching and found him with Vincente down at the paddock. The stable hands worked the young horses on lead lines. Vincente didn't say much but saddled a yearling with quick, steady hands. "Want to try him out, princesa?" he called, his legs planted wide, skinny as saplings.

I smiled, ponytail brushing the back of my neck. "No, thanks—I just had breakfast."

Vincente heckled me in response.

"Just because he doesn't have one of these," Papi patted his round belly, "he thinks he's immortal." He leaned against the fence, his forehead smooth. "Look who decided to get up," he said, and caught my ponytail's curly end. I breathed in mint and pine, toothpaste and aftershave. His eyes twinkled as they followed the cantering horse. "Excited for your dinner party tonight?"

I prodded his forearm. "I want to learn to shoot a gun," I said.

"A gun? Why do you want to do that?" His voice wavered with a suspicious lilt. I told him that ever since the bus robbery, I'd been having nightmares.

"Guns kill people, Mercedes."

"No kidding. I want to learn to shoot one. I would feel better knowing, just in case."

"I'll talk to Luis," he said. "He can teach you sometime."

I bristled. "Why can't you teach me?"

"Because I keep my handling of guns to a minimum. Although I suppose I could get around to showing you. It's not a bad idea, you learning how to use one," he said slowly. "I just don't want you to have fantasies of being a James Bond girl. It's completely serious."

Dust kicked up along the path leading down from the coffee fields. On the far end of the paddock Luis and Guillermo rode up hard, dismounted. Guillermo unstrapped a leather sheath from his side. Sunlight glinted off the machete's handle. "I want to learn now," I said.

"Today? Fidel's around. He'd be the best." Papi studied me, one hand gripping the fence and one on his hip. "What's happened that you all of a sudden want to shoot a gun, eh?"

"Nothing. Just what happened with the bus. And all the news talks about is the hijacking."

He squeezed my shoulder and said, "Those applications are in the U.S. by now. Soon you won't have to worry anymore."

The ghost of his grip lingered after he withdrew, those strong fingers that had squeezed many triggers. Or so I imagined. My legs felt watery, light. My feet slipped on the gravel, and when the ridgebacks trotted up I knelt down and buried my face in their velvety, warm fur.

Fidel guided me up the hillside behind our house, up the ridge along the trails where we sometimes rode horses. Coffee grew around us, and we came upon a small clearing with a target I had never known was there—the outline of a man's head and torso with concentric circles like the inside of a tree trunk. I had sometimes heard gunshots from up the hill while growing up and had assumed the jefes and hired guards target-practiced, but I had never seen where. The target sagged crookedly against a scrap of plywood and was riddled with bullet holes. Fidel removed his 9mm from the holster at his waist, and then the clip. Approximately twenty bullets rested inside; he plucked some out and dropped them into my hand for examination. Then he showed me how to load the clip.

He stepped up and fired a few shots, each one a crack that echoed over the valley. He stood with a firm stance and grip. It did not seem possible that this man, who marked the target and landed the bullets in the center of the shadow's chest, was the same man who drove me to and from school every day, whom I often had to shake awake when he fell asleep with his newspaper on his lap. He fired another round, and I plugged my ears until he finished. He turned to me and pouted. "Not too bad," he said. "Your turn."

This time I loaded the clip—a struggle. The bullets were slippery, the case tight, the smooth gun more cumbersome than I had expected. He adjusted my grip and instructed me on how to line up my sights. My first shot flew way off and didn't even hit the target; the kickback filled me with terror and power. My next clipped the white border of the figure. But my third hit the right shoulder. I fired a half dozen more shots. A few hit the target. One pierced straight through the heart. Fidel praised me. I felt proud, even though the act of shooting felt wrong to me.

We loaded the clip again. Fidel practiced his shots rapid fire, his shooting second nature. I wondered about him, his military—or paramilitary—past. I recalled the comments he had made about my father, Manuel's promise fresh in my mind. What I needed was more solid information about Papi that could be confirmed by other sources.

"You were a captain, right?" I asked. "Did you ever kill anyone?" He nodded, staring at the ground as he loaded more bullets.

"Who? Guerillas?"

"Some FARCs," he said. "In the mountains."

"What does that feel like?" I said. "To kill someone?"

He pressed the gun into my hand, and it felt even heavier this time. He said, "You feel like you are God." I swallowed hard; the wind kicked up and blew a piece of my hair across my eyes. I brushed the strands away. Far below the slopes of coffee lay our fields. The workers looked like tiny dots in the black soil. "You see what God sees every second of every day," he continued. "To see the life leave someone is just as beautiful and gruesome as a woman giving birth."

The glint of sunlight reflected in the crucifix around his neck. "So you don't feel bad?" I asked. "As far as it being a sin?"

"I don't think it's a sin if you're following orders." He shrugged. "At first it felt like nothing. I wanted revenge. I had a wife and two kids. The FARC took over our village, and they were killed in the fighting." He clutched his arms to his chest. "But then it felt like ripping open a wound every time. After a while, I felt sick about it. That's how your father and I got to know each other. Our troop had come through here, remember?" The gun was growing damp and slick in my hand. "One night I told him about it, and he offered me a job as soon as I could get out. He's a good man, more than you know."

Fidel's regard for my father reminded me of my conversations with Inez; I trusted her opinions more. "But my father," I began, not knowing what I wanted to ask. "Guerillas killed his parents, you know that?"

"Of course. Your father and I have exchanged much in confidence."

"What can you tell me about his past? About my mother and grandparents?"

He glanced at me, then away. "Ask someone else. Now, are you going to shoot or what?"

We shot a few more rounds, and I managed to land a few bullets across the target's torso. By the end, the cutout resembled a sieve rather than a person, its outer edge jagged and torn. We picked our way down the stony trail. I was surprised at my exhaustion, how the gun had drained my concentration. I told him this.

"Shooting can be a meditation," he said, "when you don't shoot to kill."

For a few long moments we trudged in silence. Then he said, "Your father went sort of crazy after he lost your mother. I know that for a while he was very different from the man you know—bitter, enraged. The guerillas who killed your grandparents, it was no random kidnapping and execution. The FARC abducted them because your father had become their enemy."

"But that was years ago, wasn't it?" I suddenly felt lightheaded. "Who would threaten to hurt me now?"

We had neared the trail's end, following the fence of saplings twined with barbed wire. The horses were out to pasture, the paddock vacant. Unlatching the gate, Fidel said, "Your father takes measures to protect the both of you, but he has enemies." He adjusted the 9mm in the holster, resting his fingers on the top. "And because he has enemies, so do you."

The maids had worked a half-day; no one was upstairs. The door to Papi's room remained shut. I brushed through the clothes in his closet, but nothing unusual struck my eye, just shirts, suits, coats. The dresser contained bottles of cologne and a wooden box of cuff links, tie tacks, and a few tarnished rings. I opened the first drawer—nothing but socks. The next drawer held T-shirts and underwear, the next, only jeans. The door blew open and thudded against the wall, and I jumped. But it was just one of the dogs nosing her way in. I started to tiptoe away but decided to open the final drawer on the bottom.

It was full of cash. Bundled Colombian pesos and American dollars. I shut the drawer fast, shooed the dog out. In the hallway, I listened to be sure I was alone before closing the door behind me.

Heart pounding, I once again tugged open the drawer, sifted through the stacks. On the bottom lay a folded up piece of legal paper, worn, with figures scribbled in columns and my father's handwriting along with someone else's I didn't recognize. There were amounts in the hundreds of thousands. The months were listed, with five-figure sums subtracted and the balance tallied. Payments of some kind, but for what? Nor could I tell if the numbers represented pesos or dollars, a huge difference. Was the money for illegal payouts? I replaced the paper carefully, rearranged the stacks overtop. The bundled dollars held fifties and twenties. It wasn't such an outlandish thing for a man as wealthy as my father to keep cash on hand: to pay desplazados who came and went as migrant workers, or for emergencies. Businessmen liked American dollars, or so said Ana's parents at their dinner table.

I climbed to my feet. Where else might Papi hide his most personal possessions? Forgotten dog toys and bunched-up mosquito netting occupied the space underneath the bed. I checked his bathroom, but his personal items with their distinct manly fragrances unnerved me: shaving cream, a damp towel and underwear flung atop the laundry basket. Inside a toiletry pouch I found condoms and a small bottle of rubbery smelling clear liquid; hastily I zipped the bag shut, replaced it by the sink, and exited. Sitting on the bed, I gazed at my mother's picture, traced her face in the frame. Had she really never tried to contact me? Might her parents still be alive, and did they wonder about me, their granddaughter?

The handgun nestled within his bedside drawer didn't come as a surprise, for I'd known he stored one there since I was a child. My father had shown me, with a stern eye, which things about the house I was never to touch.

Bullets rolled along the bottom as I pawed through the contents, half-queasy at what else I might find of a sexual nature, but the drawer was more empty than full. Like me, that was where Papi kept his passport. His had stamps from Costa Rica, Panama, and Venezuela—when had he gone there? Several years' worth of birthday cards from Tía Leo had been jammed in the back. As I was sorting through these it fluttered out—a photo of me as a baby, standing on fat legs between my parents, who crouched in the sand of a beach somewhere. For the first time I took in this version of Paula in color: the chestnut brown of her hair, the lilac bathing suit against her pale skin. Papi looked much younger, not as lean and boyish as Manuel, but shockingly sinewy, his face rounder, his bright eyes narrowed at the camera. A few inches separated them, but they were smiling. Her arm was around his back; my tiny hands grasped both of his. On the back was written, "Cartagena with Mercedes, ten months." English, the handwriting neat. Hers.

For several moments I sat there, barely able to breathe, studying the picture, grappling with the irrefutability of the three of us together at a single point in time. The image somehow made Paula more real than the portrait I'd revered throughout my childhood, her gaze as distant and lofty as that of a movie star. Did the lone family photo lay jumbled inside the drawer, forgotten, or did Papi keep it within reach to mull over before bed some nights? Even if he did, I could not return the print to its place in that musty drawer. I crept across the hall, and after examining it a few minutes more, slipped it among my cherished keepsakes, where it belonged.

Manuel rumbled through the gate on his moto at eight o'clock. I was hunting around the house for a jacket so that I wouldn't freeze on the back of the bike. Papi emerged from his room and held out a leather jacket. "Try this on," he said. "Your mother left it here." I took it from him gingerly. So she had left something behind. Aside from the photo I had found earlier, I had never come across a single object that I thought might have belonged to her. I slid the jacket over my tube top, yanked out my hair from underneath the collar. Papi folded his arms, his face flushed pink with embarrassment or nostalgia; I didn't know which. I told him thank you and hugged him good-bye. The jacket smelled musty and faintly of cedar. I fervently probed the pockets. All empty.

I asked him how late I could stay out. "We were thinking about going to salsa clubs afterward."

"You'll be back right after dinner. Midnight at the latest. Got that?" Papi looked over my head at Manuel as he said this. Manuel regarded us warily from the bike, helmet underneath one arm. I teetered down the steps in my heeled sandals. Papi followed me out but remained on the porch. The cool air kissed my face as I approached the bike. From his motorcycle Manuel waved and Papi held up his hand in return, but both kept their distance. "How's the social justice coming?" Papi called out.

"More or less," Manuel replied. "The message of peace, that doesn't change. To persuade sinners to face their actions is another story."

But my father only leaned against the beam and removed a cigar and matches from his shirt pocket. I climbed onto the back of the chugging moto; heat radiated off Manuel as I wrapped my arms around him. The leather of his jacket rubbed against mine. "How's the finca?" Manuel called out.

"Always the same. Too many displaced." Papi's cigar flared orange-red. "Midnight, don't forget."

We zipped out the gate. The roar of the engine made it impossible to talk, so I settled into the comfort of his jacket, the dewy fragrance of the ripening cane cutting through the bike's oily fumes. We roared around the bends and drops, onto the autopista and the night ahead.

The Mirador overlooked Cali from a mountainous suburb—quite a commute for Gracia and Esteban. Insects droned as we wound through the rainforest, and my ears popped. We turned down a driveway into a partially-hidden lot and parked next to the vehicles of wealthy caleños and gringo diplomats: Gallopers, open-top Jeeps, Land Rovers, Peugeots. A guard with an automatic rifle was perched atop a tower; another two patrolled on foot. Fountains and waterfalls lit as brightly as Christmas trees bordered the great stone staircase as we ascended to the clatter and laughter of the restaurant. Inside, it smelled of steak and yuca. The hostess whisked away our jackets and led us past candlelit booths to a long table by the dance floor. Ana and Carlos had yet to arrive. Of the dozen or so friends gathered, I recognized only a few. The ponytailed peace activist drank from a tall mug with a metal straw—maté. How predictably hip. We sat at the opposite end near Emilio, more handsome than ever in a snug dress shirt, next to the seats reserved for the guest of honor.

Manuel gently led me over to the enormous picture windows. My breath grew shallow, misted the glass. The city lights outshone the stars; on the hillside above, the statue of Cristo Rey glowed. I had never seen the statue so close before, nor a view of Cali more spectacular than from above the hacienda. "This restaurant is like our relationship," he joked. "Difficult to reach but once you arrive, very much worth it." He pinched my side and we laughed.

"Isn't it beautiful? Like a view from heaven," Ana said. She stood in a too-tight black dress, her neck and wrists adorned with glittering emerald jewelry, one arm around Carlos. "Feliz cumpleaños!" everyone cried. The table erupted into applause and birthday heckling, Carlos blushed and shook his head. He leaned over and kissed Ana on the cheek, but then quickly released his hands from hers. Something between them caught me—perhaps if Gracia had not said anything on our pharmacy excursion, I might not have noticed. As soon as they sat down, each of them struck up conversations with different guests.

Musicians tuned up behind us: the melodic trill of guitars, the staccato rattle of drums. A white-haired man, arms sun-spotted, struck the claves, a lanky young man plucked the bass. Emilio was engaged in a lively conversation with a pretty, curly-haired girl from the tent meeting, like the last man on Earth who would take religious vows—top buttons of his shirt unfastened and cuffs rolled up, exposing the sculpted arms all three brothers shared. "The priesthood is too high a calling," he was saying. "If priests didn't give up marriage and family, we wouldn't be able to serve humankind so completely."

"But how can you make a vow when you don't know what will happen? Your feelings may change," she argued. The tattoo of a peace sign flashed from the inside of her wrist. "Plus to deny yourself—celibacy is extreme, that's all I'm saying. And old-fashioned."

I leaned over and whispered into Ana's ear, "Won't not having sex be too much of a struggle for him, if it isn't already? Don't you think?"

"You might be right," she replied. A small smile played across her lips, and she swirled her wine with the expertise of an adult.

Emilio kneaded the tablecloth. Mid-sentence, the girl reached up and flicked a bread crumb from his shirt. The other hand threaded the back of her hair. According to him, adultery meant sex outside of marriage was a mortal sin.

"But isn't that unnatural," I cut in.

Emilio faced me, forearm pressed onto the table. He said, "Imagine that when your life is centered upon God, all your relationships are like stones held in a glass bowl. But when you let something, or someone else, become your focus instead of God, your life is nothing more than a pile of stones with nothing to contain them. Sex is natural, beautiful, but it has dangers."

The dancers filed out and circled each other, the men removing their hats, the women flapping their long skirts—la cumbia. Our plates arrived, steaming rice, yuca and inch-thick steaks, one portion enough to feed a family of four in the hovels at the end of our cane fields, and the talk turned to Gracia and Esteban's talents as the two of them performed a flamenco number.

Manuel slouched toward me in the high-backed chair; underneath the table, he brushed a hand across my lap. I caught his fingers and bit my lip to keep from grinning. Into his ear I said, "I shot a gun today."

"Why?" His head shot up.

"I talked it over with Papi, and we decided it would be a good idea for me to know how to use one." I paused, toying with my napkin. "But there's another reason." I started to describe the guerilla's call. At the mention of the death threat, Manuel motioned for Emilio to listen.

"Scare tactics," Emilio said when I finished. "Not that this means we should ignore them entirely—you did the right thing by telling us right away."

"We should report it, though, don't you think?" Manuel asked him. "I know it's not going to change anything we're doing, but still."

"Don't worry, I'll take care of all that." Emilio said. He picked up a roll, pointed it at us. "No matter what, you can't flinch. Because that's when evil wins."

"I didn't tell Papi," I said.

"No, you shouldn't," Manuel said. He stroked my hand with his thumb. "You can't trust what he might do."

"We each bear our cross, don't we?" Emilio said. He looked at me as he said this, buttering his bread. I wasn't sure exactly what he meant.

Manuel drew closer to me. His stubble scratched my cheek. "So, you a good shot?"

"Too early to say," I said, and sipped wine. "I have found out some things. Tell me what you think." Emilio reached for more yuca, his gaze tracing the dancers, but I knew he was listening. I told them how the FARC had abducted and murdered my grandparents in retaliation toward Papi, although for what I didn't know. Fidel had been either a soldier in the Colombian army or a para; if so, Papi's connections might lie there, as we had housed uniformed troops before. I described Fidel's remarks about Papi taking measures to protect me, although that could mean paying off someone or just Fidel's double role as driver and bodyguard. The only thing I left out was Papi's confession.

They asked the most questions about the troops—how many men and how long had they stayed? Did I remember the names of villages, or where they were going? I shook my head. Manuel touched his napkin to his lips to hide a smile, and I raised my eyebrows at him questioningly. "Nothing," he said. "Just that you're getting to be pretty observant. It's encouraging to see. Especially in someone who for so long hasn't noticed what goes on."

"I'm a fast learner," I said.

Dessert was being served, flan and arequipe, and coffee with Bailey's. Ana had taken her share of wine and any resentment on her part toward Carlos had apparently been forgiven; she now perched on his lap, his hands clasped around her waist as they kissed and talked. The girl with the peace sign had squeezed in the far end, she and the student activist telling a story. His hands animated the air, her curly head shook. I rested my head on Manuel's shoulder, grateful for the chatter drowning out our secrets.

That's when I brought up the hidden cash, describing as best I could the note and rough estimates of the figures jotted down. "What do you think? If we're talking American dollars, that's a lot of money."

"If the amounts equate dollars, yes," Manuel said. He asked if there were any other clues on the paper, maybe I could make a photocopy of it. "But that might not be a balance sheet for payments. It could be a tally of sugar bushels—a private cash arrangement he has with a refinery somewhere, you know?"

"But why keep that hidden away in a drawer?" Emilio countered. "If it doesn't have to do with coca, or paras."

"Is it possible he's tied to the paras?" I asked. "But why would he be paying them?"

"Many reasons," Emilio said. He leaned forward, the candlelight dancing across his face. "Perhaps he has friends there who offer him protection from his old enemies in the cartels, or the FARC. Or he may have enemies in the paras, too, who he pays to keep off his back. I know what he's told you, but none of these men get out of that business, once they're in. At least not alive. In the very least, he operates well beneath the radar, pays off politicians like so many other big ranchers. Why else do you think we're so adamant?" He cupped his chin in his palm, and his face softened. "I'm sorry."

My stomach clenched at this, how true his words rang. "Still," I said weakly. "I have to hope."

Manuel nodded, rubbed my arm. "I wouldn't ask Fidel anything more, if I were you. It sounds like the subject came up today fairly naturally, but I don't think he's to be trusted. Even though he's your driver."

I nodded. The lights behind us went out, the dance floor dim and deserted.

"Anything else?" Emilio asked. He swirled his glass, the remaining wine coating the inside like blood. I tried to picture him performing the Eucharistic ceremony like the wizened priest I had seen, now that I'd glimpsed a few La Maria masses. I couldn't.

We sat in silence. The waiter brought the checks. "I found out I was baptized," I said finally, a hopeful upswing in my delivery.

"Alleluia!" Manuel cried. He slapped the table's edge and the silverware bounced. Emilio and I laughed. "You know I only date baptized Catholics. If you had found out you weren't I was going to have to end things with you, or Emilio would have to take this water and fix things quick." He dunked his fingers in a half-empty water glass and flicked the droplets at me. I flicked him back and made a face. I was still laughing as we stood up to leave.

CHAPTER SEVEN

The first week in May, the ELN released seven more Avianca hostages and a statement. I strained to hear the RCN broadcast, which included President Pastrana's response, as Fidel drove me home that day. The ELN lashed out at the corrupt government and the elite for doing nothing to ease the disparity between the social classes; the guerillas stated that political exclusion justified their actions as a means to an end. But the president issued an equally harsh response: "The national government ratifies its rejection of using atrocious crimes like this with the intent of achieving political goals or benefits." More desplazados clogged the roadsides and stared as we drove past. Barefoot children splashed in a puddle and exchanged a dead fish no bigger than their hands; one boy wrenched it from another and skimmed its pale body across the muck.

On the precious few hours after school when I met Manuel, I discovered with the rains that Fidel tended to lose track of the time—I would often rush to the car only to find him drooling onto his shirt, asleep. And he would accept my lateness without question if I brought him a churro, his favorite snack. Manuel and I roamed the squares of the historic district, ducked under awnings to share arepas and Fantas. We held hands like good Catholic youth even though I did not consider myself one, baptized or not. One day we took shelter in the cathedral; the echoes of our footsteps reverberated up into the corners of the grand ceiling.

Manuel educated me on the Church's history of mediating peace talks both formally and informally—they had been doing so for ten years, after violence against the Catholics intensified and Bishop Jaramillo was murdered in 1989. Countless bishops, priests, nuns, and missionaries had been kidnapped or killed; I had never realized this. I asked about Sister Rosemary; if her life was in danger.

Manuel said he didn't know. "But I worry for Archbishop Duarte," he said. "Everything he does is a risk. He acts out of pure love." Cali's archbishop was one of the most blunt, harsh critics of those who committed or contributed to violence against civilians. "I don't want to say it since I'm afraid it will come true, but mark my words—Duarte's going to be killed."

Some days we headed straight for the apartment, where our talks continued. Emilio explained why clergy and volunteers must not appear to take sides—partisanship brought brutal consequences. Beyond facilitating negotiations, a priest's role was to inform the groups as to what was and was not Christian behavior without mention of the controversial issues that pitted the sides against one another. To this cause Emilio intended to dedicate his vows.

On other afternoons Manuel and I escaped the rains and entered the quiet, shadowed rooms above the carpentry shop. We retreated to his bed without words; only our lips and hands spoke, like the way Manuel crossed himself and pressed his fingers to his lips when he entered a church. I always liked the way he delivered the kiss, as if God was truly his beloved.

Yet he continued to hold back from sex. There were other releases, substitutes, although I found these acts only partly satisfying, like drinking coffee without sugar, or eating cake without icing. Where exactly were the moral lines being crossed? The final act itself equaling sin was absurd. What about the rest? Did the Bible state that any touching of intimate parts with another person needed to be confessed, or was merely going beyond kissing wrong in the eyes of God? No wonder Manuel was so confused. But I kept these thoughts to myself. I didn't bring up the prospect of losing my virginity to him again, either. Pregnancy terrified me, and loomed over every embrace in the stuffy bedroom above the wet street. Then the much-awaited day arrived on the calendar, and each morning I swallowed the tiny pill. Still,

I held back from asking him, and practically speaking, Emilio and Carlos needed to be gone.

One Saturday night late in May, La Maria hosted a street festival. Ana's parents had taken a private plane to their beach house for the weekend—I didn't mention this to Papi. Manuel and I could leave the festival early, sneak into a guest room. I buried the pills in my bag, drunk with the giddiness of love, of marrying one day, the delirious hope of forever.

We met outside Ana's gate. Carlos dragging Ana along because he didn't want to miss the Ciudad Jardín orchestra, Ana rolling her eyes behind his back, Esteban and Gracia gushing over the booths of indigenous crafts. Manuel and I fell behind, laughing. The streets had been barricaded off from motor traffic, and the air thick from close bodies and greasy street food. An endless procession of musicians and revelers packed the roadway: a Mexican mariachi band, kids performing la cumbia in overly made-up faces, then gigantonas—oversized papier-mâché figures. A witch, bobbing and whirling, bumped into me. The operator's face peeked out, barely visible, hidden behind a flap underneath the giant head.

In the mob we quickly lost sight of our friends, and picked out our favorites of the comical figures—devils for Manuel, voodoo queens for me. Soon he fell quiet, however, his gaze flitting over the revelers. Speakers blared dance music from truck beds. He said, "Let's get out of this craziness," and led me through the churchyard. Young people straddled the stone wall, legs dangling. They slung their arms over one another and their teeth gleamed bluish-white. I inhaled hairspray, popcorn, cigarettes. A boy snatched an ice cream cone from the girl at his elbow; she squealed and ran after him, gleefully swinging her purse. Ahead the rose garden awaited, a dark oasis. I skirted roots and watched my steps, but Manuel hurried as if late for a bus. We were walking past a banyan tree when he pulled me to him. He kissed me deeply, tugged up my shirt and slid his hand underneath. But his expression was solemn, distracted.

"We can go to Ana's," I whispered. "The guard will let us in." A hundred meters away the brass horns died, and the orchestra struck up Vivaldi. I walked ahead and held out my hand behind me, but he didn't move. "You don't think we're going to do it in a churchyard, I hope?" I said, my tone playful.

He caught my arm, slid his hand down until he grasped my fingers. "Not tonight. I'm sorry, I know it's good timing in some ways. Just that back there, in the crowd, I felt like something was wrong. Don't you ever get those feelings?"

"What kind of feeling? Something about us?"

"No, more like something bad was going to happen. I don't know, maybe I've just been going to too many meetings. About us—maybe. I don't want you to get hurt." He stroked my thumbnail, let go and touched my hair. "Maybe you should go to school in the United States."

"Is that what you want?" A sinking, panicked feeling rolled through me.

"For you to leave? Of course not." He ran his fingers through my hair, combed out the tangles. "We're planning a peace march next month, and I want you front and center beside me."

His fingers hit a snag. I caught my breath as he gently tugged it smooth, pictured myself holding up a banner and marching. I saw Papi watching us on the news and heard the ring of the phone late at night. The dreams of rifles, thirst, death.

"I didn't even like being on stage at the last rally. Next time I thought I would join the crowd." I shifted, the ground uneven. "Let's get out of here. No one will be at Ana's."

"In a minute. The music." He nodded toward the orchestra. He edged closer, running his hands up and down my back. We rocked a little. "Don't you realize what a powerful presence you bring?" he said.

The statue of the Virgin stared serenely, so close I could reach out and feel the moss on her robes, if I wanted. I lifted my head from his shoulder. "What are you talking about?"

His breath warmed my ear. "Oh, come on. The daughter of Diego Martinez, speaking out for peace?"

"Is that what this is about?" I asked slowly. "Your Church cause?" I recoiled and when he tried to draw me back, I wrenched away, arms crossed and clasping my elbows tight.

"My God, Mercedes," he said, voice gritty with exasperation. He ran a hand through his hair and clenched his brow. "Of course not. But think of the thousands in this country who have no power, no voice. And I shouldn't have been pressuring you. I'm sorry. It's my calling. You choose yours." His tone sounded like the President's address to the guerillas—convicted and irrevocable. I recalled Ana, her lilting cadence and dancing eyes. *Manuel, he's a good one. Passionate, too—if you can handle that.*

"Cause?" I echoed. "I don't even know who I am, or anything about my family. Do you have any idea? So excuse me while I take some time to figure that out. Then maybe once I've cleared up a few things, I can serve soup or lead marches, or whatever else you think I ought to be doing. Okay?"

He hung back for a moment, arms loose at his sides. Then stepped forward, palms outstretched. "I'm so sorry," he said. "That was unfair. I wasn't thinking." He kissed my temple, gently. "Forgive me?"

I touched his cheek. "Let's go to Ana's."

He glared at me hard, his jaw set. "What if you get pregnant?"

"I won't. We'll use something."

"No, now's not the right time."

The shrieks of the teens pierced Vivaldi—one that I knew from Papi, *The Four Seasons*. A balloon had floated over and hovered a few feet above the grass, half-deflated, a desplazado lost among the trees. I started to walk away then, but he didn't follow. "I'm going back to the festival," he said finally.

"I'll be at Ana's," I called over my shoulder. "Tell them I don't feel well." Which was true. I reeled with dizziness as if I was one of the zigzagging parade figures. I didn't look back once, but picked my way through the darkness of the churchyard, the roots and rubbish near the wall. In a waste bin at the end of Ana's street, I threw up.

In the mansion's guest room I lay awake for hours, tossing and trembling. How had the evening gone so terribly wrong? Instead of caressing in his arms, I was alone in a strange house of empty green rooms. The urgent way he had kissed me, his proclaimed despair—was that what had been driving him to seek comfort with me? How much of his interest was wrapped up in my status as the daughter of Diego Martinez? I held on to the slim chance that I might hear the front door open, a soft knock outside my bedroom, and it would be him. But when I did hear the door and footsteps on the stairs, I caught the laughter and whispers of Ana and Carlos, Esteban and Gracia—no Manuel. It must have been two or three o'clock in the morning. They stayed up playing Latin pop music in the upstairs living area, horsing around, and made hushed attempts to be quiet for my sake. Finally each couple retreated to their bedroom. I shoved my face into the pillow and wept. Love could be lost as easily as the drop of a coin in the street.

I awoke at eight-thirty, dressed, and gathered my things. In the bathroom, I swallowed my pill with a handful of water and inspected the foil pack, half-empty, two rows of blue and white pills remaining. What good did they do? In the hallway I paused, unsure if I should say good-bye or leave a note. I crept outside Ana's door—nothing but silence. I found paper, scribbled something apologetic about getting sick from the festival food, and slid it underneath her door. When I passed the next bedroom I paused again at the stir of weight on the bed, the soft talking and moans; Esteban and Gracia were making love. I lingered only a second longer to listen—wistfulness, curiosity, and jealousy converging in me at once—and headed downstairs to wait on the damp curb for Fidel.

I didn't see Papi when I got home, and Inez said that he had been out all morning, even though none of the jefes or workers tended the fields on Sunday. I asked if anyone had called for me, but she said no. Upstairs, I spread the English books across the office table and popped the dialogue tape in the player. I stared at sentences with missing nouns and verbs that required conjugation, dull as music notes.

Around noon the phones rang and Inez yelled for me to pick up. I answered and tried not to sound too eager, hoping for Manuel. But it was Ana. She spoke in a panicked, rushed voice—something about the church, a big kidnapping. Sirens wailed in the background. "Which church?" I asked, but even as I said the words, my limbs felt impossibly heavy.

"Turn on the TV," she pleaded. "It happened this morning, at the end of mass." I raced downstairs, phone pressed to my ear, and clawed the couches for the remote.

The Cali station declared breaking news. Police cars and hysterical civilians swarmed outside La Maria—I glimpsed the tent where the social justice meetings took place, and the statue of the Virgin. Thirty guerillas had rolled up in canvas-covered trucks at the end of the Eucharist ceremony and stormed inside. They shouted that a bomb had been planted in the church and they were going to detonate it. By this ruse, they loaded the entire congregation into trucks, including the priest, then fled south into the mountains above the town of Jamundi with army troops and police commandos chasing the caravan. The authorities, still in pursuit, did not yet know which rebel group was to blame, FARC or ELN. The guerillas had littered their escape route throughout la Ciudad Jardín with homemade land mines, and the authorities had been forced to stop and disarm the devices.

"They've got Emilio," Ana said.

"What about Manuel? Is he there?"

"They left. He and Carlos ran in and took the keys to the Land Rover. I told them not to go, that all three of them will be killed, but they've lost their minds." She heaved; I could barely understand her and tried to calm her down. "They would have stolen the car if I hadn't given it to them. Oh, Mercedes, what could I do?"

"How do they even know where they're going?" To the west and south, the high peaks jutted against the blue, and craggy rock broke out among the rainforest green. She said Manuel knew because of what Emilio had found out through mediations—that it was the ELN, and they were taking the hostages into the Farallones National Park. Possible scenarios swarmed my mind—the brothers getting lost in the dense, steep rainforest of the Farallones, the guerillas capturing or shooting them on sight. The possibility of never seeing Manuel or the others again.

"They're crazy to go after those trucks," I said. "What else did he tell you?"

"Only that he said he loves you, and is sorry for not leaving the festival with you. Did you get into a fight?"

"Sort of," I said. I groped my way to the couch. The mutts were out with Papi, but Zulu and Shaka had sneaked up to nap; Zulu rested her chin on my thigh. Why had I failed to imagine the real extent of the phone call weeks ago, its implications? Perhaps a childish part of me hadn't wanted to accept the anonymous threat as real. I'd told the brothers and they'd all but jeered at it—to a bad end. If they'd misjudged something this serious, what else might they be wrong about? Had I trusted them too easily? Here I thought I'd be safer with Manuel. Maybe not.

Ana rambled on about how she wished her parents would fly back, but she also feared for them. She begged me to come and stay with her. I told her I couldn't. The jefes listened to their radios in the fields. Once Papi found out, if he didn't know already, he'd keep me home.

"Any other week, it could have been me and my parents," she said, "or my grandmother." I pictured them marching through the jungle, hands on top of their heads, and lying in the dirt at night, even as I wondered what would happen to Emilio and the congregants. Guerillas were notorious for letting many hostages go at first, but also for holding others ransom, often for years, and carrying out brutal executions when demands were not met. Papi's ties—might he have a hand in the kidnapping, however inadvertently? Might he even have known that this was going to happen, and when?

This possibility drew me back upstairs, to the office. I tore through the files in the cabinet near his desk and Rolodexes of names which meant nothing to me, sifted through HSBC bank statements, bills for horse feed, invoices from sugarcane refineries, shipments out of Cartagena. Everything appeared legitimate. My previous hunch had been right—records of illegal activities or cash payouts wouldn't be kept in an office. They likely weren't kept on record at all.

I had just rolled the last drawer shut when I heard voices in the courtyard, and the patio door opening. I was pretending to study, bent over the grammar book. When Papi entered I bit the inside of my cheeks. But as soon as my eyes met his, I asked if he'd heard the news.

"In the truck—I only caught part of it. Inez said someone called and upset you. Was it the boy?"

It crossed my mind to ask what work he'd been doing on Sunday, but instead I told him about what Ana had said. He shook his head slowly, face clouding over. For a moment I didn't know if he would yell, or if the incident made him think of his parents' fate, but I couldn't ask because he squeezed me in a hug, and I burst into tears. He smelled of stale sweat and wood smoke, as if he'd been near a campfire. From below, one of the jefes laughed to another, started up his truck, and rumbled off. Papi handed me his bandanna; I wiped my eyes. He said, "You know, sometimes the most you can do for others is to take the best care of yourself."

"What's going to happen to them?" I asked.

"How should I know? That wasn't very smart of Manuel and his brother to go chasing after guerillas into the mountains. Although they'll probably run out of gas before they get killed or captured, thank God."

"Can you do anything?" I said, looking up at him.

"Don't be ridiculous." But his eyes darted back and forth, searching my face, his lips parted. I held my breath. "Listen," he said, leaning over again. "This is what happens when you try to stand up to guerrillas, to cartels, to any evil. I know all about Manuel's little youth group. And what of it? Let him choose his destiny. You choose yours." He gave my shoulder a quick, hard squeeze, and left.

When I came down for dinner that evening, the patio door stood ajar. Papi and the jefes sat back, silently chewing their cigars, their fanned-out poker cards lowered. The television blared in the living room. The ELN had claimed responsibility, as Manuel had predicted. Within hours of the kidnapping, Army General Mora had sent helicopters and swarms of troops over the mountains and forced the ELN to abandon eighty-four abductees. I lobbed Zulu a ragged toy; she whipped it back and forth in her jaws. Emilio might be among the released, on his way home with his brothers even now.

The jefes discussed the incident, their earnest voices peppered with inquisition, and I squinted at the TV, straining to overhear. How much had Papi told them about Emilio's abduction, if anything? "Looks like the Third Brigade needs to set up its own Cali branch," Papi said. Low chuckles followed. Luis mentioned giving Uncle Charlie a call. Who was that? "Do you know an Uncle Charlie, a friend of Papi's?" I asked Inez. She was setting two places at the table.

She shook her head. "Charlie," she repeated slowly. "Isn't that sometimes what the American soldiers are called?"

This felt familiar. Had Luis meant that it was time for the Colombian military to call in American forces? Possibly, although I found this hard to believe: American troops summoned to Colombia to eradicate guerillas who had kidnapped a church. Papi stood up and excused himself, told the men that tonight he was eating with me. Inez served us first, then the men, and shut the door after her, cutting off their smoke and talk. He dug into his roast chicken but I picked at mine. It was nightfall; had Manuel and

Carlos returned home yet, or were they still roaming the national park? Was Emilio to unite with their family, or did he face a night in the chilly elevations of the forest with nothing but a thin shirt? I could see him leading people in prayer, his voice steady and eyes downcast. Ana would have called if there had been news. The live coverage talked about a wave of terror, that nowhere in Colombia was safe. "What's next?" a man Fidel's age cried to the camera. He was stopped on Avenida Sexta, pushing a stroller. "Are they going to abduct people at supermarkets? Movie theaters?" Many spoke of Bogotá as the site of the next, undoubtedly greater, guerilla attacks. Would Gracia's parents let her accept a dance scholarship if violence erupted in the capital?

"The ELN is going to start riding into downtown Cali," Papi said. "In broad daylight. Office buildings, courts, schools. What's to stop them?" He was eating with vigor and drank quickly, appearing tired but rejuvenated. I asked what he had done earlier, and he said he had helped move some desplazados who needed medical care to the mission, and hauled scraps of lumber to their makeshift camp. "Otherwise they're cutting down my good trees," he said. "I'm afraid it's going to turn into a Cali slum down there. Little Aguablanca, Luis calls it." He spoke with a mixture of nonchalance and pride, a glimmer in his eyes—the only bright spot in the otherwise grim day. He added, "I want you home right after school every day from now on. And no more rallies or festivals. It's just too dangerous."

I pushed the rice around on my plate. "Can my friends come here?" I asked. Papi raised his glass but paused. "I would prefer you not see Manuel anymore," he said. "However peaceful, his activities make him a threat. Sorry."

I dumped my plate and trudged upstairs. This time when I tried the brothers' apartment, Carlos answered, his voice hollow and weary. "We just got back," he said. Emilio had not been among those the ELN had been forced to abandon. Carlos handed off the phone to Manuel. The two had driven through the national park for hours, the helicopter gunships whirring low overhead, the military and police tearing past, family members of other abductees careening behind, the roads in chaos. Darkness fell, and the authorities warned them to stop searching; the guerillas may have rigged the roadways with homemade bombs. So the brothers came home.

Then he broke down, and I could picture him hunched on the edge of his unmade bed, fist against his forehead. I told him I was sorry over and over, asked what he was going to do now. "Everything I can," Manuel said. "More rallies. I'll use whatever connections the priests have to the guerillas to negotiate his release. Pray. I'm already a wreck without him." He apologized for the night before. "That's the only other thing I thought about today. I want to talk to you about it."

"I wish I could see you," I said, lowering my voice. "But I can't right now."

On the other end I detected rustling, movement. "I'm coming there," he said. "Can you meet me outside the gate in thirty minutes?"

"I'm too exhausted," I said. My stomach growled; I rubbed my temple. The last thing I felt like doing was sneaking around the property. "Let's talk tomorrow."

"No," he said. "We're supposed to leave the lines open here, in case of calls. I'll be fine. I'll meet you on the road."

Soon after, I crept downstairs in my mother's jacket. Papi regarded me like one of the dogs waiting for the maid to fix her food bowl. I said that I was going to go for a quick walk to calm myself, that I'd spoken with Ana and she'd given an update. "A shame," Papi said once I told him the brothers' pursuit had failed. "But martyrs seek to become martyrs. I'll bet even more than Manuel, this Emilio wants to either be archbishop, Pope, or Jesus Christ. Am I right?"

"He's studying to be a priest," I said. "Isn't that what Catholics are supposed to do? Follow Jesus?" I shrugged. "There are worse things."

"Do you know what happened to the twelve who followed Christ and preached his messages?"

I rolled my eyes, spun the globe. It whirled a few times before I jammed my finger on top to halt it. Italy's boot.

"All of them but one died terrible deaths. They were tortured, their limbs pulled apart, eyes plucked out," he said. "Follow anyone, and you better be aware of what your choices may lead to, as noble as the cause may be." Wind muffled the microphone, whipped the TV reporter's hair. She plucked aside a piece that had caught her lip, smoothly prattled on about the next potential attack. Papi pointed the remote, and the set flashed to darkness.

I was halfway down the driveway when the ridgebacks sprinted up. Papi's voice bellowed above, along with a rousing Middle Eastern album. He had rejoined the card game. "Shaka, Zulu, go home," I hissed and pointed back to the house. But they trotted alongside, ignoring me. The guard stepped out of his tower, a hand on his hip and a Fanta in the other. "What's up?" he said.

"I'm going for a walk to see the alpacas," I said. "I don't want these two following behind."

"I'll hold them while you go through," he said, and hit the button inside his booth.

The gate opened slowly as the door to a tomb. He swung down the steps, grabbed the dogs' collars. Shaka and Zulu whimpered but sat down on the driveway. "Shush, now," he said. "One of these days you two are going to get loose, aren't you? And don't you know how upset your papa will be then, huh? No, we don't want that." He knelt, rumpling their ears. "Enjoy your walk, princesa."

Minutes later the motorcycle's lone headlight flashed out of the cane. Manuel glided up, parked the bike behind trees. We embraced. He crushed me to his chest and buried his face in my hair. A faint odor of dried sweat clung to his shirt, and something sweet that had spilled, like soda. "I've missed you," he said. "All I could think of today was how could I be so stupid, to let the chance to be with you slip away. That it wouldn't be wrong. I love you—how could it be?"

I traced his cheek. "Maybe there's more than one truth to everything," I said, "and that's the highest truth of all."

"Forgive me?" he asked, his forehead against mine.

"For the other night at Ana's? Of course. I love you." I let my hand rest on his shoulder. In the shadowed pasture, the two alpacas sleeping beside one another stirred. The smaller one wobbled to its feet, approached the fence. Its companion awoke and followed, sluggish and sleepy. "It's the actions that are stupid and rash that aren't easy to forgive. You might have listened to those warnings."

"What do you mean?" His grip loosened upon my waist.

"That when I told you about the phone threat, neither of you took it seriously. And now look."

Even in the darkness I could see the color drain from his face. "Why do you say we didn't take it seriously? How would you know?"

"What I mean is, nothing's so simple. Didn't it even cross your mind what might be at stake? For yourself? Not to mention everybody else—that whole congregation."

"I can't believe you," he said. I stepped closer, arms extended, hushing him to be quiet, the guard, but he jerked away. "I had no idea Emilio would be taken, or anybody else. You can't blame me."

"I'm not blaming you. How could anyone have known they were going to kidnap a church?" I said. The watchtower cast its beam a few lengths away. We circled each other in the grass. "But you can't pretend that your lives haven't been threatened. That you've got to protect yourself."

"You know what, Mercedes? You know nothing, I'll tell you right now. You're a spoiled, sheltered rich girl." He stalked off, kicked the fence. The alpacas snorted and flinched, trotting away. I crept toward him, squeezed his shoulder. He whirled around, his face streaked with tears.

"I'm sorry," I said. "That was unfair." I felt like the valley was caving in on me, the chilly air hurting my lungs.

He sank down and I did the same, our knees digging the moist earth. I smoothed his forehead, and he mumbled that he forgave me too. His eyes blazed pink; I rubbed away his tears. "Go home," I said. "Papi doesn't want me to see you anymore. We'll have to find another way."

He nodded then, in the grateful way that children do when you clean up their wounds, and allowed me to lead him to the bike. We hugged again, hard, and for a fleeting moment I wanted to jump on and escape down the road—but to where? How? Inside the gate I brushed past our car, cool and vacant. The rosary beads shone black in the dark.

CHAPTER EIGHT

Fidel palmed the wheel with one hand as he drove, flicking his cigarette ash out the window with his left. "Can you believe those rebels would stoop this low?" he said. The veins in his neck bulged and the radio's blare overtook his voice; he appeared to be talking more to himself than to me, even though he glanced back over his shoulder as he spoke. "To raid a mass, and during the Eucharist no less. Idiots." He grunted, took a long, hard drag, and pitched the butt. On the radio the monsignor of the Colombian prelate was speaking in a tone bridled with shock and indignation. The Catholic bishops were seeking excommunication of all ELN members for this insult and mortal sin.

"What's the big deal?" I asked. We struck a pothole; the rosary shimmied and swung.

"The ELN might as well have pissed on the back of Christ himself," he replied.

How little I understood because I had not been raised Catholic. I slumped against the door. We took the downtown exit and the car balked in stinking city traffic, the cathedral dome and columns blinding in the early light. In a radio message, the ELN leader Gambino stated that occasionally the wealthy urban elite must experience the consequences of war, and not escape the horrors that thousands of peasants face every day. Might the threatening callers wait for me after school, grab me as I crossed to the car and Fidel? We inched up the avenue, where an intersection was blocked off. A police van and officers on motos surrounded an empty, sun-bleached Renault abandoned in the middle lane. One officer held his white helmet underneath an arm and with the other, waved in a bomb squad van. At the revolving door to an office building, a private guard adjusted his automatic rifle as he conferred with another, who stared ahead through mirrored sunglasses, chewing gum. I counted five outside the Banco de Bogotá alone.

Fidel startled me then, remarking that I was quiet.

"I'm just worried about a friend. One of the young people who was taken yesterday at the church. He's studying to be a priest."

"Sorry to hear that," Fidel said.

"Do you think they'll release him? If his brother works hard to negotiate?"

Fidel shrugged. "The guerillas will keep anyone they think is valuable. You'd better pray." After we sat gridlocked for another ten minutes he swore under his breath. I thought of a remark Sister Rosemary had said, *Patience is a form of action and often the only route to take.*

That afternoon, the nun brightened when I inquired about Papi's recent visit to the mission. She said he'd arranged with one of our tenants, a poultry farmer, to donate what eggs and meat she didn't sell at the Saturday market. That way the displaced children would at least have enough protein and a chance to concentrate on their lessons during the week. Dozens didn't have shoes; he said he would speak to the zapateria owner. "He probably doesn't tell you this, but he stops in to check on their progress every afternoon," she said, "even if it is just for five minutes." She smoothed her skirt as she said this. A beaded anklet dangled from above her sandaled foot. Birkenstocks. I hadn't known such ugly shoes existed.

"Sounds like he's bored," I said.

She looked at me quizzically. "Why do you say that?"

"Papi? He doesn't know how to relax. Even when he has his cigar, he's jabbering with Luis or someone, complaining to Inez about the maids. Or bothering me." I flipped through the EFL workbook, frowning.

"But look at the big operation he runs. That's got to be stressful."

"Stressful, sure. I just wouldn't get too excited. Stopping by for five minutes? Telling some lady to give away a few crates of eggs? If he really wanted to, he'd do a lot more, that's all." I sat back, twirled my pencil in the air. "He's amusing himself."

She bit her lip, picked up the workbook, and set it back down. Then she withdrew some lotion from her bag and dabbed a dot on her hands, rubbing them vigorously. Lavender steeped the air. She kept her fingernails short like Inez but her hands appeared delicate and smooth, the freckles faint. My mother's hands, how did they compare? Did Paula get manicures, carry a nail file and lipstick in her purse, like Ana's mother?

"Aren't you ever afraid about guerillas raiding the mission and capturing you?"

"I think about it sometimes," she said slowly. "Who doesn't? But fear is the ultimate test of faith."

"Faith. I don't even know what that means."

"Faith means believing in the best outcome for all situations. And we are all being tested, especially right now."

Hesitantly, I reached for the lotion, eyed her for approval. She slid it toward me. "Never forget to moisturize, even in the tropics," she said, head bowed toward me. "And you should be using sunscreen." She was so jaunty, assured. And still pretty, with her clear skin, blue-green eyes, and cropped blond hair.

"Have you ever been in love?" I asked.

A long moment of silence passed. She marked crosses on the scratch paper in front of her, and at the mention of love she traced a heart. "Once, when I was your age," she said. "But we never truly got together. The timing was never right—or maybe we thought we had so much time. We each lived in other countries for a while. And then he married someone else. But it was love." She drew a sky of stars over the crosses and the heart so that it resembled a graveyard.

"How terrible," I said.

"Perhaps. But I learned I could go on, create another life. So here I am." She smiled and set the pencil aside. "How is your Manuel?"

I told her what had happened to Emilio as she gathered her belongings; any minute Fidel would enter downstairs, ready to drive her back to the mission. She paused as she collected the books. "Do you want me to pray with you about it?" she asked, her hand light on my shoulder. Downstairs the dogs barked and scuffled on the tile. I touched the paper with the stars, the crosses and the heart, shook my head, and said no.

There had been little news of Emilio or the others. Manuel took over the youth group, their mission now to organize parishioners whose family members had been taken and launch a series of peace rallies and demonstrations; Carlos was doing the same on his campus, joining forces with the student organizations there. Overnight the ranks of La Maria Juventud swelled, the public outcry against the guerillas infiltrating a church and defaming the Catholic faith showing no signs of slowing down. To pull off such a large-scale attack the ELN would have had to plan for months, according to Manuel. In hindsight, he didn't think the phone threat had much to do with what happened—the ELN had a much larger agenda than the two of them. He was working past midnight every night, coordinating with the victims' families, negotiating with church officials and the Red Cross for the release of as many captives as possible. While the ELN would likely hang on to a few dozen hostages they thought they could hold for ransom, the leaders settled on a date. Manuel had less than two weeks to arrange that Emilio be among those released.

One Saturday I phoned Tía Leo. Her tone was full of concern over the mass kidnapping, and she said that all of Costa Rica was saddened and alarmed at the news. "Have you spoken to Papi yet?" I asked. "About me finishing school there?" A deluge of afternoon rain created a tinny white noise on her end; Costa Rica was just beginning its long wet season. I strained to hear her.

"Didn't he tell you?" she said. "I called him weeks ago, not long after I talked with you. Although he didn't love the idea."

"Why not? If the schools are as good as you said."

"He said it wasn't far enough away. I guess he's afraid with all the targeted kidnappings and violence that someone may even come after you here." She laughed a little at this, adding, "But nothing like that ever happens in Costa Rica. Just petty theft." A beat of silence followed, and the drum of rain. She asked, "Don't you have a school vacation coming up?"

The first two weeks in July my school would be on break. Had Papi told her, because how else would she know? What had they discussed about me?

By what I could tell they spoke several times a month, lamenting about daughters, griping over tenants. Not much else.

"Come visit and I'll tell you what I know," she said. "But if you're worried about your father, there's no need. You're all that he has in the world."

I roamed the house then, restless as the dogs. I needed to walk, and so climbed the slippery trail to where I had shot the gun with Fidel, then farther. Shading my eyes, I peered over the hilltops but spotted no evidence of coca production: campesinos stripping plants of the stimulating leaves, stuffing the crop into giant bundles. But that was only my imagining of an illegal drug operation. Perhaps I had no idea what to look for, and the evidence lurked in front of my face, coca flourishing among the coffee. But when I trekked back down I saw only our house, the road snaking through the valley of cane, and the smoke rising from the desplazados' campfires beyond.

A vehicle that I had never seen before was parked in the driveway—an open-top military Jeep but unlike the ones I remembered the commanders dashing around in last year when the troops streamed through and bunked with us. Those Jeeps had been splashed with shiny camouflage, plush seats, and the latest dashboard conveniences. This one had a skinny black steering wheel and gear shifts so tall they looked like golf clubs, the numerals and lettering on the dashboard dials printed in old-fashioned font; up close, I guessed the Jeep to be decades old, a relic from the civil war that had raged since Papi's boyhood. Approaching the house I strained to hear but couldn't. Motor fumes and grass choked the air. Black bandannas hid the faces of the three workers fanned out over the lawn, weed-whackers buzzing.

The man who talked breathlessly on the couches beside Papi and Luis had a receding hairline and reddish face. Gold-rimmed sunglasses jostled from the breast pocket of the stranger's military fatigue shirt, but the frayed hems and dated style told me that similar to the Jeep, the shirt had been out of commission for some time. He looked younger than them by a few years—not quite as young as Fidel. Cellophane and glittery ribbon crumpled upon the coffee table, a bottle of Flor de Caña, Papi's favorite rum uncapped. Ice clinked. All three lowered their cocktail glasses, looked up. The raucous exchange ceased. Papi gestured for me to come and sit down, his eyes dancing over me as he chomped on ice. "Mercedes, I'd like you to meet Uncle Charlie," he said.

We shook hands. "I like your Jeep," I said. "Interesting."

"It's a memento from La Violencia," Uncle Charlie said, referring to the decade-long period of bloody civil unrest preceding the war. He spoke pure Colombian Spanish. No chance he was American or even another Latin nationality. "Passed down to me from an uncle who fought against the first guerilla groups, 1958, so occasionally I take it on driving tours."

Luis smirked, holding his sides. "Driving tours?"

"That's how I like to put it," Uncle Charlie replied. The corners of his eyes turned up slightly, and his lips revealed horsey teeth. He faced me and spoke as if we were the only ones having a conversation. "I don't drive it around much, only on special visits to see old friends."

"How long have you three known each other?" I asked. "Since Florida?"

Papi shot me a surprised, sharp glare. "Actually, sometime after. Uncle Charlie is here on business, hopefully to assist in the problem your Manuel's brother finds himself in."

"Oh, in the negotiations?" I asked. "What do you do?"

Luis and Uncle Charlie chuckled, but Papi frowned and shook his glass.

"Like I said, your father called me in to help. He said things down here in Cali needed straightening out. So here I am," Uncle Charlie said. He shrugged, palms upturned on his knees. A handgun peeked out from his shoulder holster. He must not have driven any sort of distance in that Jeep alone, in open bandido country. Inez was setting the dining room for four. On the patio, two men in rumpled camp shirts and chinos looked down upon the cane, jabbed cigarettes to their lips. A haze of smoke swelled up and out. One limped over to the table where the men played cards, set down his automatic rifle before he sank into a chair.

"Mercedes will be going to school in the United States soon," Papi said.

"If I get accepted," I said quickly. "I still have to take the EFL test."

"A change of scenery, good," Uncle Charlie said. "My kids, as soon as they turned nine, BAM!"—he slapped his knee and grinned like a little boy—"off to the best schools in England."

"England?" I said, wincing.

"Much colder and a longer plane ride way," Papi said. "See how good I am to you?"

I rolled my eyes at him, leaned back and propped my foot on the edge of the coffee table. Outside, the bodyguard lightly stroked the barrel of the rifle, cell phone to ear. I asked Papi for a sip of his rum, and he fixed me a small glass. "Don't your kids miss home?" I asked. "Where do you live?"

Uncle Charlie pointed upward as he sipped. "Córdoba," he said. "North of Medellín. My life's crazy, so my kids only want to come back on vacations. They have their friends and boyfriends there. My daughter came back with a British boyfriend, can you imagine?" he said to Papi. They exchanged a knowing look.

"Uncle Charlie will be staying with us for a while," Papi said.

Over dinner the men talked of military operations that I didn't understand, although I recognized some of what they spoke about from the news: the Third Brigade, which was part of the military and headed by Army General Mora, who'd been interviewed by Caracol Radio Station yesterday afternoon. Uncle Charlie had been in touch with General Mora and was working to set up something called the Calima Front. They rattled off so many names and rankings, I couldn't remember a single one. They spoke of who was retired and who was not, and men Uncle Charlie referred to as "active in the north," under his command. Other times, he referred to his cattle business the way Papi referred to his cane. Head woozy, I sipped the now watered-down rum and lime juice. Tilapia grew cold on my plate. By then their conversation sounded tedious. Why wasn't I a better spy? At a lull, I asked him the most benign question I could think of, about how many head of cattle he owned, and which breed.

Uncle Charlie shoved down a heaping forkful, waved off my question as he chewed, then swallowed. "How's your English?" he asked—in perfect American English, just the way Sister Rosemary spoke it. "Studying hard, I hope?"

I gulped some water. The candles flickered. White slabs of fish floated atop buttery puddles. "I need to practice more," I said, my mouth dry and sticky, the English thick.

"Do you have a boyfriend?" He spoke with no hesitation, no accent. Was he a Latino American, down here as a special agent in their drug war? "If you do, forget him," he said. "Get out of this South American shithole while you can."

"Manuel, her boyfriend, plays guitar and has an amazing voice," Papi said. In English—I had never heard him speak it before. Inez leaned across Luis, asked if he was finished with his plate. He pinched her cheek, complimented her cooking, then sipped silently, his gaze roaming. Papi said, "You would appreciate hearing this young man. She still hasn't invited him over to play for me."

"You said you didn't want me to see him anymore," I exclaimed.

Papi's eyes narrowed at me. He set down his glass with a shove.

Uncle Charlie drained the last of his rum. "Bring him over. I love a good guitar." He'd reverted to Spanish, his delivery commanding, final.

"You'll find this young man interesting, Carlito," Papi said. "Exceptional. He'll make your hair stand on end."

Uncle Charlie beamed. "How about Friday night?"

"I'm not sure. He's been working nonstop for his brother and the others—the hostage release." I shrugged. "I haven't even seen him lately."

"But she talks to him every night," Papi said, exchanging bemused glances with the men. I set my jaw and squirmed. To me he asked, "I'd have thought you'd be eager to see him, no?"

"Of course," I said. "I'm sure he'll want to come. He's just preoccupied."

"Then it's decided," Uncle Charlie said. "Friday night. We'll have a little fiesta."

The humidor lid clapped shut, the men filing outdoors. Upstairs, I jotted notes in a math notebook—what had sounded like the most crucial points. I wanted to call Manuel right away and tell him everything before I forgot any details, but with strange men lurking around, I didn't trust the phone. If only we might be left alone, I would love nothing more than him coming to visit. But the way Papi had described Manuel rolled my stomach. Instinct was undeniable.

The next morning Uncle Charlie joined Papi and me for breakfast and ate two plates of eggs and gallo pinto. He made fun of me for "sleeping in" until six-thirty and bragged that he had arisen at four. I asked him why he got up so early and he said, "To rally the troops, of course!" He sipped his coffee in the courtyard, his arms crossed over dark green fatigues and his sinewy legs planted wide as he talked with Papi and the jefes. In the coming days his Jeep and bodyguards appeared and disappeared—where did he go? What business was he conducting in the Valle de Cauca? One evening he peeled up the driveway in the chugging antique Jeep, the bodyguards cradling their automatic rifles like lovers in the crooks of their arms. He'd gone to the gym for a Zumba class, he said. Papi called him Jane Fonda for the rest of the night.

Ana was going to La Maria every afternoon to pray until the hostage crisis ceased, and one day I met up with her. I'd made up a lie to tell Papi about a meeting for International Club, claiming I might join since boarding schools looked favorably on such activities. Manuel picked me up outside school on his moto. I told him about the dinner conversation, the Third Brigade and Calima Front, and Uncle Charlie's mention of his little army. "What do you think?" I asked, hugging his middle. We were stopped at a big intersection. On the corner a squat woman sat behind a table, hollering for passersby to purchase lotto tickets.

"It sounds like paramilitary movements to eradicate the guerillas from the mountains south of here," he said loudly, over his shoulder. "And that will mean more bloodshed for villagers, more displaced. If your father's wrapped up in that, it's an ugly business." The light changed, and we raced toward la Ciudad Jardín.

Manuel dropped me off at Ana's gate, then sped to the church—he had another meeting to attend. Ana had changed out of the blue uniform of my former high school. She greeted me in a brown jersey dress, knee-length and modest for her taste; I couldn't help teasing. "Is this your church outfit? Sister Ana?"

"Shut up," she said, elbowing me. "And you should talk. Manuel's at the chapel every time I go there, when he's not on the phone in that apartment."

I was struck with both gratitude and envy at hearing this—Ana knowing more about his routine than me. "I see him whenever I can. Papi's just so protective." I paused. "How's Carlos?"

"A mess," she said. "Manuel is handling things better, I think. Carlos has lost so much interest in God. You heard him the night of his birthday, when we were talking about priests and sex. He just questions everything to death and gets fed up. He wasn't prepared for this. But neither was I," she said, shrugging. "Poor Emilio. Who knows what he's going through in those mountains, with those guerillas? They murder activists who criticize them, you know."

"So do the paras," I said.

She glanced at me quickly, apparently taken aback. "If it weren't for Carlos, I might apply to those boarding schools along with you," she said. "No matter what I do, I'm terrified. So I just pray. For my family. For Emilio."

"I didn't realize you were so close to Emilio."

She slowed and stared at me, her knuckles clenching the book she carried—a missal. She touched below her neck out of habit, but no emerald necklace gleamed against her skin today. "I don't know him well, but Emilio is my brother in the church," she said. "We are all God's family. You, too." She took deep breaths even though the climb was not very steep, and her eyes flashed at the sidewalk—someone had scrawled *Cristo es Rey* in chalk in front of the church. "Emilio will be my brother-in-law some day. And if you marry Manuel, we'll be sisters." She squeezed my arm above the elbow. "Not that I don't already consider you one." We had reached the cool stone entryway. "Be good to Manuel and your father. They both love you so much." She genuflected at the altar and the crucifix before us.

A saint's card skidded underneath my shoe as I descended the path to the rose garden. I wedged it among the flowers and photos crowding the bottom of a nearby tree. Bouquets and candles bunched at the Virgin's feet and a garland was draped around her neck. Manuel had said to wait for him there. I didn't wear a watch but I guessed that we didn't have very much time. Time—how much we wasted on pointless entertainments and invented tasks that didn't matter: the school subjects we studied but would never put to use, the repetition of cable news reports, the hours spent complaining, gossiping about the failures of parents and friends. And then all of a sudden there wasn't enough and you were chasing time, stretching to pick up every scrap of it you could, willing to give up your life for fifteen minutes of a warm hand grasping yours or gazing at another's face. Racing to share your love, because that was what mattered most.

Manuel and his bike flew like a black fly along the valley road. The gate opened and the bike coasted into the courtyard, its rumble reverberating off the stonework and mosaics. It was Friday night. Manuel had ridden with his guitar case strapped across his back, something he didn't like to do as it wasn't safe, but he had reluctantly agreed. He swung the case down and stretched before he wrapped his arm around me. "Ready for the evening's adventures?" he whispered.

The maids had set the table for six. Manuel extended his hand to Papi. "Thank you for inviting me back. I'm afraid I put you off last time, without meaning to."

Papi said, "No, no, all is forgiven. Please, sit down. Tonight is all about music and good times." Underneath the table, Manuel squeezed my leg, searched for my fingers and clutched them hard. Fidel strolled in, claimed the seat across from Uncle Charlie.

"Captain," Uncle Charlie said in greeting Fidel, who improvised a quick salute in return but flushed red and stared down, embarrassed. So they knew each other—Fidel had served in one of Uncle Charlie's little armies if not under his direct command. I was waiting and hoping to see how Uncle Charlie would introduce himself to Manuel but when they shook hands he stuck by the nickname. I declined the aguardiente, the potent grain alcohol too much for me, but Manuel poured himself a short glass. Inez set down two crystal serving bowls of ceviche, one of scallops and the other of shrimp. "Ah, the real Peruvian kind!" Uncle Charlie cried. "Soaking it overnight in lime, that's the secret. Not like the slop they serve in these cheap places, with ketchup and mayonnaise."

"I am Peruvian, remember?" Inez patted his shoulder as she passed by. "For you, only the best."

Citrus and fresh cilantro wafted up, mixed with the honey aroma of dripping wax. Luis lifted his plate, Uncle Charlie the ladle. The clear juice and pale chunks of seafood pooled onto plates. Manuel said, "Shall we say grace?"

Uncle Charlie folded his fingers together loosely and glanced at Papi, who set down his fork and did the same. Fidel bowed his head and sat up straight. Luis slouched and shut his eyes.

Manuel recited a quick thank-you to God. "I look forward to playing tonight," he said, picking up his fork. "I apologize beforehand if I'm rusty. But I've been distracted by other obligations lately, as you know."

"What a coincidence, so have I," Uncle Charlie said. "But that is always the case. Sometimes I dream that I am alone on San Andres Island with a volume of Mario Benedetti's poetry in one hand and a beautiful whore in the other." Luis and Papi chuckled at this, although Fidel didn't even crack a smile. "My apologies if I've offended you," Uncle Charlie said to us.

Manuel smiled, tight-lipped, and raised his brows. "My brother is studying for the priesthood, not me," he said. He took a bite of ceviche.

"Your brother, yes—what's the latest?" Uncle Charlie said. "The FARC killed my father when I was a young man, you know. To think you can't sit down at a table in this country without everyone having suffered some tragedy. All because of these cowardly thugs."

The men chewed and stared down in silence. Luis cleared his throat, his face somber. He shoveled ceviche into his mouth, gazing off. The sun sank orange into the mountains. So he'd lost someone too. Maybe he acted boisterous and aggressive because he didn't know how else to deal with it. I lifted the water pitcher, offered him a glass.

"Sorry to hear that," Manuel said. "What do you do now?"

"I'm afraid I'm not at liberty to say." Uncle Charlie sipped his drink as if it was a fine wine, patting his mouth afterward. "You might say I work behind the scenes. Right now, I'm tackling the problem you are facing, but from another angle."

"I never realized Mercedes had an uncle," Manuel said. His elbow brushed me, pressed into my blouse. "Are you American, from her mother's side?"

Luis and Fidel burst into laughter at this, and Papi and Uncle Charlie chuckled under their breath and exchanged a private look of amusement—the way I had seen Manuel and Emilio share glances. Papi smiled behind his folded hands. "He's not really her uncle," he said. "But Uncle Charlie is an old, very good friend."

"I hope you don't mind me asking this," Manuel began, "but do you see a path for peace? Or should we just forget it?"

Fidel's eyes appeared glassy, already midway through his second pour. "The million-dollar question," he said, "for the million-dollar man."

Silence fell. Luis sucked down ceviche. I halved a scallop, and the slippery white flesh shot across my plate. Papi glowered at Fidel—had the remark been intended as an insult? Uncle Charlie asked, "Do you read, Manuel?"

"Sure. Mostly theological books by Catholic writers and activists. Orianna Fallacci, Dorothy Day."

"But you don't read literature? Poetry? Fiction?"

"Not really," he replied.

"In literature lives the heart of the human being, even more than religion," Uncle Charlie said. "Don't get me wrong, I go to mass." As he spoke he popped shrimp between his lips. His teeth appeared too big for his mouth. Everyone sat up waiting to hear what he would say, myself included. "Our great writer Garcia Márquez has said that Colombia is in the midst of a Biblical Holocaust, and I believe he has it right. There are only three outcomes that can result from violence: one side will win out eventually and rise to power. Or the sides will get tired of fighting and killing and drop their weapons. Or lastly, the fighting will go on, fed as it is by the gringo appetite for drugs, and the larger, corrupt interests of the multinational corporations and U.S. government—until we have killed each other off, every last one."

"But which do you think is going to happen?" I asked. I took a teeny sip of Manuel's aguardiente, and coughed.

"Do you think I know?" Uncle Charlie cried. "I want peace but at the same time there are economic realities. We must defend ourselves, our families." His fist drummed the table.

"Isn't that playing both sides?" Manuel asked.

"If you play both sides, you never lose," Papi said with a shrug. "Ask the Americans. They've been doing that for years here and all over the world. Their citizens don't even notice."

"They're too busy getting high on our coca," Luis said.

"Exactly," Uncle Charlie said. "And yet when we protect our farms, we're criminals?" He and Manuel began to argue about the Americans' latest role in the drug trafficking. Papi wandered to the humidor.

I took another sip, throat burning. "How are your displaced?" I asked Papi.

"What's this?" Uncle Charlie interrupted.

Papi offered each of them a cigar, passed around the cutter. Only Manuel declined. Papi lit his off a candle, slowly savored the first toke. He resumed his seat with legs crossed and touched his bandanna, freshly pressed, in his shirt pocket. "There's a camp in the lowlands, past the cane. I've let a few dozen displaced stay there in exchange for working the fallow fields."

"More like a hundred," Luis said, staring at the end of his cigar.

"And you will have more," Uncle Charlie said. "That's good of you. Saint Diego, see what I'm talking about?" He looked at us, but reached over and thumped Papi on the shoulder.

"That's very kind," Manuel said. He toyed with the cutter. "So you believe in faith in action?"

"What other type of faith is there?" Papi said. "I wish I could offer them more. But we all do the best we can, don't we?" A twinge of mockery hung on the words, quickly eclipsed by his suggestion that we move into the living room for the guitar show, if Manuel was ready.

Manuel sat before the fireplace, patted the place beside him for me to join. As he strummed, the valley fell more deeply into darkness except for the glittering stars and scattered lights of small farms. Soon the jefes arrived, each stooping to fetch a beer at the mini-fridge Papi kept stocked on the patio before ambling in. All wore guns at their waists. Uncle Charlie waved in his bodyguards. His reddish face turned even darker with the blood rushing to his capillaries. "Should we wait for the girls?" he slurred.

The maids darted about, collecting glasses and emptying ashtrays, and the dogs cavorted and barked at the jefes who tossed toys for them. The men leaned in the doorway and against the couches: wiry Vincente, rolled cigarette hanging from his thin lips; Guillermo, with the high cheekbones and indigenous features of Inez, ceviche piled onto his plate; Fidel, the youngest, sulky from too much drink, Uncle Charlie, or both; Luis, who laughed a lot but adjusted himself and poked his head outside to spit in the lawn when he thought no one was watching; and Uncle Charlie, the latest addition, who now sat in Papi's chair across from us with his hands clasped upon the arms, and his feet flat on the ground like a gentleman about to watch an opera, or a king—all of them different versions of Papi.

Headlights flashed and gravel crunched underneath tires. The maid threw open the front door. A half-dozen women pranced in. One wore the highest heels I had ever seen, her shimmery camisole straining to cover her augmented breasts; from the wrinkles in her cleavage she appeared to be the oldest. Another wore jeans so tight that the crack of her backside peeked out the top. A dainty tattooed tree frog leapt beneath the strap of her hot pink thong. She paraded around like a cat proud of her sleek, thick tail. The prettiest had straight black hair that swung down her back and a beauty queen smile that gleamed when she sidled up to Guillermo and stole a forkful of ceviche off his plate. No doubt she knew the tricks Ana knew—how to rub Vaseline on your teeth, and coconut oil in your hair. She couldn't have been more than nineteen or twenty.

"I hope you don't mind," Uncle Charlie said. "But I called some friends." He spoke sloppily, swept his arm toward the bar where the women poured one another aguardiente. Papi loitered in the kitchen, talking to Inez as she scrubbed.

Manuel pinched my knee, and I flushed. "Who are they?" I whispered.

"Who do you think?" he scoffed. "Prostitutes." Then he began to play.

Everyone fell quiet. Papi hurried over and slipped into the chair beside Uncle Charlie, face smooth and fixed upon us. Putas—did my father go to bed with such women, and was this the kind of behavior that had driven my mother away? What was the relationship between Papi and Charlie for this bizarre old friend to waltz in, bunk with us for however long he liked, and order prostitutes at his leisure?

Manuel played for about an hour—intricate classical pieces, lively rumba numbers, plus his own compositions. When the most recent round of applause died, Manuel took my hand and said, "I wrote this last song for the love of my life." Whistles and murmurs erupted. Papi shifted, chin in his palm and his other hand clenching the bandanna.

Manuel played a new song he had sung for me once in the brothers' bedroom. The faces remained still under the soft lamplight, the maids and Inez standing in the back, arms folded. Fidel hastily wiped a tear. Guillermo stared down into his drink, entranced. As the last notes reverberated, Uncle Charlie looked like he'd just closed the covers of a wonderful book. "You have inspired me to double my efforts against the ELN on your behalf," he said.

"My brother Carlos and I were going to record this month," Manuel said. He arranged the guitar in its case. "But that's all been put on hold until we get Emilio released."

A thick cloud of perfume filled my nose and mouth. The prostitute with the enormous breasts hovered over Manuel, praising his performance, Vincente behind her, extending his hand, grinning and nodding enthusiastically. His other hand rested on the woman's lower back, her skin too-tan even in the dimmed light. Guillermo and Luis crowded around, and then the others. Only Papi and Uncle Charlie remained seated.

That's when Uncle Charlie leaned over to Papi and whispered, "You weren't kidding about his talent. Or his potential." *Potential.* I stood there, passing around Manuel's CD and meeting the women's envious glances, straining to hear my father's reply. *Que encantador*, the pretty one with the shiny teeth said to me, tilting her head toward Manuel. I complimented her tacky purse, pretended to listen as she prattled on about where to get designer knock-offs. Did Papi view Manuel not as a threat, but someone he might win over to his employment—like Fidel? I backed closer to the couches, but heard nothing more.

When at last I broke away, Uncle Charlie had left. I started to breeze past Papi but he caught my side. Tears glistened in the creases of his eyes, bandanna crumpled on his knee. I grabbed his other hand. "I love you so much," he said, voice trembling. He squeezed my hand so hard that it hurt. "I'm sorry I'm not a better man."

"You're fine," I said. "I love you, too." My throat tightened and to my surprise, I said, "Like you said, we do the best we can."

A bitter cigar haze clouded the downstairs and Shakira's "Suerte" rollicked the speakers. I coaxed Manuel outside, shut the din behind glass. On the couch Uncle Charlie sat wide-legged, hugging two women, their shirts unbuttoned and bras exposed—the one with the tree frog tattoo and one of our maids. He groped her white pants and she scolded him, wielding her cup of guaro overhead, the two of them laughing. "I sort of like him," I said, nodding over my shoulder. "Uncle Charlie."

"Of course you do," Manuel said. "He charms people. I know his type, and he's dangerous."

The grass chilled my ankles as we descended the lawn for the stable, the noise of the house falling distant. My father had disappeared. Had he gone upstairs to bed, alone? I didn't see the young one with the glossy hair anywhere—was he with her? The stallion whinnied and snorted, knocking around his stall. "We have a flair for finding ourselves in the company of animals," Manuel said, bemused. "In more ways than one." He stared into the dark foothills, traded the guitar case from one hand to the other. "I should go," he said. I knew he was worried about Emilio, wondering if someone had called with a message, even at that hour. I begged for him to stay. He shook his head, dug out his keys. At the paddock fence we kissed. The horses stamped their goodnights.

CHAPTER NINE

Midmorning, I shuffled downstairs and was startled to find Papi there—he never got off to such a late start. The skin underneath his eyes bagged, and he clutched a large water glass. At these signs of hangover, I snickered even as I skirted the thought of my father possibly having spent the previous night with a prostitute. "Shut up," he grumbled and chugged some water, attempting to hide his sheepish grimace. I asked if I could accompany him to the fields. He threw back his remaining tinto and said Uncle Charlie was supposed to join him, then regarded me with a grave, exasperated expression. "What happened last night was not my idea, okay? Charlie makes his own rules, if you can't already tell. But he's one of the most intelligent, dedicated men I've ever met. He's on our side."

I wanted to ask, *and which side is that?* But I was afraid of his answer.

Uncle Charlie claimed the wheel of the army Jeep, Papi the passenger seat. I perched upon a bench behind them, no safety belt, and clung on. Papi reached back and tugged my ponytail. The bodyguards, silent as their weapons, climbed in the back. "We're on the property, no need to worry," he said to Uncle Charlie, but already our houseguest shifted into gear and we lurched forward. Papi jumped out to talk with a man and woman clearing brush with machetes, middle-aged, but their faces appeared as worn as pirate's maps. The bodyguards chewed gum and their glances pierced as if the workers might attack. Papi swung back into the

Jeep. It balked, and I lurched as if on a carnival ride. A Jeep from 1958. How much blood had rolled underneath its tires—our country still at war after forty years?

The peeling seatback scratched my grip. I leaned into the front. "You said your father was killed by guerillas?" I asked Uncle Charlie.

"Kidnapped and killed," he corrected, "just like Diego's. I was your age, sixteen."

"That's a lot of years of fighting," I said.

"Revenge can fuel a man for a long time. Especially after loss." He steered widely around a patch of deep ruts. "At least it did for me. But then just like this Jeep, it runs out."

"Has yours?" I asked. Bullets and a Rambo knife, its leather tassels nubby and worn, bloomed along his cracked belt. "I suppose you've killed many men."

"Fighting guerillas is one thing," Papi said. "Selective murders are another." The road dipped; my stomach dropped. His mouth remained hard as he stared ahead. The fallow fields smelled differently than the cane—of compost and animal dung. Desplazados stooped, planting. We rumbled past a clattering ox-cart, the driver a boy about twelve. He wore only a pair of faded shorts, raised his switch in greeting.

Charlie beeped. The oxen plodded on. "Who wants to keep fighting? I'm tired. I want to yell at my daughter about her grades and her boyfriend like this one here." He elbowed Papi, who smiled reluctantly, staring off.

I asked if conditions had improved in the camp, and if the children had shoes yet at the mission. Papi shook his head. "I only have so much time to play saint, and there are too many to count. You should hear the stories."

"A necessary evil," Uncle Charlie muttered. "God will reward you ten times over me."

Papi rode with his arm raised, palm open as if catching the sun's rays. "I don't know about that."

The wind whipped my hair and eyes. I could not see his face. We drove along in silence. Uncle Charlie braked hard; a goat trotted off the road, bleating. A handful of children scurried after it. I said, "But won't the orphans of those killed swear revenge on the guerillas, or the paras? Then it will never end."

"You are perceptive for your age," Uncle Charlie said, glancing back. "That's been my struggle, since I killed the brother of the FARC leader. In his house I found five more children. I thought, I will have to kill them all or they will grow up to do the same thing. But I couldn't."

We turned sharply, the sun beating my face. Squinting, I swiped the sunglasses from Papi's shirt pocket. "I've heard the paras cut people's heads off," I said, and slid on the shades. "Anyone who provides services to a guerilla is a sympathizer. A Marxist."

Papi huffed. "You don't even know what that means," he said, and snatched the glasses back.

"How do you know? Don't people deserve trials if they are going to be accused? Especially if the punishment is getting their throats slit and their bodies dumped in rivers?"

"See what I'm talking about, Carlito?" Papi said, leaning over. "This Manuel, he's a fanatic. The brother kidnapped—who do you think is next?"

"No one knows what is in a man's heart," Uncle Charlie replied. "Only God." He shifted gears, and we hurtled toward the tree lined refugee camp. I saw what Papi meant. The shacks had tripled in number and now reached the field's edge, plastic bags ballooning over the makeshift windows. Flames leaped high above an open fire tended by a woman, middle-aged, with a poncho skimming her ashen knees. Noxious fumes stung my eyes and throat; I held my breath. She pressed a cloth to her face as she poked the trash curling black: crushed Styrofoam, tin foil, and—I cringed—a flattened, dead cat. The road ahead disappeared in an enormous puddle, as big as our patio. We splashed across. The stench shifted—vegetable rot and standing water. The rains collected here at the low end of the fields. Uncle Charlie lectured as he drove, children and dogs darting away from the tires on either side, until we charged uphill, back into the cane. According to him, the war wouldn't stop until the narco-trafficking did. "When that happens," he snapped his fingers, "our economy regulates. But cocaine will only stop when the users do."

We rolled past the whitewashed farmhouses of concrete block. A grey-muzzled fila brasileiro ran along a fence and barked at us. At another, children in swimsuits kicked a soccer ball; they'd made goal posts out of sawhorses. Papi and Uncle Charlie talked in low voices about the Autodefensas. So Papi was aligned with them, his old friend not merely an off-color, harmless, entertaining *tío*. Wasn't Uncle Charlie merely living out his view of the world, warped by a tragic past? How could I judge him for that—and judge my father? And how could I not?

The following afternoon I remained glued to the rally on TV. The assembly marched from the Iglesia la Merced to the Catedral de San Pedro, holding a white banner which read, JUVENTUD PARA PAZ Y LIBERTAD PARA TODOS—Manuel in the center, chanting the refrain in a voice that must have gone hoarse so late in the day. To his right marched the young woman who'd argued with Emilio at the birthday dinner; every time she raised the megaphone to shout, her wrist flashed the peace sign. A mounted policeman trotted alongside, sun glaring off his boots. The news repeated a clip of Manuel's speech from earlier: "So many will try to destroy us. This has happened to those who speak out on the verge of great change. Christ is just one example of the thousands throughout history who have been attacked for speaking the truth about peace and love. This is a time of greatness for Colombia. And in this time, we cannot be broken." I snuggled farther underneath the blanket. Cocoa stirred at my feet, circled, and slumped back down.

Uncle Charlie flung open the patio door, Papi at his heels. Papayas and mangos were wedged under their arms like footballs. Uncle Charlie plunked a mango onto the counter, sliced it with his Rambo knife as he spoke. "That one is destined to be a rock star, no? Or a saint. If he doesn't get kidnapped first. I can see why you're in love with him." His brow lifted as he chucked the mango cubes into the blender.

"His intentions are true, I won't argue there," Papi said. He eyed me warily as he unbuttoned the top of his shirt and stretched his legs. "You want to marry this boy?" he asked matter-of-factly.

"Why not?" I asked.

Ice knocked in the blender; the blades whirred. Papi snatched the newspaper from beneath the cigar and horse magazines, thrust the front page onto my lap, and jabbed at the black-and-white face by the main article. "Read this."

Duarte had indeed condemned the rebels to be excommunicated, and ninety-five percent of the ELN guerillas were Catholic. Gambino claimed he had not authorized the kidnapping of a congregation but had ordered his subordinates to execute a high-profile attack in retaliation for a paramilitary slaughter of a village on the Venezuelan border the day before. The leader reiterated their demand for a safe haven in return for the twenty-five hostages still in captivity from the Avianca hijacking, as well as the fifty-four parishioners, Emilio among them. I read Gambino's quote aloud: "'We're not enemies of the Church. We beg forgiveness from all the faithful for this act, and we are sure that many will understand.'" I looked up. "What does this mean?"

"If the Church excommunicates those five thousand ELN, things will not be good for Manuel nor his brother," Papi said. Uncle Charlie whisked around and set a smoothie into his hand, and Papi drank. "Ah, perfect. Forget the words of remorse. Those guerillas will be humiliated and enraged. Although that is their own stupidity for not expecting such a public outcry and consequences from the Church. So, don't be surprised if the ELN retaliates by executing a few noteworthy captives. Manuel had better negotiate fast for his brother's release." I pictured Emilio with the gun at his back, his lips moving in prayer. Manuel would think he hadn't done enough to free the hostages—he would blame himself. I grabbed the smoothie Uncle Charlie set in front of me and drank. Tangy sweetness drenched my throat, and I shivered.

"And those guerillas watch everything, or they have informants," Papi continued. "You had better believe they are viewing this broadcast right now and taking note of Manuel."

"Oh, I despise the ELN just a hair less than the FARC," Uncle Charlie exclaimed. "They make me so tired of defending myself." He guzzled his smoothie, slouched toward me and said, "You could always date the son of one of your neighbors. When you come back from the United States in a few years, of course."

Inez walked in and began yelling at Uncle Charlie for making such a mess with the blender. He and Papi retreated to the stable. I slipped into Papi's room, knelt, and tugged open the dresser drawer. At first it refused to give way but when it did, the lightness startled me, so I knew a split-second before I looked what I would find: the bottom clear, the cash gone.

Uncle Charlie didn't show up to dinner that night. I asked Papi why. "He's finished his business here, went back to his cattle station in Córdoba," he said.

"That's a long way in the dark," I replied. Although I had no doubt Uncle Charlie knew those mountains all too well. I imagined him rattling along in the Jeep with the crazy dials, half of them broken, Papi's cash stashed in the back in burlap sugar sacks, the armed guards mute and wide-eyed as jungle cats.

As much as he distrusted my father, Manuel said he valued his foresight about how the ELN might react to Duarte's decision. Some hostages' families had received messages from loved ones through guerilla contacts or negotiators. But no word on Emilio. We talked about this later that week near Emilio's desk, now Manuel's, our island in the midst of committee meetings taking place. As for Uncle Charlie, Fidel's comment about him being the "million-dollar man" had Manuel doubting that he might be an undercover U.S. drug official, as we had first thought. Instead, Manuel thought Charlie might be the elusive and notorious Carlos Castaño Gil, leader of the Autodefensas Unidas de Colombia, the AUC—the most ruthless and well-funded paramilitary. "The AUC was only formed a year ago," Manuel said. "If Uncle Charlie is Castaño, that means he was hiding out at your hacienda. Because he is a wanted criminal with a million-dollar tag on his head. Your father could be arrested for harboring him."

"He can't be Castaño. Papi would never take that risk."

"You sure about that?" He looped an arm around my waist. "Look, Charlie may be someone else—a subordinate in the Autodefensas. But the AUC is funded by landowners and corporate interests in exchange for protection. Your father fits the type." Someone cranked up the radio and the latest Shakira hit rocked the air, breaking the industrious mood until Ana turned it down.

Incense burned nearby. A wave of nausea rocked my stomach, and I stepped over to the printer. Would Papi act so recklessly, if Charlie really was Castaño? What were the ties that bound him to this old friend—and was Charlie less a friend than an enemy? Copies of flyers spat out, crisp and warm, summoning caleños to that weekend's rally.

Manuel lifted off the top sheet. "La Maria has hired so much security, you'd think the President's coming," he joked. "But the Archbishop's nobody to fool with, either." He gently turned me to face him, smoothed my hair. "Promise me that you'll get away for this. I'll never ask you again, I swear."

"Helping you out here is one thing," I said slowly. "Those crowds—even with a thousand snipers and helicopters overhead, I don't feel safe."

His arms fell to his sides. "You think this place is any safer?" He lowered his voice and stepped closer; his lips grazed my ear. "You can be sure the ELN and the FARC, and I've no doubt whoever else is watching this block, are well aware that all the motos and cars parked in the alley don't belong to customers shopping for their next bedroom set."

I set down the flyers, now cool. "Okay," I said. "That still doesn't mean the rally is any less dangerous."

"It's not," he said, and sighed. "But you're part of this too. Aren't you?" He held up the flyer, eyebrows raised, and dropped it onto the stack. Then sank into the chair and rubbed his face, his eyes puffy and hair mussed. He badly needed a cut. "It's just that you're my girlfriend, and it's that much more important to me. Not having you there feels like—almost like you don't exist." He stared at the wall, then up at me.

I caught his hand, threaded my fingers through his. "You know that's not true," I said. "And if you feel that way—how terrible." From the kitchenette, the coffee machine gurgled and hissed. The girl with the peace tattoo emerged, pot steaming. She approached the ponytailed university activist, then Ana, cheerily poured coffee into Styrofoam cups.

"I'll find a way to get there," I said.

"You will?" Manuel drew me close, buried his face in my middle. "Thank you," he mumbled. The tattooed girl ducked over, asked if we wanted coffee. He waved her off, kneaded my leg through the thick folds of my skirt, making me flush.

While dressing for school the next morning, I sifted through my jewelry chest. Pearl earrings—I had only worn them for Christmas and New Year's so I had easily forgotten about them. Papi had given them to me last year, for my quinceañera. "A lady wears pearls always," he'd said. "And one day you'll be one. This valley—you'll own everything you see."

Now I popped open the velvet box with the pearls and set it on the console. They stared back, lustrous and unsettling, a pair of voodoo eyes. Fidel and I were sitting in the car outside my school with the doors locked. A vagrant black man passed by with so many things hanging from his jacket he resembled a hat rack: a pair of sneakers swinging from ties, a rainbow scarf, head phones over his ears, minus the cord, and his jacket, which appeared to be made out of aluminum. Fidel said, "I can't take these, princesa. Weren't they your mother's?"

I hadn't thought of this. But too late. Even if they had belonged to her, this was now. "I need to go somewhere on Sunday," I said. "We can leave mid-morning. I'll be home before the men finish shearing."

He gripped the wheel, even though we remained parked. "I don't know," he said. "It's not for certain, is it, that the shearing will be this weekend?" He glanced down at the pearls, then at me. "You're going to another peace demonstration, aren't you?"

"So what if I am? Can you drive me or not?"

"Where will you tell your father you're going?"

"I'll figure out some excuse by then. Don't worry."

He raised his eyebrows and cocked his head, still studying the pearls. "Okay," he said, tone resigned. He pocketed the box. The pearls had to be worth several hundred dollars, about a month's salary for a driver. Fidel might receive more for his protection services, but not much.

"Why do you get along with my father, but not Uncle Charlie?" I asked.

A classmate jumped out of an armored Mercedes, called out to another. Heads together, the two girls hurried into the school. "Uncle Charlie believes in a warped view of God," Fidel said. He raised his pointer finger to his temple and twirled it. "Crazy. Your father is not."

"What happened between you and Charlie?"

"I'd rather not discuss. But his name's not Charlie."

"I know. Was he your leader in the military?"

"Sort of." He yawned. "What's this, an interview? Get to school."

Grinning, I rapped on the window. He groaned and unlocked the doors, and I bolted into the daylight, the tropical sun already strong at eight a.m.

Had the pearls belonged to my mother? Later, I crept back to Papi's room when he was in the fields, not to rifle through drawers but to study her face—her tall, angular body and perfect paleness. I thought I'd managed okay without her growing up, even when I had gotten my first period and had to run downstairs and find Inez. But lately I found myself fantasizing about conversations with Paula: taking walks or afternoon tea where we might talk about the loss of virginity, birth control, what to expect with men, and perhaps she would have spoken about American men, too—just how different were they from the men I knew? I pictured her wrapped in a shawl not unlike Sister Rosemary, delicate and beautiful as a bird. Would we have been able to discuss such things? Might we still?

On the patio Inez rocked, her hands rhythmically working in her lap. Her bluish veins bulged as she scuffed the two halves of the carders together. A sack of alpaca wool overflowed at her feet, buried her shoes.

I sat beside her, drew one knee to my chest. "You know, I didn't realize there could be so much disagreement right away, even if you're in love with someone. That one person could need another to do things, you know?" Her gaze shot up, and I shook my head. "Not what you're thinking. I mean how you fit another person into your life, what they expect. Not that I'm fighting with Manuel or anything."

"Ah, yes," Inez said, and clicked her teeth. "You disagree, good. You don't want to be the kind of woman who just goes along with things. That's just as bad as fighting all the time."

"It is? How?" I'd been rocking and stopped.

"That's how you lose yourself. And the other person. *No* is like a magic staff. If you don't use it, well—" Chin tucked, she raised her gaze and her mouth slightly turned up. "Exactly what is Manuel wanting you to do, huh? Is he not behaving himself? If you say no and he doesn't understand—"

"Believe me, you don't have to worry." I pushed off and rocked hard, my thighs creased and sweaty against the leather. "My mother and Papi, were they always fighting? Or did that happen mostly at the end?"

"Fighting? No. They sat out here and laughed at night."

"Laughing? Like me and Manuel?"

Dust clouds flew upward as she scraped. "They spoke English, I didn't know what they were saying." She shrugged, flicked her braid, a silken cord of silver and black, over her shoulder. "But she began to get sick right away—the different foods." Inez picked off the carded wool thoughtfully, set it into a basket. "You don't know homesickness. This was a strange place to her. My parents, they left Peru, came here as a couple—young but not too young. Before la Violencia, of course. My mother made Colombia her home just fine. She loved the valley and being close to the ocean. But for my father—" Inez shook her head. "He missed living high up, above the world. His whole life, this country was like a shoe meant for the other foot. No amount of jamming will make a right shoe fit on the left foot."

"But my parents—how did things go so wrong?" I asked. "Between them, I mean?"

"It's really none of my business," she said. "And look, I was busy. Because once the downstairs was finished, they had me cook these big dinners—twelve, fifteen people, everybody speaking English. The driver took your mother everywhere— to la Ciudad Jardín, the English bookstore, the synagogue if she wanted. And the horses, she loved. She went out at first, but she didn't have an easy time, being pregnant. Your father tried to help, sure. When she was sick he paced around like crazy. But she was living here for him. See, that's what I mean."

"But she left me. Maybe she didn't have family at home to help raise me."

"No, no, she had parents," Inez said. "You think your father would let her take you? To lose you both? 'Do you want to kill me?' he asked her—this I heard, him pleading in Spanish. He has some wild animal in him, always has. But—" and here she lowered her voice, angled her head toward me. "With what he was involved with then, he would have gone up to the coffee groves, put a gun to his head, and pulled the trigger. They had this argument the day she left—you could hear them in the fields." She frowned, plucked the bristles and brushed wool into the basket. "Make no mistake, you saved him. And the hacienda. They'll be shearing this Sunday," she added, "now that Carlito's gone."

"Oh?" I said, picking up a fallen bit of wool. "You were right, you know. I wasn't really ready for love. At least not how fast it moves." I arose and hugged Inez, her scent comforting—laundry soap, dried sweat, and dust. So there would be little chance of Papi missing me that weekend. And

Fidel would not be missed, either, as he spent Sunday afternoons drinking beer at the local cantina, watching fútbol. The men would not listen to the radio because the shearing made so much noise, and handling the docile but easily skittish alpacas required total attention. Papi would not return to the house until nightfall.

The sky blazed pink. I had always believed my father's story of what happened and not asked him hard questions. But was his depiction of my mother accurate? Did he really not know Paula's whereabouts, nor have a single phone number that might lead me to her? Inez closed up her sack of wool. Below, the jefes sprayed the mud off their boots and lined them up to dry on the porch.

In the flat yard of the alpaca station I told Papi that I was going up the mountain with Fidel to target practice. Jug of water under one arm, Papi nodded and yelled for Guillermo to grab his end of the flapping tarp they were laying down. An hour later Fidel dropped me off. The Ciudad Jardín streets were packed with demonstrators. I stepped over the bouquets strangling the sidewalks and archway. A reporter wearing heavy makeup crouched beside an older woman. She tucked her shiny sneakers beneath her as she spoke, her baggy T-shirt printed with a wedding photo of a young couple. The reporter scrawled in a small notepad. The woman was a member of the abducted congregation—one of the lucky few who'd been released that same day. "My son and his wife are still being held captive," she said, her voice rasping. She brushed her cheeks, her nails long and sharply oval, the professional manicure crowned by her ring, several carats. "Leaving them behind was the hardest thing I've ever done." A dozen steps away, a group wearing similar T-shirts and sashes held hands, a man in a sport coat and loafers leading them in prayer by the temporary platform La Maria Juventud had erected in the churchyard.

On the platform steps Manuel gave me a quick kiss hello. Someone called his name and he stepped away. The chatter in the churchyard increased as more people gathered; the prayer group quieted, and a moment later, broke out softly into a hymn. Manuel returned, extended his hand to me from above. "Come on up. You don't have to say anything."

Ana rounded the tent then, paused to talk with Carlos, who was running the sound check. I nodded toward her. "I'm fine hanging out with Gracia and Ana," I said.

"I don't mean for the whole time. Just while the Archbishop is speaking." He stood firmly, muscles defined beneath his taut La Maria T-shirt, palm steady and open. "You can stand in the back, next to me."

"This isn't fair, Manuel. You said my being here would be enough." I hugged my chest. In my anxiousness to get away I'd forgotten to stuff my T-shirt in my purse, and now was the only one among the youth group in a Polo shirt. Gracia breezed through the gate; a police officer clapped his hand on her shoulder, gestured for her to open her bag.

Manuel's arm dropped to his side. He climbed down, looped his fingers through the belt buckles of my jeans. "Because I'm going to be your husband," he said. He ran his hands down my sides. "If you want me. My mother got married at sixteen. If I marry you right after your birthday, then what can Papi do? Nothing."

"Get married?" The microphone shrieked. I winced, clamped my ears. "You're serious?"

"Why wouldn't I be?"

"You're a master of persuasion, you know that?" I laughed, shifted my weight. "Better than Emilio. Wow."

"So yes?" Chin lowered, he peered at me, brushed my hair behind my face.

I nodded, smiling so hard my cheeks ached. We rocked in a long hug. This is what it means to love someone, I thought. When you miss them so much it hurts a little even when you are together.

Manuel hauled me onstage, steered me to the back. A La Maria priest spoke, then Duarte climbed up, pectoral cross hanging down from his white collar and pressing against his black cassock; sunlight glinted off his large ring as he clutched the microphone. "Violence is a disease. And when our enemies attack us, or refuse our demands for peace, I will be ready for their stones. I belong to you, my fellow Colombians." He called the ELN guerillas "miserable and mean," threatened to excommunicate anyone who defiled the Church. Thousands bowed their heads; the speakers crackled as he led the prayer. Manuel's grip grew warm. I lowered my head. At the periphery of the crowd, a covered truck lumbered; I let go his hand, braced to run. But it was a police vehicle, not a canvas truck about to open fire. "We ask God that the guerilla fighters in Colombia may feel deep sorrow in their souls for the evil they commit," Duarte droned. "That they understand that theirs is not a just war, but merely a repetition of the savage acts from the saddest time in human history." From below came muffled weeping; a baby wailed. A news camera clicked, loud and rapid. Manuel squeezed my hand again. As soon as Duarte headed for the steps, I jumped down and pushed my way to Gracia and Ana.

More speeches followed, then Manuel and Carlos took center stage. The audience broke into the chorus, clapped their hands overhead, and Manuel whipped the microphone around. The wind rustled the branches above, the blossoms brilliant and the palms iridescent. Ana, Gracia, and I linked arms and sang along, rocking back and forth. I thought, *I am fifteen, in the most beautiful country on Earth, and in love.*

When the show was over, the fans surged the stage. Manuel and Carlos climbed off the back, but before they could reach their guitar cases, the news reporter stuck her microphone in Manuel's face, asked him if he knew that because of his music and speaking out for his kidnapped brother, he was becoming a household name. A young woman, wavy hair highlighted like Shakira's, called out, "Manuel, if you rescue my brother I'll make it worth your while!" Laughter erupted. Above the mob he shouted for me and mimed putting a phone to his ear. I waved, face hot with tears.

I met the car in front of Ana's. Fidel scanned the pedestrians streaming past and barely greeted me. I assumed he was anxious about getting back before dinner, or how to navigate the barricaded streets, or both, but he said nothing. We zigzagged out and left the rally behind, and in silence sped down the autopista, free of traffic, heading home. Papi enjoyed the gentle alpacas and no doubt would be in a good mood after shearing. The men would gamble over their cards and joke, and I hoped for a quiet evening with few questions.

But as soon as we turned down our road bordered by rising cane, there rolled a long line of military Jeeps. Fidel dodged the convoy. The soldiers peered down at us as we passed, their faces smooth with youth and smeared from forehead to chin with camouflage paint. Machine guns sprouted from their dark green fatigues. On the upper left arm of each was knotted a white cloth band with Colombia's colors: blue, yellow, and red. One wore a necklace of bullets draped around his neck like a boa constrictor. He hung over the creeping wheel, this creature of the mist-covered mountains, waved and shouted at the Jeep ahead. His armband's black lettering read *AUC*. The line crawled to our front gate.

"What's going on?" I asked. Fidel's gazed pierced the rearview mirror.

"You'll see." His tone was dark and definite. The antique Jeep awaited us on the other side, and Uncle Charlie's bodyguards rocked in the patio chairs.

Fidel's footsteps crunched outside my door. I didn't move; he grasped my shoulder, gave it a gentle squeeze. "I'm sorry, princesa." He guided me out to face him, bit his lip and slightly shook his head.

Weak-kneed, I climbed the steps. The dogs slid across the tile, tore in between my legs. Papi and Uncle Charlie sat in the living room, a map spread before them, Uncle Charlie in full, crisp fatigues and matching cap but no insignia or identification. Their heads jerked up. News reports jumped across the muted TV. Papi pushed himself from his chair, fists clenched and knuckles white, his face as drawn and convicted as the Archbishop's hours earlier. "Welcome home," he said.

The ridgebacks trotted off to rest at Uncle Charlie's black-booted feet, the mutts to the dining table, plastered with maps. The soldiers gathered there, chewing sandwiches, fell silent. One eyed me over the rim of his Fanta can, lowered it slowly to his knee, pretended to stare off at the view. Another soldier leaned in the hallway outside the laundry, out of sight of the living room, and gawked at me. Had the troops who had come through before worn armbands—which kind? Inez husked corn by the sink, rinsed each ear without looking up, steady and robotic. Uncle Charlie stooped forward, frowning. My limbs felt impossibly heavy.

Papi said, "What do you have to say for yourself, daughter? And don't bother to lie, since I know where you've been." He jerked his head toward the muted TV, hands on hips.

I swallowed hard. Fidel crept behind me, slipped the keys onto the hook, turned to leave. Papi called to him, "And what did you think you were doing today? If I didn't know how crazy my daughter is for this Manuel, I would think something was up with the two of you."

Fidel brushed his palms against his jeans and stood there, staring at the floor—he and Papi the only ones in regular clothes among camouflage. Like hostages.

"What am I to do with you?" Papi paced, breathing hard, and ran a hand through his hair; his face and neck flamed purple. "Do I just let you run around with peace activists? Until one day you're sleeping on the ground, some stupid teenager's gun in your face?"

The can of Fanta snagged the map when the soldier set it down. Our eyes met. He had similar features to Manuel with the exception of a higher forehead and thinner legs—what Manuel might look like if he ever put on a camouflage uniform and paint. The young man bent over and whispered to Shaka. She popped up and jogged over; vigorously, he scratched her head.

"What about this?" I said, my voice husky and shallow. "What's going on here? Or should I find out on my own?"

Uncle Charlie settled back, arms folded.

"Do you appreciate nothing? I tell you exactly what will happen." Papi marched as he spoke. Spittle flew from his lips, struck the map. "But instead you sneak around. And to the exact events I've warned you about. Do I have to pull you out of school, keep you prisoner?"

"No, Papi," I cried. The soldiers shifted. One tapped another. They stepped out to smoke.

"Mi hija," he began, and his tone took on an even but steely edge. "You're not leaving this room until you tell me what I'm to do with you. Or else I'm putting you on a plane tomorrow, for the U.S., no goodbyes. You can sit in Pilar's apartment in L.A. while she's in China or wherever. You think I'm kidding? Or that Manuel's going to fly there and see you?"

"Diego, may I—"

Papi's hand sliced the air, silencing Uncle Charlie. The soldiers stirred, slid open the patio doors and filed out, backs to us. Uncle Charlie's ears turned red but he sat calmly, one leg crossed over the other.

"Then let me die," I said. "Because I'm going to be with Manuel no matter what."

"You can't be with him if you're dead!" Papi yelled.

"Fine. No more rallies, okay? But you had better tell me what's going on. Unless you want to lose me like my mother." I brushed past the soldier who lurked in the hallway, his eyes boring into me as if he couldn't wait to see me undressed, and ran upstairs. The banter and acrid smoke of his friends floated up, and the slap of boots upon stone. I clutched a pillow. What right had Papi to let a private army use our home for a base camp? Was his fear of losing me to some violence so great that he would risk his freedom to protect me? Yet within the hour the voices below faded, and Papi passed my door in silence.

CHAPTER TEN

Gunfire echoed from high above, as rapid as coins cascading onto a stack. Sister Rosemary dropped her pen on the practice test. She and I exchanged yet another troubled, uncertain look; frowning, she adjusted her shawl, picked up the pen. The convoy of Jeeps had remained parked at the bottom of the trail for several days, partly hidden by the house and thick vegetation. I imagined what the secluded hills looked like—soldiers crawling on their bellies, Uncle Charlie barking orders. Countless targets lining the coffee shrubs. The EFL test was a week away, and I'd hear back from the boarding schools any day now. Manuel and I needed to make plans, if we might indeed run away and get married.

That afternoon Ana called. She had received a death threat from the ELN. So had Gracia; since the rally, all of La Maria Juventud had reported warnings about bombs in their mailboxes or workplaces. Ana asked if I had received one. "Since this Sunday? No," I said, and clutched the kitchen counter. The floor felt like it was shifting underneath me.

"I'm so scared," she said. "Carlos says the guerillas want the rich for ransoms. That's how they fund their war. What if I'm on a target list?"

"I'm sure you're not," I said.

"Well, I'll still help however I can. But Gracia and I were just talking, and—no more demonstrations. I told Carlos," she said, and exhaled. "I can't face telling Manuel."

As soon as I hung up with Ana I called him. Manuel had received a phone threat, too, and told the police, but wasn't going to let it dissuade him. "We'll have gone from thirty-five people to five the next meeting," he joked, but his laugh sounded fatigued and forced. "Thank God they haven't called you again. I feel like such a jerk for dragging you on stage now, when you didn't want to go up there."

"Things have changed here. Let's just say Uncle Charlie is back."

"Ah," Manuel said. "For a minute there I was worried." Our hacienda likely made an ideal stopping point for the paras, headed to the Calima Front to cleanse the south of the ELN. He didn't know about Emilio's chances for release. Even though their family wasn't rich, Manuel had a bad feeling that Papi had been right—the ELN might keep a church mediator as a power play, to test the Archbishop's decree that the Church would not pay ransoms for clergy or just for spite because of the excommunication. "Please meet me at La Maria on Thursday," he said. "I can go through this without you. But I really don't want to."

I rarely spoke to Fidel beyond our time in the car. And I wondered what he must do all day, for surely Papi, workaholic that he was, was not the type to employ anyone part-time. That afternoon I descended the slope to the jefes' farmhouse. Papi had forbidden me from hanging out there—young ladies had no business witnessing the crude talk and habits of unmarried, middle-aged men. But they were still working the fields; the quarters should be empty of everyone but Fidel. Dirt-caked rubber boots listed across the top step, and I set them upright, scooted them aside. Further down, the breeze had blown a work shirt onto the porch's edge, half of its body flapping toward the machine shed. I draped it over the back of a rocking chair, careful to avoid the butts blooming from the ashtray nearby. At the last unit, a radio broadcasted faintly, coupled with an odd machine-made chugging sound.

Fidel sat in a swivel chair at a plain desk, facing the window. His 9mm handgun lay next to an adding machine which spit out paper as his fingers punched the keys, and a ledger spread open before him. He regarded me with surprise and abruptly halted, his short-sleeved shirt unbuttoned down the front to reveal his torso, a slight thickness collecting around his middle. "What do you want, princesa?" he asked, his tone businesslike but upbeat.

There was nowhere to sit but the narrow bed, the sheets unmade. A limp pair of boxer shorts lay in a heap at the foot. I propped upon the mattress's edge, taking in the stark room, desk and chair. "What are you doing?" I asked.

"Payroll. I keep the books for your father."

"He's never told me that."

"Well, now you know. Is it so shocking that I'm not just a driver?"

Several bound stacks of bills stood next to the adding machine, American dollars. "I need to spend the next afternoon in Cali," I said, "for when the hostage list is released."

He folded his arms. "I was afraid of this. I sympathize with you, I really do. But can you imagine if your father found out that I had lied about that?"

I hugged my chest, nodded. Noises boomed from the fields, louder than at the main house. "How would he find out if you didn't say anything, though? As long as the car doesn't crash." I forced a hopeful smile.

He snorted but shook his head. "I'm sorry."

The screen door lifted and shut, and the drone of insects competed with the pickups' engines rumbling, the shouts and whistles. Someone in the cane was singing but I couldn't make out the words. I approached and placed a hand on Fidel's shoulder; he didn't look at me, his breaths long and steady and the only sound between us. I felt detached from my body, an observer. Perspiration glistened on his hairless chest, the saint's medal and crucifix half-hidden underneath his ribbed undershirt. A desk fan fluttered the adding machine tape; the cool air passed over my arms and stomach. All of his life was now contained in that shabby little room, once an old horse stall: the hard twin mattress, the messy sheets, the scratched gun. A stuffed toy dog, grubby, one eye missing, propped on a chair in the corner. "Do this for me, please," I said, squeezing his arm. "I know you remember what it was like to have someone you really loved."

He removed my hand, clasped it. "I'm sorry. But I can't."

I swatted him off, said, "I thought you might be on my side," and pounced for the door.

"Wait."

"Why?" I spun around. "All I had to give you was the pearls. So what will it cost?"

He rested his elbows on his knees and pressed his thumbs against his forehead. "This is crazy," he muttered. But then he sat up. "Your father keeps cash in the house, American money."

I stepped closer. "Yes, I know."

"You do?" His eyes flickered with surprise. He grabbed a bundle of dollars, held it up.

"Bring me one of these in fifties. No one can know, okay?"

"You don't think he'll miss it?"

He tapped the ledger with a pen. "I handle the money," he said, "for all his businesses."

What did this mean about me, if I was willing to steal from my father? Or was this an exception where a higher law triumphed, like Manuel said? If the cash wasn't there, where else would I get the money? But when I tugged open the drawer, a dozen bundles of American cash jostled loose in the bottom. I snatched a stack of fifties, stared at the rest at moment longer. A missing one might be more noticeable when so few remained. The phone rang. Inez yelled up the stairs that it was Manuel. I stuffed the stack under my shirt.

Did Papi notice? The morning of the hostage release, he kissed me good-bye and wished me a good day at school as usual.

I pulled out the package as Fidel turned off the downtown exit. Not knowing how to disguise it I had decided on the obvious—wrapping paper—so it resembled a gift, although the only kind I could find sported balloons and bears wishing happy birthday to a child. He examined the neatly wrapped bribe and burst out laughing. "You may make an undercover agent yet," he said. "Ever thought of that?"

"I need all afternoon," I said. "You understand?"

We exchanged a handshake, brief but firm. My moist palm tingled.

Hours later, the howls of anguish and outbursts of joy reached me even before I entered the churchyard. A crowd milled outside the doors, listening to a priest read names off a paper. Two teenagers who looked like sisters hugged, jumping up and down. An older couple lingered under an archway with a priest and a young child; the husband pressed against the stone as if holding up the weight. The wife shook her head, tousling the hair of the grandchild who began to wail. A few others had wandered into the rose garden. Carlos sat beneath the statue, cradling his head. Ana approached, and he waved her away. Manuel drifted among the eucalyptus trees, hands in his pockets like a pensive, anxious politician, his back to me. I called his name and he whirled around, his face red and swollen. His eyes blazed with a look I had never before seen in him—wild, desperate. "Is he alive?" I asked.

Manuel nodded. The wind gusted hard. Branches rustled; the glistening leaves cast their shadows. "For how much longer, who knows? They're aware we don't have money. And we sure as hell aren't going to pay a ransom even if we did. So yes, they're keeping him for other reasons." He snatched a bouquet of yellow roses from beneath a tree and threw it. The petals dashed apart, the holy card cartwheeled in the wind. I crept over and placed my hand on his shoulder; he collapsed in my arms, weeping. A sibling who was also a best friend—I could only imagine his despair. Soon he quieted, squeezed me hard, and led me to his motorcycle. Fidel leaned against the car on the shady side street, reading his paper. We rounded the opposite corner, sped past Ana's. She and Carlos, single file, trudged up the front walk.

Manuel locked the door behind us. We backed our way to the bed; in another minute we lay free of clothes. He held my face; on his lips I tasted tears. Through the barred window, thunderheads gathered, rumbling in the distance. He moved against me more slowly, then inside; I whimpered. The bedroom fan whirred. His kisses deepened, grew more urgent. I guessed he was fully inside me, my lower half pinned in a queer mix of pleasure and pain. He smoothed my hair away from my face and I moved against him, but the pain took my breath away. I went still again, but my response must have excited him; he buried his face in my neck and kept going. Just when I thought I would scream that we had to stop, the tears trickling from my eyes, he pulled out. A wetness like hot wax sprang onto my stomach.

I lay there, stunned, but he rolled off, caught his breath, and kissed my shoulder. He left and returned a moment later with a roll of paper towels. "You're bleeding," he said, tearing off sheets. We dabbed them against my body. Should I tell him about the pills?—No. He lay down next to me, traced my neck and collarbone. "I'm sorry. But it hurts girls at first." He handed me another towel, and his forehead furrowed. "I hope you're not pregnant."

"I have a feeling I'm okay. What about you?"

He rolled onto his back, his hair falling in front of his eyes. "God breaks his own rules sometimes. I guess it's just a question of how merciful he is when we break them."

"With me, that's how you feel?"

He stroked my hair. "Never. That's how I know you are meant to be my wife."

"If we get married, where will we go?" I asked. "We can't stay here."

"I don't know. Maybe Medellín. But we might have to leave the country to be safe, ultimately." He didn't say *from your father*, but the words still rang in my head. I described the drills and target practice conducted high above our house, the number of troops—several hundred, by my estimation, the AUC armbands and types of weapons they carried. His face searched mine with each answer to his questions. He lay with his hands behind his head and stared at the ceiling as if in a grassy field, gazing at the stars. I drifted to sleep. When I awoke the sun's rays no longer illuminated the bed; the clock read quarter to five. He stirred awake and kissed my neck and shoulders. I whispered that I had to leave. "What do you think you'll do about Emilio?"

"Oh, I'll get him out. Even if I have to meet the guerillas myself."

"You wouldn't do that." I sat up abruptly.

"Wouldn't I?" he said, staring out the window. Then he kissed me again, my neck and breasts, and I dragged myself away and into my school uniform. The skirt, the vest—it felt like a dress-up costume, an outfit belonging to a child.

Beyond the cane fields the smoke arose from the desplazados' camp and from the hills as the troops cooked their dinners. I had been praying that Papi would be off somewhere with Uncle Charlie or the jefes. But he was home, the news blaring live footage of the hostage release facilitated by the International Red Cross and the Catholic Church: "Buses transported the ELN hostages from the Fallarones to the Cali fútbol stadium where family members embraced their loved ones," the reporter stated. I rinsed my bloodstained underwear in the bathtub and changed into jeans, my hair flowing with Manuel's scent. In the foyer, Fidel said something about the water pump going bad, us having to pull into a garage. The mechanic would send Papi the bill.

Papi and I ate half-facing the TV. His appetite had returned in recent weeks, and his face filled out again. "Visited the mission lately?" I asked.

"No. Not lately." He took a long drink of water. "So, was Romeo's brother released?"

"He wasn't on the list," I said. "From what I heard."

Papi shoved aside his empty plate. "The only way to save the rest now will be blood. Rallies and talks mean nothing."

"Do you know anything? Please? I know you don't like Manuel, but any help—"

"Help Manuel?" He drained his glass, refilled it. Water splashed the tablecloth. "That boy wants one thing from you."

"Ha—that's what you think! He has more love for the world than anyone I know."

"I'm sorry then. Because he'll leave you."

"What? No he won't. He's devoted to—"

"Devotions, yes." Papi thudded his fist; the water sloshed. He jumped up and spoke rapidly. "It is precisely his devotions that will take him away from you. To break away and return, that is the struggle. I know what it is to be Catholic. You don't."

"Fine. What about the displaced? But I suppose it doesn't matter what you do."

He dropped the door to the humidor, and I cringed at the slap. Somewhere in the darkness, Jeeps revved. "Maybe I should let you try and save yourself," he said, and shrugged. He slipped outside and sat alone. He stuck the cigar to his lips but made no attempt to light it.

That night, as Manuel's family mourned Emilio's ongoing captivity, I stepped out of the bathtub a woman. Any remnants of the girl I had been swirled down the drain. Toweling off, I played Manuel's CD. Gracia had recently given me a photo she'd taken of us the night of the street festival. When the phone rang I was outstretched on my bed, naked, admiring the snapshot. I picked it up and said hello. "Mercedes Martinez, we warned you not to attend any more rallies with La Maria Juventud. Tell your boyfriend he had better shut his mouth unless he wants to join his brother next time. You, too."

My hair, cold and wet, clung to my back. I trembled. "Next time?" My voice rasped, barely a whisper. "You're threatening to kidnap us?"

"You can't ransom the dead," the stranger warbled, and hung up.

After the second death threat I began skipping school several times a week. Manuel picked me up the next day at noon. He'd been working fewer shifts in his father's shop so he could organize the campaign to free the abductees—much longer hours since the numbers of La Maria Juventud had dwindled. Peace signs tipped against the walls. His pencil scratched rapidly across the legal pad; now and again the phone rang. In his bed I waited, counted down along with the silent red numerals of the clock.

One day we danced naked to salsa. Another day he played his guitar, and I peeked through the blinds into his Colombia: the man on the corner who pushed the cart of shaved ice and squeezed Coco Lopez and cheap fruit juice on top to sell to the kids after school; the teenagers in the chained yard who lifted barbells and bench-pressed weights. Later, astride him in bed, the discomfort dissolving into pleasure for the first time, I whispered into his ear that I wanted him to release in me. "What?" he said, gaze searching me. I told him it was fine, that I was taking the pill. He turned his face away. The brightness of the room flooded over us.

Afterward, I slipped into the bathroom. When I emerged, he lay propped up on his elbows. He asked, "How long have you been taking the pill?"

"A couple of months. I know you don't believe in it."

"When were you planning on telling me?" he said, an edge to his tone. "Or were you just going to let me believe—never mind." He fell back, shaking his head. "No, I don't like you taking those pills, putting hormones in your body. Tricking nature. It doesn't seem right." He paused. "But I don't know what I believe in anymore." He knit his hand in mine, kissed my knuckles. "I'm going to the mountains to bring back Emilio."

"What?" I twisted around to face him. "Why not keep negotiating for his release with the others? You said they just want ransoms. That once they're tired of waiting, they'll let him go."

"Or we wait, and they kill him," he said, eyebrows lifted. "I'm giving the talks one more week, and then I'm going."

"If you don't come back, what will I do?"

He touched my temple, lifted a piece of my hair. "Then you get away from here. You go to one of those American schools, and you take care of yourself. Right?"

I nodded and laid my head on his chest. The breeze through the louvered glass rustled the pages of the books, open to where Emilio had left them.

Nights, I still dreamed of camouflaged soldiers so vivid that I awoke and could not fall back asleep. So I read the Bible. Emilio, despite his intention to enter seminary, really wasn't as much of a holy man as Manuel. I read again the story I knew best from Hebrew school about Moses on Mount Sinai, how he came down from the mountain transformed, a man marked by God. If Manuel succeeded in meeting the ELN by himself and survived, would he abandon me for missionary work, traveling and preaching, as Papi had predicted? Could he have such a change of heart, despite the magnetic connection between us?

By now a couple of weeks had passed. I was due to get my period. On the toilet I stared at my underwear, praying for blood.

And then the troops left. One Saturday I awoke to the birds chirping outside my window, the men's shouts, and the roar of the Jeeps, one by one, leaving. I ate my breakfast alone. Outside in the courtyard, the maids swept up the cigarette butts and the hundreds of discarded shells, gleaming metallic in the sunlight.

I continued practicing with Fidel. I no longer needed his help to load the clip. We didn't talk much, until the end. Shooting, like sex, has a language all its own. He wore his saint's medal and the sun glinted off its surface, too. I fired my last three shots, lowered the gun, and we ambled over to the frayed target. "You believe in the saints, don't you?" I asked. "How can you tell if someone is one?"

"I've asked them for protection," he said. "Who else can you ask when you are caught between these?" He tapped the holes in the paper. Most of my shots had landed on the torso.

"They have to be dead first, before they can be proven. But I think of your father as one."

"You're kidding."

Fidel clasped his elbows. "I can't explain it, but that's part of why I believe it. He lives out his convictions, he fights for them. And he is prepared to die for them."

"But what about the troops who just left?" I bent down, pinched a shell, warm from the earth, and held it up. "He still does wrong."

Fidel took the gun from me. "One day I pray that he will redeem himself. He saved me. And I'm going to get out of here soon."

"Me, too, but not the way he thinks," I said, and caught myself. "Don't tell anyone."

"That's okay," he said. "We both know each other's secrets. We're friends."

Far below, a young horse circled the paddock on a lead line. Vincente lightly flicked his whip as he talked to the head stable boy, who looked on. In what ways were Fidel and I friends—the time we were forced to spend together in the car? Our banter? Or did we have a deeper trust and understanding, now that he'd shown me how to shoot? Now that he'd taken me to certain Cali streets in secret? The pearls—what had he done with them? "I have nothing left to pay you with," I said.

Fidel scuffed the dirt, hung his head. "Don't worry, princesa. You have paid me enough. And I know what it is to be in love." He turned his back and braced himself on the balls of his feet with every cautious step of his descent.

Shakira and the Virgin Mary with her halo of stars stared down at us. Naked, I straddled Manuel on his couch. There had been no word on another release date. He was arranging his visit to the ELN compound via the Red Cross; the organization dropped off blankets, medicine, and supplies weekly for the hostages. He didn't know how long he would be gone, nor if he would inform the Church—they would likely advise him against it. He also didn't know if he would tell his parents. Carlos had argued but relented. Both wanted their brother returned, and both of them couldn't go. To put all three of their lives in jeopardy wasn't worth the risk. Besides, someone had to stay and oversee release efforts. So Manuel would make his journey alone; the only question was when. I'd be leaving, too—off to spend the upcoming school holiday in Costa Rica with Tía Leo. Papi had booked my flight for that Sunday, right after the EFL test. I wouldn't return until mid-July. Two weeks. "Aren't you afraid?" I asked. We leaned our foreheads together, his hair light and soft in my fingers, our breath intertwined.

"Terrified," he said. "Even Jesus sweated blood in Gethsemane. Before the crucifixion."

He kissed me. We made love on the couch, where countless volunteers had bickered over ideas and spilled Cokes and cried for their captive relatives; the cushions stung my knees. Then a key rattled in the lock, and Carlos's face flashed, his big soft lips an "O" before he slammed the door shut. I ducked, too late. What had he glimpsed—my bare shoulders moving up and down, the unmistakable thrusting of bodies, our moans? We collapsed, rocking with laughter. "Thank God it was Carlos," I said, gasping. "And not Emilio."

Manuel's grin vanished. "I wish it had been Emilio," he said.

I folded him in my arms then, and we dozed. When at last I stood up, a trickle of blood ran down the inside of my leg. My period, thank God.

As I was cleaning up, the phone rang. Manuel handed over the portable—it was Ana. "Your father just called here," she said. "He's furious."

"What did you tell him?" I said.

"I didn't know what to say, so I told him you were here but in the bathroom. He called me a liar and said he knew where you were, that you had better get home. Your school called him about you missing classes. He was screaming at me, Mercedes. I'm shaking."

"I'm so sorry, Ana." I yanked on my clothes, hopping. "Look, I've got to go." I chucked the phone aside. To Manuel I said, "He's going to kill me. School means everything to him. I should have known."

"Does he know we're having sex?"

"No—how would he?"

"I just don't think that would go over too well."

Papi stood inside the gate, his arms crossed. The purple bandanna was tied tightly around his forehead, and the breeze fluttered the loose flap covering the top of his head. He started barking before the car glided to a stop. "What were you doing out of school, huh?" He sounded like when he scolded one of the ridgebacks after she had wandered for hours.

I breezed past but he chased after me, grabbed my arm and twisted it. I yelped. He forced me up the steps. "Where were you? Tell me the truth."

"I was at Ana's."

"That's a lie." He squeezed my arm harder, pushed me to sit on the couch.

"Fine, you know then. What's the big deal?" I wrenched away.

He grabbed my chin to face him. "And what were you two doing all afternoon?"

"Nothing. Just talking and playing music."

"I'm not stupid." He swiped my purse from the coffee table, dumped it upside down. Wallet, gum, and the sleeve of birth control pills fell out, the foil pack of holes like the bullet-torn target. He waved the empty pack like a prize. "Mercedes?"

"I'm sorry," I said. And it was almost true: I was sorry for having lied to him, but not for what I had shared with Manuel.

Fuming, he tried to rip apart the pack but it refused to tear, so he crushed it instead, saying, "What a fraud, this Manuel. An apostle one minute, in bed with you the next. Are you that blind? Can't you see?" Droplets of spit sprang from his lips as he spoke. He threw the pack and it skidded across the tile.

"He's not—so what if he struggles with what he believes, like a million others? Like you."

Papi rubbed a hand over his face, puffy and in need of a shave. "I'm partly to blame," he said at last, solemnly. "We've never talked about it, and I suppose this was bound to happen. For once I wish your mother were here."

"Just for once?

"This isn't about her." He held his head in his heads, closed his eyes. "Or maybe it is. Maybe I'm to blame for all of it."

Nearby the dogs resumed their places on the tile, the mutts at Papi's feet. "I'm sure you're not. But you could talk to me more," I said. "Why don't you tell me what happened with her?"

"I can't talk to anyone," he said, shaking his head. "Don't you understand that words sometimes fail? Action, that's what counts." His eyes popped open. "Why do you think the guerillas and the army are still fighting?"

"Maybe we've got to try harder," I said. My lower abdomen cramped. I ducked into the bathroom, swallowed an aspirin. The pill left a bitter spot on my tongue.

As I descended the stairs for dinner, Inez waved me over, TV remote in hand. "Isn't this where your friend and her boyfriend perform?" she asked, and made the sign of the cross before turning up the volume. Police lights glowed at the bottom of the screen: "BOMBARDEO EN EL RESTAURANTE DE MIRADOR." Chunks of debris blanketed the sports cars and luxury SUVs in the parking lot, the windshields splintered. People sobbed and clutched one another, and when the camera panned up to the night sky, smoke plumed from where the roof had been. Everything inside me turned cold; I tried to turn up the volume but fumbled the remote.

My hands shook so hard I had to dial twice. First Manuel's number, then Ana's. All busy signals. I left voice messages, kept trying. The ELN claimed responsibility—the death toll at fourteen and rising, the police still recovering bodies.

Finally, someone picked up at Gracia's house. I didn't recognize her voice, she sounded so subdued and serious. "We're lucky," she said. "We usually don't work that shift." The police had yet to release an official statement. But another young couple, good friends of theirs, had been performing when the bomb detonated—the woman now in critical condition, her partner instantly killed. "I'm moving to Bogotá and then the U.S. or Europe, first audition I can get," she said. "I'm out of this hell."

I reached Manuel next. He had spent hours in the offices of La Maria priests and the archdiocese. But another hostage release had failed to be drawn up. All evening he'd phoned and rallied the frightened, disenchanted La Maria Juventud: *We must not let the guerillas see that their fear has won.*

I didn't say anything. After we hung up, I pored over the brochures again: the too-wide grins of teens playing Frisbee and frowns of students in lab coats and goggles, raising chemistry beakers. I couldn't picture them crying in each other's arms, leading candlelight vigils and marches for kidnapped relatives. I kept hoping that the attacks and threats would stop, but at what point were the forces too much? When did you know that the best thing to do was to save yourself and leave your country, your home, and loved ones behind? The night at the Mirador had been so magical—all destroyed in mere seconds. Did I wait until the next bombing to tell Manuel that I wanted to leave, and for him to come with me? Gracia and Esteban had just escaped losing their lives. I cast aside the brochures and picked up my airline itinerary: two short flights to the serenity of a country that had no standing army, no paras or desplazados. What had Sister Rosemary said? *Sometimes in order to see your life clearly, you must leave it.*

Twisting in my sheets that night I pleaded silently for help. I didn't want to die. And I thought another voice answered me from within, one of reassurance and love. *Estoy aqui*—I am here. Was it God, or simply my weary imagination? The cocks crowed in the darkness, and at last I fell asleep.

The EFL test took place in my school's library at eight o'clock. I stared down at the test booklet as if it contained hieroglyphics. When the proctor called my name for the oral section, my hands shook. She hit the record button on the tape deck, and even though the dialogue was one that Sister Rosemary and I had drilled, I faltered and gave simple, short replies. As I exited, I knew I had earned a mediocre score at best.

When it was over I hurried to Avenida Sexta and hailed a cab. I had lied to Fidel and told him the test would run until mid-afternoon. As we rounded the corner into Manuel's barrio a light rain speckled the windows, blurring the glass. The corner butcher swung a hog's head onto a scale, wiped his apron red. The crowd in the apartment spilled down the stairs to the street; I could make out Manuel's voice, as passionate and articulate as Papi on a tirade. I sidestepped two girls in platform sandals crouched on the bottom step, pushed past the book bags and jackets of the university students, and slipped inside. The air thickened with the musk of bodies, cologne, cigarettes. Manuel's eyes locked on me as I squeezed into a spot in the back.

How long ago it felt, that first rally I had attended in the Plaza de Cayzedo two months ago, when Emilio had addressed the crowd and Manuel hung back, only to emerge with his guitar. Now Manuel explained how the victims' families giving into the ELN's ransom demands perpetuated the kidnapping culture—"You're making a deal with the devil," he said. Shouts and questions flew. "How else do you expect us to get our loved ones back?" asked a young man, cross-legged. "My parents and grandfather?" He brushed aside his dirty blonde hair, eyes relentless, defiant. Flannel shirt cinched around his waist, he looked like Kurt Cobain. One young woman explained that her mother had only been returned two days ago, once her family had sold their house to pay off the terrorists. Mascara traced grey rivers down her face.

Interjections began. Manuel shushed the crowd and held up his hand—"Let her finish," he said sternly. More people wordlessly crowded the doorway; the scent of rain drifted in. Manuel reiterated the Church's policy to not meet ransom demands for its priests. We ought to adopt the same rule in the community, let the guerillas know it up front. Tomorrow he would lead another demonstration. But he did not mention any plans after that, and the secret known by only a few of us twisted my heart—nothing was going to stop him from meeting the guerilla leaders in the southwestern mountains.

Most filed out then, fliers in hand. The grungy kid grabbed a skateboard resting inside the door, others the motorcycle helmets, lined up like skulls in a row. A few stragglers hovered around Manuel, barraging him with more questions—why not demonstrate every day until the ELN released every hostage—and then hung on every word of his replies, their stances bristled. From down the hall the toilet flushed, and the young woman emerged, cheeks powdered except for tiny black specks near her eyes. She sipped coffee from a Styrofoam cup, grasped Manuel's arm and implored him to do something for her brother who remained captive. I sank onto the arm of the couch. A forgotten sweatshirt lay flattened against the cushions.

Manuel guided them out, slid the bolt. The candles blazed as hot as a campfire at the little shrine. I picked up the matches, hesitated, then tossed them aside. We held each other. I cradled his face; my breaths grew tight. "Please," I said. "Don't go yet."

"What do you mean?"

"To the mountains. Wait until I come back from Costa Rica first."

He kissed the inside of my wrist. "I love you," he said. "But for now I've got to live as God calls us to live. Sometimes people have to be apart before they can live together, to accomplish what they each have to do."

"I'm not asking you not to go at all." I was crying now, quietly. "Can't you do this one small thing for me?"

He didn't answer, but I let him put his arms around me. Silence passed. Then he kissed the top of my head and whispered, "I won't go yet, okay? I'll wait another week, until you're home." I nodded, dried my tears on his shirt. "But things may be different when you return. Remember to be aware always."

"Always?" I said.

"Always," he repeated. "That is our greatest calling. To become the eyes of God."

The clear pools of wax overflowed, the flames leapt high. Were we fooling ourselves and delaying the inevitable? Suicide and martyrdom—one cut you off from God, the other joined you to Him. What was the difference, when both resulted in death? Why hadn't I asked Sister Rosemary? I prayed to the small space of calm within me, *Please show me what to do.* Manuel hugged me tighter. I blew out the candles, and the room fell into shadows and half-light.

CHAPTER ELEVEN

The plane descended into Costa Rica's Central Valley. San José sprawled for miles within the rugged volcanic mountains, like home. Vast plots of cleared rainforest, cattle, and sugarcane dotted the city outskirts. Here, young Americans hauled surfboard bags around the baggage claim, flip-flops slapping the floor. A retired couple clipped past toting a matching red luggage set, trailed by two gangly grandchildren in T-shirts which read: "Costa Rica Pura Vida." In rollicking Italian, a woman scolded a teenage boy and girl with white-blond locks. The taxi drivers who clamored against the glass shouted in both English and Spanish.

Tía Leo stood behind them, waving, her dress flapping in the breeze. I had never seen her wear pants, even in photos from years past. In her late forties, her cheeks and chin had grown rounder along with the rest of her stocky figure, but her smile reminded me of Papi's. After we hugged and she exclaimed how much I had grown up since Christmas, we climbed into her old Galloper and headed past chicharróneras and men selling peppers and lotto tickets, then left the traffic for the narrow two-lane which wound around the hillsides of grazing Brahman cows to the high whitewashed walls of her house in Piedades de Santa Ana.

We ate at the picnic table under the rancho, a jungle oasis tucked away: empanadas, pico de gallo, and fresh mango juice. Cats trotted along the railings, and a pack of neighborhood mongrels awaited slivers of pork to drop; Tía Leo shooed them off. From the hills above, a workman sang and rapped his hammer; below, the stable and paddock where my uncle's beautiful Paso Fino horses had frolicked during my previous visits remained empty, the stalls dark and grasses high. I asked her about them. She clutched her arms across her chest, and a frown clouded her pretty, carefully made up face. "I had to sell them," she said. "And we still aren't making enough." I sensed her loneliness, too, as she said this, and strained to remember my American uncle more clearly, but couldn't. His desk in the corner overflowed with bills, paperwork, and an adding machine; when he was alive the desk had been organized, the ledgers stacked. Above hung faded pictures from the 1970s and '80s: his pink face in the sharp pilot's uniform, my cousins as chubby toddlers in their bathing suits, a bikini-clad Tía Leo lifting a wineglass, family pictures around a Christmas tree somewhere I didn't recognize, in the United States. A family together—would I ever know what that was like?

I chewed slowly, savoring the steaming potato and spicy pico de gallo, the mango sweet and cool on my tongue. "Papi raves about your empanadas, you know," I said. "Nothing compares, he says."

She gripped her glass with both hands. "How is he, lately?"

Below the pool, a workman stepped out of the cluster of cottages by the chicken shed and stretched. "Well, I wish all he was up to lately was raving about your cooking," I said. "But I'm afraid not."

"What do you mean? When we spoke last week, he talked about the alpacas. And that you'd had a few visitors."

"Visitors. Is that what he said? Well, I'd like to hear your side of things first. About the trouble he got into in Florida. And how he met my mother."

Tía Leo gazed at the fruit trees bordering the footpath, stirred her juice, and began. My grandparents had four children: Leonora, the oldest; Diego, two years younger; and Pedro and Jorge. Growing up, my father, Diego, had dreamed of owning the hacienda near his parents and buying the farmland their family leased from the wealthy landowners. Papi had always been bullheaded and independent; he did not want to have to work in the city, pay rent, or answer to anyone. But their family was middle class, tenant farmers, and such a dream remained impossible. Tía Leo shared a similar streak of rebelliousness; she and my father had been close growing up. Leo wanted to travel. She wanted more than to get married like her girlfriends, so when she finished high school she applied for and landed a stewardess position with Taca Airlines. When she came home she shared stories and photos from her stopovers—Puerto Vallarta, Havana, Miami. Papi was entranced by her trips to the Mayan ruins and the beaches of Cozumel, the colorful foreigners she met, her constantly improving English. So as soon as he finished school he took a job with a commodities company out of Cartagena, which involved travel to Fort Lauderdale and Miami. The job was perfect—he needed to learn English, but more important to his employers was his extensive knowledge of sugarcane farming and refinery. There was a chance he would even be offered a permanent position in the United States someday, if he desired.

Leo wrote to Papi often—she sent postcards to an apartment address in Cartagena. And for a time she was assigned to fly a route there, and if my father were home they would visit. He kept a charming apartment with flower boxes tended by an elderly landlady, on a side street a block from the waterfront and restaurants. But after a year or two, Leo noticed that whenever she asked about his job in Miami, he grew more evasive. She knew the commodities company paid well, but his clothes grew increasingly more expensive and tailored: white suits, black Italian ties and shoes, a silver Swiss watch. It was the 1970s, and Colombia was ravaged by civil war with no end to the violence in sight. Many of the upper and professional classes were fleeing to Panama, Venezuela, or the U.S., desperate to escape if they hadn't already. From her travels and talks with fellow Colombians, airline crews, and travelers, Leo knew that Miami was becoming a hot spot for narco-trafficking. She suspected that her brother had somehow fallen into working for the Colombian cartels. But she turned a blind eye and didn't ask. He still never missed a Sunday mass, at least not when she visited.

Just when she ought to have been paying more attention to Papi's activities, she was transferred to another route and fell in love with an American pilot fifteen years her senior—my uncle. With no more Cartagena stopovers, she only saw her brother on holidays. One Christmas Papi announced that he had bought his parents' land and presented them with the deed; their mother wept. Leo asked how his business was going, and he only said that he spent more time in Miami and made enough to save and invest much of what he earned. By then, Leo and my uncle were engaged, and my uncle commented that Papi must be involved with drug smuggling. "An apartment in Cartagena and another in Miami," my uncle had said to her. "And those shoes he's wearing? South American commodities companies don't pay that well."

They visited my father in Miami once, on their way to their honeymoon in the Bahamas. Unlike his modest second-floor quarters in Cartagena with frayed but quaint secondhand furniture, in Miami he lived in a white high-rise with the latest in home decor, huge abstract paintings, security in the lobby. They drank mojitos, never more than two because Papi was such a purist. He hated overindulgence, although his one vice back then, as now, was tobacco. They lounged on the balcony overlooking Biscayne Bay and talked in English, and to her surprise his command of the language rivaled hers. *Who has my brother become?* Leo wondered. But their visit only spanned an afternoon, and nothing in particular struck either Tía Leo or her new husband as direct evidence that her brother was involved in illegal activities.

Still, Papi's Miami lifestyle proved a topic of conversation for some time. "When I brought up the fact that my brother would never take drugs, my husband shrugged it off," she said. "He told me a smuggler doesn't have to do drugs to be involved in the business. Many don't touch the stuff." Their suspicions had been correct, although my aunt would not discover this until years later. Leo quit working when Pilar was born. She didn't talk to my father as much, but when she did, he always mentioned his most recent purchase of land back home, in the Valle de Cauca. He was buying up the hacienda from the family whom his parents had worked for their whole lives: three hundred acres here, five hundred acres there. He intended to return, build a house, and run a sugarcane plantation. He flew back to Cali often, and every six months or so he made another purchase. Only just before my mother left Colombia to return to Florida did she tell my aunt that our farm, the trucks and horses, the house, had all been bought with drug money from his position with the Cali cartel.

How had it happened? Like many young, single colombianos who landed in Miami in the 1970s, Papi had been motivated by the opportunities to make money in America and bring it back to Colombia to make his dreams come true. In Miami's Colombian-run bars and clubs, he befriended caleños who persuaded him that he could operate as a middle-man, under the radar; he would never have to even see marijuana, and later, coca. The cartel paid him for his shipping connections to Cartagena. He had been keeping up the ruse for nearly a decade when he met my mother at a rich man's party on a yacht. Paula was twenty, a student at the University of Miami, and he was almost thirty. Over the course of several conversations with Paula, my aunt learned that despite my father's illegal dealings, he had remained steadfast in his goals. He treated both his commodities job and his position as a narco-trafficker as a business; when he fell in love with Paula, all he talked about was returning to Colombia to farm and to start a family. It was the 1980s, and the drug wars in Miami had turned brutal. He wanted out.

"But did my mother know?" I asked. "About his narco-trafficking?"

"She suspected it like the rest of us," my aunt said. "She was a clever young woman, and your father, as you can imagine, was extremely charming. He hasn't changed. And you should have seen him in those white suits he used to wear. All my friends were in love with him."

Tía Leo said that one day she got a phone call—she and her husband were living in Costa Rica by then, so they could be close to her family but not raise their young daughters amidst the violence of Colombia, which had only escalated with the drug trade fueling the civil conflict and guerilla factions. Their mother said that Diego had quit his job in the U.S. and returned home for good, that he was finally going to start his farm. He had brought an American girl with him, and they planned to get married in four days at the church. What the family didn't know—Tía Leo found out this part of the story from my mother much later—was that the U.S. authorities had planned to arrest my father in Miami. But someone in the cartel tipped him off first, and he had called up my mother in her dorm and told her that he was leaving that night. He confessed about his involvement with the cartels, and he wanted her to come with him because he could never again return to the U.S. In exchange, he promised he would leave narco-trafficking behind forever; he had poured his profit into land and wanted to farm. And she agreed, dropped out of university, and left with him without saying good-bye to her family. Later, she wrote a letter to her parents, telling them she was in love and not to worry, that she would return to visit.

So this was the reason for my parents' hasty departure from Florida and marriage in Colombia rather than the United States, and why Papi did not mention visiting me at boarding school. Because he couldn't.

"If he tried to go back, would they arrest him at the airport?" I asked.

"I don't know," she said. "Probably. But why would he ever risk that when he can live in his country and remain perfectly happy? And obviously he was not such a high-ranking criminal that the U.S. authorities would go after him like they did Pablo Escobar. The Americans arrested many cartel members, but many escaped, too—or negotiated deals. He was lucky. And foolish." We sat in silence, the rain beginning to patter the roof and banana leaves. Paula had trusted my father to keep his word—why? She must have believed him a good man, that he would honor his promise to cut ties. But to pick up and flee to a new country where she did not speak the language, leaving her friends and family behind—she had loved him.

"What about your parents?" I asked. "Did they not suspect anything?"

"Oh, yes," she said. "They were uneducated but not stupid. Before the wedding your father confessed to the priest and to them, too. Got down on his knees and begged our parents for forgiveness, for how he had deceived us all. But he promised he was finished. And he didn't lie. He worked hard to start that farm."

"They forgave him?"

"Don't you know the story of the prodigal son?" Tía Leo asked, surprised. "Everyone loved Diego. We were just happy to have him home."

"Then how did Papi get into trouble again, if he started the farm?" I told her about Uncle Charlie, how he was not an old cartel operative from my father's days in Miami, but someone from the more recent past.

"I don't know," she said. "He's always been devoted to that farm, from what I can see. Why he'd be hosting someone like that, perhaps as some kind of protection—who knows?"

Papi had bought the plot with the main house that had belonged to the original owners, but he wanted to modernize and so tore the rooms apart; he and my mother lived on one side. As Inez had stated, my mother was a city girl unaccustomed to a standard of living outside the U.S. While he broke his back replanting the hundreds of acres of cane and shouting down from horseback to hired workers, Paula had no interest in digging the dirt or gathering eggs from chickens. Tía Leo and her family spent that Christmas in Colombia. Diego and Paula were clearly in love—they teased each other, and even when they spoke with straight faces, a charge snapped between them. Shortly thereafter, my mother found out she was pregnant, but she didn't appear excited to be having a baby, according to my grandmother. She would sit in a corner or by a window and stare off, and didn't talk about possible names. She battled morning sickness throughout her pregnancy and had every reason to be miserable, although she didn't complain. Tía Leo said she was not surprised when she heard shortly after my birth that Paula had left my father and me behind. Nor was she surprised that in his depression my father let his fields turn fallow and the strays run through the house, until the Cali cartel once again lured him back.

Rumors rippled on the tongues of relatives: Diego's heart had turned black with bitterness at my mother's abandonment. The Church granted him an annulment but the finality of the divorce propelled him into greater despair. He stopped going to church, lost his faith in God and even his interest in me, his newborn daughter. Inez and my grandparents provided care throughout my infancy. Not only had my father returned to the Cali cartel, buying up the mountainside behind the house and the acres of coffee, but he convinced his brothers, Pedro and Jorge, to also get involved.

My grandparents didn't believe this at first, but some relatives refused to associate with the three Martinez brothers any longer. While Papi's operations remained behind the scenes—he supplied money and infrastructure for smuggling via his sugarcane operation—his younger brothers became more immersed. The Cali and Medellín cartels had started warring against one another, and one day both of my uncles were taken out by hit men, their bodies dismembered and strewn across the fields less than a mile from their birthplace. In retaliation, my father carried out a hit on their killer and succeeded, ordering the rival trafficker's body meet the same fate—the ghastly deed which resulted in his eventual excommunication, as told by the former Cali operative-turned-priest.

The death of two sons at once, and the loss of a third to the dark side of the cartels, proved too much for my grandparents. The hacienda was thriving by then, one of the largest plantations in the Valle de Cauca, and Papi mourned the deaths of his brothers perhaps most of all. Tía

Leo reached out to Diego over the phone. "I forgave him," she said. "I knew my brother, and that all of this was in defiance—that he had made a promise to God to lead a good life as a husband and father, but he lost your mother anyway. I asked him, 'How much more damage do you want to do before you lose your daughter?' This caught his attention, even though you were too young to understand what was going on. He knew he could not keep up his recklessness. What could he do? Papi asked Leo. He had lost the love of his life, his brothers, and severed his tie with the Church. His parents refused to see him. But she told him to go and beg forgiveness once again to their parents, show his remorse for having drawn his brothers, who would have been content to work as jefes for the rest of their lives on the hacienda, into the narco-trafficking business. She waited but didn't hear from him for days. When she called their parents and asked if they had spoken to Diego, my grandparents admitted that he had stopped by and begged for their mercy but they needed to pray about it before giving him an answer.

And then she received the news that the FARC had swept through the Valle de Cauca. Her parents, along with a few neighbors, had been kidnapped. Weeks, and then months, passed.

The guerillas did not ask for a ransom, unheard of with a family member as wealthy as Diego Martinez had become. Even though she was terrified to leave her two daughters and husband, Tía Leo flew to Colombia. I imagined her visit, my father and his sister facing one another—the last remaining members of their family.

"He kept saying how he had killed them all, he had allowed evil to overrun his soul. He said he would spend the rest of his life trying to make things right with God—his life and yours," she said. "I pitied him and hated him at the same time, yet there I was because I still loved him. What choice did I have? We were the only ones left. I asked if he was sure, and he said there was no doubt. Rival traffickers had slipped under the authorities' radar and joined the FARC—this is when the U.S. officials and the authorities down here had started to crack down. Rather than kill Diego, his enemies had targeted him where it would hurt him most—his loved ones. We talked about me taking you because things were so dangerous, but he said without you he had no reason for living and would kill himself. So I left, alone. But

I knew by the look on his face that he had finished with the cartels for good. Don't you remember any of this?"

"Nothing," I said.

Tía Leo and Papi spoke little after my grandparents' deaths—the bodies were never recovered. The remaining relatives fled Colombia out of fear for their lives; no one wanted to live within five hundred miles of Diego Martinez. When the authorities killed Pablo Escobar in 1993, my aunt called Papi. "Did you have something to do with this?" she wanted to know.

"Only in the smallest of ways," he said. The Colombian authorities had contacted him and promised to drop charges—they had a file on him two feet thick—if he would help put a group together to take down Escobar. I guessed this was how Uncle Charlie—Carlos Castaño, if that's who he was—and Papi became friends. After his family's slaughter, Papi insisted to Tía Leo that he no longer profited or participated in drug trafficking. But he had funneled money to bring down those in the Medellín cartel who had been responsible for their deaths, including Escobar.

In the years following, Tía Leo and Papi rekindled their relationship. With the obvious expansion of the sugarcane production, his management of the tenants and now the desplazados, and his concerns for me, she believed his actions had proven his promise to be true—he had left the world of narco-trafficking behind forever. "But tell me what's going on," she said. She regarded me with an imploring, clouded expression, her palm pressed flat between us.

"There's so much," I said. I told her about Papi's confession to me about his smuggling, and the convoys of military trucks that had appeared last year and again, just weeks ago, but this time under the command of Uncle Charlie. She shook her head at the mention of his name and description, although she added that Papi's jefes had all, at one time or another, been involved in the cartel. There was my father's constant fear—paranoia, even—for my welfare and my involvement with Manuel. But when I asked her what she thought, she just shrugged.

"I wish I knew the answers," she said. "But if Diego is still involved, how would I have any idea? His life seems quiet to me."

"The troops at our house weren't quiet."

"Well, I would not be surprised if he's paying off old ties, as your driver said. And who knows—those ties may be paramilitary like you suspect, or they may be in government. Everything down there is so entangled. But I know he's afraid for you, with all the violence. If I were you, I would leave Colombia as soon as possible. And you are welcome to stay here for as long as you like. Don't feel you have to go back, if your life is in so much danger."

The rain drummed the roof now, and tiny rivers rushed from the gutters and downhill through the yard. The construction workers' singing and hammering had stopped, the valley view turned to thick gray mist. Suddenly the journey coupled with the hearty empanadas and the rain caught up with me; I yawned. Tía Leo asked if I would like some coffee, but I declined. As we arose I asked, "Did you keep in touch at all with my mother?"

"Not anymore," she said. "She called me a few times after she left. All she had thought about when she dropped her life in Florida was being with your father. She didn't anticipate how difficult living in another country would be, away from her family. And then to get pregnant, care for an infant. I don't think she went back to school for a while, she was so sad about it all."

"But even if she didn't feel ready to be a parent, why wouldn't she try to get in touch with me, at some point? He's always sworn she hasn't, that he has no idea where she is."

Tía Leo didn't pause from gathering utensils and stacking plates, just shook her head. "That's what he says. Knowing Diego, I suppose he's terrified that if he encouraged you to contact her, you'd leave."

"Then he's being silly," I said. "Even if she did forget me and ran off somewhere, don't you think my grandparents would have wondered about me? I'd like to meet them, at least. Would you help me find her?"

"I don't know if I would be of much help. Are you sure that's what you want?" She bent over and scraped the remnants of an empanada into a dog dish on the porch's edge.

I stood and listened to the lull of the rain. I wanted sleep, to disappear into the soft world of dreams and wake up without such difficult choices to make. I felt as if at any moment, one slight decision would take me down a wrong road, but I never could tell which decision would reap such a result, so on I plunged into vagueness. My mother, another person with the depth of an ocean inside her.

"Maybe I don't," I said.

I slept hard for an hour and awoke, groggy and disoriented, in Pilar's bed. Photos of my oldest cousin's travels covered the walls: Pilar horseback riding on a white beach, her auburn hair swept back, kayaking before a glacier, flying in a balloon above an African savannah at dawn. She worked for the National Geographic cable channel, in production. If I didn't become a flight attendant, what kind of path might open up, that I couldn't yet see? Paula's story, how similar it could be to mine—a quick departure and marriage to a passionate, conflicted man, a domestic life. What if I was I doomed to repeat my mother's mistakes and unhappiness?

Jacki arrived before dinner, her freckled skin tanned and her reddish-brown hair pulled back into a scruffy ponytail. We disappeared to her bedroom, absent of her sister's magazine-quality photos and neatness; Jacki's creased snapshots stuck out every which way from her dresser mirror: blurry pictures of her dancing at clubs, or arm-in-arm with friends. A string of Buddhist prayer flags and posters of famous surfers on enormous waves draped the walls. I asked to see her flight attendant uniform, and she held it up to herself with pride. "Hard to believe, huh?" she said, and raised her eyebrows suggestively. "And I have to wear these." She dug in her jewelry box and held out pearl studs, smaller than my pair but newer, more lustrous than the ones I had given to Fidel. I could see Paula leaving an ill-fitted jacket behind—not valuable earrings. Mine must have been from Papi. I fingered the uniform and told Jacki I hoped my English would be good enough one day for me to become a flight attendant.

"Aren't you going to boarding school?" she replied, surprised. "Mami says that's all Tío Diego talks about lately."

"I don't want to." I flopped back on her bed. "I won't find another one like Manuel."

"Really? I wish I'd studied in the U.S., like Pilar. Sometimes you just don't realize what a big difference those choices make. She has such an amazing life."

"So do you. You're much cooler."

"Am I?" Jacki laughed. She straightened the white blouse on the hanger. "I never thought I'd work for Taca. But as far as jobs go in Latin America, it's not so bad, I guess." Then she drifted downstairs, calling for Tía Leo.

We traveled east. Downtown San José's dingy sidewalks and buildings reminded me of Cali, homeless and junkies sifting through garbage bins. But Costa Rica was not so far removed. We'd passed the Multiplaza mall near the Escazú exit, billboards for Fendi and Prada beckoning. "Colombian drug money built this," Jacki said. "Money laundering. They do it with tons of places—hotels, nightclubs, restaurants." I rode in silence. How much of the everyday had the drug trade built, worldwide? This was just one movie theatre, one mall.

We climbed the narrow highway through the Braulio Carrillo National Park, the dark canopy and thick mist hugging the mountainsides. It was like looking back at the Earth millions of years ago, when dinosaurs ruled, easy to imagine a pterodactyl swooping down. A pair of hikers, backpacks towering, trudged along the shoulder. I would never want to descend into that abyss; how would you ever come out? "Every year visitors die in this park," Tía Leo said. "The most renowned hikers and guides get lost. Even the rangers can't find them because the forest is so endless." My pulse quickened. The Fallarones—why had I never considered the terrain as a threat? What if Manuel took the wrong trail and couldn't find his way back? It would not take long to perish with panthers lurking, poisonous tree frogs and snakes. Were the Fallarones this impenetrable? How foolish we were, knowing so little, even nothing, about our backyards. We clustered in cities and imprisoned ourselves behind fences, cut off from nature.

But Manuel was still in Cali, not the Fallarones. He had assured me he would wait, and would be there when I returned.

Then we drove across the flat land with nothing but pineapple fields and banana trees, speckled with workers' villages. Some teenagers rode bikes, balancing younger brothers and sisters on handlebars, their clothes faded. Other children, barefoot, played in the lanes paved with puddles, the dwellings like our tenants' homes—concrete block, many little more than tin-roofed shacks. For miles we drove, and still the banana trees and pineapples ran across the lowlands to the distant mountain slopes, whoever owned the fields and employed these squalid villages a mystery. As we neared the Caribbean coast, we came upon yards of shipping containers stacked one on top of another—Chiquita, Dole, Del Monte.

We passed through Limón, a grungy port city much like Barranquilla, where many desplazados had been driven by the paras, and where the poverty was even worse. In sleepy Puerto Viejo, Jacki and I watched the surfers on Playa Negra and Salsa Brava, the famous break. She had brought her surfboard and plunged in, but I lounged in the shade and the warm sand. Tía Leo flipped through magazines; water lapped the fishing boats pulled up to shore. A dreadlocked young man limped up and down the beach, gesturing for sunbathers to browse the shell necklaces that draped his arm. Manuel and I could live here, and disappear. But what would we do in such a place? The glistening coco palms swished over the turquoise water. A guide on horseback led a gringo couple up the beach. For a while I dozed, until a hollow thud jarred me. Then another. Howler monkeys clattered above, lobbing coconuts onto our bungalow roof.

Jacki and I traveled on our own then, to the Pacific coast. One night in Jacó Beach, dozens of high-heeled Latinas swarmed inside the hotel casino—prostitutes like Uncle Charlie's "girls." One of them, red-headed, was struggling to yank down her top and flaunt her artificial bust before some older gringos, sunburned and round-bellied, when she swung around, her big purse knocking my Coke. She and I fussed over the spilled drink, embarrassed, apologizing to the cocktail waitress. At the roulette wheel a group of younger men roared in English and burst out laughing, the loudest in a T-shirt that read University of Colorado. He swaggered up to the redhead, called, "Venga! Let's have a shot—this guy's getting married in a few days!" The waitress brought another Coke; I declined. Would the bride suspect the groom had paid for sex? Gracia's father had twice kept mistresses, once with his secretary and then with the housekeeper, before her parents divorced. Her mother had pretended not to know. This was not unheard of, and far more common than Uncle Charlie's preference for prostitutes. Did all men behave this way, gringos included?

"What happens to these women?" I asked my cousin. "Do they have families?"

"Some do," Jacki said. "They need the money, obviously. A lot of them get abortions. It's illegal, but you can find places, you know? A girl I knew from high school got one in San José, downtown. The store front looked exactly like an eyeglass shop with a doctor and everything, but in the back they had tables with stirrups."

At an Internet café in Quepos I bought a phone card and called the brothers' apartment. But there was no answer. Nothing about Emilio or another hostage release date had turned up online. The guerilla violence had only increased.

When we arrived at the hotel in Manuel Antonio National Park, the clerk greeted us in English. We responded in Spanish; he startled and switched, tossed both languages back and forth when he passed us on the footpath. This same routine was repeated later with a waiter and zip-line operator. We jostled in vans beside gringo couples who asked about our families, and upon discovering we each had an American parent, appeared baffled at why we didn't live in the United States. They rattled off compliments about what natural beauty Costa Rica possessed, how friendly the Ticos were, and so on.

"Will you be going to school in the U.S.?" one thick-legged, graying man asked. When Jacki said no, he shifted to me. His eyes twinkled beneath his floppy hat, a marlin leaping above the brim, his wife's sun-spotted hand rested loosely on his knee. Her chin drooped, and she napped against his shoulder. All I could think about was the man leaving a casino, a puta leading him by the hand like a child. I told him I hadn't heard back yet but listed the schools. He raised his eyebrows. "Impressive," he said. "Much better than what you've got down here, and Colombia's so unstable. I bet you can't wait to get out. You'll love America." And so forth. I faced the window, gritted my teeth.

One morning a slender, dark-haired gringa around forty sauntered by the pool. I watched her while pretending to read my magazine. But her body curved in the wrong places, and her skin had a bronze undertone. Not Paula—although her features may have changed, of course. What if she wasn't even living in the United States? She could be in France, or Japan, anywhere, with a new husband and family. I might have brothers and sisters; I might not. If Papi really knew nothing about her current whereabouts (and indeed, he might not), how else might I track her down? If she didn't want to see me, what then?

We stopped in Quepos again to check e-mail and make calls before the ride home. Tía Leo said I had no messages from Manuel or Ana. When I dialed Manuel's number, the machine answered for the third time that week—the brothers' apartment was never so vacant. I tried to reach Ana, then Gracia, but got hold of neither and left messages telling them to call me at Tía Leo's number. We sped past the palm forest; the rows endless and dark, a dizzying blur. If only I could disappear into those rows. I'd walk and walk and never come out.

That evening, Gracia called me back. Jacki and I sat with Tía Leo. I sipped ginger tea. A cat sprawled, warm and heavy, on my lap. Gracia asked how the trip was going, but her voice was too high-pitched. "Have you talked to anyone?" she asked. When I told her no, she said, "I have some bad news, Mercedes. Are you sitting down?"

"Yes," I said faintly. "Please, what's going on?"

"Manuel left for the mountains. Did you have any idea?"

"You're kidding me." I heaved off the cat; he yowled in protest. "He'd promised to put it off. Until I got back." Tía Leo and Jacki stared wide-eyed, listening. "When did he leave?"

"A few days ago. I can't believe he wouldn't tell you." Gracia paused. "I'm so sorry."

"Me, too." I traced the rustic wall, the grain rough and deeply grooved. "But of course, he wouldn't tell me. He knew how upset I would be, that I would beg him not to go." She asked when I'd be back, and I told her my flight wasn't until Sunday. I couldn't wait that long, though; I'd change my ticket, come home right away. "There's no other news, from Carlos or anyone?" I asked. "I can't believe Ana hasn't called me back yet."

"You haven't talked to Ana? You don't know what's going on with her?"

"No. Is she okay?"

"Sort of. But I'll let her tell you."

Before we hung up, I asked whether or not she was still moving to Bogotá with the spike in violence. "A thousand guerillas wouldn't stop me," she said. She was finished at the Mirador; the restaurant was in shambles and closed for now. Last weekend she and Esteban had flown to Bogotá and found an apartment. They planned to move at the end of August.

Tía Leo found the airline number, arranged for a morning flight. I called Papi, told him my change of plans. "Tired already of the good life?" he asked—*la pura vida*, a Costa Rican saying. He sounded either drained or disappointed.

"No, something's happened with Manuel," I said, stuffing my suitcase. "I found out tonight."

"He's alive, I hope?"

"I don't know. He went to negotiate his brother's release."

"That's unfortunate. Of course, come home right away."

Ana called late. Manuel had been gone five days. Carlos had taken over La Maria Juventud and tried to compel the diocese to do something on behalf of his brother, but they were overwhelmed, their hands tied. No one had received any more death threats from callers claiming to be ELN, but no one had heard anything about the brothers, either. She wished she had more news. "You must be so mad at me for not calling you sooner," she said. "I can't believe it myself, that it's taken this long for me to call you. So much has happened lately."

"Like what? Gracia mentioned something. She said you'd tell me."

"Well, Carlos and I are getting married next month. August twenty-first."

I froze above my suitcase, speechless. "You're getting married in a month? How did this happen?"

"Carlos brought it up, actually," she said, the words rushing out. "I guess he's realized how much his family means to him now that his brothers are gone. I laughed at first when he said he wanted to talk to my parents about it. One night at dinner, he brought it up. It was pretty easy. And of course, I was surprised my parents would give permission while I'm still in high school, I won't even turn seventeen until October, but—"

"What happened?" I said. "Are you pregnant?"

She fell silent, then let out a shaky sigh. "Yes. Gracia really didn't tell you?"

It had happened sometime in May, she said. She had missed her period right before I left for Costa Rica, and one day after school she took a home pregnancy test. But she had only gone to the doctor with Gracia and broken the news to her parents a week before. "Are you sure you really want to marry Carlos?" I asked, although my burning question was, *Do you really want to be a parent, when you are not yet an adult?*

"I have to. What else? My mother cried, and my father didn't look at me for three days after I told them. But then they talked with me and Carlos and his parents. We arranged the date right away with the priest."

A photo hung crooked—Pilar in a sari, bright-eyed and surrounded by brown children. "Isn't there anything else you could do?" I said. Then mentioned the doctors Jacki had told me about—the abortionists.

"Mercedes, how could you? That's murder. I know you're not Catholic, but—"

"I'm not saying you should do it," I said. The idea of the act done in such a place, with who knows what kind of doctor or method, made me cringe. "But is that the only option, when you're still in high school? To marry Carlos?"

"Who else would I marry?" She laughed. "I've gotten over the shock, you know. I wouldn't have a baby and give it away. Besides, I want a family, so it might as well be now."

"What about school? Will you finish?"

"I don't know. That doesn't seem like it should matter much, if I'm going to be a mom, you know? My parents said they'll hire a tutor soon. That way I can just stay home, not have to face everyone at school."

"Well, I'll be around. I'm not going anywhere until Manuel comes back."

"What if he's gone, Mercedes?"

Slowly, I rolled up my underwear, tucked it in the corner of my suitcase, and wedged my make-up bag on top. "I don't know. You'll call me as soon as you hear something, right?"

"Of course. That was awful of me to say that, just now. I wasn't thinking."

"It's not your fault."

"He's only been away a few days. No reason to think the worst."

"Thanks," I said. "Are you sure you're okay?"

"I'm great," she said. "When I first found out, I wasn't. I wanted so badly for you to be here, but at the same time I was embarrassed to tell you, or anyone. And I was so embarrassed to face Gracia. She asked how it happened, and I told her it was just carelessness, a couple of times without condoms. I hope you don't think I'm stupid. I'm sure everyone does."

"If there's anything I can do," I said, and straightened Pilar's picture. My bikini hung from the towel bar, rinsed but damp.

"I'll be fine," she said. "Anyway, it's too late."

At noon the next day I kissed Tía Leo and Jacki good-bye, boarded at the Taca gate. As the flight attendants readied the beverage cart they gossiped loudly about a crew member. For the remaining two hours, they took turns up and down the aisle, collecting trash, and in the back, passing around a celebrity magazine—one the maids frequently left in the laundry room. Jennifer Lopez and Penelope Cruz were on the cover. I might as well serve coffee in a restaurant.

The man snoozing next to me had stowed a crinkled *La Semana* in his seat pocket. Peace talks between our government and the guerillas had been postponed. While the ELN continued to hold its hostages captive, the FARC had launched an attack against fifteen towns, one just thirty-five miles south of Bogotá—bombing banks, bridges, and power lines; they barricaded roads and attacked police barracks. One army official called it "the largest and most demented guerilla offensive in the past forty years." I crushed the paper back inside the seat pocket. The sunshine illuminated the field of clouds, the landing gear groaned. We flew through blinding white, then broke through, the lush ranges and flat ranch land rushing up below.

CHAPTER TWELVE

We sat in our usual places: Papi in his chair, me on the couch, cross-legged. A late lunch sizzled, fried pork. Inez knelt on her hands and knees, cleaning the floors. "We ate at the best chicharrónera," I said. "Jacki took me. You've got to have her take you next time you visit." He nodded, frowning, and stroked the purple bandanna in his pocket. His face had thinned, the skin sallow; he'd been smoking too much. "Maybe when you come see me, at my new school."

Inez dunked her sponge. Water trickled hard, slowed to a drip. Papi eyed me like a shying horse and said, "Do you have any idea of your test scores? And your grades this term—none of those schools could even make an exception. Did you do this on purpose?"

Angel and Cocoa panted on the tile. Outside, the parrots squawked. "I'm sorry," I said. "I did my best, I swear."

"I know who is to blame. Hardly a surprise he's gone off to stir up trouble." He let out a wavery sigh. "Well, you'll study more. Reapply."

"But why can't I finish school in Costa Rica? I'd be much happier there. Closer, too."

"Mercedes, you must never choose the easy route—it only proves longer and more difficult. And Costa Rica?" He shook his head. "It's just too close."

"*You* want this. *You* want me to go away," I said, my voice rising. "What about me?"

"Enough!" He snapped his fingers at me. "When I phoned your school, I pulled you out. Sister Rosemary's going to be here, five days a week."

"What?" My head grew hot. "How could you?"

"I'm sorry." He arose, rubber boots squeaking on the shiny floor. "To make it up to you we'll have a big birthday party with your friends." He forced a hopeful smile. "How's that?"

I frowned, picked at a nail. "If Manuel could come, sure. Otherwise, I don't care."

"Manuel? No way." Papi flicked his hand. "Although I suppose if he makes it back alive that counts for something. If he still has all his fingers, and can play the guitar." His lips twitched.

The mix of fried pork and lemon cleaner nauseated me. I closed my eyes, sucked the air through my teeth. "About the test. I was so upset after the bombing. I'll reapply."

"Good. You see how easy that was?" He clapped, startling the dogs. "What else do you want for your birthday? Tell me." Before I could answer he crouched, made a face at the mutts, and skidded a bone across the tile.

The day I resumed my studies I wrote about the poverty in Costa Rica. I left out the prostitutes, guessing that topic would raise too many questions with a nun. As Sister Rosemary marked the essay, I told her about Manuel's journey. "He probably shouldn't have gone," she said, shaking her head. "You poor thing."

I asked if Papi had visited the mission lately. "He has," she said. "Would you like to come with me one day and see for yourself? It's not far."

"Maybe. If I ask you another question, will you promise to keep it a secret?" She straightened and slid the essay aside. I said, "I'd like to try and look for my mother, but I don't know where to start. Could you help me?"

"Why not ask your father?"

"He has no contact with her, as far as I know. I'd like to do it on my own, without him knowing." I paused. "He might not be pleased."

"I see. And do you have any idea where she is?"

I told her what I had learned from Tía Leo: my mother was from south Florida and had been a student at the University of Miami sometime in the early eighties.

"Of course, I will help however I can," she said. "But I will need some kind of documents to start with, perhaps a copy of your birth certificate? And an address, if you come across one."

I didn't know where Papi kept my birth certificate. I left my studies and combed through the cabinets. In one I found a thin file marked, "Mercedes—Personal," containing tuition receipts for the schools I'd attended, progress reports, immunization records— and my birth certificate. An unremarkable document, it listed the Cali hospital and date, the doctor's scrawl, Papi's jagged signature and my mother's feminine one, neat and sloping: *Paula Meyerhoff.* Seeing her signature for the first time made the decision real, and I felt a heightened uneasiness about what might happen if the nun were to find her. But I copied the certificate on Papi's machine and handed it over, then returned to my geometry, grateful for the exactness of numbers and proofs.

In the hour before sunset, I walked. Sometimes I wandered down to the paddock or the pasture fence and called one of the horses to me, stroked its coarse mane and stared into its large, otherworldly dark eyes. Other days I hiked the hill, past the target practice area and coffee until I reached the gravel road's end. Often a feeling brimmed inside me like I wanted to cry but I couldn't, as if I had been clinging to something but now it was caving in on me, crumbling. I picked up fallen mangoes and inhaled the sweet splits of their skins, looking to nature for answers but finding none. Should I tell Papi of my conversation with Tía Leo, so we didn't have to pretend any longer? Part of me desperately wanted to clear the veils we lived behind, and to push him to reveal more about my mother. I was reminded of the story of the tree of the knowledge of good and evil, from Genesis; knowledge is irreversible. When I thought of Papi, a tide of fear and distrust welled for what disaster he might still be capable of carrying out. You could learn so much about someone only to find yourself on the precipice of the soul's abyss, grasping nothing but air. And so I sought to please as well as to avoid him.

Mid-week, Ana called after dinner, breathless. "They're back," she said. "Emilio and Manuel." I was completing my homework outside. Upstairs,

Papi dressed for a neighbor's party while listening to Mozart; relief and joy flooded over me on the faint strings of the music. "They're with his parents," Ana said. "Come over."

My hand trembled as I attempted to work out the geometry proofs; I could hardly keep still. Minutes later, someone slid the glass door open behind me. Papi's cologne carried on the breeze. Even in dress shirts he appeared a caballero, just a crisper version. I tossed down my pencil and said, "I need to go to Ana's tonight."

"Tonight? Why?" He settled into a chair nearby, unfurled his tobacco pouch.

"She wants to see me. Just a short visit. Can I go?"

"Can't this wait until the weekend?" His gaze narrowed as he wetted the paper's edge.

A gust lifted the hair from the back of my neck. "I've got to see her. Ana's pregnant."

"Oh dear God," he said, leaning back. Frowning, he lit the cigarette, and took a long drag. "Well, that's it for her. She's dropping out of school, I suppose? Who's the father?"

"I don't know if she'll stay in school. But she's getting married next month. May I go?"

He cleared his throat. "I'll tell Fidel. But I want you in bed by midnight." He shook his head slightly as he smoked, pinched his lower lip pensively as I gathered my books and crept inside.

Fidel and I zipped through the streets empty of traffic. A helicopter flew low overhead, blades chugging, and passed us, flying south. How much weight might Manuel have lost, and had he been beaten, tortured? Emilio, too? What about him might have changed? Cars lined the block; a camera crew packed up a news van outside Ana's house. The guard in his narrow booth greeted me, tall and alert instead of bent over his newspaper or radio. Midway to the steps the din inside grew, and I slowed. So we wouldn't be reuniting with Manuel and his brother alone, with just family; how naive I'd been in my eagerness. When the maid answered the door, all of La Maria Juventud looked up. Snacks spilled across the dining table: sandwiches and empanadas, roasted chicken and refried beans, chips, soda, and beer. Ana's parents met me, their faces flushed, her father gripping a cocktail, her mother a glass of red wine. Sparkling water fizzed in Ana's glass, although she appeared her usual self: curvaceous, wearing a tailored pair of jeans paired with a dressy sateen shirt. Any excuse for a party—that was Ana.

A reporter, shirt cuffs rolled up, held a recorder to Manuel who was talking energetically at the head of the dining table. "Excuse me, can we pause for just a moment?" he said, and arose as I neared, his face twisting slowly into happiness as if he had just been told a welcomed secret. We embraced, rocking; he smelled of dampness and soap, his body warm and firm beneath the shirt. *He's here*, I thought, *he's alive*. How was it possible that the universe had delivered him back unharmed, and with his brother, as he had intended? Emilio's eyes were rimmed by dark circles. I hugged him next, his collar bone digging into my shoulder.

Manuel ushered me beside him, as friends patted my back and exclaimed how relieved I must feel. Sandwiches crammed their plates. Emilio picked at his food, but Manuel sat erect and ate with ceaseless vigor. He appeared no leaner than before, yet his demeanor had changed somehow—the fire of innocence gone, replaced by an irrevocable knowing, a more callous determination. Staring ahead coolly, he took swift sips of his drink, and made no move to brush my hand or knee beneath the table.

"You said you were able to hitch a ride with the Red Cross?" the reporter asked. "If you don't mind continuing."

"Yes, I met them near the Fallarones, an outpost by the National Park. Then I rode with one of their trucks to a village." From there Manuel caught another ride on a farmer's ox-cart. It was difficult to imagine him traveling without his moto, but how impractical that would have been on the slippery mountain passes, while not knowing in what condition he might find Emilio. Manuel asked the farmer the way to the ELN. Rattled, the man refused to say until Manuel explained his mission and convinced the farmer of his faith. The farmer, a devout Catholic, admitted that he disliked the ELN who had controlled the village for a long time now, but the paras had proven more brutal. The ELN's camp was very high, a half-day's hike—he pointed Manuel to the jungle path where the guerillas unloaded their trucks and marched abductees up the mountain, single-file. The Red

Cross unloaded their supplies in the village below, and the guerillas transported them from there. The farmer had proven correct. The path was steep, the air thin, and Manuel had to stop numerous times, fatigued and nauseated. He could not imagine elderly captives making such a journey in street clothes, without rest, proper hydration, or medication. Partway to the summit he ran into three young guerillas, armed and making their way down. Guns raised, they surrounded him, pivoted, and marched him to the summit.

Dozens of tents pitched across patchy slopes. Captives lay on worn sleeping bags or huddled in groups, talking. A handful of guerillas unloaded Red Cross canned goods, blankets, and medical kits from a truck bed, guns slung loosely upon their backs. Manuel learned later that the guerillas had carved hidden roads down the mountain, unknown to the authorities, paras, or military. "I didn't see Emilio right away," he said. "But a few parishioners wandered over. One of them assured me that he was alive and well, and praying with a sick woman in a tent."

"No better practice for the priesthood than being captured by guerillas." Emilio's face cracked into a grin. "Although I don't recommend the diet. Too bland."

The three teenagers escorted Manuel to the ELN leaders: Gambino, two others who'd orchestrated the church kidnapping, and a handful of other high-ranking members. "I told them I wanted my brother back," Manuel said, "and they gave me this dazed look. They couldn't believe a civilian would climb a mountain into their camp. Several were very agitated, as you can imagine." He made it clear that he was not just interested in negotiating for his brother's release, but for the others as well—and was committed to understanding the ELN's objectives.

Several leaders recognized Manuel from the TV coverage, and they wanted to march him back down or punish him for his audacity, but couldn't agree. With the Archbishop promising to excommunicate their organization, a Catholic youth activist showing up was like a blowfly to a flighty horse. But Gambino waved them off. He liked the idea of Manuel visiting and reporting back on the fair conditions, or so he claimed. But they would not allow his brother's release for nothing. The soon-to-be priest had kept up the wealthy hostages' spirits, and the hostages were valuable—

therefore, Emilio was valuable. Manuel could leave whenever he liked. The guerillas didn't starve or beat the captives. Blankets, no matter how many, provided little comfort on the damp, uneven ground. The beans and rice served twice a day contained little pork and almost no vegetables, and the limited diet had weakened many. The ELN had released those with severe ailments in mid-June, but since then new maladies had flared up: an older woman whose leg wound refused to heal with ointment from the kits, a middle-aged man who had twisted his ankle just that day and needed X-rays. In one tent a young woman lay, her cough wracking and incessant, her fever mounting. The hostages' outlook was one of boredom, with almost a lack of interest at the prospect of rescue, like a far-fetched dream one mustn't speak of too often. With Emilio tending to the captives' needs, Manuel decided to stick by the leaders, find out what he could to aid him in gaining Emilio and the others and prevent future attacks, under the guise of befriending the guerillas if needed.

The brothers had long known that the ELN funded their operations through kidnaps and ransoms, not coca, unlike the FARC, who levied a ten percent tax on peasants and operated as middlemen, selling the crop to traffickers. A no lesser evil. But the ELN also held classes and meetings in the villages under their control; Manuel had attended several. They educated the poor in literacy and health and encouraged the farmers to plant crops besides the more profitable coca. Many farmers loudly protested this—using valuable land to plant bananas, corn, coffee, or yuca, which might each take several years to harvest, brought in far less income than pure coca. But the guerillas insisted that this was the only way for the villagers to eventually free themselves from the drug economy and multinational corporations who otherwise controlled the lives of the poor.

"Surprising, isn't it?" Manuel said. The brothers' respectful openness, fortitude, and resolve worked. By week's end, Manuel had convinced the leaders that he and his brother would be better off on the outside, as advocates for a truce between the government and guerilla groups. Gambino agreed to the release of Emilio and a handful of the weakest captives—on the grounds that the brothers would speak the truth. The ELN desperately wanted to be seen as campaigning for human rights, higher education, and social services among the rural poor, and not solely be condemned as killers and kidnappers of the urban elite. The brothers were blindfolded, loaded into the back of a pickup, and driven down the mountain before dawn, to a main road in the National Park. "What the leaders said makes sense," Manuel said, shrugging. "For the poor to prosper, the common man must be self-sufficient, grow his own food. Take back the land."

"But you can't let them fool you." Emilio shot us all a warning look, the journalist trailing his chin with the recorder. "These guerillas play both sides. That's why they're doomed to fail. You can't preach self-sufficiency and peace and kidnap civilians at the same time. Or in the FARCs case, take your cut of the coca. After six weeks their hypocrisy gets old, believe me."

"They need a different vision," Manuel said, thumbing his napkin. "A new leader."

"It will never happen," Emilio said. "They are too misguided, and distrustful of the government, albeit with good reason. The only thing that will make those men lay down their arms will be time. Things will naturally fall apart for them, you'll see."

"Exactly." Manuel said. The tablecloth scrunched underneath his forearms. "So why can't that happen sooner? All it would take is someone to bring new thinking to the leaders."

"Are you volunteering?" Emilio drained the last of his Fanta.

"I'm going back for the others," Manuel said. "Aren't you?"

"Not if I can help it," Emilio said, and crushed the soda can. "Knowing what I do now, the next round of peace talks I lead will be very different." His back and shoulders rippled as if he was casting off an uncomfortable coat. "I pray to God I never see that mountain again."

I left without a word or glance and headed upstairs. What was Manuel talking about, going back for the others? Why couldn't he follow his brother's advice, stick to reinventing the peace negotiations as Church mediators? In the bathroom, I wet my fingers with cold water and pressed them to the back of my neck, blinking into the mirror.

A footstep creaked in the hallway and stopped; Manuel said my name under his breath. "I know you must be shocked," he said, his voice low outside the door. "I wasn't going to bring that up until I'd talked with you first. About me going back."

I flung open the door. "Just when were you going to tell me, then? Or tell me what I want to hear? Because we both know you're going to do what you want, anyway."

"I want to pay them another visit, yes. But not yet. We've got to get the new peace talks going first. Look, I came back for you. I'm sorry about not waiting for you to get back from your trip. I tried, but the way things were going, I couldn't wait another day." He leaned in that way I liked, the sleeves of his T-shirt exposing the muscled curves of his arms. "Please believe me. I'm not making a move without taking us into account."

"I find that hard to believe, with you running off into the mountains to make friends with guerillas."

"I can't just abandon my battles. We'll be together." His eyes fluttered with exhaustion. "How could we not?"

"I want to believe you," I said. "I just don't know if I can."

"I love you," he said, his voice breaking. He smoothed my cheek. "Please—"

I jerked away and stormed into the guest room, him following. The door clicked shut behind us. I sank onto the bed, let him hold me as I stroked the silky green and gold leaves of the comforter. Below us throbbed laughter and electronic beats; how long-ago that party on Holy Saturday, months past. The ceiling fan circled, a mild gust. I told him I loved him and how much I had thought of him while he was gone, and then we apologized a dozen times the way lovers do. Guests slammed car doors; engines rumbled. He raked his fingers through my hair, tugged out the knots. I asked if he'd found out anything about the threats we'd received from the ELN. "They might have been made by lower-level operatives, just carrying out scare tactic orders from above," he said. "Why?"

I told him what I had learned from my aunt, and how the threats to my life were very real. "I need to leave." I ran a finger down to his shirt's V, the skin smooth. "Will you come?"

"I promised those hostages I wouldn't give up on them." He caught my hand and kissed it. "But we'll make a plan. If you leave, I leave."

Someone knocked on the door then—it was Ana—and in her polite voice told us that the time was past eleven o'clock, and my driver was pacing outside the gate.

In the days after Manuel's return the hacienda formed my prison, the fields and mountainside my walls, Fidel and the jefes my guards. I fidgeted and made mistakes in my coursework, drifted behind. I wanted the sensual world, not books, concepts, indoor air.

More distracting was the mass exodus of peasants flooding the valley, the spike in violence having uprooted thousands. Papi had hired extra workers for the upcoming harvest. Up and down the road entire villages begged, refusing to scatter until the jefes fired shots into the air. The mission had erected tents, Sister Rosemary told me one day, but the nuns needed more volunteers, and the soup kitchen didn't have enough food. "You don't know how difficult it is to turn hungry people away, and when you know you have enough to eat," she said. "I understand how your father feels." She joined us for dinner often, she and Papi discussing their problems of how to feed people, find them decent work, urge them to move on. They were becoming friends.

While I struggled to fill my empty hours, the brothers contacted upper-level Church and political leaders about using their insider knowledge of the ELN to resolve conflicts. President Pastrana's officials were assembling a Civilian Facilitation Commission and chose Manuel to serve—the youngest member. The huge rallies he had led in May and June had earned him a reputation as a young peace activist not only in Santiago de Cali, but Bogotá as well. One day he appeared on the front of *La Semana* with the other panelists as they emerged from a meeting downtown. I barely recognized him in a suit and tie. The panel met in the afternoons. I hadn't seen Manuel since the night of their return; if I could make up an excuse, a necessary errand, I could meet him somewhere. I cast aside the paper. "I want to buy a new dress for the party," I said to Papi. "May I go with Ana this week?"

He picked up the publication and glowered. "Why doesn't Manuel focus on becoming a rock star instead of a revolutionary hero? This country is in no way ready for peace."

"I was talking about a dress," I said, dejected.

"You realize that while President Pastrana says he wants a cease-fire, he is preparing for war?" When I didn't answer, Papi shook his head slowly. "I didn't think so. And neither is he aware." He thrust a finger on Manuel's image, mid-stride. A close-up captured the brothers conferring on the government building steps, the caption summarizing their recent release.

"You mean this peace panel is all fake? A waste of time?"

"I live and breathe this country. My blood tilled the soil. How long do you think until the guerillas see this panel as just another government move to appear to do something on their behalf, but really is an insult?"

I snatched back the edition. Manuel's eyes were locked on Emilio's in that way I knew so well—the earnest, optimistic gaze he shared with me. The sharp scent of ink mixed with my longing. "I can't just forget him," I said softly.

Papi drew the paper closer; his fingers curved over the photo. "I'm not asking you to forget him," he said. "I'm just telling you to say good-bye."

That evening I obsessed over how I might roam the streets with Manuel like we had months earlier, eating churros and arepas, laughing and teasing. How long ago that felt. And to where would he and I escape now? Duck inside a church, rent a cheap, bug-filled hotel room for an hour, or ride his moto to a park? The youth group operated out of the apartment again. Our days spent naked and entangled above the honking traffic and electric saws of the shop below, bodies glistening, had slipped out of sight like the sun on the horizon.

Ana would have preferred to shop at one of Cali's upscale malls, but Fidel dropped us off at a shopping center downtown. She rolled her eyes at the teen shops—"So cheap," she quipped, "Latin American rip-off brands," but when we passed a baby and maternity store she paused. I charged ahead, forgetting her predicament in my eagerness; we had two hours to find me a dress and meet Manuel. When she didn't follow I spun around and squelched a pang of irritation—my best friend being suddenly and carelessly pregnant. "Don't you want to think about the wedding first?" I asked.

She pressed against the glass. "It's such a small thing. Once we were together I knew I'd marry Carlos. But the baby," she said, exhaling. "Sometimes I'm so scared."

"What if your parents didn't give you permission? Could you still do it?"

"Why wouldn't they?"

"What's the age?" I asked. "To get married by a priest?"

"Sixteen, I think. Why?"

I asked if she wanted to browse, but she turned back to the sidewalk. We walked on, a woman with a gray chin crying out on the corner, selling tamales. Ana said, "Your father will go crazy if you run away and marry Manuel, you know. Is that what's going on?"

"I don't know. But if I leave, he's coming with me."

"He'll never live with you without being married. Those brothers aren't like Gracia and Esteban. Even if their will power crumbles when it comes to sex." She laughed weakly. "So does mine."

"It would be easier," I said. "To just leave."

"Even Carlos insisted we get married right away. He wanted the priest to marry us even before he told his parents I was pregnant—imagine that!"

A deep purple dress in a window caught my attention—oddly, the handbags and outfits on display were for middle-aged women. But the dress had satin spaghetti straps and trim and a wide, flat belt, and the matte fabric contained a faint pinstripe print. "Classy," Ana said. "A real cocktail dress. You should try it on."

The dress proved the perfect color—"You look so gringa," Ana gushed—and made me feel taller than my average height, like a model. In the mirror, my small breasts pushed tightly together in the bodice, my thin shoulders squared. I thought yes, *this is who I want to be*—a young lady, self-possessed. Papi would be taken with it—he loved fine things, rum, designer shirts, cigars—but also flustered. In the ravishing dress I was undeniably no longer a child. I needed him to recognize this perhaps more than I needed to flee. From the envelope of pesos he had given me to go shopping, I paid for the dress.

Ana accompanied me as far as the government building but then pointed to a café, said she was tired and needed to rest. I handed the dress to her, but not before Manuel's voice boomed behind me: "What's in the bag? Something for me?" He touched my waist; I inhaled his cologne as he kissed me, and his warm hand interlaced with mine. I missed the scent of wood shavings and tools, and his arms in the T-shirts he usually wore, now covered in the somber suit jacket.

"It's a surprise," I said. "You'll have to come to my party to find out."

After he greeted Ana we headed for the Plaza de Cayzedo, where she agreed to meet us in an hour. In silence we wove through the sidewalk traffic, past a market of farmers lugging produce and clucking chickens, and a coffee stall, where a giant roaster stirred and groaned, the beans shiny as rosary beads. I could feel each moment end before the next began, the seconds slipping away like water through fingers. Things were going well with the new commission, he said. The remaining hostages should be released in a couple of weeks, and he intended to head up a new dialogue with the ELN.

"What about the feelings you were having?" I asked. "About something bad happening?"

Manuel stared above me at the monument of Joaquin de Cayzedo, an early fighter for the republic, and gripped his chest. "You know, since my trip those feelings have disappeared. Isn't that weird?" The Juan Valdez impersonator heckled passersby with his plaster burro, and some teenagers in school uniforms loitered, eating mazorca asada, roasted corn. Manuel removed his jacket; we sank onto a bench. "This is killing me, not being alone with you," he said, and lifted my hair, carefully placed it behind my shoulder. "I talked with the priest. You'll need to get someone to sign a piece of paper, stating you have your father's permission. I wish we didn't have to. But I'll ask the Lord forgiveness later, among other things." He touched my cheek. "Do you know who might do that for us?"

The only person who popped to mind was Fidel. Would he betray my father so blatantly? There was no way to tell, and no one else to ask. "Possibly," I said. "But I still have to leave."

"So we'll go to Medellín. Live with my cousins, keep a low profile."

I rested my cheek against his. "Papi could have friends there. Or enemies. If I just disappear, he'll be crushed. I don't hate him, you know."

"Of course not," he murmured into my hair. "But I only want to stay in Colombia if you can be safe, too. Otherwise you'll be wound so tight, a hundred hours in bed won't free you." He pinched my nipple through my shirt; I squealed and swatted him away. He might not have felt a heaviness, but I did—a sense that this could be the last time we would stroll through Cali during the day, past the quilts and newspapers unfurled on the sidewalks, vendors straightening their cheap handbags, packs of underwear and gym socks. I didn't know Medellín, could not picture us living there as I could Costa Rica. How might such a future become a clear and tangible escape? When at last Ana arrived, nibbling an ice cream with my dress bag slung over her shoulder, I saw only the party—me in the dress and heels, Manuel singing to his guitar.

He walked us to the corner where Fidel had pulled up, waiting. Fidel emerged from the driver's seat, waved his newspaper, and said, "Have you heard?" As he helped me hang the dress bag, Manuel hovered beside the car, reading. Fidel said, "Archbishop Duarte finalized the excommunication of the ELN. I hate to see what those guerillas do now."

"It certainly won't help things with the Church," Manuel said, immersed in the article. "But they did it to themselves. Gambino knows that."

Ana climbed in the car, Fidel slammed the door after her and took the paper back. "Gambino might, but what about the other leaders?" he said. "He can't control them as it is." He shook his head. "Those poor hostages from La Maria. They're screwed."

"We're too close," Manuel said. "I'm not giving up on them."

"You couldn't pay me to go near the ELN when they're this pissed at the Church," Fidel replied. "You've got some balls, man." He thumped Manuel on the back, urged me to get in.

The night before my party I rocked on the patio, making bows for the dogs' collars, when Uncle Charlie putted through the gate. He swung down from the driver's seat; the bodyguards' automatic rifles and elbows jutted out the sides of the Jeep. I dropped the ribbon, and it rolled across the patio. His fatigues reeked of stale body odor and dank rainforest as he suffocated me in a giant hug and pinched my cheek. A grin spilled across my face, but it quickly fell when he asked how I'd been and which schools had accepted me. I told him I hadn't gotten into any. "What, your father didn't make them a good enough offer?" he said, surprised. He swayed with his stocky legs wide apart, his balled fists on hips, head wagging back and forth. "Saint Diego, what will we do with him? I'll straighten him out on this, don't worry."

"But it's my fault. I didn't pass the test."

His eyes flashed and he gripped my shoulder. "Don't ever let anyone, or some stupid test, tell you what you can or can't do." His voice softened then. "You're a young girl of tremendous intelligence and insight. You'll go where you're meant to be, given the right circumstance."

"I don't want to leave," I said dimly. "But I don't want to stay, either."

His horsey, reddish face and slightly bulging eyes pierced back. "Colombia will find peace someday. You will want to return, raise your family here." He skimmed a hand, gentle and firm, down my cheek. "I hope that will be the case for my children, and that they will bring their education back with them. But peace won't happen anytime soon. Not until your father and I are dead."

"That won't be for a long time," I said.

"I'm not so sure, princesa." He chuckled softly, adding, "Let's hope." Then he tromped indoors and called for my father as if he was arriving at his own home, sniffed underneath his shirt, and ordered himself to the closest shower.

I was relieved the next day when I peered down from my window to spot him in a Hawaiian shirt, Panama hat, and crisp shorts, chatting with Papi and scratching the dogs behind the ears—the antique Jeep would be hard enough to explain to friends. Although the night of the putas was never far from my mind, I was partly pleased to see him again, this short, eccentric man; charming and deceitful as I guessed he probably was, he promised to never be boring.

Papi wore white pants and a blue-and-white striped shirt, the cuffs rolled up to his forearms; he might have stepped off a yacht at a beach resort. He carried a ladder around the patio, adjusting decorations. Clean-shaven and dressed in fine clothes, he appeared younger—a different version of himself, free of farm duties. The jefes looked sharp, too, as they roamed between their quarters and the beer cooler at the patio fountain. Luis wore a new pair of jeans, shirt tucked over his belly, and Vincente, his dress caballero boots with the silver spurs. In his tight-fitting V-neck shirt, Fidel appeared ready to hit a salsoteca; maybe he planned on meeting a date in Juanchito after the festivities. Their handguns were prominently displayed in their holsters, each as fixed as a wealthy man's watch.

I admired the new dress in my full-length mirror, complete with high heels and makeup. Inez had pinned up my hair in a twist, so my neck and shoulders felt exposed. "You must wear lipstick," she said, fluttering to my bathroom. She found one, dark plum, and handed it to me with a knowing look, saying, "That's the secret." The way she said this made me wonder about my mother, what it would be like to have Paula here, helping me get ready. Sister Rosemary's efforts at tracking her down had turned up nothing yet. I blotted my lips in the mirror, my earlobes starkly bare. Fidel had pawned the pearls by now, surely. I couldn't ask for them back.

Car horns beeped. Ana's parents glided up in their armored Volvo, followed by the old Honda Manuel and his brothers shared, dented and missing a hubcap. A woman with salon-dyed red hair exited with Ana's parents—Gracia's mother. Manuel emerged from the back of the Honda, lugging his guitar case, and Emilio from the other side. I grimaced. Another guest as outspoken as Manuel. Too late now.

Other vehicles rolled in: the blue pickup of our neighbors to the south, also cane farmers, and the faded green Galloper of the plantation down the road—they had raised mangoes for generations. Esteban buzzed up on his moto, Gracia straddling the back. Voices traveled across the foyer and up the stairs; I descended carefully in my heels, and Gracia cried out, "There's Mercedes!" But it was Papi's face I searched for, his lips parted in bewilderment and pride. He encircled me in a stiff embrace. "Your birthday dress," he said. His eyes shifted, searching for the words. "You didn't show me what you bought."

"Isn't it nice?" I asked.

"Nice, yes. Very grown up." He didn't look at me as he said this, just squeezed my shoulder once more, his roughened palm cool and firm.

Everyone crowded around to greet me: Ana's parents, bearing gifts, Ana in a loose red dress, Carlos beside her, guitar slung on his back, soaking in the grand, rustic room, his jaw hanging loose. Gracia flushed pink, her lips and Esteban's cold from their brisk motorcycle jaunt when they pecked my cheek. If only Manuel had come on his bike, we might have escaped for a quick ride. He greeted me last, sliding his hand down my back, and I kissed him. In my ear he whispered, "The letter—you have it?"

I pressed my lips together, shook my head. "Soon," I said.

Emilio edged over and wished me happy birthday. "I hope you don't mind me inviting myself," he said blithely, "but I figured I could use a fancy party after a few weeks of camping out." Already his skin looked brighter, more plump. His lips brushed my cheek, and that sensation, the mix of like energies, washed through me; he carried the same familial scent as Manuel, wore the same cologne. "I'd like to meet your father," he said. "And is that Charlie?"

The guests plucked shrimp ceviche from the crystal bowls the maids brought around, talking of the problems with the desplazados desperate for work. On the couch a pair of wives chatted, their necks and fingers flaunting the bulbous gems worn only behind gates. Uncle Charlie's laugh boomed louder with each swig of guaro. Luis manned the bar, pouring juice mixers and aguardiente shots; Papi passed around cigars from the humidor like Santa Claus. I introduced Emilio to him and Uncle Charlie. "Now this one didn't come with a guitar," Uncle Charlie said. "But something tells me he's got a different talent."

"The soon-to-be Father," Papi said. He gripped Emilio's hand and beamed.

"Not yet," Emilio replied. "Or perhaps you mean my other brother."

The brothers and I laughed but Papi and Uncle Charlie appeared puzzled until Emilio clued them in—that Carlos was Ana's fiancé. "I see," Papi said. He sidled up to Ana with a funny little dance step and squeezed her shoulders. "How is our mommy-to-be doing?" he said. She patted his hand and thanked him. This startled me. He rarely spoke of babies or family, and when I broke the news about Ana he had reacted as I would have predicted—with disappointment, almost disgust. But here he was, enjoying the idea of the new young family. Weren't his hopes for me wrapped solely around school achievement? Maybe I was mistaken.

I asked Gracia and Esteban if they would dance. Gracia said she wasn't dressed for it, but nodded. "I'll make an announcement," I said, and dragged them through the cigars' haze to where the men stood talking. The mango plantation owner was saying thank God for the paras, that before them he'd been paying off the guerillas for protection, but the Autodefensas did a better job for a better rate. He raised his glass. "To hell with the guerillas!" Papi, Uncle Charlie, and the other men joined him. Emilio and Manuel hung back.

Papi frowned, swirled his drink. "Guerillas don't deserve to be heard. Not while they continue to pull these stunts. And half of them are illiterate teenagers."

"Not if there's a new revolution," Manuel said. "One of persuasion."

"Oh, I believe they deserve to be heard," Uncle Charlie said, and rocked in his heels. "But they will never trust the government negotiations, and they are right. Governments as a rule do not want peace."

Manuel lifted his face into the light. "The only way to earn the ELN's trust is to meet face to face. On their ground."

Uncle Charlie arched his eyebrows. "You'd better know what you're doing to walk into that lion's den," he said, tone ominous.

Emilio sipped, his glass of guaro sweating. "The new civilian commission is making progress. Words are words, whether spoken at a distance or face to face. Running up into the Fallarones is an unnecessary risk."

"Isn't it a greater risk not to do the harder thing?" Manuel said. "What no one has tried before?"

Emilio's elbow grazed Manuel, his faces inches away. "All I'm asking is that you see things through first." He looked at me. "I'm sure I'm not the only one here who agrees." Emilio and I exchanged a glance of tacit agreement; I quickly dropped my chin, uneasy.

"You'd be wise to listen to him," Papi said to Manuel. "If a man is to sacrifice he'd better know what, or who, he's sacrificing for. Colombia has too many dead, young men or otherwise."

Manuel faced Papi. "I listen to God," he said, "unlike most men."

"We have ourselves a prophet," Uncle Charlie said, chuckling. But his laughter died as fast as it had arisen.

"You don't think God speaks through his family?" Emilio said. His neck strained and grew redder. I tried to imagine him in a priest's collar but couldn't, even though he was less than two months away from entering the seminary. He spun on his heel with a dismissive wave, said, "Forget it, brother," and slipped outside to join Ana.

Smiling, I stepped up and said, "My friends would like to dance for us. Wouldn't that be great?" Manuel took my cue and wandered to the fireplace where he'd set his guitar.

Uncle Charlie's beady eyes flitted over Gracia and Esteban, then me. "We should oblige the birthday girl, shouldn't we, Diego?" He nudged my father. "When I first saw her this evening, I thought, who has replaced my friend's little girl with this magnificent young woman? The dress is stunning."

"It's her birthday present," Papi said. "Last year I got her pearl earrings."

"I love this dress," I said, smoothing the front. "We should find seats. The boys will be ready in a minute with the music."

Papi didn't budge, but eyed me over the rim of his glass. "Why don't you ever wear those earrings, hija? They are a special pair."

I shrugged. "I suppose I don't like to wear earrings much," I said. Then scurried away and claimed the hassock next to the fireplace. The brothers began to play, the chords slightly off. Manuel apologized, and they started again, the guitars galloping like a team of horses.

The breeze cooled the room and cleared the smoke, the dancers clapping the only human noise. Those transfixed faces—what secrets lay behind them? Papi in his chair wearing a preoccupied expression, staring off—was he thinking about the homeless on our land, or Emilio's rift with Manuel? And Ana's parents, their soft hands clasped, smiling contentedly as they listened, their pampered daughter pregnant but marrying a good Catholic boy. And the jefes, Fidel flirting with Gracia's mother in her tailored blazer and snug pants, Luis stepping out to the patio to confer with a new guard. Was it any coincidence that Uncle Charlie had not needed to be introduced to the neighbors, nor to Ana's parents? After the brothers' packed up their guitars and the aguardiente flowed, didn't the adults carry on as if they had known each other for years?

Afterward, Manuel stepped outside, fresh drink in hand, and beckoned for me to join. Papi stood up from his chair. When I brushed past him for the door, he caught my arm. His warm breath stung my ear. "I'd like to see you in those pearl earrings sometime soon. I hope you didn't lose them." He released his grasp, shot me a stern, knowing look, and headed off to the porch where Luis and some men were dealing cards and slapping down bills.

What did he mean by that? The night air chilled my bare skin. I fled into the yard.

Tiki torches flickered. Someone had turned the stereo to a salsa station and its beats tumbled down into the darkness. Couples danced in the shadows. An older woman collapsed to her knees on the grass, buckled over in drunken laughter. Papi's friends. The jefes had built a bonfire at the bottom of the yard. Manuel and I ambled toward it. Once out of earshot, I asked him about our plans to flee.

"Next Saturday," he said, his voice low. "After Carlos and Ana's engagement party. I'm sure your father will let you stay overnight at her house. Just pack one bag, otherwise we'll risk suspicion. We'll meet the priest at the chapel, leave from there in the morning."

"But where are we going? Medellín?"

"It has to be Medellín. I can't finish my business with the negotiations from anywhere else, and I've got to see those through."

I pictured a shabby, cramped apartment, tried to imagine waking up next to him on a pullout couch and the stale smell of old cooking and dirty laundry, his bachelor cousins bumbling around. A new city, streets to explore and lose ourselves in. "About the letter," I began. "Can't you get Emilio or Carlos to write it?"

"Emilio won't out of principle, and Carlos is a terrible writer. It has to sound like it came from your father." He kissed my temple and whispered, "You can do it, my little spy." I slid my hands down his forearms, and he pressed his forehead to mine. "If you would rather go to Costa Rica, then go," he said. "The only other option is for me to meet you there later. But I can't promise when, or if, that would be."

I nodded and said, "No, I'll come." Then, shivering, I said I wanted to change into jeans and a sweater and for him to meet me upstairs, through the front door, so Papi wouldn't see.

Inez and the maids lumbered between the guest rooms with pillows and towels, preparing extra beds. How I would conduct my routine on the hacienda without raising alarm? Papi, Inez, the maids and dogs, even Sister Rosemary I would not see again. And my friends. Just as the difficulties of our lives were bringing us closer, giving me shoulders to lean on for the first time, I had to say good-bye, escape Cali undetected—how? The Colombia I did not know awaited, without drivers, bodyguards, or friends behind gates.

I left the door to my room ajar and as I shimmied the dress to my feet, Manuel slipped in. He shut the door and locked it behind him. I scooted onto the window seat. "Careful," I said. "We can't be gone too long."

"Nah, they won't notice—they're all drunk." He arranged my legs around him and removed his shirt, said, "After our walk downtown the other day, I had a dream." He pressed his lips to my chest, turned his cheek. "More of a nightmare. I feel like I'm being followed."

I sat up on my elbows. "Are you sure?"

He shook his head. "Maybe I'm just imagining it. I was followed and kidnapped at knifepoint. They took me to the jungle. I didn't think they would kill me. But then I could see I was bleeding to death."

"Maybe you are just imagining it," I said. "Being followed." I threaded my fingers in his hair, drew his head to my chest.

"Maybe," he said. Then he began kissing my belly, down to my underwear. He slid those off, glancing up at me. From deep in the yard, a bonfire log crackled and snapped. Slowly he kissed the inside of my thighs. Reclining, I touched his face, lost in my lap, and let the stars fill my vision.

CHAPTER THIRTEEN

One morning after Papi left, I crossed the yard to the jefes' farmhouse. Fidel was pacing his room, talking on the phone. A cigarette burned in the ashtray alongside the closed ledger. He hung up and said, "You can't keep coming here." He sounded agitated and scratched his head. "What's up?"

"Are we friends?" I asked.

He sat down on the bed—today it was made, the blanket straight, no stray clothes in sight—and traded the phone from one palm to another. "Why? Is a friendship with a man twice your age so important to you?"

"I'm not joking," I said. I sank into the swivel chair, the adding machine dark and the fan still. "Can I really trust you? Do you know what I'm saying?" A silly thing to ask someone in his position, but I had to.

"We're friends." He stared at his sneakers as he said it, clasped his hands tight on his arms. "Do you need me to drive you somewhere? Because I can't do that."

I explained the letter I needed, supposedly from Papi, giving his permission for me to marry Manuel. "Just a letter," I said. "No one will ever know you wrote it. How could they?"

He scoffed. "There's always a way. I'm not surprised you're asking me, but do you realize how dangerous this is, what you're planning to do? I'm not just talking about for you and me, but for Manuel, your friends. Everyone." He got up and paced again, the day overcast and eerily quiet. "I know your father in a way that you don't."

"Yes I do. He's why I have to go."

"Even if I say nothing, he will find you and bring you back. He will do whatever it takes. You know what that means?"

"I would write it but it's got to sound like it comes from a parent," I said. "You're the only person I could think of."

He stared at me, then out the window. I wandered over to the tatty chair. The stuffed dog had keeled over, chest down. "If you don't do it, you know I could get you fired tomorrow," I said. "I wouldn't even have to make up something terrible. Just tell Papi that I don't feel safe with you." I picked up the toy, tossed and caught it once, twice.

"Leave that," he said, and turned over his shoulder. I replaced the dog, faced it front. "When do you need it?"

On my way out I lifted the saint's medal from his chest; it cut my grip. "Friday," I said.

As the week wore on I sent back my lunches half-eaten, and Papi commented on my poor appetite. When he asked what was bothering me, I shrugged. Let him think I was heartsick over Manuel.

I fretted about the letter until Fidel rapped on the window while I was finishing lunch one day. Inez and the maids had retired to the laundry room, telenovela blaring. He hovered by the parrot cage, pretending to inspect its screeching inhabitants. When I approached, he extended a letter-sized envelope, sealed, with my father's signature across the flap. "How did you do that?" I asked, taking it.

"His signature's easy to imitate."

"Are you sure? Does it look real?"

He didn't answer, just regarded me with soft eyes and a smile like the Mona Lisa. I yanked up my shirt, stuffed the envelope into the lip of my jeans. "I'd feel better if you had a gun," he said. "But you'll remember how to load and shoot, right?"

I nodded and clutched his arm near the elbow. "Thanks," I said.

In my room I weighed the envelope on my palm, its cool lightness and sharp corners my new future. I stashed it in the closet, between the folded

Hebrew uniform jumper and blouse, and said good-bye to that, too. Except for the bare essentials, I would soon leave my possessions behind, forgotten. I tried not to think of Papi, first in a storm of rage, tearing apart the furniture for clues to my disappearance, then on my bed, weeping, inconsolable. As Friday loomed the scene haunted me every time the stairs creaked underneath his steps.

The night before the engagement party, Papi sat in his chair after dinner, smoking and reading the latest issue of *Cambio*, the magazine owned by Garcia Márquez. I flipped through horse magazines, skin crawling and restless. My world was unraveling before me, like a cherished sweater coming undone. If he said I couldn't sleep over at Ana's, I could just not meet Fidel at my curfew—but that would set off a series of events, Papi calling Ana's house, Manuel and I hiding out overnight somewhere in Cali—no, I had to gain his approval for our plan to go smoothly. I brought up the party, how the festivities would likely go until late and I'd like to spend the night.

"At Ana's? Won't that youth group be there?"

"Probably. So what? I'll be safe there. We're not going downtown."

He closed the magazine, cast it aside. The cover featured a masked, camouflaged soldier pointing his machine gun at the camera and the words, *Guerra Total?* "All the guerillas have to do is drive by and throw a few homemade bombs over the gate," he said. He puffed on his cigar, rubbing his forehead with his thumb. "I assume Manuel will be there. Right?"

I picked up the magazine, fanned through its pages. "He won't stay overnight. You know Ana's parents."

"I do know. That's the problem. Half the time they have their heads elsewhere, and when they drink—well, look at poor Ana."

"What's wrong with Ana?" I asked. "She'll be fine."

"She'll have three kids by the time she's twenty-one, and hate the man she's married to. What's his name? Carlos? He doesn't make near the impression Manuel does. Nor the one who wants to be a priest. He's much too arrogant and guarded." I pouted, stood up. Papi caught my sleeve. "So, promise me. No going to nightclubs until three?"

"You go to Avenida Sexta sometimes."

"Sometimes—not lately."

"It's a dinner party," I said. "Ana hates being around smoke now, anyway."

The ridgebacks backed up to our chairs to be petted, and the maids gossiped in low tones as they brought in the plates from the jefes' meal.

"I know it's been difficult for you being stuck here every day," he said. "You're so grown up now, princesa. I have a hard time accepting that you're going away from me, is all. And it has been such a terrible year."

I headed for the stairs, throat aching as if I had swallowed a rope.

"What time should I tell Fidel to pick you up? Shall we say nine o'clock Saturday morning? And don't I get a kiss good night?"

He sat with one leg crossed over the other, his arms wide, his face tired and hopeful. As I hugged him and kissed his scratchy cheek, which smelled of the sun and faded perspiration, I told him, "Ten o'clock." But the morning I pictured took place hours earlier, me and Manuel in the side chapel of La Maria, the priest opening the letter and making the sign of the cross over us before we stepped out, hands clasped, to face the dawn. I retreated to my room. For a long time I sat on my window seat, the mountains like sleeping giants in the night.

Friday arrived, the sixth of August. I moved about like a sleepwalker, dazed yet jittery. Papi had left for the fields at dawn. Alone, I ate a late breakfast. A stable boy groomed a horse in the mid-morning sun. Medellín. What would I do there, if I needed to find a job? What if Manuel and I didn't have enough money to survive by sharing an apartment? Was it possible we would stay with his cousins for a year or two, perhaps longer? I had no idea of what rent, food, or electricity cost. I didn't know how he intended for us to get to Medellín, or how he planned on participating in the civilian commission from afar. I hadn't heard from him—a good sign. But I called Ana and asked her to check, just in case. She called me back a few minutes later. "He says to make sure you bring your leather coat," she said. "Did you get permission to stay over?"

As I filled a duffel bag with underwear and toiletries, I wondered what Manuel meant by the coat. Did he plan for us to ride by motorcycle through the Andes, two hundred hairpin miles north, with bandidos at roadblocks, hungry for bribes? And the bag filled so quickly—two pairs of jeans, a few sweaters and shirts, birth control pills, passport, and photos. I fetched the letter and slid it between the clothes, the zipper straining to shut. Might Papi question me?

Yet everything I had chosen was a bare essential—except for one thing I had forgotten. Money.

I had only the birthday cash, a hundred American dollars' at most, and Manuel couldn't have more than several hundred dollars in pesos saved. Probably less. In some bank Papi likely kept a savings account for me, but I had no idea where or how to gain access. The pearls now gone, I had nothing—that was how you ended up a prostitute, or displaced. Supposedly Medellín had a higher crime rate than Cali. Obviously I wouldn't be safe without a bodyguard, and Manuel couldn't go with me everywhere, so how would I protect myself? If I needed a gun, where could I get one, and had I practiced enough to defend myself? If I were forced into an alley or held up at a bus stop, could I shoot in time—and shoot to kill?

I knelt before my father's dresser and caught my reflection in the mirror—hair pulled back into a tight ponytail, face childlike without makeup, yet tense, joyless. Manuel said higher laws permitted such behavior. I jerked the handle and the drawer shuddered open. A lone bundle of fifties slid in the hollow. So Papi had used the rest.

I lifted it up and fanned the edge, trembling. What had Emilio said once? *Blackness needs to be plucked out of human hearts if we are to grow*—then clutched the bundle to my chest, rammed the drawer shut, and ran out.

All week I had envisioned my good-bye: me dressed in platform sandals and a party dress, hoisting my bag at the front door, Papi rising from his leather chair to hug me and dole out last-minute warnings. And I was dressed up, although concealed by my mother's jacket. Bulging bag in tow, I descended the stairs.

But at five-thirty, the hacienda remained dim and vacant. Inez rinsed vegetables at the sink. She said the workers were lighting the cane fields before sunset, and Papi wouldn't return until the fires died out after dark. In the sweltering coat I took a last, sweeping survey of the only home I had ever known, petting the dogs as they licked my bare legs, and pushed them away.

Fidel shifted in front of the car, smoking. He grabbed my bag, swung it into the trunk.

"Did you bring the bathroom sink?" He clucked his tongue and smirked. "Women."

"Very funny," I said.

When we exited the gate, however, he pulled onto the shoulder, in front of the alpacas' pasture. The funny creatures were napping in a heap. From the glove compartment he removed a box—the one that had contained the pearls—and set it on the console, nudging it toward me like a dog does a bone or toy. "Here," he said. "Take them."

"I don't understand," I said. "They're yours. I paid you for something."

"I overhead what your father said to you at the party." He spoke facing front, rubbing his jeans. "Please, just take them. I can't do anything with them—it just doesn't feel right. You're my friend." He glanced over his shoulder.

Gingerly, I picked up the box. He put the car in gear and jerked out of the shoulder, rosary slapping the dash. I removed the earrings, unblemished, and put them on.

Fidel liked to sail down the smooth stretch of valley road, but that evening the pickups and horses lined the ditches, and the rubber-booted men milled around the fire, their T-shirts and cotton pants dirt-streaked. They must have only lit the blaze minutes before, but the flames leaped and kissed the sky above the cane, and the smoke tumbled high. We rolled along slowly, the windows half-open. The dead leaves and underbrush crackled louder than a chorus of insects at night, drowning out the workers; the smoke stung my eyes and made them water. I had seen the valley engulfed dozens of times but still watched, mesmerized.

Papi stood talking with Luis, and I ordered Fidel to stop. He beeped and Papi spun around. I lowered the window; he leaned against the doorframe, his face shining pink and neck red, bathed in slick sweat. "Call me tonight when the party's over," he said. "Just so I know that you're safe."

"We'll be up past midnight," I said.

"Doesn't matter. I don't get many late-night phone calls, last time I checked." He smiled, the corners of his eyes crinkling, and the tears flowed harder down my cheeks. "This smoke is thick, you'd better go. You don't want to show up for a dinner party reeking like a cane worker."

I choked, nodding.

He studied me, squinting. "Isn't it a little warm for a leather jacket?"

"Sometimes we sit outside at night for the music. Look what else I'm wearing," I said, tilting my head and showing off the earrings.

"Ah," he said. "The lovely pearls. Well, just as long as you won't be going on any motorcycle rides around the block. Have a good time." He started to withdraw but stopped short and looked at me again, adding, "You look a lot like your mother."

I faced front and wiped the wetness from my scorching cheeks, but when I glanced over again he was gone. He stood back from the road and wiped his bandanna over his neck and brow, the faded purple stained deeper with his sweat; I couldn't see his eyes. The orange glow shot high and shrank, the smoke piling high. Fidel drove on, the cane half-obscured in the haze of gray-black. Even after we ascended the winding hills to the highway, I kept gazing behind me at the sunset—the valley ablaze, the world blotted out, up in smoke.

Manuel's moto was parked next to the brothers' beat-up Honda when Fidel dropped me off—the last time I would see my driver. By midmorning Manuel and I would be a hundred miles away. Classical music and bright light streamed from the mansion. Inside, the maids were setting the dining table with fine china and crystal; the aroma of roasted pork drifted out as the housekeeper let me in. An elderly lady, large emerald cross drooping from her neck, sat talking to another dressed in a white suit and pearl necklace, her hair carefully styled up—Ana's great aunts—but no one stirred to greet me. Emilio's voice boomed from the second floor. On the stairs I ran into the maid who told me Ana was still getting ready.

Upstairs, the Virgin overlooked the brothers, La Maria Juventud crammed onto the couches and cross-legged upon the floor. The university student, dark ponytail skimming his shoulders, passed along a newspaper. Emilio was speaking about the ELN backlash against the Church. A week ago the mediators had made strides. But in a few short days, the talks had turned strained, even hostile. Members of the peace panel Manuel participated in had received threats. Someone asked Manuel if he had received any. His gaze met mine as he answered. "Not yet. But

I anticipate lying low for the next couple of weeks. Dangerous times require patience."

The student leader's ponytail whipped around. "Patience? What do you mean?"

"Watchful waiting," Manuel said. "Colombia doesn't need any more martyrs to meet the obstacles ahead. Excuse me."

He hurried over and kissed me, his hands pressing my face to his so eagerly that after a moment I pulled away, breathless and laughing. He threw my bag over his shoulder, and we retreated into the guest bedroom across from Ana's.

Once the door was shut, I drew him to me and kissed him in return, long and slow. "You excited?" he asked. He stroked the length of hair down my back, his eyes shining as we stared at one another, grinning. Then he hugged me, hard, burying his face in my neck. "God, I've missed you this week. Everything went to hell. I can't wait for this to be over."

"What went wrong?" I asked, alarmed.

"You don't want to know." He stepped back and brightened. "But we're meeting the priest tomorrow morning at seven. Did you bring the letter?" As I fumbled through the duffel bag, he remarked, "We're not going to be able to take that on the bike. It's too big."

I stopped, letter in hand. "This is hardly anything," I said. Emotion welled in my chest and throat. "And you've got to be kidding me, if you think we're going to ride a moto all the way to Medellín."

"It's not that far," he said. "We'll ask Ana for an old backpack, and she can mail the rest of your things to my cousin's address."

I handed over the letter. He inspected the signature across the flap, folded the envelope, and stuck it inside his shirt pocket.

"But we'll get stopped at the roadblocks," I said. "Won't we?"

"They'll harass us, but we should be okay if they see we don't have anything valuable," he said, glancing up. "But I'd leave those pearl earrings with Ana."

In the hall Ana yelled for the maid and her door slammed shut. The laughter and chatter grew louder, Carlos playing measures on his guitar. I pictured us winding through the mist on the bike, and the bus robbery months ago burst to life: the shrieking passengers and howling children, the black-capped bandidos shouting, automatic rifles pointed, their eyes and mouths poking through the knit holes menacingly, like piranhas. "I don't want to ride to Medellín," I said. From the bag I produced the bundle of American cash, chucked it on the bed. "We can go right to the airport tomorrow and buy tickets for Taca or Avianca."

"Avianca, you think that's safer? I need my bike in the city, Mercedes. I can't take the car from my brothers, and I couldn't sell the bike in such a short time. I can't leave it behind." He eyed the cash but made no move to touch it. "And I don't know that I could ever use that. It's blood money."

"We don't know that for sure," I replied.

"You know it is."

"If we need it, we'll use it," I said. "What about your guitar?"

He stood with his hands on hips, chin dropped, gaze combing the floor. "I was going to leave it behind, or have Carlos bring it up," he said quietly. He ran a hand through his hair and groaned. "I guess we could drive the car to Medellín, and either Carlos or Emilio could drive the bike up later, and we could switch."

I fetched the wad of cash and held it out. "I just feel safer flying. Can't we figure it out in the morning?"

"Okay. But there are no guarantees." He embraced me again, pressed his forehead against mine. "Tonight is so special. Let's not argue. Please?"

We sat down to dinner. Ringlets framed Ana's face, her hair swept up in a twist. A pageant crown glittered atop her head, tipping slightly whenever she drank her diet soda. Ana's father popped champagne, and she sat tall in her lush velvet dress, took a few sips before she pushed it away, giggling. Carlos curled his arm around her, his round face solemn but content as Ana's father spoke. "That our daughter would find such a fine young man, driven and devout—we couldn't be happier," her father said, and raised his glass. An emerald and gold ring waggled from his pinky finger. Gracia and Esteban whispered, elbows on the table and hands playfully entwined; Manuel's never left my knee. Emilio smiled occasionally at a joke but his brows knit as he stared at his champagne glass, rotating the stem.

Afterward, Manuel and I carried our plates of cake to a living room corner and wordlessly ate. He managed only a few bites, the chocolate a dark, broken mound; I devoured mine. Someone begged for Gracia and

Esteban to dance, but Gracia puffed out her lip and blamed the champagne. Ana yawned. The girl with the peace tattoo and a few others played a game: dice clattered, and buoyant shouts of who wasn't playing fair. I asked Manuel if he had told anyone our plans.

"My brothers know," he said. "But not my parents. I didn't want to trouble them." He tilted his head toward Gracia and Ana. "Carlos told Ana earlier, when you called, and she got upset because Gracia and Esteban will be leaving and now us, too." He kissed my temple and felt around for the letter in his pocket. The speakers snapped to life with salsa.

"Do you want to play for us?" I asked. "With Carlos?"

Staring at the floor, Manuel shook his head. "I'm ready to get out of Cali for a while." Restlessly, he scanned the room. "I feel like going out. Let's go dancing."

"Dancing?" I echoed. "Are you sure? We have to wake up so early."

"So what?" Already he was standing up, gesturing to his brothers. Ana said she was tired but she would love to join us for a while, and Gracia had brought an outfit to change into in case we decided to go out. Emilio jumped up, performed a couple of salsa steps, and asked for suggestions on clubs.

"We should just stay here," I said. "I've got to check in with Papi at midnight."

"Why don't you just call him now?" Ana said. "It's ten-thirty."

Upstairs in Ana's room, Gracia changed into jeans while I phoned the hacienda. Inez answered. Papi had eaten a late dinner with the jefes and was still down at the farmhouse. I fingered my jacket's collar, the raw hide curled and tough, made her promise she would write a note and leave it on his pillow with the time I had called.

Hopping into her jeans, Gracia said, "We're going to have so much fun tonight. And just think, who would have thought that of the three of us you'd be the first to get married?" We laughed, and I started to say how much I didn't want to part with her or Ana, but she shushed me, saying no need for that yet. I tugged on jeans too, at the last minute remembering to remove my earrings and hide them in the duffel. Ana wanted a few more minutes to say good-bye to the guests, and insisted Manuel and I go ahead to the club. Ana and Carlos would join us within the hour, and Gracia, Esteban, and Emilio could ride with them in the SUV with her driver.

The grand mansions slumbered as I shrugged into the leather coat and climbed onto the back of Manuel's bike, the sidewalks empty. The guards in their cheap blue uniforms choked down empanadas out of tinfoil and joked with one another. The engine quaked to life, and I dropped my head back to see the stars as we peeled out of la Ciudad Jardín, but the city outshone them. When would I see my valley again, the sky a banquet of light? How did you know you were embarking on an adventure, and not a mistake? We hurled toward downtown, the gated estates turning to aluminum-shuttered storefronts. As we dipped in and out of the traffic near the river, the staccato beats of Juanchito pumped as loud and fast as my heart.

We parked and walked across the bridge to the north side of the river, drawn by the thump of salsotecas—dozens brightly lit, their doors flung open to the streets, the dank odors of stale booze and fog machines wafting out. Manuel walked quickly, and I scurried to keep up, skirting the wide ruts of the crumbling sidewalks. A pack of skinny boys brushed past, small jars of glue clutched to their chests. The youngest, no more than ten years old, stared ahead with vacant eyes; a trickle of blood ran down one nostril to the corner of his lip. Was this what streets were like in the United States? Probably not.

Manuel's hand was clammy and cool. "You're dragging me," I said, my laugh shaky.

"Sorry. Just thinking about tomorrow. And Medellín."

The music pulsated louder at the club's entrance. My vision crystallized; the sounds sharpened and muffled at once, the club a tunnel. The doorman stamped our hands. The neon light cast a greenish glow over Manuel's face as he turned to me, smiling, and said, "I can't wait to dance. Just get out of my head for a bit."

We shuffled in. The dance floor flickered, packed with the shadowy figures weaving in and out. A girl pushed past in a tight midriff top. One male dancer's loose jeans and T-shirt rippled wildly with each high kick. A relentless wind pounded from a machine; I licked my lips. Manuel suggested we have a drink first and wait for our friends—they shouldn't be far behind. It was early, and the bar was thinned out enough for us to grab seats. We squeezed lime into our Flor de Cañas and Coca-Cola, clinked glasses. The juice stung my nail; I sucked my fingertip. I was just about to bring up the getaway, how I didn't care anymore about driving or flying because I just wanted to leave Cali as fast as possible, when Manuel cupped my elbow. "That man who just walked in," he said, nodding toward someone in a black motorcycle jacket and gloves weaving through the crowd. "I think he's watching us." The man sat down at the far end of the bar, alone, and ordered a drink.

"But would someone be following you? Unless he was waiting outside the party." My teeth and chest ached, the Coca-Cola and rum ice cold.

The man took his beer, pressed his way toward the dance floor. Manuel lowered his head and kept talking, trying to act like we hadn't noticed him. "I'm sure it's just my own paranoia," he said. "Leaving Cali will be a good move." The man zigzagged, his back to us—a slight build, average height, but unfamiliar. Older than us, probably Emilio's age. Then he cut through the line piling in, toward the restrooms, and disappeared. Inside the entry, a trio of girls passed around a compact, took turns swiping on lipstick. Our friends were running late. We could pay our tab, leave, go back to Ana's yet. Meet up in the morning.

Manuel drained his glass, then mine. "Come on, let's dance," he said.

We wove through the crowd, hands linked, Manuel leading, when someone jerked my arm and knocked me down. Bodies abruptly scuffled and shouts peppered over the music. A glass fell and shattered next to me, a rainbow of disco lights illuminating the shards. Above me and no more than two meters away appeared the man from the bar. His face now hidden in a knit mask, he pulled out an automatic handgun from his jacket and pointed it in our direction. Then he stuck it to Manuel's chest and fired three times. My ears rang, the noise gone fuzzy, mute. Stumbling, the assassin fought his way through the mob, and bolted, a dark dot, into the street.

Manuel lurched and slumped to the ground, a deep grunt of agony bursting from his lips.

Then nothing.

I crawled through the spilled drinks and flailing limbs—if I could just reach him, he would be all right. He had fallen to his side, and as I pulled him onto my lap, the color was already draining from his face, and the blood seeping through his shirt above his heart, wider and wider, crept up my jeans, warm and wet. I said his name over and over but he did not answer; rum clung upon his lips but he was not breathing. People scrambled and surged into us, crying, "Ambulancia!" Hands gripped underneath me, tried to drag me off. I sat cross-legged on the filthy floor, cradling him and rocking, yelling at everyone to stay away. His blood smeared my forearms but when I pressed my mouth to his scalp I could smell his hair. Mint and cedar. Out of the haze appeared Gracia and Ana. They covered their faces and staggered back. Emilio and Carlos screamed, rushed to Manuel, and fell to their knees. Esteban guided me up, led me away on silent, uneven steps.

CHAPTER FOURTEEN

Papi didn't allow me to attend the funeral. I barely left my bed. The jefes burned the remaining fields, and the smoke hid the valley in gray and stung my throat. Had the ELN, angry at the Church, ordered the hit, even though Manuel had believed Gambino an ally? Or was it FARC radicals in the wake of their uprising, seeking to eliminate noisy peacemakers? After the police had driven me home from the club that night, Papi appeared at the end of my bed. "Why were you at a nightclub?" he said, rubbing his face. "Senseless. One step closer, it might have been you who was shot." He shook his head, his fingers spread wide over his lips. "You see now why I've wanted you to leave, before something like this happened?" I couldn't speak.

Why had I so recklessly cast aside his caution? Machines chugged in the fields; hawks circled. Someone knocked softly at my door—Inez with the tea tray. Homemade tamales, bland beans and rice. In my mouth the corn crumpled to sweet dust. The world was nothing but mad countries colliding blindly, like comets.

I could imagine the funeral well enough. Police on motos, young people, and media chocking the streets and entrances near La Maria. A reporter adjusting her stance before a TV crew, microphone in hand—the same woman who had reported on the plane hijacking months ago. Ushers and priests waving back the crowd. The line to view the casket winding down the block. A body was so much—how could anyone pretend otherwise? And yet what was a body but a window for life, what the guitar was for song? In the cemetery down the street, Emilio, Carlos and close friends from La Maria Juventud would hoist the casket into a dark concrete hole, seal shut the door. The girl with the peace sign on her wrist might kneel and light a candle, leave it and a sprig of roses beneath the weed-spotted wall.

The doctor had prescribed me a sedative. I awoke on my window seat, the breeze cold, and shuddered. Likely the local station had covered the funeral service that afternoon, but I'd slept through it. Downstairs, onions and chorizo sizzled and pots clanged—Inez on the phone, murmuring to her husband. A pickup rumbled into the courtyard. Papi greeted Luis, and they stood outside, talking. "They met him at the pickup point," Luis said. "I just got word he's back at his village. Looks like it's all taken care of, and he's far enough away."

"Let's hope so," Papi said. "I don't want trouble." One of the dogs growled and snapped at another; he scolded them to beat it. Nails scraped stone.

"Two hundred miles should be distance enough," Luis said. "And the amount you gave him will feed his family for months. Just proves that if a man's hungry, he'll do anything."

"A shame." Papi paused. "This one put a bad taste in my mouth. I don't want to speak of it again."

I lay there, breath shallow. Probably Luis and Papi were simply speaking of a displaced villager who had been harassing for work and had overstepped his bounds with threats or violence. Groggy, I crept to the bathroom, pressed a cold washcloth to my face. I barely recognized myself: skin blotchy, eyes rimmed red.

Inside the shower the smooth tile felt reassuring, the waterfall purging hot. I recalled Uncle Charlie's quip about there always being a way if you made a good enough offer. If you were smart. *My little spy*, Manuel had said. When I stepped out, my overnight bag rested on the bed—I'd left it at Ana's that night. Fidel must have picked it up. My blood rushed back. How sure was I that Papi hadn't found out about our plans to elope and run away? I dug out the pearl earrings and replaced them in my jewelry box. Papi involved somehow—no, impossible.

But then I shook out a pair of jeans, and the bundle of cash bounced onto the bed. I picked it up, inhaled the oily ink. Was I underestimating Papi? Holding on to that last bit of innocent naiveté? Or were others too quick in their snap judgments and conclusions, Emilio among them? I imagined my father opening the drawer, drinking in its emptiness. Rapping on Fidel's rickety screen, them conferring in the dark belly of the yard—what had Fidel said? My driver had returned the pearls; I had been so sure he was my friend. But now my hand trembled and grew sweaty underneath the money, and I dropped it like a burning leaf.

"Something different has come over you," Sister Rosemary said the following day. She tossed aside her textbooks and embraced me in a long, rocking hug.

The clouds cast giant shadows over the valley. "For a minute I'll forget about him being gone, you know?" I said. "And then—" She ran her hands through my hair the way Manuel used to, tugging out the knots. I pretended she was Tía Leo, or my mother, and closed my eyes, shutting out the light.

"Why don't you take a few more days?" she said gently, handing me a tissue. "What you're going through is so terrible."

I dabbed my cheeks, shook my head. "What's the latest on my mother? Has anything turned up?"

"Actually, I received a promising response the other day," she said. Her contact in the United States may have found an address for my grandparents in Boca Raton, Florida. It had been listed under my mother's name in the University of Miami alumni directory, although the listing was over a decade old. Sister Rosemary had written a letter on my behalf, sent a week ago. "I wasn't planning on telling you until I heard something more firm, so you wouldn't get your hopes up," she said. "Sometimes in these cases, families take time to respond—if they do at all. So I've been told."

The news didn't sink in: a set of grandparents I had never pictured, a city with a funny-sounding name. The possibility of a response from an old address seemed far-fetched. "Suppose I were to go to there on my own," I said. "Is it too late to be admitted this fall?"

Her eyes narrowed. "Is that what you want?"

"It seems like the best thing. If you can't find my mother."

"Are you sure? Moving to another country wouldn't be easy for you right now." She studied me a moment longer. "But no doubt you have considered that." I hovered at my chair. "Between your grades and your test scores, I'm not sure," she said, and shook her head. "You may have to wait several months, and try again."

In the hall the maid vacuumed; I arose and shut out the roar. I reached for my purse, pulled out the money that I had stolen from Papi for Medellín, and tossed the cash onto the table. The nun caught her breath. Perhaps that bundle was always marked for my escape.

"Florida, California, anywhere you can get me in," I said in a low voice. "And don't tell my father. When you find out I'll want to leave quickly."

She placed her hand over mine. "I'm so sorry," she whispered. A long pause followed, and for a moment I thought all was lost. But at last she nodded and swept the bundle into the canvas bag she carried, underneath her shawl.

Friday, August thirteenth, marked a week since Manuel's death. That evening I flicked on the news to discover Jaime Garzón had been killed—gunned down by men on motorbikes while commuting to his office. A political humorist who often criticized all sides of Colombia's conflict, Garzón had served alongside Manuel on the Civilian Facilitation Commission. "Would you look at that," Fidel said. He sipped a Fanta, keys in hand. In the closet Inez rummaged for the bags she always brought to the market. "It's too much to take anymore." He muted the set just as the reporter mentioned who the authorities suspected to have been behind the hit. To my surprise the white lettering emblazoned in the screen's bottom read AUC, not ELN.

"Beloved Broadcaster Meets Bloody End" ran the headline of the next day's newspaper. Jaime's face nearly took up the front page, Manuel's in a box beneath. The caption mentioned the young activist's murder alongside Jaime's proved the CFC was being targeted by an enemy to the peace efforts, and that in Garzón's case, he'd received death threats from the AUC. Here I had been consumed in thinking that besides my suspicions about Papi, the ELN or the FARC must be responsible for Manuel's death. But the authorities suspected the Autodefensas to have killed Garzón. So far the AUC adamantly denied any allegations of their involvement. What about Manuel's murder?

I set down the paper. The workman who'd been cleaning out the birdcage whistled—the noisy parrots gone, replaced with a pair of beady-eyed toucans. Just before he closed the door, he scraped chopped papaya into their dish.

I phoned Emilio. "The Garzón murder—do you know anything?" I asked.

"We're not sure. But yes, looks like the Autodefensas may have taken him out." His voice carried none of its usual vigor and resoluteness. "How are you?"

"What do you think? My mind—it just won't stop."

"Well, I have something to show you. Are you coming to the memorial?"

"I don't know. What memorial?" Papi's glass from earlier had left a watery ring over a close-up of Manuel leading a rally, shouting, his fist pumping the air. The colors had bled; I traced them. "Was it in the paper?" I flipped through, scanning the section.

"For sure. I thought you'd know. The Archbishop is holding a memorial tomorrow at the cathedral for Manuel, Garzón, and the other activists killed this year," he said. "Why don't we meet afterward?" I asked him what time and told him I'd get there somehow.

"It will be good to see you," he said.

I started over, carefully paged through. Someone had removed A6 and A7, where the front page article continued. I sat back. The toucans hopped and blinked, as quiet as the rest of the house, except for the dogs pacing the halls, the chatter of the maids cleaning the windows with vinegar and newspaper.

I brought up the service that night to Papi, sure that he would refuse. But he only said, "Maybe," lost in thought. He ate half his dinner, then arose and strolled the porch while smoking his cigar. From time to time he sat down in his rocking chair, bent forward, and cradled his head. The air cooled my face and neck. "What's wrong?" I asked.

He stared into the darkness, his bandanna draped over his knee like a flag. "Nothing," he said. "Just trying to figure it out like everybody else."

"Something happen lately?"

"Just the typical problems," he said. But when he looked at me, his eyes shone like wet glass. "God is everywhere and nowhere. Do you believe that?"

"I don't know. You're the one who pulled me out of Hebrew school."

His teeth gleamed white in the shadows, even though I hadn't meant it to be funny. "You will never know how much I love you, princesa. You are so grown up. I miss you already."

"I love you, too," I said. But the words stuck in my mouth like stones.

"You had better go early tomorrow," he said. "It's a Holy Day of Obligation. The cathedral will be crowded." He folded and refolded the limp bandanna on his knee, the light from indoors illuminating the worn square of cloth.

I waited for Emilio outside the tall cathedral doors, near the spot where I had first locked eyes with Manuel. But this Holy Day boasted no parade of crosses or icons, just the dozens of devoted streaming out underneath the Virgin Mary tapestry unfurled above the entry. Service over, Emilio surfaced. He hugged me; at the familiar fragrance of cologne and soap, my eyes grew moist. He led me past the dim altars of flickering votive candles and images of saints, through a door marked *sacristía*—the vestry. "No one will bother us in here," he said. Velvet and satin-lined priests' robes and sashes lined the walls, an enormous closet—insular, protected. We sat across from one another at a folding table. I described what I had overheard between Papi and Luis. Emilio appeared pale and drained, stifled a yawn. Yet he nodded intently, asked questions, jotted notes. "Astounding," he said when I finished. "You've been all alone out there, with those men—I'm so sorry." He touched my wrist. From a backpack at his feet, he drew out a folder and edged it toward me. "This won't be easy. Are you ready?"

Muffled voices, footsteps clamored outside the door. My insides shrank. "How did you get hold of this?"

"A friend in the Cali police," he said. "A longtime contact. Right after the murder, I saw him. The police asked me about possible leads, started the investigation from there. Then on the day of the funeral, I asked him for a special favor. I just picked this up today. What you're about to see are copies of official police records, so it goes without saying—you never saw what I'm about to show you, understand?"

I reached across, slid the file from beneath his hands, opened it. A photocopied picture of the hit man wearing the black jacket peered back. Velvet sleeves, thick and heavy, prodded my side; I brushed them off. "So the police caught him?"

"They did. But he was released within forty-eight hours."

"What?" The air-conditioning clicked on overhead, a blast of persistent cold. My throat went dry. "That's him, he was watching us at the bar that night. Why didn't the police ask me—"

"Why do you think, Mercedes?" He jerked the file back, flipped a few pages, slid the documents back in front of me, finger jabbing the print. He read aloud, "'Suspect works in the employment of Diego Martinez, who alleges that the Azúcar de Cauca employee remained on his property at the time of the murder."

"No," I said, and shoved it back. I leaned forward on my elbows, covered my eyes.

"It's sick, isn't it?" he said slowly. "That a life can be taken so simply." The air-conditioning droned, fluttering the pages. I shivered hard. When I opened my eyes he was staring down, vacant and resigned, legs crossed.

I sat up, frowning. "I can't believe it."

"Why not? Didn't you mention at dinner that your father's workers were burning the cane?"

"Yes—you could see it for miles."

He uncrossed his legs, sat back. "The perfect alibi. And the police took you home, right?"

I caught one of the velvet sleeves, nodding. The police and Papi had talked in the courtyard while the doctor tended to me—a long time. "Shouldn't we do something?" I asked.

"Like what?" He rubbed his face. "This is the closest we'll ever get to proof, you realize. Never mind justice."

I slumped, staring at the words in neat type. *Suspect works in the employment of Diego Martinez.* A detective's signature scrawled across the form, the long case number with the dash. POLICIA METROPOLITANA SANTIAGO DE CALI. The stamped seal as undeniable as the cash stacked in Papi's drawer.

He buried his face in his hands, tried to stifle his sobs, but couldn't. "I chose God—why not take me? I'm so lost now, without him. You don't know."

I offered my hand across the table; he didn't move. "When he went into the mountains after you, I was so mad," I said. "Not so much that he'd choose God. But that he'd risk his life for you. Not save himself for me."

"True. You don't know love until something happens to your blood," he said. I breathed long and slow, withdrew my hand. He cleared his throat and wiped his eyes. "He knew God more than anyone. I envied him that," he admitted quietly. "For many things, I envied him." He leaned forward then, reached behind my neck, and lifted my hair. He didn't run his fingers through it, but clutched the mass in gentle, careful fistfuls before releasing it down my back. I cupped his face. We held each other then and wept, surrounded by red and green and purple, all the seasons of the Church.

Another week began. Sister Rosemary was calling boarding schools across the United States, explaining that she had a Colombian student in a desperate situation, waiting to hear back.

I avoided Papi, claiming to be ill from grief—which I was. Whenever the men's footsteps clipped over the courtyard, I strained to catch their talk. But nothing sounded unusual. I no longer jumped at the phone ringing, believing it might be Manuel; the bleakness of his absence settled over life like the rains. If only I could sneak off with Fidel's gun, shoot at the gray-black target until there were no bullets left, my anger deflated like a leftover birthday balloon.

One morning I called Sister Rosemary and told her not to come, that I wasn't feeling well. Then I took my purse, told Inez I would be back before dinner, and set out along the valley road. I walked briskly but the jefes and field hands worked acres away, planting; the road stretched out silent and deserted. If someone had been waiting to kidnap me, now would be the perfect opportunity, and part of me cheered this on, welcomed the dare. The bus heaved up the highway into Cali. The seats grew packed. A grubby man selling colored pencils strolled up and down the aisle, sticking a sample pack in front of the drowsy passengers, who ignored him.

I rode that bus, then another, to Manuel's neighborhood and hastened along the few blocks to the shop, shuttered and dark, his bike parked underneath the stairs—who had brought it back from downtown that night? His parents, how were they putting their lives back together after the loss? Perhaps, like me, they were not.

Emilio answered the door. I inhaled faint mildew, stale cooking, musty carpet. A few candles burned in the little shrine; dirty laundry piled in the hallway, Manuel's clothes mixed with his brothers'. The bedroom door stood ajar; no one else was home. Emilio was wearing one of Manuel's faded T-shirts with a band's logo across the front, and sweatpants, his hair mussed. I had never seen him this way before, unkempt and sleepy. Blank.

He shut the door behind us, and when he drew my face to his I wrapped my hands around the back of his neck.

Afterward, we remained on the old couch, solemn and speechless but broken apart. Wetness pooled underneath me, the cushion rough. What happened had started and ended quickly. I was too numb for any real pleasure but comfort. Yet I felt restless or something like panic; I went to the bathroom, filled a glass with water. Carlos and Emilio's beds weren't made, the sheets and pillows askew, blankets dragging on the floor, but Manuel's was tidy and straight, like a manicured grave. My stomach clenched.

Emilio lay with one arm behind his head, the other pressed against his forehead, his features more defined than Manuel's; at twenty-six he had grown into his body, all boyishness gone. Ten years stretched between us—what did that matter? "Are you all right?" I asked, sitting at his feet.

He glanced at me, then away again. "We can't say anything about this to anyone. Okay?" He touched my cheek with the back of his hand, cool and smooth.

I blew an irritated puff into the glass, raising it to my lips. "I know that."

He struggled onto one elbow, took the glass. "Promise me," he said.

"When are you supposed to start the seminary?"

He eased back, stared at the ceiling, and shook his head. "I don't know. Nunca. I think I've lost my mind." He traced his fingertips from my shoulder down my back; I quivered and grew warm. He said, "You're such an angel. No wonder he loved you."

So these are the things men say, I thought. Still I said nothing, only sipped some water. Was this sin? The candles flickered, and a notebook lay open to where Manuel had been writing a song. I began to dress. When I bent down to kiss Emilio on the forehead, he clutched me and buried himself in my chest, kissing the bare space above the gap in my blouse. "I need to go," I said, stroking his face.

He kissed me a few more times but I pulled away, my skin dampened with his tears, and hurried to the door. He did not pursue me.

Later that week, the ELN released the last hostages. The news reports showed them bursting from the buses in Cali's soccer stadium, where the Red Cross had arranged their arrival. Reporters interviewed the rescued—stunned, gaunt, hungry for a real meal, for meat. But unlike the *desplazados*, the eyes of the freed shone; they would return to their office jobs, evenings at the World Gym, and comfortable beds in la Ciudad Jardín. Life would never again sink so low as camping out in the mountains with guerilla teenagers, who had no more than an elementary education, nor had ever set foot in a city.

For hours I switched from one station to another, transfixed. So Manuel's mission was accomplished. If he were alive, he would have been free to create a life with me in Medellín, or Costa Rica—anywhere. I shed no more tears; I had none left.

Ana and Carlos married that Saturday at La Maria, a somber event. Everyone walked to Ana's for the lawn reception. The maids served ceviche and champagne, and a band played, raucous and oblivious to the solemnity of the guests' long faces and subdued manner. In the living room Carlos's guitar case remained shut. One of their other cousins rushed up to Ana, tugged her arm, and pointed to a long piece of lace that had torn from her veil, and that she was unknowingly dragging on her heel—laughing, she hugged the child and peeled it off. Esteban led Gracia out onto the patio. They circled one another and began to dance la cumbia.

Alone, I finished the champagne and asked for another. I ducked through the crowd, searching for Emilio.

What was I seeking from him, comfort or closure? Were we hoping to keep Manuel alive—find him, somehow, through one another? In the dim downstairs hallway a toilet flushed. and Emilio exited, eyes pink and face drawn. He jumped back and we stood there, shifting our weight in silence. The musicians finished a number, the guests politely applauded. I took his hand and led him upstairs.

I'd never been drunk before; I wasn't prepared for the plunge. It was dusk when we finished. He remained still on top of me, breathing hard, before he rolled off and dressed in the lamplight. I lay facing the wall and pressed my hand to it, crying. He sat down and turned me over gently to face him. "We can't keep doing this," he said. "There's no future with us." He studied me, eyes narrowed and pleading, as he fastened the final buttons of his dress shirt.

I sat up, dabbed my face with the sheet. "I can't help it," I said.

He caressed my arm, leaned over and kissed me slowly, with hesitation and earnestness. His scent fell from my hair, my skin bathed in the cologne the brothers' shared, and even his naked body pressed against mine felt similar to Manuel's. Only his lovemaking was different, desperate and unsure.

"We both just want him back. Although I love being with you." He paused. "I'm sorry." The door clicked behind him like a clip sliding into a gun. I fell back in the narrow bed, my stomach reeling and hollow. Below, the reception's din carried on. I did not go downstairs for the rest of the night, and no one knocked on my door. I was not needed; my world could go on without me. That was what I had wanted—to give myself away, to be empty.

Sister Rosemary found my mother at the same time she found a school. Paula lived in Israel, but my grandparents would meet my plane in Miami. The transfer was already in place with the records from the Hebrew Day School, and I would have to retake the EFL test within the first term. My grandparents had agreed to pay for my tuition, living expenses, everything. Was this what was meant by the blood, the bonds of family love? I would soon find out. On the last day of August 1999, I would start my junior year at St. Andrew's School in Boca Raton, Florida. Classes had started the week before. "But you're in," Sister Rosemary assured me in the stuffy upstairs office. "And your mother wants to see you soon. Supposedly they attempted to visit when you were little, but plans fell through. They didn't explain, but with the violence back then, I can't blame them. They said they prayed you'd get in touch when you grew older, and are ecstatic about you coming.." She and I hugged and laughed, and hugged some more. I said I didn't know how to thank her. She told me to do well at school. That was enough.

I would have to leave as soon as possible, however, to get settled. She asked if I wanted help breaking the news to my father. "I've got to do it," I said. That afternoon we said our good-byes; the tutoring over, I would not see her again.

That afternoon I waited for Papi to finish his after-work cigar in his rocker, feet up as he chatted with Luis and Vincente. They left, and I strolled over. "I have a surprise," I said. "You're never going to believe it." And I explained my instructions to Sister Rosemary to find a boarding school, and the good news that she had been successful.

"Leaving this weekend? And which school?" He set down the cigar. "She didn't mention anything to me."

"That's because I told her not to—I wanted you to be proud of me, for doing this on my own." I lowered onto the rocker beside him. He didn't look at me, just scratched his beard and stared at the valley. "It's a great school, one of the best in south Florida. Episcopalian. I'll have a long break over the holidays. I'll see you then."

"What about the paperwork? Don't I have to fill out release forms? And what's the tuition?"

"We can look it up later—it costs the same as the others. Sister Rosemary's going to get the paperwork to you next week. I know it's sudden but I don't want to wait."

He regarded me with a small smile and waved me over into a hug, and I hugged him back, hard; he smelled of tobacco and horses. "This will be the best thing for you," he said. "Especially now, after Manuel." How alien the words sounded. He dug out his wallet and handed me his credit card. "Here, you'd better book your flight. I'll thank the sister next week. But I'm so proud of you, princess." He blew a hazy puff. "You are turning out to be quite clever."

I lugged out my two large suitcases plus the duffel, laid out shoes and belts, hair accessories, the mementos in my bedside drawer. Hangers swayed and the closet echoed, the jewelry boxes open and bare as if they'd been robbed. I lifted the heavy jacket of my mother's; beside the memories of riding the bike with Manuel it had never really fit but drooped too wide at the shoulders. How long would I have to wait to see her, and would I like her right away? My grandparents? At Papi's desk I waited on hold with the airline, spun his credit card over until a representative picked up. "Round trip?" she asked cheerily. "No," I said, "a one-way flight."

I was just ending the call when Papi stuck his head in the door. "How about we go for a ride?" he said. "I've got to check up on some things."

Reluctantly I trailed him, climbed in the truck.

The camp of the desplazados arose at the rainforest's edge—now a village. Tin-roofed shacks sprawled to where the riverbank wrapped around the mountain, and out of sight. Cows grazed under trees; some boys of about twelve sat on the roof of an old car, watching them. Two enormous cisterns held water, and a woman stood on her tiptoes, dipped and filled one bucket, then another; a crooked line of women and children formed behind her. Newspapers plastered the front of an old man wielding a bloody ax. The homemade sign above his shack read: *Carnicería*. His wife sat upon a crate, plucking a dead chicken. Feathers flew high, speckled the air white. A kettle boiled over an open fire; carcasses dangled from a clothesline. The air reeked of dead flesh and smoke.

"Why are there so many?" I asked.

"The Calima Front drove them out of the southern mountains. In pursuit of the ELN." The truck crept along, Papi braking for a pregnant girl about my age to scurry across the road, baby in arms. She glanced at us and smiled but quickly dropped her chin. "I hope I've done the right thing by letting them stay here," he said. The tires crunched, and he stared ahead.

"How could it not be the right thing?"

"Because they have to leave. This lowland can't support a town. We're clearing them out tomorrow, move as many as we can to the mission." He tightened his grip on the wheel. "If I had known they would grow to so many, I wouldn't have let a single family stay."

"But that doesn't make any sense. Why can't at least some of them stay?"

"And how do I explain that to them, decide which ones may stay or go?" His tone bit the air, and he glared at me as if for answers. "Tell the ones who have lived here the longest that they don't have to leave, and the rest must go? Or should it be the other way around? Tell me."

"I don't know," I said, choking out the words and turning away. I didn't want this to be my last memory of Colombia: the stench of greasy cooking and burnt garbage. But everywhere I looked, the poor filled my vision—children sloshed pails of water to their shacks, and mangy strays zigzagged in the pickup's path. Poverty was a living death, and I never wanted to be poor. I said, "Why did you bring me here, if you just were going to tell me that?"

"Because I want you to see, before you leave. The United States is like a drug that makes you forget the rest of the world."

"I don't believe you," I said. "Don't you think I know how things really are by now?"

"Of course I do. I'm just asking you to remember this, the one small thing I tried." Here he raised his hands and shrugged. "Even if I've ruined everything."

The radio, out of range in the hollow, fell silent. I lifted my gaze to the giant trees, the vines and gnarled branches a respite from the human soreness below. I wanted to ask about Manuel and if he was responsible for the murder, all I had to do was find the courage, but I couldn't. He slowed to avoid a man on a bicycle who carried an enormous pink-and-gray fish slung on a pole; it nearly reached the ground. Papi stuck his head out the window and asked where the man was going; the man called back, "To bring my family dinner, sir!"

Papi laughed, but it died quickly. He settled back into his seat. "Perhaps it's best this way," he said quietly, shifting his weight. "They don't suspect. Luis and the jefes will ride down with the horses tomorrow."

"Maybe if you just explain it to them, they'll understand," I said. "And they won't make trouble." But even as I said this and the truck rolled up the bank and out of the camp, I knew it would never happen that way.

In my room, I studied the portrait of Paula and the one taken on the beach. My Jewish grandparents—what might they look like? *Meyerhoff.* For the first time that side of my family felt real. Before America, what part of the world had they come from? Might I have had relatives in the

Holocaust, and what might they have endured—not kidnappings by guerillas, but hardships just as tragic? How had they ended up in Florida, a flat place but with palm trees and warm breezes not so unlike Colombia? "Florida," I said aloud and the syllables rolled along my tongue easily, like a waterfall down a mountain. *Florida*, the land Papi had fled and where he could never return. I packed the final essentials into my carry on. Did fleeing mean such things could be forgotten like items in a closet, no longer necessary but ready if you were to return? Like the worn leather jacket of my mother's. Only she hadn't come back but moved farther and farther away, until I caught up to her.

That night after Inez cleared our plates, the dogs trailing her and sniffing at the leftover chunks of ajiaco, I suggested to Papi that we say goodbye then, rather than the morning. "It will be easier, don't you think?" I said. The melted ice shone golden at the bottom of his glass; he was rotating it pensively, and abruptly he looked up. "Okay, then." We arose and embraced. "You won't forget me down here, promise?" he mumbled. I laughed shakily, replied, "How could I forget you? It'll only be a few months until the holidays. Maybe by then all this violence will be over with." I rubbed his back and started to pull away, but he clung to me for a few more moments, breathing long and hard—was he weeping? He turned his back quickly, patted his pockets for his tobacco, and stepped out.

Only the difficulty of some things can never be cheated. For Papi had arisen before dawn so that by the time I ate my breakfast, the only traces of him remained his dog-eared *Semana* and cold tinto cup. As the car hugged the curves on the road to the autopista, smoke rolled upward from the lower end of the bare fields—not a great opaque sheet like when the jefes burned the cane fields, but bonfires lit here and there. I lowered the window. Chaos carried on the breeze: shouts, horses, gunshots. A wave rippled from my toes to my stomach.

"What are they doing to clear them out?" I cried.

"The hell if I know." We struck a pothole; the rosary shimmied. Fidel crossed himself and kissed his fingers. "It's an ugly business."

At the airport he heaved my bags to the curb and hesitated. He slid off his sunglasses, and we faced one another, each waiting for the other to speak until I hugged him, hard but brief. "Who will you drive around now?" I asked.

"Nobody," he replied. "I'm going home to pack, too."

"You didn't tell me you were leaving." I swallowed hard. Papi, what would he do with me gone and now Fidel, his new favorite? Why did I care?

"Yes, I did. You don't remember? It just took some time for me to make up my mind."

"Where will you go? Are you going to drive for someone else?"

He shook his head, cleaned his sunglasses with his shirt. "I'm through. I've thought about this for a long time, after what happened to my family. But I've been talking to the parish priest."

"You're not going to become one of them, are you?"

"No way. I'm not up for switching one line of service for another." He chuckled. "But there's a Carmelite monastery down south. I went to visit when you were in Costa Rica. It's the quietest place. You wouldn't believe it."

"A quiet place in Colombia?" I grinned. "Sorry, I don't."

He touched my shoulder. "Good luck, princesa. I know you'll be strong and like America all right." And he hopped behind the wheel and pulled away, waving one last time, his talk radio program squawking as the car rejoined the crawling terminal traffic.

The flight from Bogotá to Miami took three-and-a-half hours—the longest I had ever taken. Above the Earth, time stopped, and I saw my life almost as if it had happened to someone else. So much of the last five months surfaced only in fragments—Manuel leaning outside the Taca office, Tía Leo talking as the rains poured down. My father's face as Manuel played his guitar, the bandanna wrapped around his fingers like he was trying to stop a bleeding wound. The flight attendants wheeled the beverage cart by—another future cut off. For whatever I would become in the United States, I felt sure I would never be a flight attendant. The young woman poured my soda, her dark hair slicked back into a bun. Was hers straight like Ana's or unruly like mine? Pearls peeked out from her ears, her makeup perfectly pressed. She was a few years older than me, but no more than twenty. Had this been her big dream, too, or if in some different set of circumstances might she have imagined more?

My knees turned wobbly as I disembarked. On the way to customs, cheery phrases beamed down, *Bienvenidos* along with *Welcome*. But Sister Rosemary and I had practiced, and I rehearsed the answers to the questions I would likely be asked. I reached the desk of the customs officer and greeted him in English. When he responded I froze. After all those months of studying the language in a bubble, it actually worked. What power.

The officer was not amused by my hesitation to hand over my passport, however. He drilled me with questions about my traveling alone, no doubt suspecting that I was a teenager-turned-drug-mule, until I dug out my acceptance letter from St. Andrew's and another letter from Sister Rosemary explaining my travels. At this, the officer's demeanor relaxed.

"Good luck at your new school," he said. "Been here before?"

"This is my first time," I said. "But my mother is American."

"Oh, well that's different." He slid my passport back. "Welcome home."

PART TWO

CHAPTER FIFTEEN

My grandparents met me outside customs, where they were holding a sign with my name on it just like in the movies. The first thing that struck me was how gringo they looked—sporting deep South Florida tans, light hair and eyes. When they smiled, their teeth gleamed as white and straight as if they had stepped out of a toothpaste commercial; I was soon to find out Ben, my grandfather, was a retired orthodontist. Tall and broad, he towered over my grandmother, Silvia. They appeared an athletic, energetic older couple, talkative and kind, and I had to ask them to slow down, for they spoke too fast for me to understand.

My mother was not there. She would arrive in another week or so. A pang of dismay struck me, hearing this. But then, I told myself, she lived in another country. Wasn't I expecting too much, perhaps, in thinking she could drop everything last minute and fly overseas? After a lifetime, a week might not be so long to wait.

I asked if she would be bringing a husband with her, if I had any brothers or sisters. Ben dropped his chin, shook his head as he wheeled my suitcase. He said, "She's never remarried, and has no other children. You have some cousins, though." Silvia beamed encouragingly, and Ben picked up his gait. My hopes deflated as this sank in: no family other than grandparents, a couple of aunts and uncles, cousins. I thought of Jacki. Cousins were not such a big deal.

Choking heat and the steamy scent of rain engulfed me as we climbed into a BMW, my grandfather behind the wheel. How did they have such a nice car, but no driver? As we glided away from the airport we passed strip malls, restaurants, and hotels—no peddlers selling cheap sunglasses and peppers, nor shantytowns of corrugated metal. My grandparents' neighborhood consisted of upscale, although not lavish, homes—mostly ranches in the Bahamian colonial style, but absent of gates and barbed-wire fences. We pulled into their driveway, and I was filled with unease. How could people in nice homes live so openly, nothing to separate their well-manicured lawns from the street? Wouldn't criminal gangs be robbing neighbors left and right? Maybe Papi had been right about poverty being different here.

Silvia had made up a room for me, smaller than my childhood quarters at the hacienda, but cozy. After a dinner of smiles and halting conversation, I tried on the uniforms she'd bought me for St. Andrew's—khakis, polo shirts, some ugly shoes called "loafers"—and thumbed through a *Seventeen* magazine she had set out. The only salsa I could find on the clock radio came in screeching and muffled, so I settled on a pop station playing Britney Spears instead. A blunt weirdness set in, now that I had arrived, of what I had done—fled the familiar for a new, uncharted life.

Before my first day at St. Andrew's was halfway through, I realized I'd had no idea what I was signing up for—a rigorous American prep school, where teens weren't running off to nightclubs or peace marches in their free time, but kept up an exhausting schedule of activities—mock trial, the Pipe & Drum Corps, lacrosse. Usually a chatty student, I became virtually mute; it took all my energy to follow the lessons in English, and I silently drifted from class to class overwhelmed and worried. As one of a dozen new students from Latin America I would have access to teachers and tutors who would help me with my studies, a small comfort. Twice a week we had chapel, the Episcopalian faith seemingly no different than Catholicism. I relished this time we were given to ourselves, a respite from the bustling school day.

Now I wonder: How did I not seek out the guidance counselors to ease the transition, let alone my shock at Manuel's death? Didn't I trust that they would keep whatever I told them in confidence? But spilling out the troubles that had brought me to Florida felt impossible, my comprehension of English barely proficient. I passed the door marked *Guidance* with barely a glance.

And how did I not fall apart? Was it my grandmother, Silvia? I came home from that first day at St. Andrew's to find her in the back of the house, where she kept an airy studio. Silvia had never pursued a career beyond raising her three kids—my mother had two older brothers, my uncles Jonathan and Hal, and pictures of them and their families were propped throughout the house. But when she was around forty, my grandmother had started to paint. First acrylics, then watercolors and oils, mostly street scenes and landscapes. She took classes from artists at nearby colleges and attended workshops in places like Sanibel Island and Asheville. She stood under the skylight, painting, when I entered, my book bag sliding from my grasp and landing with a thud. She greeted me but didn't probe about my day—a relief. Likely she could tell it had been stressful from my frown and furrowed brow. I climbed onto a stool, her rhythmic back-and-forth of dabbling the palate, then canvas, and back again like watching Gracia dance; all along she had a funny habit of talking to the canvas. "How's that?" she asked the painting, or sometimes muttered a satisfied, "There we go." From my corner I stifled a giggle. I didn't even mind the heady fumes, poorly masked by the floral air fresheners my grandparents kept stuck in the outlets ("Country Bouquet" to me, smelled nothing like the country). When she passed by to rinse her brushes, she patted my shoulder. Like Inez, she had the assured touch of someone who has countless times soothed children and knows the fallibility of words. Often I would take solace in her studio.

My grandfather, Ben, was less attuned to my struggles. He was the type of person who was as eager to practice his Spanish as for me to learn English, and asked me all about the schools I had attended before, what Cali was like, the sugarcane—but not Papi. A few times during that first week, Silvia laid a hand on his forearm and said, "That's enough. She's been in school all day, remember?" and he apologized profusely, only to forget and ask another question a few minutes later. Did I think I liked St. Andrew's, or would I prefer to enroll in the Hebrew Day School here? No, no, I said. St. Andrew's was fine. Was there anything they could do to make me feel more at home? I shook my head, smiling. No, nothing. Their house was very nice. To myself I thought, there is nothing you can do until you are no longer strangers. Would that day would ever come? Maybe I would feel more connected to them, more gringa, once my mother arrived in a few days. Alone, I rehearsed in careful English what I planned to say to her as I turned over her equestrian trophies from high school, fingered the satin ribbons in the hallway case. An embroidered sign outside the bathroom said, *No Smoking*; the cat emerged, tail silken and teasing against my calf.

When my mother arrived Labor Day weekend I was wearing the pearl earrings—the gesture small and silly, but I didn't care. I had opted to wait at home with Silvia while Ben picked up Paula at the airport, wanting our first moments together to happen in private. I dressed in a skirt and blouse for the occasion and couldn't stop pacing. Every time a car swooshed down the street, my heart leapt. Would some part of me recognize the woman who had carried and cared for me in my first months of life, and would I see myself in her? Was it possible that we might grow close yet, maybe even closer than I had been with Papi? I knew almost nothing about Paula except that after she had left Colombia, she pursued an education at the University of Miami and now ran her own psychology practice. She had been an Israeli citizen for a number of years now and lived in Jerusalem.

My first glimpse of Paula was of her back, as she wheeled in a large suitcase. Her figure struck me first—the skinny legs, narrow hips. Oddly boyish. I approached hesitantly. She abandoned her luggage and took a few steps, then froze. She was shorter and more angular than I'd thought, her skin hardened from the sun. A few gray pieces streaked her long brown hair. Nothing like the vibrant, youthful picture beside Papi's bed. We exchanged a hug that we both cut short, the words I had so diligently rehearsed now vanished. Ben gestured to me and said something like, "She takes after you"—and I suppose I did; no wonder I looked so different from my curvy Colombian girlfriends. She held me at arm's distance and studied my face, her mouth slightly upturned. "Her eyes are his," she said, lips parting in a polite smile. If the pearl earrings struck her as familiar, she didn't say.

"Nice to meet you," I finally said.

"Yes," she said. "It is nice, isn't it?" She exchanged glances with her parents. Everyone was smiling hard, stuck between words. My grandfather bent over and fussed with her bags. I drifted to the couch and started to sit, expecting her to follow. But instead she sighed and said that she couldn't even think of visiting after such a long flight until she took a shower. She asked me a question I didn't understand, something like, "How does that sound?" and, not waiting for my answer, wheeled her suitcase down the hall. Moments later, the water blasted.

I sat there, waiting, stunned at how differently everything was happening from what I had expected. There had been no tears, no gushing, no dramatic exclamations from either of us; I felt no twinges of remembrance, no instant familial electricity. If I hadn't known she was my mother, had never seen her name on my birth certificate, I might not have believed it. Nothing more had occurred than the awkwardness of strangers meeting for the first time, because that was who we were. Only she was my mother; if we didn't like one another, what then?

Silvia busied about the kitchen while Ben mixed a cocktail. He joined me in the living room, turned on the TV. The shower stopped. Paula padded down the hall, shut the door to the guest bedroom past mine. A long time elapsed, and she didn't emerge. Ben went to check.

He returned, shrugging, and said, "She fell asleep."

So I sat there, sipping an iced, tart drink called an Arnold Palmer that Silvia had brought, waves of disappointment washing over me, and the three of us watched a special on the death of Princess Diana.

Paula emerged several hours later. The three of us had just finished dinner. When Silvia asked if she was hungry, she said not really; she'd just have some hot tea and eat something light. Her hair was still damp from her shower and sleep, and it hung in long strings down her back, and over the front of the loose, pretty, embroidered garment she was wearing—a caftan. She looked better now that she had rested. I didn't even know her age. Was she forty yet? She sat next to me, apologizing for having forgotten her Spanish. I said it was okay, that I didn't think she would know Spanish. She drew a leg up, clutched her knee. Silvia brought over tea for both of us, chamomile, which tasted like soapy weeds, then my grandparents slipped off to the living room. I asked about Israel, why she enjoyed living there.

She lifted the mug with both hands, blew onto the top. "It's lovely," she said. "Jerusalem is, I think. There are beautiful beaches, great restaurants.

It's the kind of place where once I had made a few long trips, I couldn't see myself moving back."

"You don't like Florida?" I asked. "To be near your parents?"

"Oh, of course," she said quickly. "You never forget the place where you spent your first years, before moving on. I visit whenever I can." She sipped. "How do you like Florida so far?" I told her I was not used to how flat everything was, and the intensity of the heat. I still had not been to the beach, only a few miles away. "But I'd like to," I said.

"Well, then, we'll have to go." She set down her mug. "In a way, your arrival is good timing. I usually come for a few weeks every year, for Rosh Hashanah."

I bobbed my teabag, unsure how to feel about this. Did she mean our meeting had occurred out of convenience—that I was not special? If not for the holiday, would she have put off reuniting for weeks, months?

She asked if I was familiar with Rosh Hashanah, the Jewish New Year. "Kind of funny, isn't it?" she said. "A time of new beginnings, and here we are." She flashed an inviting smile, but her voice wobbled and her gaze dropped, flitting over the table. "You know, the people who contacted us didn't tell us much. Just that you were in trouble and it would be best for you to leave. If you don't feel like talking about it now, that's fine." She blew on her tea pensively, and sipped. "But there is one thing we need to know, that is important, in case we need to get you help." She explained further. Apparently she and my grandparents had thought I might have been abused, or raped, because the call had been so sudden and urgent.

"I wasn't hurt," I said, the words rushing out. "Not the way you are thinking."

She exhaled, and her face relaxed. "That's good," she said. "I was very worried, as you can imagine. We can talk about whatever happened later, then. When you're ready."

"I'm not some girl who makes trouble. It had to do with Papi."

"Did it?" she replied. This time her gaze fixed on me. "I was afraid of that." She paused, set down her mug. "We did contact Diego about you, years ago. It didn't go well, so we thought we'd wait. I'm sorry."

Silence fell. My questions felt impolite to ask. How to get to know someone, when what you really needed was their secrets, the past they didn't want to face, let alone you? "Maybe later, I'll tell you," I said. I asked about her practice, and then she asked about my favorite subjects, both of us relieved by the easier conversation.

When we said good night in the hallway and hugged, I remember thinking how bony she was, how fragile. How miraculous and maddening life could be, for I had spoken all evening, in English, with my mother. I curled up in bed and stared at the photo of my father, and me for a long while.

The night of Paula's arrival remained one of the only times we spoke privately, however. Days were spent with my grandparents, skipping through photo albums, and hearing stories of events and people who felt as unrelated and distant to me as ancient history. Our relatives hadn't suffered in the Holocaust; Ben's family had come to America at the turn of the century, and Silvia's had narrowly escaped Germany just before Hitler's rise to power. We had a barbecue, my first experience eating hot dogs and corn on the cob. School kept me busy, and so we dined out (another costly drawback, I thought, to not having a cook at home—not realizing how expensive it is in the States to hire what Americans would call 'a personal chef'). In one week I experienced sushi, along with Indian and Thai cuisine. Rosh Hashanah was that weekend, and my uncles flew into town—Jonathan, from Manhattan, and Hal, from L.A., and their wives, and the house became a flurry of activity. My maternal family was not particularly religious, but they observed the high holidays; Silvia and the aunts cooked a big meal of traditional foods. Two of my older cousins came, also—dark-haired brothers recently finished with university, more interested in horsing around in the back yard and wrestling the ram's horn from one another than in getting to know me, a sixteen-year-old who spoke halting English. I got the impression they had showed up out of politeness, for their parents made a fuss over me. How unlike Manuel and Emilio these young men were, glued to the TV or computer when not diving in the pool, their conversations revolving around American football and movies they wanted to go see. Beyond that, they acted uninterested in the world, immature. At their age, most young men in Colombia would be working, raising young families.

My arrival became the center point of the holiday, with my uncles toasting the year ahead, "To Paula and Mercedes, as they get to know and love each other, and Mercedes, a warm welcome into the family." There was a sheet cake with my name, "Bienvenidos" and "Welcome," and what was supposed to be a llama in a Mexican sombrero, a glaring error I purposefully ignored. My uncles and aunts singled me out, but we talked little beyond the subject of school and the questions adults typically ask of teenagers whom they don't know. Did I play any instruments, or sports? Now that I was at St. Andrew's, did I hope to get into a top university like Harvard? Each steered clear of mentioning Colombia unless it came up in a general way, and I wondered what, if anything, they had been told about me, beyond my hasty escape. What activities had I participated in there, they asked. What did I do for fun, with my friends? To such questions, I shrugged and said, "Nothing, really," feeling my face turn red, for how could I explain what my life had been like in Cali, shouting cries for peace with La Maria Juventud, helping my first love, now dead, proofread letters to a guerilla leader? That I had danced at clubs and drank cocktails until 2:00 a.m.? One by one, our exchanges faltered, each of us making an excuse to get away. Quickly and happily, my newfound relatives fell into talking with one or more of their own, laughing, my uncles poking fun at their sons, the sisters-in-law chatting among themselves. Of the grandchildren I was the youngest, and the lone girl.

What I longed for was to speak more with my mother, to walk on the beach, just the two of us, which we had not done. Upon my uncles' arrival my mother had grown aloof, quiet; perhaps it was her brothers' more boisterous personalities, or maybe, like me, she was bothered by our failure to connect, the relatives a distraction. Silvia had set out plates of apples and honey; I whisked mine to the corner where my mother stood, hugging her chest, absently watching the commotion. "When do you think I can visit you?" I asked, in between bites. "In Israel?"

She jerked her head, as if lost in thought. "Oh, anytime," she said lightly, but then shook her head. "Although trips take planning, and I have my patients. Some are very difficult to leave, or take time away from, if you came for a long stay. We have plenty of time for that."

"But why can't I live with you now," I said slowly, the picture forming in my mind as I said it. I was sixteen, not a child who needed babysitting. "Couldn't I go to school there?"

She regarded me with a peculiar, quizzical expression I had seen her give her brothers when they had disagreed over a political issue, or in reaction to a tease—brow furrowed, eyes sharp and narrowed. "I don't see how that would be a good idea," she said, a defensive edge to her words. "The culture there would be even more of an adjustment than the States, and you'd have to learn Hebrew as well as English." She shook her head. "Plus, I'm unprepared to—no, you must stay with your grandparents. Learn what it is to be American. You are one, you know."

"Hebrew, I can speak that," I said, my tone upbeat. Honey trickled its way down my finger. I licked it and tossed out a few phrases I remembered from my former school.

She smiled weakly in return, told me it was a good start—that it would come in handy on a trip.

"What trip?" Silvia said. She headed for the kitchen, sticky plates in hand. As she placed the dishes in the sink I told her that I hoped to visit Israel soon. Paula was still standing there, her back to us, one hand pressed onto the counter as if she needed to hold herself up.

"Paula," I said, and when she didn't respond, I said, louder, "Mom." It was the first time I had ever called her that, and she spun around, mouth slack, staring. I stepped closer, asked how she thought I would like Israel.

"How would I know?" she said, so low I could barely understand her. "I haven't the faintest idea what you would or would not like." Without looking back she darted into the thick of the living room, where my uncles' families huddled around a board game, laughing. Silvia sidled up beside me, drying a plate. "You're here," she said. "Where does she think she's running off to?"

For the next ten days, I scrambled to balance school and getting to know my mother, who lounged poolside reading up on the latest in psychology and sociology when not at the computer, e-mailing others in her field. She was consumed by the effect of the past on her patients, former soldiers and civilians, many of whom suffered from PTSD and other disorders prevalent in conflict zones. A few of her patients had survived street bombings years ago and still battled anxiety about routine public outings. I longed to just "hang out," as my American classmates called it, but to Paula everything seemed to need a purpose; if I approached her she wanted a full report on my day at school, the very thing my fatigued mind wanted to forget. She was extremely conscious of the time, checking her watch often and announcing that it was now time to do something—time for tennis at the racquet club, time to make her packing list of things to bring back, time for a nap. This struck me as bizarre. What tasks were so urgent that they needed to happen on such a schedule, including sleep and chores? I was still struggling to grasp why my grandparents didn't employ at least one servant. But when I asked, Silvia laughed and said that hiring such help in America was too expensive, and therefore reserved for the truly rich. Besides, she loved cooking, so why pay someone?

This made me smile, but underneath I wrestled with some difficult truths. For I was getting along better with my firm but kind grandmother than Paula, whose humor I did not get, and whose stiff demeanor made it impossible for me to relax.

Evenings, after dinner, Paula would look at her watch and say, "Well, looks like it's time for a Jeremiah's"—this was an Italian ice stand several streets over. While my grandparents went for a swim, she and I walked to the stand, where we shifted in line as babysitters scolded toddlers and neighbors chatted loudly with one another.

One night as we awaited our cones, she asked, "So, tell me, which one of your classes do you like the most so far?"

I told her Spanish.

She gave a genuine groan, and declared that I wasn't allowed to pick that one. "There must be some other class you look forward to, besides Spanish."

I mentally ran through my day, but in every other course I was hanging onto the teacher's words so intently that I couldn't tell what subjects gave me pleasure or not. I'd been placed in the highest-level Spanish class, and enjoyed the poetry and short stories we read.

"Math," I lied.

And then she was gone, the day after Yom Kippur. I came home from school, flopped on the couch, and exhaled in relief, followed immediately by remorse. Was Paula always so rigid? I found this hard to believe; Papi was fun loving, for all his workaholic ways, and would not have fallen in love with her had she been purely neurotic and cerebral. She must not know how to behave around teenagers. Maybe she would be more at ease when I visited her in Israel. The dishwasher chugged and swished, and the cat leapt upon the back of the couch. I beckoned for her but she turned around, trotted down the couch and away.

We had said good-bye to each other that morning; she told me good luck with school, and that she planned on visiting again in December; maybe we could go to Miami during the holiday break. Why didn't she say something deeper, more meaningful? But there was nothing deeper to say, and certainly not "I love you." At the mention of Miami, I clouded over inside, for we had not spent a day together, just the two of us, nor discussed the circumstances which had brought me here. Maybe she, too, was waiting for my English to improve in order to share more fully. Yet I desperately wanted her to pry.

I feel more now for my mother back then. The abrupt arrival of a daughter left behind, a foreign girl she did not know, thrust upon her. The resurrection of her guilt long buried, the judgment of family saying, *See, I told you so.* What to say? How to act? At the time I was too dismayed by what had failed to happen—long intimate talks, tears and laughter, instant connection—to see how my mother's struggle was different than mine, but equally difficult. How frightened she must have been. No wonder she acted the way she did, distanced yet overbearing, behaving the way she thought a parent would act. I could not see then how I was the one who had shown up, wanting something she could not give.

Soon after my mother's departure, Papi called for the first time. It happened before dinner. I was at the dining table, studying. I wasn't yet confident enough in my English to sign up for clubs or activities, and so had thrown my energy into schoolwork as an escape. The phone rang and I didn't move to answer it; I never did, because the various American accents confused me. My grandfather picked up. Immediately I recognized the bark on the other end, relentless and enraged, unmistakable even in English—Papi. A quake of terror rocked through me, and I sat paralyzed, my hand crushing the pen. So a mere few weeks had passed, and he had found me. Either he had badgered Sister Rosemary for the number, a thought which made me cringe, although I could not see her giving into him. Or more disturbingly, he had known how to get in touch with my mother's family, all this time. I couldn't make out his exact words, but I got the gist of his accusations: how dare my grandparents and Paula think they could do this, and get away with it—who did they think he was, an idiot? I hadn't called once since I boarded the plane from Cali, didn't they think he would look up the school, call the administration? Then to find out I wasn't a boarder at all, but enrolled as a day student, living with my grandparents, my tuition paid for. What were they doing, hiding me as if I was some kind of refugee, when he had given me everything, my whole life, spoiled me, even? And what was I running away from, that I had lied and deceived him so brazenly? How could I treat him this way?

The textbook page grew damp, stuck to my palm; I felt like I was suffocating. *But you robbed me of Manuel*, I silently screamed.

Ben could not get a word in. When he finally spoke, his voice was measured, calm. "We don't know why, Diego," he said, "but what about the sixteen years you've kept her from us? What about the letters we sent through the U.S. consulate, trying to arrange for her to visit? You were not exactly cooperative—not to mention how you treated Paula." My father was ranting again, and Ben raised his voice. "I have no idea why she's here. She'll tell us when she wants to. All I know is that our only daughter is damaged because of you, and we're happy to have Mercedes, for as long as she'd like." Papi interrupted, and Ben paused, looked at me. "Do you want to speak with him?"

I thought for a moment—Papi's voice grating in my ear, his demand for impossible answers. I shook my head and mouthed, *No*.

Papi began ranting again, how already they were filling me with lies, poisoning me toward him. How if they thought this was the last they'd heard from him, they were fools as well as kidnappers. "Mercedes is free to speak with you, whenever she wants," Ben said, "but until she does, please don't call here again." And he hung up.

My pen rolled across my notebook. I didn't know how to thank him for what he'd done. "It was silly to think he wouldn't find me," I said finally. I worried about Sister Rosemary, if my father would blame her for arranging this, and punish her; maybe he had done so already. At last I was seeing what he was truly capable of. I said, "He's going to keep calling. And who knows what else."

"Let him call," Ben said, shrugging. "We'll change the number." He replaced the phone on the receiver, flicked his hand over his shoulder. "What can he do, anyway? He can't get on a plane and show up."

"No," I said quietly. "But there may be other things he can do. He knows people."

"Even if he does, Silvia and I will handle it."

"I'm sorry," I said. "I don't want all this to bother you."

"Bother?" he echoed. "We are only concerned that you are well, and can concentrate on your studies." He squeezed my shoulder. "Are you okay?"

I nodded, staring down at my textbook: twentieth-century U.S. history, spread open to Teddy Roosevelt. A wild man, controversial. I was supposed to be writing a paper on the Spanish-American war, the Battles of Las Guasimas and San Juan Hill. My crisp Social Security card had recently arrived in the mail. My U.S. passport would soon be on its way. I was fully an American now.

I was right about Papi. He kept calling, at different hours. He called twice more that week, once in the mid-afternoon, when I was visiting Silvia in her studio. She had answered so coolly, I might not have guessed it was him at all, the way she said, "No, not at this time. Mercedes isn't taking calls." I jumped at every trill of the phone. He called on Saturday morning, perhaps trying to catch me off-guard. Over the next week or two, his tone became less angry and more desperate, pleading. He would not accept just hearing reports that I was fine. Why did they treat him like a criminal, didn't they understand that I was his only daughter? Sometimes I started to leave the room but couldn't, as if addicted to his pleas, and the crumbling they ignited inside me. While I was becoming fond of my grandparents, my new school, and ironically, as Papi had impressed upon me so many times, the American way of life, I missed the hacienda terribly—the ridgebacks and mutts, my walks to visit the horses, my sunny room, the meals cooked by Inez; for all the novelty of eating out, nothing in Boca Raton tasted like home.

Still, I refused to speak with him.

I didn't speak with Ana or Gracia, either. Whenever I did pick up the phone that autumn, I hung up before dialing, at a loss over what to say. I hadn't given a thought to how hiding the truth from my friends would make subsequent communication tricky, for they would surely press me about why I had left so abruptly, without saying goodbye—and what reason could I then conjure up to explain my looming absence over the Christmas holiday, and the school breaks to follow? How could I explain that I wasn't speaking to my father, without telling them why? Best to leave those friendships behind.

After six tumultuous weeks at St. Andrew's, my social life and studies were thriving. My grades that quarter were better than ever; I had never before focused so intently and enthusiastically on them. I stayed after school often, obtaining help from instructors but also to work on group projects with classmates. I was surprised how my English improved once I was immersed, acting out *The Crucible* with my American literature class and inserting myself in lunchtime gossip. Once or twice a week I would talk to my mother before bed—we timed our calls for when she had neared the end of her workday—and kept her updated on my progress. When I told her that I had been selected for National Honor Society, she claimed to be delighted, although she remained standoffish and strained. "I look forward to celebrating your achievement when I come for Hanukkah," she said, sounding rehearsed, a robot-parent. In a follow-up e-mail, she asked that I make a wish list: things I might want her to bring from Israel, clothing items I would like as presents, meals I would like us to have. It was not even Thanksgiving.

So I tended to avoid her nightly calls, pretending to be in the bathroom or already asleep when she phoned, preferring to deal with the awkwardness between us over e-mail, rather than in person. Maybe all we needed was a few more visits, I thought, and warmer feelings would arise. Papi's sporadic, incessant calls continued for several more weeks, until my grandparents changed their number and upgraded their security system, "Just in case," Ben said. The ensuing silence on my father's end was at once a relief, and unnerving. Did I want him to forget me so completely, even when he had done wrong? Would he forget? Because as the days wore on, Ben taking me to obtain my learner's permit, teaching me how to drive around our subdivision, Silvia preparing for Paula's arrival at the onset of Hanukkah,

I found it impossible to shake my father from my thoughts. I could hear his voice, saying, You have made your choice, daughter. So be it. And after his bout of frenetic rage, then what? He would settle in, accept my estrangement, run the hacienda and conduct whatever sordid business he carried out, as he had always done. As he would continue to do, so long as he was able-bodied and able-minded.

What might I discover from my mother and grandparents, now that I felt more confident in my speaking? In December, Paula stepped off the plane with a new hairstyle, the gray streaks gone. Her hair, now a shiny brown, skimmed her shoulders. When I complimented her, she said, "It's my natural color. I thought you might like to see it." She was still hesitant toward me and unyielding in her routines. But several nights into her stay, a different side of her emerged. The four of us gathered around the menorah, candles dancing, and exchanged gifts—my uncles' families would not arrive until the last three nights, and I relished this calmer, more intimate time. My mother sat on the couch, sipping red wine, legs tucked underneath her, the most relaxed and enthused I'd seen her yet. My grandparents gave us each a framed, black-and-white photo taken during the previous visit. "Our first mother-daughter picture," I said. "It only took sixteen years!" The three of them laughed a little, but their smiles bore a hint of sadness. I told them how Papi didn't hang photos, not even of me—with the exception of Paula's portrait by his bed. Did my mother have any idea why?

At first, she said she didn't know. The Diego Martinez she had known had been high strung, a younger man who worked nonstop, held ironclad grudges, and was consumed with business, prosperity, and stability. His ambition spilled over into the drug trade, and he could not cut loose. "The last thing he wanted was the eyes of family staring down from the walls," Paula said. "And no wonder. You can't separate family from God. When you've angered them both, well, where does that leave you?" She frowned, staring into her glass.

"He has a bad temper, that's true," I said. "But if he gets angry, it's usually for a good reason. Was he so different when you knew him?"

"Different?" she scoffed. "The littlest thing would go wrong, a worker not showing up, or trouble with a farm animal, and he'd blow up. The way he yelled at the maids—I'd cringe." She shuddered and rearranged herself on the couch. "Of course, it was his humiliation and guilt over his deals that caused this terrible anger. But others took the brunt."

"What about with you?" I asked, thinking back to my grandfather's remark when Papi had called. "Was he mean?"

"No, no, I can't say that," she said. My grandparents gawked and murmured in protest at this, and she added, "Not while we were married. If anything, he was aloof in his self-centeredness, and not really attuned to my emotional struggles. He was upset when I left, but ultimately he respected it—he could have prevented my going by force, if he wanted to. Hired someone with a gun to watch me, day and night, that sort of thing, you know? But I wanted to honor our agreement, that if I left, he would keep you, and I would not use the U.S. consulate to get you back."

"But that wasn't the end of it," Ben said, his voice tense and hollow. "You ought to tell her, Paula."

My mother idly swirled the inch of wine remaining. "I'd prefer not to. But she should know."

"What?" I asked, looking from one face to the next. "Just tell me what it is."

A few years after their divorce, my grandparents wanted to come down to Colombia and visit me. "I wasn't sure if I would," my mother said, tracing a cushion. "I was earning my degrees, in the middle of these very difficult modules. You were with your father, where you belonged." They contacted Diego, broaching the idea of a visit—perhaps we could meet up some place neutral, like Cartagena or Santa Marta, have a beach vacation. But my father refused. Did they think he was that stupid, he said, when clearly they were planning on coming to take me away? No, they insisted. A simple visit had been all they wanted. To have some kind of relationship with their only granddaughter. Was he going to be so selfish, prevent his little girl from knowing her only grandparents, since his own parents were gone?

Their talks became heated, then ugly. When Paula contacted him, he insisted that she must have regretted her decision to leave by now, and so was behind this clever ploy of sending her parents down to whisk me on a plane and bring me to the U.S. "He called me names," my mother said. "He had never done that before. Did I have any idea what it was like, he said, to watch our little girl grow up without a mother, raised by maids?

Did I ever think about how I had abandoned you both? That was when we decided," she glanced at her parents, "that we would get you back. I had my career, but my parents said they'd help raise you."

They contacted the American embassy in Bogotá, started working with Consular Affairs.

The Chief of Citizen Services advised them to cease contact with Diego Martinez, so they did. Then a few months into the proceedings, they found out that the Foreign Service Officer who'd been handling their case had been killed in a suspicious accident, the coworker with her critically injured; later it was revealed their car had been tampered with. The case was delayed, reassigned. Months passed. Then they received word that the main official working on the Colombian end had been killed, shot in public while buying a newspaper. The late 1980s were a bloody time for those in Colombia with government positions; the murders may well have been coincidence. "But it was enough. I couldn't stand the thought of more lives being lost," Silvia said, shaking her head. She patted Ben's knee. "We withdrew our case."

"We don't know that he had anything to do with it," Paula said to them. "There's no proof."

"I'm sure that he did," I said.

The three of them regarded me with bewildered, curious expressions. Ben said, "You never did tell us why you left." He leaned forward with clasped hands, elbows on knees. "Were we wrong, to drop the case?"

The candles on the one end of the menorah curled and smoked. I studied their pale faces across the dim light, so eager to hear my story, my struggles with this man they only knew from a distance. A voice on the phone. "He was a good father, mostly," I said, surprised at the huskiness surrounding my words. My friends and I had gotten involved with a peace activist group this year, I told them, and one of the young leaders, a close friend, had been murdered. I had been shown proof of my father's involvement. Alarmed and frightened, I asked my tutor, a nun, to help get me out. That was all.

Why did I not tell them the whole truth—that Manuel had not been a friend, but much more? That he had not merely been killed, but had left this Earth while I cradled him on the bloody floor of a nightclub? About

Uncle Charlie's para troops training on our land, and the jefes cleaning out the dezplazados? I only knew that I sensed the heaviness that would come with such a lengthy telling; I would have to relive the events all over again, and I didn't want to. Perhaps they sensed my reservation; neither my grandparents nor Paula asked many questions, and as the conversation waned, Silvia arose and said, "All that's behind you now. Don't feel you ever have to go back, unless you want to."

Their story about Papi and the consular murders changed things. As the picture of his deeds grew, I saw what my mother had come to realize as his wife—for me to truly thrive as she'd done, my estrangement from him must be permanent and irrevocable; there was no other choice. I remained slumped in my seat as my mother collected the glasses and wrapping paper, my grandparents having already said good night. "What a shame," I said, a phrase I had recently picked up. "Because I know he's not entirely a bad man."

"Oh, definitely not," my mother said. "There is a deep warmth to Diego. I know it, more than anyone." Her eyes were shining above the candlelight, and her tone softened. "But he is angry about where his ambition led him, and because he is ashamed and distrustful of himself, he turns that brutality onto others. It is an unbreakable cycle, and I'm afraid he will never stop." She picked up her framed photo of the two of us, peeled a piece of tape from the glass. "But you're right, it is a terrible shame." She leaned over then and blew out the candles; the menorah a strangely shaped object, absent of its light.

During that first holiday season with my mother, I asked again about visiting her in Israel the upcoming summer. She assured me it was very possible, and we would make plans the next time she came, for Passover. Throughout the Florida winter, in between passing my driver's test and earning As, I surfed the Internet for photos of what Israel looked like—imagined myself floating on the Dead Sea, wandering the ancient streets of Jerusalem, shopping with my mother in open markets. Our phone conversations hovered on the surface of things, however, rife with strain and awkward pauses, as it was difficult to find common ground outside of school and her work. A few weeks before Passover, she canceled her trip—she claimed to be too stressed to travel, and would not be in good spirits for a visit. I pretended to take this in stride, but privately ached with grief. Wouldn't spending time with me raise her spirits? Already I had been wrestling with memories surrounding Passover, for it marked a year since I'd first glimpsed Manuel in the Cali square. By now Ana would have had her baby. Emilio may have been in seminary, and Gracia scouted by the big dance companies. But I had no way of knowing.

The prospect of my visiting Israel dropped away by spring's end, my grandparents suggesting we visit college campuses instead. So that's how I spent my first summer break, listening to undergraduate tour guides drone on about their school's statistics, sun beating against my neck. As we whisked along the highway, jazz station playing and air-conditioning blasting, I rested a hand on the empty seat beside me where my mother might be sitting, were she not spending her weekends on the Mediterranean with friends. When she'd wished me luck earlier that week in choosing a college, I'd thanked her, adding "Mom," and she'd caught me.

"Not yet," she said. "Call me Paula."

CHAPTER SIXTEEN

The bus broke down as we were heading south from Ramla, into the desert. Exaggerated groans and eye rolls were traded among the forty-nine passengers as we jostled along the aisle and sprung onto the sandy pavement. The tour educator paced, cell phone to ear, and minutes later announced the company was sending another coach from Tel Aviv. The mechanical trouble would delay our itinerary for a couple of hours; meanwhile, she suggested we stick to the shade and eat our boxed falafel sandwiches, which would otherwise spoil in the absence of air-conditioning. On the opposite side of the bus, traffic whooshed on the two-lane road. Some of the group shifted and eyed the armed security guard, who was talking intently with the driver; I guessed being stranded in a volatile locale was a new experience for my fellow Jewish-Americans, nearly all in college or recently graduated. Each morning the company coordinated our itinerary with the military's "situation room." If not for the chance to take a free birthright trip to Israel, most wouldn't be there.

I dug into my sandwich, determined to shrug off any worry. While tense in atmosphere, Israel was stunningly beautiful. Since our arrival several days before, vigilance had met us at every turn, reinforced not only by the armed guard riding up front but the heavy police presence on street corners and entrances to historical sites, the stern way our tour educator outlined the safety protocol on day one. Several weeks earlier, a Palestinian suicide bomber had struck a packed billiard hall in the Tel Aviv suburb of Rishon le-Zion. It was late May 2002, the summer I would turn nineteen, and hardly an ideal time for such a trip. In the year leading up to the September 11 attacks and in the months since, Israel had been plagued by terrorist violence. Barely a few days passed between attacks carried out by the most notorious militant groups: Hamas, Al Aksa Martyrs Brigades, and Islamic Jihad, among others. I felt like I'd stepped back in the Valle de Cauca of several years before. So why on Earth was I there?

Throughout high school I'd pressed to visit my mother. But then there had been the senior class trip to Europe, graduation, college preparations—I had chosen the University of Florida, wanting to be close to Ben and Silvia and within easy proximity for Paula's holiday visits. Before the millennium Israel had been relatively calm; there was no reason to believe I couldn't visit any time without fearing for my life. But as the violence escalated, talk of such a trip disappeared, replaced by my grandparents' pleas for Paula to come home, just until things quieted down. She refused, said what did they expect her to do, stop living her life? Shut down her practice, desert the onslaught of new patients, when her fellow citizens were most in need of counseling and treatment? I resented this at first, jealous of these traumatized foreigners who got to spend time with her, and perhaps knew her better than I did. I was unable to see how her stubborn streak matched my own, when Papi had insisted that I leave Colombia.

I was still determined to make the trip, a request emphatically and repeatedly denied by both her and my grandparents. With suicide bombers strolling up to Jerusalem bus stops and cafés, she could not let me explore the city, or do anything much outside her apartment, she said. My boredom was not worth the risk.

Staying inside her apartment was fine, I countered, although I fell silent when it came to relaying why. What I wanted was time for just us, the activities I guessed mothers and daughters did together—cook meals, watch movies, confide in each other. How to explain that I already knew what it was to risk one's life? To board a bus that might explode was nothing to be with someone you loved. Or might love, since I wanted to feel that way about Paula, if I just had a real chance to know her.

After an upperclassman at UF told me about the "free trip to Israel" she'd taken several years before, I eagerly broached the idea to my grandparents one weekend, and they agreed I shouldn't pass up the opportunity—in a few years, perhaps, once the violence ebbed. On her end, Paula also disapproved. I quoted her own words back to her about not giving in to terrorists, carrying on with your life. What if there would never be a perfect time to go? Besides, the student trips were carefully orchestrated and monitored, and likely the safest way to travel. I was eighteen, capable of signing up on my own. The birthright tour would pay for the airfare, and I could extend my stay. Would she refuse to see me if I showed up in Jerusalem?

My grandparents, listening from the dining room, wore heavy looks. When I hung up, triumphant, Ben said wearily, "Maybe you should think about becoming a lawyer."

Now, months later, despite the threats and having to eat my lunch in the roadside dust, my water growing warmer by the swig and legs sticky with sweat, I was enjoying myself. In the three days since our arrival, we'd seen incredible sights. When most of the group boarded the plane back to JFK, I'd be spending two more weeks with my mother, just the two of us for the first time.

I wasn't used to the pounding desert heat, however, and after eating and chatting for a few minutes, climbed inside the bus and claimed the seat behind the driver's. Inside was stifling but shady, and at least the open door provided some air. Someone else must have had the same idea; in the seat behind me, a young man napped. I didn't recognize him at first, and it wasn't until he stirred and opened his eyes that I realized he was one of the half-dozen or so young Israelis who had joined the group the day before and were to accompany us for the week ahead. He peered over the seat, squinting. I told him about the bus breaking down. "Long night?" I asked. He was badly in need of a shave. We'd spent the previous night in Tel Aviv, and most in our group had stayed out late, clubbing.

"I wish," he replied, stifling a yawn. "No, I just came off duty with the IDF."

Of course, I thought. How easy to forget that the Israeli youth traveling with us either were attending university or fulfilling their mandatory military service. "What's that like?" I asked. "Exciting, at all?"

"More like a job." I liked his accented English, and his build, tall and athletic but not stocky; in the U.S., he might have been a college baseball player. We made introductions, chatted about upcoming excursions. His name was Asaf. I asked if a lot of the youth stayed on to visit family.

"Sure, although not as many lately, for obvious reasons," he said, frowning. "Are you?" I told him that I was going to visit my mother, that she was Israeli. He seemed suddenly awake, eyes wide. "How are you on this trip, then? You should be in uniform, too, if you're Israeli." The ends of his mouth turned up as he said this, however—a flirtatious jab.

"It's complicated. She's only recently become a citizen, a few years ago. But I'm definitely American." I smiled, back to the window, enjoying the warmth between us.

"And your father?"

Through the tinted windows, the armed guard waved toward the traffic as the new coach pulled up, gears shrieking to a stop. "I was raised by my father," I said. "In Colombia."

"He's Jewish?"

"No. Just Colombian. It's a long story." Rising, I suggested we grab our stuff.

His forearm brushed mine ever so slightly. "So that's where the accent comes from," he said. "A Jewish girl raised in Colombia. I'd love to know more."

The bus trouble made us late for that afternoon's camel trek, a comical and bumpy affair. I made sure to select a camel next to Asaf's, and then wished I didn't—riding one is anything but attractive, and to my dismay I was placed ahead of him in the long line winding across the desert, so my every lurch and yelp occurred in full view. Nonetheless, I took full opportunity to shout one-liners at him, welcoming this unexpected turn. I hadn't been with anyone, or even been remotely interested, since I'd left Colombia. My two years at St. Andrew's were spent in an exhilarating whirlwind of keeping up with my Ivy League-bound peers, and I found relating with American boys a challenge, culturally. Dating consisted of attending school dances with a friend. Certainly for the first year, and most of the next, I grappled with Manuel's tragic end—replaying that night in the club, wondering, in hindsight, if I could have done anything to dissuade our going there, and maybe he'd still be alive. Fantasized about the afternoons we'd spent in his apartment, or with friends. Most of this yearning had quieted by my freshman year at UF. Not much had happened there beyond the occasional drunken party hookup, which I made sure stopped short of sex. Maybe because I had learned early on what connection and good sex could be, and I knew I wasn't missing anything in such encounters; Manuel had left an indelible impression. And I'd become a little prudish, since diving into my studies full-force—I liked taking morning classes, and hated being hungover for them.

But that night, on the cusp of beginning a new chapter with my mother, the first of what I foresaw as many more trips to Israel, once the jihadists calmed down, I squeezed in with Asaf's group during dinner—a Bedouin feast. We ate under a tent, cross-legged, enjoying the live music, wine, belly dancers. He and I continued to poke fun at each other about the camel ride, and soon we had edged away from the others, who exchanged knowing glances at what was brewing between us. What he did as a soldier intrigued me, but when I asked him about it he waved me off. "Not now," he said. In the dim light he offered me a soft round fruit—a fig.

"No thanks," I said. "I don't like them."

"That's too bad." He took a bite. "They're an aphrodisiac, you know."

As we staggered from the tent I cornered the couple of girls I'd befriended, their names long forgotten to me now, and asked if someone had a condom. One of them said, "No, but I'm sure he does. You know he must get with a girl on every trip."

Maybe that was true. Maybe not. He knew a place, away from the tents, and led me there. I'd never seen anything like the desert at night. Past the toilets the camels rested, their saddles from the trek earlier heaped together. First we sat atop the saddles, talking and pointing out the stars; the blankets and leather smelled of dust and animal sweat. He hadn't meant to be rude when I had asked him about his role in the military, but recently he had been recruited for an elite special operations unit, which meant he'd be embarking on a full-time defense force career. He didn't want everyone knowing about it yet, but he had wanted such an assignment for a long time. "Why's it so important to you?" I asked. He gazed at me, surprised; we had slid down and reclined between the saddles, hidden from view. "My sister's best friend was killed this year, in a restaurant bombing," he said.

"Plus I have other family members who've suffered, uncles who died fighting, who I never met. Haven't you? In Colombia."

"Yes," I said, "although it didn't exactly happen like that." And for the first time, I told him, a stranger, the story about Manuel. How I had been in love with a peace activist who was taken out by a hit man, shot dead in front of me at sixteen. How this had prompted my flight to the U.S. I left out the part about my father's involvement, as it seemed too much to explain. "It's not something I've told my American friends about," I said.

"How devastating for you," he said, tucking a piece of my hair behind my ear. His eyes never left my face. "I'm so sorry. But that's what I'm talking about, see? You know the stakes we face here. These American kids don't. You'd make a good Israeli." His grin gleamed in the moonlight.

"What about peace?" I asked.

"Peace? Eliminating the troublemakers before they blow up a marketplace, that's peace." We were kissing then between the saddles and blankets; I let him remove my top but stopped there. Sometime later I sneaked back to my quarters, grateful to find my roommate's place absent; hushed laughter sounded from neighboring tents. I told myself not to expect anything more than a pleasurable fling, although by the way we had talked I sensed something beyond chemistry. Had he, as well?

Over the next few days, Asaf and I tried to keep some distance between us as we hopped on and off the bus, hiking the Ein Ovdat National Park and the Roman Ramp at Masada. While romances often sparked within the group, Asaf said the tour educators didn't appreciate them being flaunted, especially when one of the parties involved was Israeli and represented the organization. On the bus and at mealtimes we were careful to choose seats apart, only daring to shoot one another the infrequent conspiratorial glance. Ultimately, however, we drifted nearer, and at certain locales, could not help but pair off. In Masada we descended the Snake Path to the Dead Sea, strolled until we found a deserted spot, entered the water together. I thought I had never encountered a natural phenomenon so bizarre, with its chunks of salt like snowdrifts on the banks. Asaf laughed at my attempts to swim strokes. "You don't swim in the Dead Sea, you float," he said. "Here, let me help." He bobbed closer and slid a hand under my bikini bottom, giving me a playful squeeze. Salt choked the turquoise water; flecks crusted our lips and eyelashes. A half-moon scar graced his forehead, just above his right eyebrow. We forgot who saw us. His mouth tasted of lip balm and salt.

The minerals and strong sun made me relaxed, blissful. As the bus barreled toward Jerusalem, our destination for the remaining days, I wondered—what my mother's apartment and neighborhood would look like, if I would feel at home there. How she must be preparing for my arrival, even now. Our previous visits had always included my grandparents; how would she be different once we were alone, on her territory? A new, unexpected side of her might emerge, cultured and nuanced in ways I couldn't expect. She would introduce me to her Israeli friends, speak Hebrew. Surely she knew some restaurants where we could dine out of harm's way, in hidden courtyards or behind walled gardens. Had she delayed my visit for so long because she had been afraid I would fall in love with her adopted country, despite the latest carnage, follow her to where she had escaped the past and reinvented herself? For I had taken to Israel on my own, and what could she do if circumstances eventually brought me here as an adult? I'd slept with Asaf, one evening while my suitemate stayed out, and I was already fantasizing about a possible future with him. Premature and risky, perhaps, at so early a stage. But also not far-fetched, as I knew couples met under similar circumstances, followed lovers to other countries all the time.

That evening after dinner, most of the group was getting ready to go out. I stopped by Asaf's room and knocked, but heard only silence, and left disenchanted. Minutes later, he slipped a note under my door: *Just got back. Roommate is leaving. Come over.*

He led me inside; we undressed each other in the lamplight. After our excursion earlier in the Dead Sea, we were eager and deliberate. I pulled off his T-shirt, he loosened his jeans, and I caught my breath, taken aback by the slim holster circling his abdomen, the concealed automatic. I asked what make and model it was, and if he always carried it. "What, you think the security guard is the only one who's armed on that bus of fifty people?" he replied, shaking his head. His eyes flashed in amusement as he tugged off the belt and I recalled Fidel crossing the yard, jerkily unbuckling the holster and 9mm from his waist as he strode to his quarters. Skimming a finger along the barrel, I told Asaf I never would have guessed, and how had he kept that hidden when we'd undressed above the beach that morning? Grinning, he said, "That's the whole point," and kissed me deeply, his fingers kneading the hair at the nape of my neck, drawing me toward him. Like Manuel, he exhibited a sureness that I responded to, although the look in his eyes was different, warm but calculating, a trained swiftness that Manuel had lacked. He told me a secret then—that this tour would be the last for a while, those following having been placed on indefinite hiatus, as the violence showed no sign of diminishing.

When it was over, we talked more about his upcoming training. What kind of life he would lead, as a special ops soldier, the equivalent to our Navy Seals, the years ahead imbued with discretion, secrecy. He would be well compensated, his family taken care of. But whomever he married would have to accept the fact that only a portion of him would be available to them; the dark side must remain dark. "What do you think about us—about Israel?" he asked me. As we spoke I lay curled inside his arm, the automatic staring back from where he'd left it on the table. Emboldened by our electric day, I decided to confide more in him as well—prove that I was a woman who could handle ambiguity and danger in her lover's occupation, after all, I'd done so before. I told him more about what had happened in Cali— how I'd been shown evidence that my father had arranged for my boyfriend's murder. That my father had committed many crimes, likely still did, and this was why I'd estranged myself from him. My life lay elsewhere now, in America. And perhaps, one day, in Israel, for my mother didn't appear to be leaving anytime soon.

He had been running his fingers through my hair, and as I spoke he did this more slowly, until he stopped. I told him more than was necessary, certain that he would find my background intriguing. "That's some startling information," he said at last , a thoughtful look on his face. "I'm glad you told me."

Since it was getting late and the others would be coming back soon, we ended our night. Inside the door we lingered, and he kissed me just as intently as before. Both of us grinning, he brushed my backside as I slipped out.

By the next morning, something had changed. At breakfast Asaf chose another table, which would not have bothered me except that he barely met my gaze and nodded hello when we both lined up for coffee. Our morning excursion was to the Yad Vashem Holocaust Memorial, followed by the Children's Memorial, the Valley of the Communities, and the Boulevard of the Righteous among the Nations, and for the duration he acted preoccupied and aloof; I attributed this to the solemnity of the occasion, as silence had descended upon the group. But by the time we had moved on to Mt. Herzl, which held the graves of Theodore Herzl and other Zionist luminaries such as Golda Meir and Yitzhak Rabin, along with young soldiers who gave their lives to create and protect the State of Israel, his behavior toward me was unmistakable: I'd joined my roommate and a few others, Asaf among them, and after a moment or two of conversation in which he had looked everywhere but me, he meandered off.

Everything inside me felt like it had been hurled over a cliff. I marched over to him, asked what was going on.

"Nothing," he said, his tone one of forced nonchalance. "Just that we should probably get used to being separate, since we only have two days left. I don't want to give you the impression that this was going somewhere beyond this trip."

"I don't understand. Last night, the way we were talking—"

"Never mind last night. Look, I like you a lot, Mercedes." He glanced at me briefly, then beyond, toward the soldiers' graves. "It's just that you're not going to be my wife, that's all." I stood there, dumbly, aware that our frowns and curt, private exchange had caught others' attention. So I had mistaken a holiday fling for something more, hardly the first woman to do so, but it was the confusion that stung more than the humiliation. Did Asaf share his secrets so freely, with whichever girl he singled out on each tour? Or had I done something to put him off? I replayed the recent events, but could think of nothing that had occurred, no moment of awkwardness or misspoken ridicule. Just the salty sea, laughter, lust. I climbed the bus, groped for my seat, my whole body throbbing with the loss. A few rows up, he was chatting animatedly with another girl about heading down to Eilat, a raucous beach town, at tour's end.

That night, Asaf and the other Israelis of the group planned to lead an excursion to Ben Yehuda Street. At the end of dinner I said I was feeling unwell, and as I headed for my room caught his eyes following me. I thought maybe he would knock later, or slip a note under my door offering some further explanation or condolence. But he did not.

The following day, our last, we toured the Supreme Court building and the Knesset, Israel's parliament, but as the guides detailed the political system and challenges faced when combining ancient laws and traditions with modern life, I hardly listened, I was so consumed with heartbreak. Later, we made a farewell visit to the Western Wall. I found a spot, as alone as I could make myself from the group, rested my forehead on the ancient rock, and wept; those nearby must have believed I was very religious, indeed. The outpouring served me well, for after I composed myself I was at least able to enjoy a pleasant dinner, seated beside my roommate and other new friends. The tour educator said some parting words and announced that at the close of dinner the young Israelis who had accompanied us would be departing. When Asaf arose and left, I pushed in my chair and hurried after him. Apparently he had checked out already, for in the lobby he shouldered his duffel bag, exiting for the street.

I called after him, jogged up. He turned around, regarded me without a flinch.

"So that's it?" I asked. "You weren't even going to tell me good-bye?"

"I thought it might be easier not to," he said, shifting his weight. "Who wants unhappy memories, right?"

"It was cruel what you said the other night. About how I would never be your wife." I swayed on the sidewalk, hands on hips.

"Cruel, yes. I didn't mean to be anything but honest." He hung his head.

"What the hell did you mean by that? Is it because I'm not religious?"

He lifted his chin. "Not at all. That could be easily corrected." The last word piqued my attention, such a conscious choice. *Corrected.* "Just please, forget it. I wish you a wonderful time with your mother. And, if you feel called to it, I hope you might someday become one of us." He smiled warmly as he said this, clapped a hand on my shoulder. He turned his back, walked away.

"Tell me, will you?" I said. "No matter how personal. I want to hear it."

He stopped, slowly faced me again. "Fine," he said, and approached. He stepped close, so that I could see where the points of his scar disappeared, his breath on my cheek and voice low in my ear, even-keeled. "When I take the assignment I told you about, I'll be in the absolute highest level top-secret clearance, and I'm afraid we Israelis have even stricter standards than the U.S. If I'm with a woman whose father is an international criminal, tied to drugs and terrorism, and who knows what else—it's impossible. I don't want to be associated with that. Unfair, I know, and you can hate me for it. But the person you should really hate is your father, from what it sounds like. For how he's tainted you." He kissed my temple, and the top of my head. Then he said "Shalom, kol tuv," and walked away.

I stared into the space where he'd been, long after he was gone, feeling battered and bereft, mute with shock at something so unforeseeable and hopeless. Was this how it was going to be—opposition and judgment whenever I shared my ordeal? Then I would never be free of my past. I had been foolish to speak so freely about such a grave aspect of my life with someone I had fallen for, but barely knew. Yet the others were waiting for me inside; I had to pick myself up. Say more good-byes, pack. Dial the local number my grandparents had given me, the address not far away. Pray that no one would detonate a bomb while I was crossing the street.

So it was under these circumstances that I reunited with my mother: pitched forward by disaster.

Paula met me outside the hotel the next morning. We embraced as the taxi driver loaded my bags—our most heartfelt hug yet, but her clothes couldn't hide the weight she had lost, and she had let her hair fade to gray again. As we set off through the streets, I asked her why she'd stopped the fashionable cuts and dye-jobs. She pinched a piece, lifted it up into the sunlight streaming in. "Hair," she said absently, "who has time for it?" She let it drop, said, "I've been worried sick about you all week."

"You didn't have to be. They didn't let us out of their sight."

We headed out of downtown, toward Knesset and the government precinct to the west. So she didn't have a car then, I thought, feeling somewhat sad to watch the shops, cafés, and quaint pedestrian streets of the city center fall away, replaced by bland hotels and office towers.

Nor did she live in one of the hip, pedestrian-friendly areas where I had spent the last several days; only now did I become aware of how much I had been picturing this—that while strolling with the tour group around

Zion Square and King George and King David Streets, I'd been imagining my mother around the corner, shopping or having tea with a friend. Ducking through a back alley to an apartment, worn, with chipped fixtures, but charming. Flower boxes and cobblestones. A fantasy. I asked where she lived, if she usually took the bus.

"West Jerusalem. I'm afraid it's not very appealing, after where you've been staying. As for the bus, yes, I do. But cabs are safer these days."

"Isn't that how most people get around, though? By bus?"

"Of course. But I don't recommend it right now." She shot me an imploring look.

"Just wondering. Papi never let me take the bus in Cali, either."

"Well, I'm sure he had good reasons."

We took a broad avenue, twisting and turning. I asked where she worked, and she pointed out a western hilltop and the Hadassah Medical Center—her practice was part of that complex. She also pointed out the nearby campus of Hebrew University, and I craned my neck to spot the buildings. I envisioned studying there for a graduate degree.

Just as I was hoping we'd continue past a cluster of high-rise apartments, we pulled into one. I murmured something about how convenient this must be, for her to live this close to work, fighting back my plunging disappointment. Across the street there was a park; on the corner, what appeared to be a convenience store and snack shop. Nothing else but the roaring highway, the bus stop. Inside, a sour-smelling elevator lifted us to the seventh floor.

Her apartment was neat and clean, but spare. The furniture and décor dated from the 1980s, and I guessed she must not have bought new things since she first moved here. Herbs, vitamins, and boxes of tea bloomed beside the fridge; she ran water in the kettle, set it to boil. Above the couch hung a large abstract painting, swirls of dark pink, blue, and white. Fallen books occupied the shelves, spines slanting in diagonals. The latest *Jerusalem Post* headlined the most recent attack—a car packed with explosives had hit a bus traveling from Tel-Aviv to Tiberias, killing seventeen and injuring thirty-eight. In the hallway, a photo of my mother in scuba gear, surrounded by friends, gave me pause. "I had no idea you did that," I said.

"Only on occasion. Diving helps me relax."

My room, with its narrow window and twin bed, had a musty odor. An ironing board perched at the footboard. Paula rummaged in the hall closet, handed me a stack of towels. "Well, here you are then," she said, her smile brief. She asked if I had laundry—while she washed clothes, maybe I ought to take a nap? I dug out my soiled clothes, handed them over. At last alone, the door shut, I let out a shuddering breath. I couldn't believe the life my mother had claimed for herself was so bleak—a drab apartment, a lifeless street. Did she not care how she lived? Did she find her thrills elsewhere? Maybe she entertained friends, guests. I knew nothing of her romantic life. She must earn a good living. Perhaps she lived frugally in order to afford diving trips, dinner parties, airfare to Florida and my university degree. Although I had been told my grandparents were helping to pay for that.

But when I shook out a towel the edges were frayed, the terrycloth thin and taut. I flung it aside and decided to shower later. Inside the sheets, I inhaled the sharp scent of dust, stale air. The phone rang; she did not answer. I recalled that in the vacation photo, she appeared around thirty. So this was what she had built, the life she had left me for, and continued to choose. I was so shocked and appalled, I could not even cry.

For two hours I slept deeply, and awoke to the aroma of sizzling meat and vegetables. I fumbled for my toiletry kit. The bathroom sink exhibited no signs of feminine routine, the soap a stiff brown cake of scummy cracks that refused to lather no matter how hot the water. I had run out of toothpaste and borrowed hers, a foreign brand, licorice-flavored. On my way out I flipped back the shower curtain, relieved at the natural sponge hanging up, jar of salt scrub, shaving gel. Another photo, of Paula on a sailboat with friends, albeit dated, hung above the toilet.

She greeted me but kept focused on the stove, asked if lamb was okay. I said sure, even though my diet veered more toward vegetarian lately, something I had announced during our last visit, which she had apparently forgotten. I asked what she had planned for us to do.

"Nothing too involved, I'm afraid," she said. "I would have taken a few days off, but we can't go touring, so what's the point?"

I was chewing an olive, and considered what she meant by this. "But

I'm sure there's some place we could still go, that's not likely to get bombed. How's Jordan these days?" I said, attempting to joke.

She continued, glib and clear voiced, as if she hadn't heard me. "It's too bad you came at such an unpredictable time. We'll catch up at night, though. I've told everyone you're here for now, so they'll be leaving us alone."

"I won't be meeting your friends?"

Her lips parted in surprise and she stepped back from the stove, dumbfounded. "My friends? They're all older and married. I didn't think you'd care to hang around them."

"But that's why I'm here. Why else did I come?" I slouched against the counter, dropped my chin. The table could seat six; it was set for two. There would be no gatherings to anticipate, I realized, no one to pester about her social life, dates gone awry, or funny vacation stories. So she expected me to do nothing but stay there all day, not even visit the homes of the friends she alluded to? Now I wondered if she had any. Did she intend on showing me nothing of her neighborhood, her office, places we could visit in cabs or by trusted rides?

"You can read, relax. There's an exercise room and pool downstairs." She arranged the lamb, couscous, and vegetables on plates. Midway between carrying them over, she paused. "I hope you're not going to hold this against me, that I work long hours, because there's nothing to be done. Before you came, you said you'd be fine with that, and I'm betting you had plenty of fun on the trip you were just on—knowing the Israeli youth, probably too much. So under no circumstances should you be out. Please, just give me that peace of mind."

"Fine," I said. Nineteen was too old to sulk.

Dinner conversation consisted of me telling her about the places I'd seen over the last ten days— the rugged volcanic mountains of the Golan, the soft-sand beaches of Tel Aviv, the intense heat of the Negev. But when she probed about whom I'd met, if there had been anyone special, I pretended to be stuck chewing a fatty piece of lamb. As the meat rolled in my mouth I was reminded of Asaf; the last time I'd eaten lamb had been as a guest of the Bedouin villagers, that surreal night with him underneath the tent, and later, the empty, starlit desert. I longed to tell my mother, yes, I had met someone—and there she waited, as ready to hear the story as I was willing to tell it. But was I? I had never told her nor anyone besides Asaf the full story of Manuel's murder, how exactly Papi had ordered Manuel killed; as far as Paula knew, I'd never had a boyfriend. So how could I explain this sudden, intense romance with Asaf, and why things had fallen apart? She would furrow her eyebrows at me in that unusual manner of hers, press me further. I swallowed the lamb, drank some water. "No," I said. "Maybe next time."

The next morning I slept in, although Paula's morning routine woke me. Coffee gurgled and the radio spat a report in Hebrew; I guessed my mother listened for news on the latest attacks before she went to work. I stayed in bed, not wanting to emerge and receive a last-minute lecture on why I was to remain indoors. She left, the flat once again silent. In Florida, we only listened intently to news radio when a hurricane threatened the coast.

When I arose later I plopped in front of the TV—the channels all in Hebrew, a few in English, nothing I cared to watch. One by one, I sifted through her books, mostly mental health texts, and skimmed through for photos or notes that might be stuck inside, clues to the life she led now. Nothing fell out but the occasional index card with a scribbled question or author to look up. Brimming with the desire to find, do something, I combed through the bathroom and her bedroom, careful to replace each item I picked up. Her closet teemed with stylish clothes now several seasons out of date; same with the shoes. A pair of flippers leaned in the corner, coated in a glimmer of dust, next to worn hiking boots, and a faded one-piece swimsuit drooped from a hanger. Perhaps my mother was more of an outdoorswoman than I'd thought.

More telling were the items lacking. Paula kept a small pouch of cosmetics, a lone, full bottle of Estee Lauder perfume on her dresser. In her bedside drawer I found no clues to her sex life like one might expect—just an eye mask and earplugs. A scuffed underwater camera rested in a case. I sat back on my heels, chiding myself for being surprised. My mother had left her old life behind to come here; why would I think she had held onto what she had sought to forget? Maybe because I hoped she would have wanted to cling to something, no matter what pain it brought.

But by afternoon's end, I'd torn her room diligently apart and back again. There was no mistake—she owned no photos of me nor Papi, not a scrap of anything I would have recognized from the hacienda. She had done everything she could to purge my existence from her reality, and in its place erected a scholarly spinsterhood dashed with intermittent adventure. Now I was an unexpected addendum to this life, someone she would accommodate like a patient but not fully embrace; after such purposeful reinvention, she was incapable. She did not even consider me worthy enough to take time off work, or to impress with new towels.

In this mood I fled the apartment for the pool and gym. Both turned out to be just as dour and unimpressive as the rest of the building. Residents were still at work; the workout machines stood empty, the stained chaise lounges vacant. The pool overlooked the sea of concrete rooftops and antennas that sprouted down the hillsides of the New City, as this part of Jerusalem was called. In the strong, inviting sunshine I read one of my mother's nonfiction titles called *Reviving Ophelia*, about troubled adolescent girls. Had she purchased it thinking of me, believing she needed to figure me out? The book profiled girls who were anorexic or cut themselves, and couldn't be further from my experience. How nice that must be, to have the sort of troubles that could be looked up in a book, prescribed remedies. Cleaned and sewn like a cut.

That evening I wanted to talk to my mother about possibly visiting her office one day. But there had been yet another attack—three Israelis, including a pregnant woman, killed, and five injured when an armed terrorist infiltrated the community of Carmei Tzur, south of Jerusalem. Hamas claimed responsibility. "That's not far at all," Paula remarked before the TV, rubbing her hands. I guessed going anywhere would be out of the question, so I remained silent.

Still, I didn't listen to the news reports, or stay inside the apartment like my mother.

The following morning I ventured out to the living area shortly after Paula's key clicked in the lock. The early light streamed across the carpet, the traffic rushed below. Twenty minutes away, one of the most ancient cities in the world awaited, a treasure I hadn't fully explored—was I going to spend nearly two more weeks holed up in stale rooms, or tanning on a concrete rooftop?

I dressed and hopped in a cab, asked to go downtown, to the Jaffa Gate. Once there I roamed the Old City, hiked along the ramparts and peered down, into the hidden courtyards and alleyways. Our birthright tour had focused on the Jewish Quarter, synagogues and the Cardo; in the coming days I visited the Islamic shrines and mosques on the Temple Mount, the Church of the Holy Sepulcher, and the Dome of the Rock. I snacked at hummus parlors and bakeries, viewed the city from the top of the Petra Hotel, sipped fresh carrot juice and explored the Ethiopian Monastery. Every morning when I left, the only rule I set was to explore something new—not a difficult task in an intricate, four-thousand-year-old city. The wave of suicide bombings made the crowds in even popular sites nonexistent. I constantly surveyed my surroundings for signs of danger, but I also relished this tempting of fate, fueled by my anger. If not for these mad countries, I thought, I might not have lost Manuel, nor Asaf. Wasn't this my birthright, to pursue a vibrant life without fearing other human beings? I had survived such a place before; I would do it again.

Looking back, I cringe at my rashness and naiveté—not for leaving the confines of the apartment, but for never leaving a note, so that in case something happened, my mother would have had an idea of where to find me. My conviction that all would turn out well, that I would not be blown up, turned out to be correct, if only due to luck. Whether my decision to wander on my own was foolish or courageous, I had no regrets about my boldness on that trip. The greatest affair of your life is when you fall back in love with yourself. After Asaf, I badly needed to find my center. I doubt I would have if I had remained on a roof, tanning and reading pop psychology books, obsessing over his rejection.

I made sure to cut my afternoons short and return no later than four-thirty, just in case Paula arrived home early. But she didn't, and as my trip wound to a close yet another letdown grew in place of my longing for her. At six she showed up with a bag of groceries or take-out; after the meal we stayed up talking, but mostly about larger topics—Israel's situation, the position with the U.S., my grandparents' and her brothers' opinions. I could barely keep from flaunting my exploits to her. One night I said, "It's a shame there's so much unrest. I intended on traveling more." I paused. "I've been thinking I want to spend spring semester in Argentina. What do you think?"

A long moment passed as my mother took this in. "Argentina? Why there?"

"Because I've always wanted to go there. And if I major in Latin American Studies, it's a requirement."

She frowned, made her funny look as if she smelled something bad. "I don't think that's a good idea. Not at all. What about that English class you told me you loved? If you have to study abroad, why not go to England? Or Spain, at least?"

"Spain isn't Latin America. And I don't think you'd be acting this way if I said I was interested in Judaic studies."

She tossed down her napkin, massaged her temples. "Don't you think it would be much healthier for you to go in a totally new direction?" she said. "Because I do. You think by studying, you'll find what you're looking for. But believe me, you won't."

"Since when have you ever considered what was healthy for me?"

Any other parent would have retorted something then—*That's enough*, or called me a spoiled brat. I willed her to, but she did not. She abruptly arose, scraped her plate into the garbage, and drifted down the hall. Moments later, I heard her laughing on her phone, the bath water running.

The news flickered across the TV; since my arrival at Paula's a pipe bomb had exploded in a restaurant north of Tel Aviv, and children had been injured from a roadside bomb. Earlier that day, while I had been admiring Bedouin embroidery in the bazaar, nineteen people were killed and more than seventy injured in a suicide bombing on a bus just outside of Jerusalem. The bus, which was completely destroyed, had many students on board. Cali of 1999 paled in comparison to this, a suicide bomber detonating every few days. Guerillas in Colombia didn't dream of blowing themselves up. While my mother tried to soothe her fears, I began to pack. For all the beauty I'd found in Israel, I didn't plan on returning until the bloodshed stopped. I had no reason to.

That fall at the University of Florida, I began the research that would evolve into my senior thesis on Colombia's history of violence. Most revealing was what happened after the cartels' collapse. That after Pablo Escobar's death, the collapse of the cartels and the vigilante group, Los Pepes, numerous former leaders went on to head paramilitaries. Others disappeared: were either killed or slipped underneath the radar. I stumbled upon the names of the men who for years had worked for my father, held various positions overseeing the farm, and likely still did. When I was a little girl they had spun me over the lawn, my arms outstretched like airplane wings, until I burst with squeals of laughter. They had brought me gifts: trinkets, stuffed toys, foreign candy. For weeks those names kept me up at night: *Guillermo*, *Vincente*, *Luis*. Only I couldn't remember their faces.

I found out, too, that Archbishop Duarte had warned priests not to become personally involved in the civil war. In the 1980s and '90s, many clergy had mistakenly taken sides when the leaders of opposed rebel groups contacted the bishops to seek the Church's assistance in mediation, with brutal consequences. Duarte had warned Colombians about speaking out directly against the atrocities committed by the insurgents. Many individuals who publically denounced the ELN, the FARC, and the AUC became targets, their names placed at the top of hit lists only to be kidnapped, killed or "disappeared" soon after. Activists spoke out at their own risk.

So I had never fully understood the dangers Emilio, and ultimately Manuel, took on under the auspices of *La Maria Juventud Para Justicia Social.*

One night that fall—it must have been early in the semester, as I hadn't decided about Argentina yet—I had been invited back to a party in a dorm room. A bong was passed around, thick marijuana smoke sweetening the air, and one of the rich American boys, freckle-faced and with the collar of his polo popped, brought out a mirror trimmed in gold. I never touched drugs, so this was rare for me to be amidst them. The boy was no older than Manuel had been; I had known him for a year. He laughed, asked if he could rest the mirror on my lap. Because I liked him I said yes, even though I knew what he was going to do. Perhaps because I knew, I sought the experience. And he set a plastic baggy-covered white rock on the mirror. He broke off crystallized chunks with a razor as if the rock was an iceberg, and I couldn't take my eyes off of the thing—the blood-stained jewel of my country was not diamonds or emeralds, but cocaine. The boy asked if I minded as he diced up the crystals into furrows. "Go ahead," I replied.

One by one the fraternity brothers bent over the gilded mirror that might have been from Ana's house and snorted line after line of the crushed white powder from my lap. With each raggedy inhalation and tossed back head, I saw the faces of the desplazados along the muddy road, the bandidos with rifles pointed at the bus as babies screamed, Manuel's bloody torso on my thighs where the cold mirror rested, the beginning and the end. I recalled Uncle Charlie's words about the drug war stopping when the gringo appetite for cocaine stopped. I peered through the remaining crystals like scattered snowflakes at my reflection, my dark hair adorned as if covered in the white lace of Ana's bridal veil. Only my first love was behind me, along with my father and my homeland, and the mirror, hardly magic, showed nothing extraordinary.

Nothing, yet everything. For that was when I knew.

I would become an expert.

CHAPTER SEVENTEEN

My mother and I were having dinner at a restaurant my first week in California when she told me she was dating someone. She laughed and turned her head in embarrassment as she announced it, hiding her mouth behind her wrist, awaiting my response. I sat back, smile frozen, dumbstruck. My hand hovered over the artichoke appetizer, leaf pinched between my fingertips. For several days we'd been huffing and grunting up and down the stairs of my new apartment, between jaunts to Pier One and Target; she'd had plenty of occasions to tell me, although the visit had been rife with spats thus far. I turned twenty-five that week, and we were supposed to be celebrating my birthday, as well as my doctoral studies at Berkeley's long-established program which would start in several weeks. After earning the PhD, I hoped to land a research or policy position in the public or private sector, probably in Washington, D.C. or South America.

Behind our booth, a pianist played airy notes. The restaurant was filled with warm chatter, aromas. Her news momentarily knocked aside the irritation and fatigue of the past few days, my curiosity a liberating reprieve. "You've met someone?" I asked. "Who? Where?"

"You couldn't tell?" she replied, and sipped some wine. "I thought the whole world could read my face." And it was true, she looked different this visit, although I had determined her more relaxed demeanor to the diminishing hazards of living in Israel, now that the surge of the early 2000s had ceased. She was no longer rushing around her office, seeing patients back to back—families traumatized by the loss of an entire branch, adult children, in-laws, infants. She actually had time to go out for lunch, the Jerusalem eateries bustling again with security guards posted at the entryways; maybe this accounted for the filling out of her face and middle. While I was in college, my mother's hair had turned a silvery-grey, and on nights like tonight, when she wore her shimmery cascade of curls clipped back, she looked attractive, sophisticated. She was seeing an Israeli she'd met on a rafting trip last year in Turkey, she said.

I raised my glass in a toast, congratulated her on meeting a nice Jewish man.

"Oh, no," she said quickly, our glasses chiming. "He's Arab."

"You're kidding. That's not problematic?"

"Not yet. He's a Christian Arab."

I raised my eyebrows, took a sip. Throughout dinner, I asked more questions—what did he do for a living? Did he have a family, and what were they like? If he had been married, what had happened to his wife? Was he a practiced outdoorsman, or an amateur, like my mother? I wanted to know about his personality, his looks, picture him in my mind, even if I'd never met him. And all the while wondering how similar or different he might be to Papi, if in some way, this stranger would measure up, or surpass him. Or maybe my yearning didn't have as much to do with Papi as the promise of my mother sharing her life with someone who might also one day matter to me. By the time dessert arrived, I'd exhausted the topic. "I imagine you'll be meeting someone soon," she said. By the upswing in her tone this sounded like a deliberate diversion. "Hopefully more your equal than the last one."

She was referring to Gabe, my boyfriend of two years at UF, and I couldn't suppress the grin creeping across my face. "He wasn't so bad," I said. She shot me her funny look and I erupted into giggles, nearly spewing my coffee. Gabe and I had met studying abroad in Buenos Aires, a haphazard affair ignited by romping around an idyllic setting late at night, after too many drinks—a carefree romance that rekindled on campus the following fall. Half-Dominican, half Jewish, he'd been what my mother called "cute but crunchy"—a slight-framed, mop-haired young man who headed up a student environmental club, skateboarded and trotted around barefoot like his musician idol, Michael Franti. Gabe had been mellow and affable, unfocused at times, but I accepted this in exchange for his easy-going nature. Early on I'd sketched out the briefest details of my past to him, something he never questioned, maybe because he didn't have to. He graduated a year before me, our parting sad but expected. Easy come, easy go, I thought, wondering where Gabe was now, halfway around the world in some village without electricity. Aside from commenting on his sporadic Facebook posts, we hadn't reconnected since he'd taken his Peace Corps assignment in Africa. The latest I'd heard was that he had signed on for another two years.

"I'd like that very much," I said. "To meet someone, fall in love." I gazed into my coffee, stirring its contents. "But that's not why I'm here." The waiter returned with Paula's credit card. She scooped up the pen and signed. "How about you?" I asked. "Are you in love?"

Her eyes darted over the receipt, and she set it down. "I don't know yet," she said. "Nothing's quite like the first love of your life."

I thought of Manuel, us hand-in-hand in the Cali streets. The chilly nights on the back of his motorcycle, my cheek pressed against his jacket. "No," I replied. "It's not."

She leaned across the table, into the light. "I know it must be hard even now, but don't let it be one of those things that haunts you the rest of your life," she said. "It's not worth it. He was a perfectly nice young man, if unremarkable. I know I've told you many times. Good ole Gabe." She sighed, rising, pulling on her coat. "He just wasn't a keeper."

The week in Berkeley marked a turning point between us, although I never would have predicted that from the outset. My mother had offered to accompany me in getting settled, claiming that my grandparents, now in their seventies, couldn't very well assist with a cross-country move. I suspected the real reason was because she was feeling guilty, in hindsight, for missing my graduation from UF the previous year, due to a conference in Sweden. Never mind that she had known my graduation date a full year in advance. Paula had never approved of my career decision and battled it all the way, even when I graduated with accolades from my program, a five-year BA/MA in Latin American Studies, and received a Fulbright to spend the next year in northern Ecuador. At the time, I could only read her skipping out on my graduation as a snub—her attempt at having the last say. But as we hung pictures and instructed delivery men on where to place the mattress, she was nothing but supportive. My decision to embark on the PhD may have at last won her attention and respect, or maybe her new Arab lover had convinced her otherwise; I'll probably never know.

One night when we were unpacking boxes, however, I came across the only photo of me and Manuel, bent-edged. Gracia had taken it the night of the street festival, before the argument that drove Manuel and me our separate ways. I propped it against my dresser mirror. Throughout my stay in Ecuador, I'd sensed the Colombian border pressing upon me like an invisible storm from the north, something I both hungered for and resisted. In my Fulbright proposal I'd stated I wanted to study the effects of the narcotics trade and desplazados on the rural villages of the Ecuadorian Andes. But I knew even as I was writing it that I could have chosen anywhere—so why a few hundred miles from my birthplace? "I always thought I never wanted to go back," I said, studying the photo. The childlike smoothness of my face, the shining eyes—expectant, trusting. "But lately I'm not so sure."

"Going back doesn't mean you have to visit anyone in particular," she said. "Unless you want to. Remember that." She took the photo from me gingerly, asked who the young man was.

"Just an old boyfriend. In Cali."

"Really? He's got a striking look in his eyes." She handed the photo back. "I'm sure your career will bring you there sooner or later. Then the decision will partly be made for you."

"I don't think it will be that easy."

"Did I say it would?"

I didn't answer. I stuck the picture inside the mirror's frame. She resumed unpacking. "If you like, you can call me Mom," she said. "It's taken long enough to get here, I realize. But I think I'd like that."

My Advanced Portuguese class met on Tuesday and Thursday afternoons. I sat in the back with the handful of other grad students, where we teetered in our chairs and cracked jokes under our breath. Portuguese, although required, wasn't officially part of our coursework like the Core Colloquium and Seminars, and therefore crowned the fun class by tacit agreement. After taking a few semesters of the language at UF, I considered myself proficient but not fluent. I wanted to take an Advanced Brazilian literature course, however, and needed to brush up. Unlike my peers who obsessed over Brazil's rise as a developing nation, and could talk endlessly about deforestation and the pitfalls of ethanol, my interest stopped at Elizabeth Bishop and the samba. I was already too busy preparing my proposal for a Tinker Summer Research Grant to El Salvador.

Jeremy, who sat to my left, was one of the Brazil enthusiasts. During class he would lean in and politely ask me to clarify a grammatical construction or pronunciation. He spoke with a North Carolinian drawl that took me some time to adjust to, and dressed as if on his way to someone's lawn party for a mint julep—seersucker shirts, chinos, flip-flops. Sometimes he wore oversized glasses that I guessed were fashionable somehow, and he had a way of smoothing back his silky brown hair that I found charming. I'd never met anyone like him; how he had developed such a passionate dedication to Brazilian studies remained a mystery. All I knew was that we were both on track to finish our PhDs in three years, he with a focus in City and Regional Planning. I also spoke better Portuguese than he did, and this made him jealous in a subtle, gentlemanly way. Then a few weeks into the semester, he found out from someone that I'd won a Fulbright the year before. The next time he sat down beside me he wore a bashful smile and said, "So why didn't you tell me you're the new darling of the program?" After that he joked less openly in my presence, and I sensed him regarding me with a quiet awe, one that left me both flattered and uncomfortable.

Camaraderie aside, I felt nothing for Jeremy. But it was enough to prompt my asking if he would like my help with Portuguese. He was earning Bs and at nearly every class, expressed his frustration with the language not coming easily to him. At first he thanked me profusely but declined, saying he couldn't imagine taking up my valuable time when he could just find another tutor, a native-speaking undergrad. It's no trouble, I insisted, and thought of my apartment, room after empty room, the squeaky new furniture and vast surfaces. The awkward, desperate privacy. I suggested we meet at a restaurant.

We decided on Nino's, a pizzeria near campus that also featured Brazilian fare. It was late afternoon, the dining room nearly empty. He ordered a dark beer called a Xingu, and for me a Palma Loca. We both stalled then, maybe because we realized that we hardly knew enough about one another to launch into a contrived foreign conversation. "After this," I said, and nodded toward my raised pilsner. "It helps loosen up your speaking ability, you know." He said the only thing drinking loosened about his tongue was him talking too much, and that had landed him in a fix more than once. A fix, I asked, what's that? His eyes danced at me as he took a long swig of beer. Trouble, he replied, smirking. Usually with women, but only occasionally. The afternoon was warm. He had rolled up the sleeves of his shirt, a deep blue linen, and his bare forearms rested against the table. I liked their shape. I wondered about North Carolina, asked him what it looked like—someplace I had never visited.

"Beaches and mountains, and tobacco farms in between." He traced a thumb on the foamy rim. "But anyone from there'll tell you that Carolina's the most beautiful place on earth." He said this with his head slanted, gazing nowhere in particular, but I felt like I could see right through him. He was homesick for his state the way I had been for my country, and still was—the kind of yearning so agonizing that you bury it, or else it will eat you alive. With his buoyant personality I doubted others in our program detected this.

"It must be beautiful," I said. "North Carolina sounds like Colombia."

"Is that where you're from? *Martinez*—I was wondering."

"Originally. I've lived here since high school. What about you? Travel to Brazil much?" He cradled his beer with both hands, shook his head. "But I hope to," he said. "As long as you don't snag all the summer research money." Beneath the table he nudged me with his foot. His interest in Brazil arose from his family history, he said. The Hopkins' clan had originally been Episcopalian, and while his parents' generation had long since dropped away from churchgoing, his great-grandparents had been missionaries there in the early twentieth century—they had even brought one of the first motorized combines with them, hauled the pieces in separate boxes through the jungle; to this day, his family heard the combine was still in use, the Hopkins name revered by the village elders. As for him, he had only traveled to Brazil once, on a college trip to Rio de Janeiro, and while there had taken one of the famous "slum tours." Afterward, he had difficulty dismissing the shacks and filthy children picking through garbage, and sensed his grandparents' unfinished work calling him. Only he had no interest in descending into the horror himself, but thought he might do more good on the policy end. "What was it like, where you grew up in Colombia?" he asked.

"Lots of sugarcane," I said. Beer empty, a wave of drowsiness and elation hit me. Sifting through my memory was like treading through dreams, it had been so long. Had that life even been real? Was it really possible, that had I not seen the folder proving Papi's guilt with my own eyes, that I might be riding along beside him in his pickup, discussing the crop, which fields to plant and which to leave fallow, partner and heiress to his millions—rather than drinking beer on a sunny afternoon in Berkeley? I said, "The maids used to lay out a school uniform each morning, while I was at breakfast. I would go upstairs, and it would be freshly pressed on my window seat." I laughed. "Do you know they actually helped me dress until I was twelve? Can you imagine?"

"Sounds like something out of the old South." He signaled the bartender, ordered another beer.

"Oh, it was crazier than that," I replied. But my laughter died off. He was leaning closer, gaze flitting over me, eager for more. His foot brushed my ankle again. "Well," I said, catching my breath. "I suppose we should begin."

Nino's remained on our regular rotation of study locales, a favorite haunt of the LAS students. After our Advanced Portuguese mid-term the grad students decided to meet up there. Three hours later, half-empty Palma Locas, Xingus, and abandoned pizzas cramming our table, conversation drifted to various plights—namely the bloodshed now ravaging Mexico as the drug-trafficking highways shifted north. This was my area of expertise, or what I hoped would be after next summer. The field work I conducted in El Salvador would shed light on the key players in Colombia, where much of the coca still originated. Afterward, I wanted to write an article that would double as the cornerstone of my dissertation.

"It sounds fantastic," Julie said. "I wish I'd thought of it." She was a second-year doctoral candidate, and the only other female there.

"How'd you become so interested in this, anyway?" Jeremy asked. He balanced a glass of bourbon and melted ice on his knee. "Something you experienced in Colombia, growing up?" He exchanged looks with Julie and Sergio, whose parents were Panamanian. They shifted toward me, waiting.

It was a fair enough question, one I should have been expecting. By now, everyone had shared what brought them to pursue graduate work, except for me. "I suppose it was my whole experience of growing up there," I said slowly. "Not that I want you to get the wrong impression. It wasn't like I walked in on mounds of cocaine and scales on the kitchen counter."

They laughed. "But she had maids, and a driver," Jeremy said. His face was pink and slightly damp, and he shot me a knowing look over his bourbon. "I just made up the driver part, but am I right?"

"Yes." Laughter again. I clutched the handle of my mug, sipped. "We all did."

"Maids," Julie said, a slight hint of disapproval in her voice. "I'd love to hear about it, though. How you grew up."

"Me too," Sergio said. "Probably not very different from how I was raised, in Panama." All eyes fixed on me. I couldn't disappoint them now, and it was too late to make up a reason to leave. So I sat up and told them the story they wanted to hear. That I had spent my childhood on one of the largest sugarcane plantations in the Valle de Cauca, and saw firsthand the hundreds of impoverished displaced who fled the violence of the mountains for the cities, begged on the streets, squatted in slums. That when I was fifteen, I fell in love with a peace activist who was murdered one night at a club, but that no one knew for sure who ordered the hit. Afterward I left for school in the States, enrolled in college. "You can look up the newspaper reports," I said. "The authorities never charged anyone. They thought it must have been either the FARC, or the paramilitaries." The waitress stopped by, asking if anyone needed anything, but no one looked up.

"That's so unbelievably sad," Julie said. She was leaning toward me, chin cupped in her palm. "He died in your arms. I can't imagine."

"That must be difficult, when you go back," Sergio said. "To be faced with all that. I know how weird it is when I visit Panama. Like your life is split in two."

"Well, Mercedes doesn't strike me as the type who'd be hanging out in the slums," Jeremy said to him, joking. His leg jiggled under the table and his hair was mussed from where his fingers had been anxiously running through it for the duration of my story. "I'm sure things aren't so bad on the hacienda." He turned to me. "Sounds like your father runs quite an operation. You know some characters, I bet."

"What do you mean?" I asked, frowning.

Sergio slapped him lightly on the chest, said, "Come on, it's not like her father's a drug lord." He shook his head to himself, but he was still smiling.

Jeremy brushed him off good-naturedly. "Don't be ridiculous, you know that's not what I meant," he said, waving his bourbon between them. "I'm just saying, with horses and alpacas and maids running around, that sure as hell must have been a colorful upbringing, is all."

I nodded, although a lightheadedness came over me. I mumbled something then, like I appreciated them listening so intently, and Julie said wasn't it great we could gain such a clearer understanding of where each of us was coming from in our research. We paid and shuffled out, the restaurant bustling with the dinner rush. Outside the moon was shining, the temperature brisk. Jeremy's questions, and the others', had been genuine and innocent, yet I looked down and away, seething at him for putting me on the spot. Forcing me to deliver the Hollywood version of events that outwardly my peers deemed cliché and inauthentic. Yet secretly this was the story they wanted to hear, the only story. Love and blood. I might have told all, gone ahead and given them what they wanted—my father's history as a trafficker, my knowledge of his arranging Manuel's murder. But the truth would have been over the top for them, and I would have risked credibility and resentment. I'd been smart in my restraint. So why was I still so angry?

I said a hasty goodbye, peeled away from the group. My apartment was a ten minute walk. Jeremy jogged after me, asked, "May I see you home?"

"I'm fine."

"No, let me."

We trudged up the hill, both of us shivering in the chill. He put his arm around me, but I shrugged him off. "Hey," he said, alarmed. I quickened my gait so that he wouldn't see I was crying. Under a street lamp he caught my sleeve; I stopped abruptly and we bumped into each other. "I'm so sorry," he said, and ran his hand up my arm. I rested my cheek against his chest, inhaled his clean shirt smell mixed with the aroma of the pizzeria; he held me, and we rocked for a minute. "Come on, my place is closer," he said. I clung gratefully to him. We turned down a side street, and another, climbed the porch steps. The house was a Victorian divided into apartments. He opened a door on the first floor hallway, flicked on a lamp. In the shadows I could see the room was big and white, with a white baby grand piano, and an oversized couch with colored pillows.

I'd stopped crying. Jeremy wiped underneath my eye with his thumb. He kissed me, his mouth sweet and strong with bourbon, my first taste. We backed up together through the room, collapsed onto the couch.

Piano notes pinged in the dawn. I pulled on the T-shirt Jeremy had given me the night before, crept out of his bedroom. Sunlight streamed through the parlor's tall windows, dust floating in the beams. He was dressed in a brown cashmere robe, his eyes closed and hair fallen across his forehead as he played. I hung back until he finished, then ran my fingers along the instrument's satiny edge, asked if it was his.

He shook his head, pulled his glasses from his robe pocket, wiped them. "I've got a Steinway, back in Carolina. You can imagine the cost to ship it. But this is why I chose the place. The tuner said this one's actually decent. Owner doesn't have a clue." He peered through the lenses, replaced them in his pocket. "I acted like a damn fool at the restaurant," he said. "Will you forgive me?"

"I'm sorry if I gave you a shock, with that story."

"I'm glad to have heard it."

I took his face in my hands—he appeared different without his glasses, more boyish. He reached underneath the shirt and felt my nakedness, drew me close and buried his head in my middle. "God, I've wanted this to happen for weeks," he said, his voice muffled. "Haven't you?" He lifted the material, kissed my belly.

I pulled him to stand, led him toward the bedroom. Through the walls and ceilings came the sounds of footsteps, the inhabitants shutting drawers, blasting showers. I stripped off the shirt, climbed back into his bed. As he curled his arm around me, I thought, *I am deliriously happy.*

Within several weeks we were spending most nights at one or another's apartment, when not grabbing lunch together on campus or studying in the bookstore café. All of which became an enormous effort, my mind and body having melted into the haze of falling in love. If Jeremy had the same struggles, he didn't let on—he was the type of student that professors glance to when a question hangs in the air too long. While the rest of us scribbled notes or stared off, trying to appear pensive, Jeremy jumped in with a salient point. There was a casual, almost offhanded manner in his delivery; you might even assume by the way he slouched and twirled his pen that he hadn't been listening. From the beginning I had been drawn to his intellect and lack of pretense, and later on I wondered how I had overlooked the even-keeled warmth between us as a sign of something more—that the cornerstone of a great relationship might not lie in a flush of desire, but in a trusted friend. Someone who shared similar passions and perspectives, and laughed with you at the end of a hard day.

I preferred his place, because I could study more easily in the sunny, main room with the wooden floor and high ceilings. My apartment, although newly remodeled, was smaller, and I found it impossible to write papers when he came over, or do anything much besides read, make love, or eat. One day in late October when I was working at his dining table, I mentioned Thanksgiving. I thought we might go somewhere that weekend, escape the city for wine country or a national park.

He leaned against the counter, drinking iced tea. "Won't you be seeing your family?" Trying to brush off my fading hopes, I shrugged. "Not for Thanksgiving." The holiday had never been a big deal with my grandparents, for Paula was never there; the three of us went out to the same fancy restaurant in Boca every year. I asked, "You're really going to fly all that way just for a dinner?"

As soon as I said the words, I wished I hadn't. "It's not just a dinner," he said with a disbelieving chuckle. "My mama goes all out. I promise you've never seen such a feast. All the cousins come, my sisters and brother. I wouldn't dream of missing it." He poured a second glass of tea. "You're invited, you know."

"I'll be fine staying here, really."

He frowned. "But what are you going to do here, all alone?"

"I didn't grow up with that holiday, remember?"

"True. But that just means you don't know what you're missing." He set the iced tea before me, rumpled my hair and kissed the top of my head.

I reached behind me, touched his cheek. "Please stay. I want to go somewhere, just us. See the redwoods."

He breathed into my hair, said, "Maybe." Then, after a pause, added, "How come you didn't ever spend Thanksgiving with your mother? Sounds like a weird custody arrangement."

"It wasn't actually an arrangement. Probably difficult to understand, if your family's not estranged."

He drifted away, to the couch where his laptop and papers lay strewn. "Estranged?" he echoed, and faced me, hand on hip. "My folks divorced when I was a kid, then remarried each other when I was twelve. Then got divorced again when I was eighteen. Now they insist they're the best of friends, and my father comes to every holiday and get together." He drained his tea and shoved a pillow aside before he sat down. "So let's just say I'm no stranger to the strange."

I released a breath I hadn't realized I'd been holding. "Wow. That's right out of a telenovela."

"Yeah, well, it doesn't feel like a TV show when it's happening. As you know." He didn't pick up his laptop right away, but rested his elbows on his knees, stroked his face.

I turned back to the article I'd been highlighting, but when I reached the end of the page I couldn't recall what I'd read. How did it happen, two people falling so far away from one another, and then years later, finding their way back again—was it because of children, or memories? Was there an intangible bond that could never be erased, or was love damaged once those involved had broken it—reparable, but never again the same, like a crystal bowl glued back together? Yet somehow, despite the mess, his family had struck some common ground. "Don't worry about me," I said at last. "Go home, see your family. I want to get a jump on finals, anyway."

"I'm glad you understand," he said. "But I haven't booked my ticket yet, so I'll stay." Smiling, he added, "We'll go see the redwoods."

That summer, the university approved our travel grants. I was off to El Salvador, Jeremy to Brazil for over two months. My field research on narcotic transport routes was slow-going but revealing. Mexico had become the Colombia of the 1980s and '90s, rife with kidnappings and murder—only those who disappeared ended up in mass graves, rather than delivered home in buses arranged by the Red Cross, the Sinaloa, Juarez, Tijuana, and Gulf cartels now the predominant wholesale distributors of South American cocaine. In Colombia, smaller, more agile organizations such as the Norte del Valle Cartel, had replaced the notorious alliances of my youth, and utilized para groups to protect their labs and associates. Midway through, I knew my dissertation would be sorely incomplete without conducting a field study in Mexico, and so made the arrangements. When I broke the news to Jeremy over Skype, his face in the grainy video stream turned grim. Earlier we had discussed my coming down to visit him when I had finished, spend a few days at the beach before we headed back to the States. My extension in Mexico would leave no room for that. "What about Colombia?" he asked. "Won't you be going there, to see your father?"

I paused, considering my options—to outright lie or tell some version of the truth. "I guess I've never made this clear," I said, "but my father and I don't speak. We had a falling out when I was a teenager."

"You're kidding," he replied. "Over what?"

"I'd rather leave it at that, if you don't mind."

"But a teenage falling out—can't you make amends? I was mad at my father, the second time he left, but—"

"This is nothing like that, I promise," I said. "Please, can we both agree to just drop it?"

"Fine. It's just that I love you, and I don't want to see you do something you might regret. Maybe it's my religious roots, but the older I get, the more I find most sins forgivable."

I nodded, said I love you, and signed off. *Most sins*. If I told him everything, would he believe murder to be forgivable? Plotted and carried out in front of a sixteen-year-old daughter? Never mind all the others. Or would the altruist in Jeremy press me to reconcile? For I hardly feared that he would dismiss me the way Asaf had; Jeremy had no cause. We were fast becoming the type of couple who finished each other's sentences and laughed madly at inside jokes. With him my doubts were deeper and murkier; I loved him so much, I worried I would make some grievous, unforeseeable misstep. I shook out the photos I carried with me, tucked inside my passport—me and Manuel, and the picture taken with my mother that reunion weekend. The old holiday shot with Tía Leo and Jacki—how could I ever go to Costa Rica and not think of them, take the chance of running into each other somewhere? Small countries are like big towns: climb a hill and you bump into somebody. I had not seen them since estranging myself from Papi, and who knows what they would think, if they would welcome or shun me.

The last photo was the one of me as a baby with my parents. I held it until the edges smudged. I thought of my Berkeley apartment, as absent of framed photos as the house in which I'd grown up. That's what happens to a past riddled with secrets—forced to disappear along with what it hides. Excommunicated from display.

My dissertation won an award, announced by the faculty Chair at the banquet the week of graduation. Afterward, fellow classmates flocked the table, eager to hear my next steps. Did I have excerpts forthcoming in journals, or better yet, a publisher interested in the manuscript? Would I be hitting the academic job market that fall? They had reason to be curious, for I had kept quiet that spring. I hadn't wanted to get my hopes up, or stir jealousy, but a Distinguished Visiting Professor, the former President of Ecuador, impressed by my research, had put me in touch with several contacts in Washington, D.C. Over Spring Break, I had flown out for an interview with the State Department. The job would involve rigorous research, and over the next few years, would likely take a more public turn—they wanted a bright, articulate, multilingual specialist to amass the latest reports on the bloodbaths spilling across the U.S. border, and to present before committees and dignitaries, perhaps even the press. Most importantly, the ideal candidate was to exhibit the highest level of dedication and ethics; my dissertation's focus on how the shifting narco-trade routes affected civilians had caught their attention.

"I grew up in Colombia," I told the hiring committee. "You won't find a more highly motivated candidate." For most of the process I'd held my breath, worried they would quiz me further, suddenly foist a Top Secret clearance requirement upon me, despite my initial contact for the job having insisted that I didn't need one; those more exciting avenues had been cut off, thanks to who my father was. Once findings reached my desk they would be declassified, just in need of assembly into coherent reports. The day of the banquet, the offer came.

Jeremy's parents and my mother were to attend our graduation, and I was apprehensive about everyone meeting—the questions I guessed his parents might ask about my father's whereabouts, and if my mother would act rattled and flighty. I told him to simply say that my father and I were estranged, and he agreed. His parents were flying out together, staying in the same hotel but in separate rooms. Neither had remarried. "My mother just wants to enjoy her friends, but my father"—Jeremy frowned—"he never talks about it, but I sense he's pretty lonely."

I had been half-expecting Paula to bring the man she'd been seeing for the past several years—he'd yet to make a trip with her to the States, or meet my grandparents. But when I met her in the hotel lobby, she was alone, in a long, flowing skirt and silk blouse. I asked about him, and she shook her head, stared at the floor. "It's over," she said. "I meant to tell you when we talked, but somehow I just couldn't." Sadness struck me; it was the first time I felt for my mother as a fellow woman, in mourning over love's loss.

"What happened?" I asked. "Was it the cultural difference?"

"Yes, but not entirely," she said. "The longer you're forging your way in the world alone, the more battle wounds you acquire. As does the other person. And so the harder it becomes to kindle something healthy and strong."

We met for dinner. Jeremy's parents made a stark contrast. His mother wore a short, sleeveless dress that showed off her shapely, tanned figure, and her blonde hair grazed her chin; she was talkative and laughed a lot.

Jeremy took after her in looks; they shared the same round face. But I could see more of his personality in his contemplative father, a slight, greying man who sat by solemnly as his former wife gossiped about relatives and critiqued the restaurant, but made his words count when he spoke; I liked him immediately. He played the piano, and when I brought this up, saying, "I hear you're something of a songwriter," he sheepishly waved it off.

"Nonsense," Jeremy cut in. "He's a regular James Taylor."

"It's true," his mother chimed.

Listening to them was like watching a game of badminton—comments flying, Jeremy's mother urging me to try a sip of her specialty martini, his father chewing thoughtfully, seemingly lost in his own world until he asked about my dissertation. Paula quizzed Jeremy on Brazil, leaving me to get to know his parents. I asked about his brother and sisters in North Carolina, with whom he was close. "Now that you'll be on the East Coast, we expect you to visit," his mother said. "Holidays in the mountains, summers at the beach. Right, honey?" she said to Jeremy. "You've been hiding this lovely girl from us for far too long."

"Only from you, Mama," he replied, a bemused edge to his tone. He and his father shared a fleeting glance.

"It'll be nice to be so close," I said quickly. "I only hope my new job gives me time off."

Dinner concluded, we parted out front. Jeremy's mother had drunk three martinis, but she was the one who steered his father by the elbow as they stepped out to hail a cab. By all appearances they interacted like any other long-married couple; were they really going back to separate hotel rooms, to sleep alone? What kind of scars underlay their affections, forced them apart? Was it the usual vices—drinking, infidelity—or another, more sinister, less visible thorn? They offered for my mother to ride with them; as Jeremy hugged them goodbye, she and I walked around to the other door. Embracing me, she said in my ear, "I couldn't imagine two people better suited. It's clear he adores you."

"He does, doesn't he?" I said. A warm breeze kissed my face, rippled through my mother's silver hair.

"I never would have predicted this when you announced your major, and I'm sorry for the hard time I gave you back then," she said, her voice trembling. "But lately I've taken a lot of solace in your happiness—and now with this position in D.C." She shook her head, smiling; her tears glistened in the twilight. Climbing in, she said, "You'll have everything I never had." She tucked her skirt after her and slammed the door.

CHAPTER EIGHTEEN

We drove to D.C. cross-country, and for the first time I experienced the expanse of America—the steep valleys of the Rockies and bleak towns of the northern plains. Washington D.C. I'd barely glimpsed on my quick jaunt for the interview. Nothing could have prepared me for seeing the pillared monuments and famous buildings up close, the well-laid boulevards and outdoor cafés buzzing with youthful energy. Hastily we settled on an apartment in Arlington, too pricey for our budget, but I fell in love with the neighborhood. With the recession, we hadn't been sure about how long Jeremy might have to search for a job. But in three weeks, he landed a position at a program funded by the Department of Energy and a large foundation to bring solar lighting to the developing world. They needed someone to head up the Brazilian sector; occasional travel was required. He was ecstatic, and I couldn't be happier for him.

The bigger adjustment remained my job. With the violence in Mexico hardly waning, and Arizona citizens in an uproar as the cartels dumped bodies across the border, pressure to assess information pouring in and develop new strategies had reached an all-time high. My small team of bilingual experts fielded calls and viewed footage from Central American authorities—street battles with police, mass graves of disfigured victims, and high-profile arrests. The disturbing images and long, rigorous workday drained me; I felt as if where I'd lived until now, Florida and California, had been a somewhat sleepy and unreal existence; here was the real thing, the mission I was meant to pursue, in the trenches, as the saying goes. Such footage made a grim reminder that real lives hung in the balance. Soon I came and went dreading what landed upon my desk, but also addicted to it.

Most importantly, however, the move steered us to discuss marriage and eventually, children. We were both twenty-eight, and still in love; I couldn't foresee anything obstructing us.

In a few years we'd move to the suburbs, both of us having reached higher, hopefully more influential positions, be able to trade back and forth as needed with childcare and travel; perhaps our children could even accompany us. I wanted it all, and why not? In the grocery store I glided my cart past the fruit display, the bright labels curling atop the pineapples and bananas: Dole and Chiquita.

That November, we spent Thanksgiving in North Carolina. Jeremy's mother had retired to Asheville, although she still kept a summer home in the Outer Banks. As we wound through the mountains, the leaves brilliant and bold, I couldn't quash the fluttering in my stomach. I didn't say much, and Jeremy noticed. "Nervous?" he said, grinning. He'd been excited about this for weeks, not only the "Southern feast" as he dubbed the dinner, but finally introducing me to his family. He kept assuring me that I'd fit right in; they were a warm and welcoming bunch, "practically South American" he joked. I didn't know quite what I was so shaky about—nothing had been as nerve-wracking as meeting my uncles' families that long ago Rosh Hashanah, with my limited English, the customs so foreign. And I really was looking forward to meeting his brother, sisters, and their spouses, who ranged in age from twenty-five to thirty-three, plus the cousins; at long last, I'd get to know what it would be like, having an extended family which included people my age.

We pulled up to a spacious, log-cabin style house. Two young women, one with a baby nestled against her shoulder, talked and rocked on a porch swing. Both were stylishly but comfortably dressed; a Ralph Lauren logo peeked from underneath the younger woman's cascading honey brown hair. Jeremy introduced the woman with the baby as Kat, the oldest of his siblings, and the other sister as Jill, almost thirty and finishing school to become an obstetrician. At the door his younger brother, Wade, met us, a taller, thinner version of Jeremy, without the heart-shaped face and high forehead. In looks, Jill and Wade most resembled their father, while Jeremy and Kat took after their mother.

Every seat in the living room was occupied by a relative: wrinkled, fresh-faced, and every age in between. Children squealed over toys by the fire, and two fluffy cats perched on tabletops. Jeremy introduced me to his grandmother, a frail eighty-nine-year old who smiled and took me in with pale, watery eyes, although just as quickly, her gaze fell back to the cacophonous room. "She's not very lucid anymore," he said softly, "but she likes to be with family." I nodded, wondering if that was true, or if the hubbub might be too much for an elderly person—for the house was like a festival unto itself, delightfully swarming with food, laughter and chatter. We entered the kitchen, shaking more hands and kissing more cheeks, and I tried not to be overwhelmed. So many cousins, great aunts and uncles, I had never fully imagined what a close, extended family looked like. Would my father's family have once resembled this bunch? Jeremy's aunts stirred and stooped, delivering casseroles from the oven; after hugs, his mother poured us some red wine and refilled hers, the pours more than generous. His father hovered in the hallway, drink drooping. His eyes lit up when he saw me, and I asked if he would play the piano for us later. "I don't usually, but I will," he said. "Hardly anyone ever asks."

At dinner Jeremy and I sat among his brother and sisters, and stuffed ourselves. Conversation revolved around how we were adjusting to D.C.; his sisters reminded me of their mother, whose attention fixed on whoever was new to the circle, and Kat, especially, was no exception. Kat's slight overbite was offset by her rather beguiling green eyes, and she asked questions with a certain amount of disarming, offhanded charm, like Jeremy. But when he left with Wade to watch football, an awkward lull arose. "It's so nice that your father's included," I said quickly. "Even though he keeps to himself."

"We wouldn't dream of not inviting him," Kat replied. "That is, Mama can't stand to be seen as inhospitable, or rocking the boat."

"Really? I guessed there was more to it than that. More between them."

"They're good about coming together for the big events, like weddings and Kat's baby," Jill said. "The small things that need tending between two people, that's where they fail."

I drank this in, along with my coffee. "You're lucky to have them in the same room at all. And to host this big dinner. You do this every year? And for Christmas, too?"

Kat looked up from the baby, whom she was feeding. "Doesn't yours? Otherwise I'm curious where you've been, with Jeremy just bringing you around now."

"Of course we do." I explained how I usually spent Hanukkah and Passover in Florida. "But it's very different, unfortunately. My parents don't speak."

"That might be a blessing," Jill said. "If you were spared years of fighting. I know I'm not the only one traumatized by all the bickering and name-calling." She excused herself then, off to check a football score.

Frowning, Kat turned to me. "Isn't your family Catholic? I hear they go all out in South America, for Easter. You must have a ton of family down there."

"I don't know," I said, pouring cream and stirring.

She laughed. "What do you mean, you don't know?"

"Just that my family was scattered years ago, during the civil war. I don't know those relatives." I sipped the coffee and set it down, not really wanting more.

"How awful—I'm sorry. That's so difficult to imagine."

"Is it? Well, I suppose no family is spared their share of tragedy," I said. "Whether it's divorce, or something else." Jeremy's father caught my eye from across the room, pointed at the piano. I waved, rising, and asked Kat if she wanted to come and listen to him play.

"No thanks," she said. "I've heard enough, watching him go broke and us too, fancying himself the next Billy Joel. Never did I think I'd have to watch my father spend his retirement working for the Home Depot." She adjusted the baby, shook her head. "But you got it right. Some families' tragedy is just the quieter type."

My career took off that year, in ways I couldn't have imagined. Our first summer in D.C., I'd begun contacting literary agents who represented nonfiction about my dissertation manuscript, and by the winter I'd landed one who was willing to work with me on a revision to give the book a more commercial slant while still remaining an "NPR book" as she called it. "Drug trafficking is a sexy topic, mysterious and dangerous," she said, and insisted it would sell. For the rest of the winter and spring I toiled over the manuscript, with Jeremy providing feedback. Together, we invented a new title, *Cocaine Highways: The Changing Lanes of Drug Trafficking from Colombia to Mexico*, sent it to the agent, and crossed our fingers. In September, a little over a year since I'd accepted the job, the manuscript sold to a mid-sized but respectable imprint of a major publisher. The advance wasn't huge, but we went out to dinner and clinked champagne flutes nonetheless. "What do you think I should do with the money?" I asked. "Maybe we should go on a trip someplace."

"A honeymoon, you mean?" he said, leaning in. "We could definitely use the money for that, get married this year or next."

"Maybe we should elope. Get everything over with at once."

"Elope? That's for sissies. I want to do things in style."

I raised my champagne, the bubbles tickling my nose. A wedding, yes. But more important was the book, and what it meant for my career.

The day after I received my copy of the contract, I marched into my superior's office and proudly showed it off, announcing the book's release date the following year. Timing can sometimes prove uncannily optimal; in my case, the media liaison position above me had just opened up, and I expressed that I wanted the job. Within two weeks, I was no longer straining my neck over incoming reports but overseeing my former team, and shortly after that, presented before my first committee. Then we got word of another wave of horrifying violence: forty-nine mutilated bodies dumped on a highway in northeastern Mexico, a hundred miles from the U.S. border. CNN contacted our office, wanting an expert for a live segment that afternoon—me. As I dashed off to meet the cameras, I texted Jeremy—*Making my debut on national news at one p.m.!* He wrote back, *You're a star.*

The segment only lasted a few minutes, but felt like an eternity. Somehow the lights and microphone signaled me to step outside myself, into a role. Was this what I'd been seeking, the glorious authority of a public persona? My nerves jumped as I waited, but when the host spoke through my earpiece at last, posing the first question, the answers formed easily. Yes, Mexico had deployed military forces and bolstered police, but the latest incident proved that doing so had limited effectiveness. I disagreed with the other guest expert who insisted we must do more. The U.S. could not curtail the violence or send troops, I said, but must assist Mexico however possible in finding a solution on its own. The segment rounding to a close, I was given "the last word." The host said, "Some say this really isn't as big a problem as it seems because the drug criminals are only retaliating against each other. Is that true?"

I lowered my chin slightly at the camera. "Fifty-thousand lives have been lost so far, including innocents caught in the crossfire. It's a downward spiral, and everyone is affected, eventually. Who wants to invest, let alone stay, in a lawless nation?"

The earpiece cut out, the camera turned off. I was sweating underneath my blazer and scarf. In the restroom, I couldn't wipe the smile from my face. Not yet thirty, with a book coming out and interviewed as an expert on CNN. I guessed Jeremy was right: I was a rising star.

On a Saturday soon after, the foreign embassies opened their doors and showcased their countries with free food, music, art, and lectures. Jeremy and I wandered embassy row with Julie and Sergio, our fellow Berkeley alumni; both had acquired jobs in D.C. after graduation. Tired but exhilarated, Jeremy and I parted from them in the late afternoon. He insisted we stop by the Peruvian embassy, where they were giving away sopaipillas and picarones, the dough greasy, coated with powdered sugar and too hot to eat. He paced impatiently while I finished mine and wiped my fingers, then dragged me over to where a vendor was selling miniature stuffed llamas, made from real fur. Jeremy suggested I pick one out, and I laughed, asking what on earth would we do with such a thing, but the vendor thrust a llama at us anyway. Jeremy, grinning and bouncing on his heels, insisted I take it. As my hands dove into the soft fur, a shiver jolted through me—tied to one of the pom-poms around the toy's neck was a glinting diamond ring. He didn't get down on one knee in the swarm of people, thank God, but tugged off the ring and shakily proposed marriage. I croaked out a yes, too surprised for words and yet not—for hadn't our lives been unfolding in this direction since we first met? With the foreign weight of the gem on my hand, we strolled toward the Metro, arms linked, soaking in the day's magic. Those who know the harmony of shared silence are a great treasure. Jeremy was such a person, and I'll be forever grateful for that.

My happiness was short-lived. The following evening, we each called our immediate family members to share the news. Paula's congratulations sounded heartfelt but weary, and I asked her what was wrong. She dreaded having to tell me this, she said, and hamper such a special phone call. But Silvia had been diagnosed with advanced bone cancer, her prognosis grim. In her late seventies, she refused to undergo chemo and radiation treatments. The doctors predicted she had a year, eighteen months at most, to live. As soon as Paula finished arranging a leave of absence from her practice, she planned to spend most of the coming year in Florida, assisting with her mother's care. I told her I'd arrange a trip one weekend, meet her in Boca. "They probably won't say anything about this when you call," she said. "The last thing Silvia would want is to dampen your good news. Remember that."

I hung up, but couldn't bring myself to phone them. My chest felt impossibly heavy; how could I hear the voice of the only grandmother I'd ever known, who had consoled me so many times throughout high school and college, and not burst into pieces? Instead I crawled into bed with Jeremy, where I rested my head against his shoulder and sought comfort in his words. When he suggested that we might get married sooner than later, before Silvia grew too ill, I didn't say anything. I was too overwrought thinking about how worried and terrified my grandfather must be for her, and himself, after decades together, at losing what I had found—that rare, kindred spirit with whom you bear the storms of life.

Jeremy's mother threw us an engagement party that July, to coincide with the Fourth. I arrived late, my plane delayed from Mexico City, where I'd spent the week at a Latin American summit. Along the coastal road the houses of the Outer Banks lit up: cars lined the driveways, laughter spilled from porches. I hurried up the steps, wheeling my luggage behind me; as media liaison I traveled more and more. Exhausted, my mind halfway in Mexico, I longed only to see Jeremy, have him whisk me away to a soft bed with clean sheets. Inside, someone played a piano. A rush of gladness washed over me upon entering the packed room, Jeremy bent over the keys, hands flying. No one noticed me except his father, who stood nearest to the door, and we exchanged smiles. I waited until Jeremy finished before I rushed forward and embraced him, cries of welcome greeting me, everyone offering congratulations. Few asked about Mexico, what I had been doing there—or my book, scheduled for release in two months. But I brushed this off and focused on being happy for Jeremy's sake. Family meant so much to him.

I fixed a plate of food. His father offered me a beer. I asked if he'd been playing the piano much lately. "No, not really," he said softly, and I strained to hear him over the party's din. "There's this one bar where I still get booked, Saturday nights. But I'm pulling six shifts a week as floor manager."

"Sorry to hear that. All passion and no play, that's no way to live."

"I may not be young anymore, but I'm no fool," he replied. "You think we don't get CNN in our stock room? Lots more people are going to recognize you, soon." He winked, raising his beer to his lips, then asked if he could preorder my book yet.

As I shared with him the hectic schedule I would be taking on as I squeezed in speaking engagements and book promotions with work, a thought occurred. If my father was still alive— and somehow I felt surely that he was—could he have seen me on TV? The hacienda had received American channels and the cable news stations via satellite; I had been invited to speak on all the major networks since assuming my new position. What might Papi think if he saw me now?

I touched Jeremy's elbow; he was talking with Kat and Jill. The subject of the wedding date came up. "We haven't settled on a date yet," I said. "What's the rush? I'm not going to drive myself crazy and plan a wedding in six months."

"Well, you can't keep us all waiting," Kat said. "Weddings are a big deal in Carolina!" She rattled off venues, glancing expectantly at Jeremy as she listed each one, adding that we could also have it right here, on the beach.

Jeremy raised his eyebrows, said, "Those places are all well and good, but I think Mercedes may have a few of her own in mind." We exchanged a conspiratorial smile; neither of us having talked much of the wedding yet. "Maybe later this weekend, we can discuss it."

"I'm thinking we might do a destination wedding," I said. "Italy, maybe, or Ireland."

All of them, Jeremy included, gawked at me. "Destination wedding?" Kat echoed. "But we've got so much family. They couldn't possibly all fly to Italy." She faced Jeremy, her tone one of betrayal. "What about all your friends from home?"

"I'm sure Mercedes isn't serious," he said. "We're just tossing out ideas, right?"

"Sure," I said. "But what's wrong with a destination wedding? It would be unique, and fun."

Jill placed a hand on her sister's shoulder, but looked at me when she spoke. "It would be lovely, I'm sure. What about someplace in Florida? Isn't that where you grew up?"

"That would make things easier for your grandparents," Jeremy said. "Think of that." His expression was one of shock; I guessed my seriousness at pushing an unconventional wedding had alarmed him, as it had me—I hadn't realized my feelings about it ran so deep, until now.

I hugged my sides and stared at my shoes. "I guess I've been picturing something small and intimate, just immediate family. No big dress and mounds of lace. I'm afraid I've never been that type of girl." I glanced around, smiling hopefully. But their faces remained fallen.

Kat scoffed, shaking her head in disbelief. Staring at me, she said, "This wedding seems to be the last thing on your mind."

"That's not fair," Jeremy snapped at her. "Not to mention untrue."

"Let them plan what they want," Jill said, insistent. "Not every bride has a book to promote. Mercedes has lots of family and friends to consider, I'm sure. Doesn't your dad live in Venezuela?"

I abandoned my beer and fled out the back door, for the beach. A few dozen yards distant, neighbors huddled around a bonfire and smoke carried on the breeze. Sand ran over my shoes; I yanked them off. Someone jogged up behind me—Jeremy. "Who does your sister think she is?" I asked. Hair rippled across my mouth. "I'm sorry, but I just couldn't take it anymore."

"Kat can be nosy and overbearing, I know. Why don't you both give each other a break?"

"Sure, but I don't think either of them will forgive me for shooting down their *Gone with the Wind* fantasies." We trudged for a moment in silence. The noise of the bonfire grew faint. "Is a big wedding really important to you?" I asked. "Because that's the last thing I want."

"That's what I was picturing," he said slowly. "Maybe it was foolish of me, without us talking about it first. But why are you so against it?"

"Why do you think? Imagine how embarrassing it's going to be for me—two hundred people on your side of the aisle, five on mine. How do I explain that? Your sisters apparently believe I have hordes of relatives and a caballero papa in Venezuela."

He laughed, walked on. "I wouldn't take that personally. They don't know you well enough yet. Jill didn't mean—"

"I feel like some Latina they think you've rescued from the slums."

He caught my arm. "How can you say that?" he said. "And what's your fixation suddenly on this destination wedding idea? We can have a smaller wedding, if you want. But are you so scared of my family that you're trying to make it difficult for people to come? It would break my grandmother's heart—Silvia's too—if we married on the Amalfi coast or somewhere."

"We could have it someplace closer, I guess. Maybe Key West—I'd be okay with that. Just a few family, whoever could make it."

"Key West?" he said, incredulous. "Look, if this is about your father and relatives, why don't you reach out and invite him? Your wedding is the perfect occasion for—"

"No." I jumped back; the waves tumbled and crashed. Cold water rushed against my ankles. "Don't you know me at all?"

"I've been wondering that myself," he said, his voice eerie in its steadiness. "Are you ever going to tell me the whole story about how you grew up? I know I haven't made a big deal about it—I guess I've always figured you'd share more eventually. But lately wondering if I've been too generous."

"Why is it so important to know?"

"Are you kidding? Because I love you. If you can't confide in me about why you fled your father, how am I supposed to feel as your husband?" He kicked the sand. The wet clump exploded, granules grazing my calf.

"I just don't want other people to know more than they need to. Your family included."

"You don't think I would keep whatever you had to tell me in confidence, if you asked me to?" He jerked away, shoved his hands in pockets. "So you really don't trust me. Great."

I grabbed his arm, panicked. "Fine. I'll tell you, okay? As long as you don't run to Kat and your mother. I don't think it's healthy, everybody talking so much, knowing one another's secrets."

He peeled my hand off his arm. "It's called love," he said. "I'd have thought that because you barely have anyone, you would be more accepting of my family—enthusiastic, grateful even. We're not perfect, but I won't apologize for our openness. It's the one thing I believe we've done right." He turned his back, trudging toward the house, his strides long and determined.

"I do appreciate them," I said, running to catch up. "But you're right. I'm not used to so much honesty. I promise you, I just need more time to adjust." He charged ahead, and didn't look back. "Or is that it? You're giving up on us?"

He slowed, and after a few steps, turned around. "If that's what you think you need, fine." I hugged him, and he smoothed the top of my head, rested his chin on my hair; when he spoke, his breath warmed my skin. "But I don't know if time will make a difference, if you can't trust. You've got to understand that."

I didn't tell him about my father that night, and all that had led me to flee Cali. Nor did I bring it up in the weeks afterward. For the rest of that long, humid summer, we went about our routines and jobs as before, and neither one of us brought up our fight on the beach. Maybe he had pushed it aside in his willingness to give me another chance. But when I was alone on the Metro or in the apartment, Jeremy on a work trip to Brazil for ten days, the ugly questions of that night flared up. Was my understanding of love flawed? How might I come to cherish his warm, garrulous, imperfect family, rather than shrink from them? Maybe I simply needed to not worry so much, and let the events play out. One day, when the timing was right, during a quiet night at home or in bed, I would tell him everything that had happened. He was not going to abandon me.

Meanwhile, I poured my energy into the book's release: *Cocaine Highways* would be nothing less than a success. I mapped out the tour dates with the publisher and pressed my job for the time off, arguing that the book bolstered my worth and the reputation of our Department; after much negotiation, they relented. I set up a Facebook fan page, Tweeted twice a day, narrated a book trailer. With the help of a publicist and my own media contacts, I appeared on "Good Morning, America" the week of its release, relaying the glamorous studio interview in a breathless blur to Jeremy as I caught the train back to D.C. He helped me organize several parties and readings around Washington, and nearly every weekend that fall I spent out of town—L.A., Denver, Phoenix, Houston. Nights, I fell asleep without dinner on the couch, only to wake at midnight with a thin blanket over me. Or alone, if he'd flown to Brazil where he traveled more lately. I couldn't help but wonder if he did so on purpose.

By Election Day, we'd been engaged six months, and still hadn't set a wedding date. Family and friends had stopped asking, and I was too overwhelmed to think about it. A wedding seemed as implausible and remote as an African safari.

One night, I swept in to find him in his boxers, eating cereal, his hair askew and eyes glued to the computer. Dishes piled in the sink, unfolded baskets of laundry lined the hallway. "You won't believe it," I said, jubilant, flopping on the couch. "Guess who CNN has agreed to be their new Senior Latin American correspondent?"

He didn't look up from the screen. "My guess is you. What does this involve?"

I explained that a bump up to official correspondent meant not only higher pay and prestige, but more TV appearances, and best of all, my own reports. "It's setting me up for a remarkable career," I said, searching his face for a mere flicker of approval. "I can't very well turn it down."

"I suppose not," he said. "So you went after this?"

"Yes. But I'll still be based in D.C."

"I'm just wondering when our life might resemble something more normal, or whether I should be taking a mistress."

"Don't be silly," I said, but my stomach clenched. I sank back into the couch, rambling about various ideas I had for reports—in-depth features from the front lines of the drug war, showing how the conflicts of Central America spilled over into the United States, the troubles inextricably linked. When he didn't respond, I arose and peered over his shoulder as he furiously pecked the keys. He was playing a game. "Did you hear anything I just said?"

"Does it matter?" he replied. I placed my hand on his head before retreating to the bedroom. Minutes later, the shower blasting over me, I sobbed. All the presentations and coveted guest spots, the final checks in the mirror, the poised talking points—and already my private life was slipping away, the public mask taking over. The resentment in his voice matched the emotions welling under my skin, the yearning for our long-ago sleepy weekends in Berkeley, our first months in D.C., the simple meaningfulness of research and reports. I hadn't foreseen my career leading me into journalism. Yet I knew I couldn't decline the correspondent offer; it was too high an honor, one that would surely lead to great things. I would become a woman of influence, shed light on injustice. Wasn't that my purpose?

Silvia lived long enough to see the success of my book, and called when she finished reading it, her breathing weak and labored as she whispered praise. I spent Thanksgiving and Christmas in Florida, everyone knowing it would be her last. Jeremy understood but chose to spend the holidays in North Carolina; I didn't say anything, but couldn't help feeling distraught at this. I told my mother that he and I were going through a rough patch, but was sure we'd come through fine—after all, one couldn't expect life to go smoothly always. She agreed, said that both of us had good hearts and minds, and nothing was more difficult than holidays and illnesses. Silvia was harder to fool. "Where's that clever fiancé of yours?" she said. "Hurry up and marry him, will you, before I do." I sat beside her, patting her hand. My mother, for all her single living, had transformed into a compassionate if scattered nurse, my grandmother having decided to die at home, in a hospital bed. "He's not going anywhere," I assured Silvia. "I've been thinking we should just do it. Maybe fly down here one weekend, get a Justice of the Peace. Have a wedding later."

"Good," she said. "Everyone needs someone to come home to."

"Yes," I said, although I could barely hear myself. She rolled onto her side and slid into a morphine-induced doze. Those were the last words we exchanged. She died a month later.

Jeremy and I flew down for the services. We could have stayed longer, both of us had accrued plenty of vacation and sick days, but neither of us wanted to. On the way back to Arlington from the airport, he drove. I slumped in the passenger seat. Dark clouds carpeted the sky, and raindrops splattered the windshield. "We don't drive that much," I said, signs for Mount Vernon and Fredericksburg flying past. "There are so many places we could go, on weekends."

"I drive plenty," he said, eyes fixed on the road. "Carolina is far enough for me."

"I didn't mean Carolina. I meant exploring, just the two of us. Monticello, for instance. I'd love to go there."

"Then you should."

"I'm talking about the two of us. Some weekend that we're both home—"

He laughed with a sarcasm that made me shrink. "For us to go away, darling, you would actually have to be home. Not to mention it would require that we have a normal relationship, where we talk about personal matters and make love more than twice a month."

"That's what I mean," I said. "We could use a few days to ourselves."

"A few days? What happened to a lifetime? Remember this?" He lifted my hand, thumbed the ring, and let go. "I know who I am, Mercedes. It's you who I don't recognize anymore." The rain beat harder. He flicked the wipers on, and they groaned against the glass. "You can go to Monticello all you want. I want to break up. I can't be with someone who's so damn terrified of the past that her life's ambition is to rectify it. Never mind that you've sacrificed everything beautiful and sacred between us, rather than find the guts to tell me about it."

"I don't believe you," I said. I felt the blood drain from my face. "Let's talk about this. We haven't even tried—"

"You haven't tried." He quickly wiped underneath his glasses, readjusted them. "I'm going to find a place of my own, this week or next."

"What? No. Look, everyone says that thirty is when all these societal pressures hit—careers, weddings, babies. We just have to hang in there. Reconnect."

"You can keep the furniture," he said. "I promise I'll look somewhere other than Arlington, give us both a clean break."

It was this remark that finally caused the tears to run into my mouth. We drove like that in silence, him gripping the wheel, clearing his throat now and then and wiping his eyes, me gazing at the unknown scenery becoming familiar, as slowly the streets and storefronts pieced together, signaling home, or what had been, up until moments ago. For the first time it occurred to me that home was a creation between two people, more if you shared a family—an agreement. Living alone was something else. As we filed up the walk, the only sound was the splash of our footsteps and wheels of our suitcases bumping behind us.

I didn't believe him, even after he'd moved out and we hadn't spoken in months. Time and distance would inevitably reveal how much we needed each other, and any day I expected to receive a message from him saying he wanted to meet up, to give us another try. To stave off my despair, I plunged into my new job with a renewed fervor. I delivered my first reports as a CNN correspondent, an hour-long special in the works. With my increased visibility and platform, my book sales shot ahead, and the publisher contracted me for another title—on what topic, I had no idea, but my agent convinced me to take the deal and we'd turn in the proposal later. I became one of those Washington careerists who spend the night on her office couch, eating take-out, all too willing to avoid the apartment, silent except for the hum of the dishwasher or air conditioner.

But for all the excitement of the position, my stint turned out to be short-lived. I felt satisfied with my initial reports, but didn't care to spend long hours in the editing room, hashing out decisions with producers. At heart, I was a scholar and researcher, not a journalist; I felt more on the frontlines when acting from the inside, I discovered. After seven long months I contacted my former boss at the State Department and asked to come back. CNN said they were sorry things didn't work out, and they would love to have me on as a guest again—or as a future correspondent, if I changed my mind. Even as I returned to my former office in a new senior research position, I couldn't help feeling down about an otherwise incredible opportunity not working out. What price had I paid for chasing after what I'd insisted on seeing as a more adventurous career path, only to have my efforts dead-end? At the time, all I could think was that the correspondent job had driven the wedge between me and Jeremy, and what a waste it was. Now I wonder if losing him played a greater role than I'd thought in my failure, as with every month, my passion for news reporting diminished, rather than bloomed. He'd been my rock, more than I'd known, and instead of leaning against him, I had collided until we cracked. Now I was left alone, to toss about in the stream.

I might not have heard the news if not for Julie, our mutual friend from Berkeley, who still kept in touch with the two of us. Occasionally, I met her for lunch or cocktails. One day around Passover she messaged me, asking if I'd heard from Jeremy lately. No, why? I typed swiftly, and stared at the glowing dialogue box until her next words appeared. "His father committed suicide the other day," she wrote back. Stunned and yet oddly relieved that it wasn't something about Jeremy, I asked if she had information about the funeral services. They would take place in North Carolina, and I knew without a question that I would call off work and go. I considered calling Jeremy and began to write an email, but stopped halfway through. Words lose all impact when it comes to loss; action was what counted.

Throughout the long drive I puzzled over the tragedy, recounting, as humans do, my previous encounters with Jeremy's father, a gentle man I'd come to admire—and miss, having spent recent holidays with just my mother's family, with whom I'd never grown close. Had there been signs in his aloofness, his quiet way, to signal that he had become so desperately unhappy? We all had our personal cliffs. The trouble was determining how close a person was to the edge. And Jeremy—how was he handling this, less than a year after our break up? I was half-hoping to rekindle our connection; it was impossible to pretend otherwise. This might be our chance to salvage what we had, rather than lose it forever.

I hurried across the parking lot of the Episcopalian church, a historic sandstone structure, and joined the press of attendees, all the while craning for Jeremy. His mother dabbed her eyes, her back to the masses as she stood surrounded by her children; Kat caught my eye and looked away. Inside, I wove through the dark suits and flower arrangements, searching. Just as I was about to claim a seat, he stepped out from a throng to join his mother. I approached at a clip, then slowed. A blonde woman followed at his heels, her fingertips pinching his sleeve. His hand reached back and entwined with hers just as he spotted me, called my name. "Thanks so much for coming," he said, and hastily introduced me to his new lover. I nodded, uttering the lines required of politeness, the room spinning into a haze; a plummet of grief hitting me, my body light as air. They hurried past, to the front, as I fumbled to sit. Above the bowed heads she guided him into their pew, his hand grazing her lower back.

CHAPTER NINETEEN

Perhaps I would have reacted differently to Emilio's face showing up in the footage of the cartel kingpin's arrest, if I wasn't still reeling from my encounter with Jeremy at the funeral several days prior. But former lovers have a way of compounding the past. At first glance, the face hovering behind the handcuffed suspect plunged me into the realm of impossibility, for I could swear I had seen Manuel, resurrected in mid-life. After I paused and replayed the footage, however, I knew instantly that the chiseled face and upright physique belonged to Emilio, no less haunting. So he had abandoned the seminary to become an undercover agent, either with ANI, Colombia's National Intelligence Agency, or the Prosecutor General's office—from the footage, I couldn't tell which. How, and why? The DEA and FBI partnered frequently with such organizations in joint task force investigations. The agents I knew might very well know him.

I unearthed what I could that week, and discovered some unsettling facts. Emilio had a decades-long career with the DAS, which had been embroiled in numerous scandals, including conspiracies with paramilitaries and radical left-wing groups. He'd been charged with bribery and suspended in 2006—but the charges were dropped, apparently due to lack of evidence, and I couldn't find out more. By 2011 the President had deemed the DAS a national embarrassment, dismantling the organization and replacing it with ANI, many employees getting reassigned to the Technical Investigation Team out of the Prosecutor General's office. Lately Emilio's duties included apprehending operatives like the one in the clip, leader of one of the largest cartels in history and major supplier to those in Mexico. That we had landed in similar careers fascinated yet unnerved me, somehow; did Emilio also have something to prove, surrounding his brother's death? I thought of the long ago day in the vestry, him sliding over the file. Finding out would require a savvy strategy on my part, for calling him up cold from my Washington office would be a brazen way to confront a former friend and lover, although I didn't want to think of those painful, blurred days following Manuel's death. Yet that was exactly what we needed to discuss.

The following day I sought out my boss, spun the face I'd recognized in the footage into an urgent need to fly down to Bogotá for a lengthy investigation, conduct my own research into the Norte del Valle cartel's connections to Mexico, now the hotbed of narco-trafficking and the focus of our efforts. She made a few phone calls, stopped by my office later that week with good news. She'd arranged for me to work out of the embassy, move into temporary housing for a month, longer if I needed to extend my trip.

Bogotá had never been my city. Even so, I awakened in the middle of the night that first week, struck with insomnia, no one to call. Nothing but a pillow to clutch. An additional blow had fallen in the weeks leading up to my departure, for while I awaited my paperwork and embassy clearance, Ben suddenly died of a stroke. I helped my mother with the funeral arrangements, the absence of his steady counsel a sudden, enormous silence, the inheritance my grandparents left me hardly a consolation for their collective absence, both of them gone within a year. I wept for Jeremy, longing to call him, knowing I couldn't. He wasn't there for me now and would never be again. Instead of reporting to my embassy desk, I woke up late and roamed the apartment in a T-shirt and underwear, sipping coffee, attempting to accomplish research, and floundering. I was also supposed to be working on a new book proposal, due in two months, but when I tried to write or outline ideas, the words arrived stiff and lifeless, and I spent hours staring at a blank screen, fearing another failure like my foray into special correspondence, the inability to deliver a follow-up book a public humiliation. The days slipped by, and Emilio's contact information loomed back at me, waiting. Why was I so reluctant to track him down?

So I decided to look up someone else first.

I searched the Internet, and a professional photograph of Gracia popped up in the cast member profiles for a Bogotá dance company. So she never left, despite her talent, I thought, disappointed. I tried contacting the company, but they replied swiftly that no, they didn't give out dancers' personal information—even though I hadn't asked them to do so, merely for them to pass along my number and email. When my second email went unanswered, I decided to see a show, try to catch Gracia afterward. According to their website, they would be performing at a festival that weekend.

Thousands of guests strolled the park, one of Bogotá's largest, to the beats of a popular Colombian singer, the attendees eating and playing games underneath the many tents, similar to an American fair. I had just purchased a woolen shawl from a vendor near the stage when the flutes started up and the dancers swished to their places. One of the women poised center stage in a white peasant blouse and wide skirt, her face familiar. Gracia. Strong and slender, she had grown into womanly beauty. The dancers divided, the men and women facing each other for a Bolivian folk dance, and I grew nervous. What would she say, and would she even want to speak to me? There is always that anxiety running into long-lost friends, over whether their lives have turned out well or been fraught with disappointments—what about them has changed in unforeseeable ways. Performance over, the troupe beamed at the applauding crowd. I waited beside the stage, a Corona warming in my hand. The troupe filed off and down the steps.

I called her name. She turned her head, parted from the others, and approached hesitantly. In closer proximity, her beauty was even more striking. "Mercedes, I can't believe it's you. What are you doing here?"

I told her I worked for the embassy, that I had tried getting in touch through the dance company. "They're rather vigilant," I said, hoping she took this as a joke.

"Oh, them." She waved a hand in dismissal. "They're so overprotective and flighty. How long have you been back?" She hugged herself, skirt swaying.

"A couple of weeks. I didn't think you'd be here."

"Well, I've only been back recently too. I was with a bigger company, touring Europe."

"You and Esteban, are you—"

She shook her head, glanced at the ground. "No. We stayed in touch, though. He's with a company in Argentina, doing well. Married a choreographer, has two children. And you?"

"No." I forced a smile. "Maybe someday."

"Well, I've got to change for the next number, but it's good to see you," she said, the coal black arches of her eyebrows lifting. "I sensed we might reconnect somehow, with the Internet. Let me get your number." She ducked into a closed tent, emerged a second later with her phone.

As we exchanged information, I asked, "How's Ana?"

"What?" Gracia's finger poised over the glowing screen. "Mercedes, didn't you know?"

"Know what?"

"Ana's dead."

"Oh my God." The blood drained from my face. "How? When?"

"A few years ago. I assumed your father had told you. We had a big funeral. Everyone was there but you." She cocked her head, brow tense. "Why didn't you ever call?"

"I have my reasons—nothing to do with you," I said. "But my father and I don't speak. I haven't seen him for fifteen years. Since the last time I saw you."

"You're kidding." She fixed a loose piece of hair in place with a hairpin, swore under her breath. Someone yelled for her and she whirled around as she hurried off, saying, "We've got to talk about this, and you sure as hell better call me."

The following day Gracia and I met over tinto and pastries at the downtown feria. Farmers hauled pallets of eggs from pickup beds and rammed cane stalks into grinders, the popular juice gushing into old soda bottles, rinsed for reuse. "I always wondered why you dropped off the face of the earth," she said. "You could have picked up the phone, you know. We didn't have a clue what happened to you." Plates pushed aside, we'd been talking for an hour. I had just finished telling her the story behind my sudden departure, what Emilio had shown me after the murder, and a brief version of my life in the United States after reuniting with my mother. I'd decided to pretend I knew nothing about Emilio, wanting to see what she might offer on her own.

"I should have called, even if it was just to tell you I was all right," I said. "Maybe it was the shock, or just immaturity. I don't know." The waitress delivered our second cups and we sipped, the sunlight breaking through the clouds.

Not long after my escape, Gracia had left Colombia too. After finishing at the dance academy, she and Esteban had been hired by different companies, which ended their romance. He had wanted to marry and have children, and a well-known world dance ensemble recruited Gracia, an opportunity she couldn't refuse. She toured for a decade, working her way up to a principal position, until her father's decline prompted her to quit and return to Colombia last year. "He's got Lou Gehrig's disease," she said. "He has another year. Probably months."

Ana had stayed married to Carlos, had three children and lived in a big, gated house a few streets away from her parents. But the young couple fought often, and Gracia suspected Carlos cheated on her cousin. Five years ago, a criminal gang raided their house one night. Ana and Carlos had been pistol-whipped, bound, gagged, and left on the floor while the bandidos stole their electronics and valuables; the children had been locked in a closet for hours, the toddler hospitalized afterward for severe dehydration. "But she refused to leave," Gracia said. "Not Carlos. Or Colombia, either." Six months later criminals raided the home again, and Ana was fatally wounded. "It was big news, the daughter of one of Colombia's oldest families," Gracia said. "I hadn't seen people so upset since Archbishop Duarte was killed. Carlos couldn't deal with it." He sold the house, and Ana's parents moved to their second home in Santa Marta, la Ciudad Jardín harboring too many memories. "Her parents let go all the live-in maids, except the cook, because she's been with them for so long. But they don't trust anyone else. Too often, these gangs are tipped off by the help. At least that's what the police and newspapers say." I asked about Ana's children. "Oh, my aunt and uncle are raising them, Carlos too. But he's an engineer now for the oil companies, and works on the pipelines. A dangerous job because of the FARC, but he makes good money. He flies home to see the kids every couple of weeks." She added that he rarely played guitar anymore.

"And Emilio?" I asked. "What happened to him?"

She drained the last of her tinto. "Actually, it's funny, you running into me and not Emilio. He works here, in Bogotá."

"Really? For the diocese?"

If my surprise seemed measured or feigned, Gracia didn't notice. She laughed, brushed her lips with a napkin. "Hardly," she said. "You'll probably never guess, so I'll tell you. He's an undercover agent. Used to be with the DAS, but after they got dissolved I'm not sure—he's either with ANI now or maybe the Prosecutor General's office."

"Maybe it's not surprising," I said. "He was so good at leading La Maria Juventud."

She rested on her elbows, toyed with the hair on the back of her neck. "Do you really think your father arranged Manuel's murder, though?" she asked. "Something about the whole thing strikes me as odd. I remember your father. He didn't like you dating Manuel, it's true. But killing him in cold blood—it just doesn't seem possible."

"He was a drug-trafficker, Gracia—sounds hard to believe, I know. You should hear the stories my aunt and my mother told me, about his youth. I didn't have a clue, until Manuel and Emilio showed me documentation. There was a whole side of himself he kept hidden—the Cali cartel, paying off the paras. No way can I just ignore that. Never mind how obsessed he was with my leaving here to finish school, remember?"

"I don't know," she said. "No one was ever convicted of Manuel's murder. I wonder if there's some way for you to find out more, now that you're here?"

"Maybe. I was thinking I could visit Emilio. Do you think he'd be willing to help? Since he's an investigator?" I hadn't told her what had happened between Emilio and me, after Manuel.

Gracia tore off the end of my churro and chewed thoughtfully. "Forget Emilio. I'd go right to the source and visit your father."

"You mean call him and tell him I'm back in the country?"

"I think you should just show up. Fly down and hire a driver to bring you out to the hacienda. What's he going to do, turn you away at the gate? And so what if he does? Then you've lost nothing more than what you're going in with."

I shook my head. "I don't know. You really think there's a possibility of him being innocent? I saw with my own eyes the police file."

"You were sixteen," she exclaimed. "Those brothers were obsessed with the bad guys, so who knows what you saw? This is your father we're talking about. No matter what, he's not going to run down the driveway waving a gun at you. Sheesh." She rolled her eyes; I'd missed her humor and sensibility. "Will you quit stalling and book the ticket before I do?"

"Okay, okay, I'm booking it," I said, bringing up the Avianca site on my phone. "I'm just telling you, he might not want to see me."

"You're his only daughter," she said. "Even if he hates you, he'd still want to see you."

Afterward we hugged goodbye. I walked to the bus stop. The wind rattled the eucalyptus trees. An old man, slight yet hard-muscled under his work shirt, lips puckered over lost teeth, sifted through just-roasted coffee beans, hollered for me to purchase some.

How old would my father be now? Sixty? Sixty-two? I couldn't remember. Not a very old man, but the wind and sun took its toll. Would his hair have retained its jet-black fullness, or be streaked with grey? Maybe it had thinned, and turned salt-and-peppery. Would he have put on weight, like the belly he had been apt to gain when I last knew him, or would farm labor have kept him lean, hardened? Unless he'd battled a disease, and then he might be thinner than I cared to imagine. But it was almost too easy to picture him that way, the once strong and commanding landowner in a chair, fallen to frailty. How would I even greet him and get him talking?

Papi, I've been meaning to arrange a visit. It's just that I haven't been in this part of the world much, in the last few years. And I can't reveal details about my job, or why I'm here. But I was going to come down to the hacienda on my first vacation, I swear—

Stop lying. You turned your back and you know it. Don't cross me, daughter.

Or would we say nothing at all, but throw our arms around each other and squeeze, and sway.

All I knew was that I wanted to see him and not to see him. Eucalyptus carried on the breeze; alone at the bus stop, I shivered and tucked my shawl around me.

Up and around the winding narrow roads the driver sped outside Cali—the same route off the autopista that Fidel had taken every day, bringing me home from school. The outlying towns of the Valle de Cauca hadn't changed, but I didn't know how close we were until we turned at the zapateria with the belts and boots hanging from the porch. Only a few minutes away now; my belly tensed. We passed the bus stop where I might have been abducted all those years ago, but the abuelas with grandchildren and plastic shopping bags now waited with calm faces. City buses were not hijacked in Cali anymore.

We turned onto the valley road, the cane high and waving. Workers labored in the distant fields; I couldn't tell if they were desplazados, or if I recognized the jefes on horseback. The next moment we were stopped at the gate, the bougainvillea blooming amidst the barbed wire on top. A guard, automatic rifle in arms, approached. When the driver explained that I was Diego's daughter, the guard ordered him to roll down the back window; he was no one I knew. He said not a word, but thumped the button on the dusty call-box and pointed to the crackling female voice that answered. I would have recognized the voice anywhere.

"Inez?" I asked. "It's Mercedes. Please let me in."

"Mercedes." The box static and breathing. "Is it really you?" A pause. "How will I recognize you? It's been so long."

The guard shifted and swatted an insect from his face, his mouth slack. I was wearing a work blouse and pants, a light shawl across my shoulders. I pressed the button again and said,

"I'm wearing the pearls Papi gave me for my quinceañera."

The gate jolted and crept open, and the guard stepped aside.

We drove through. The driver parked and killed the engine. At the front of the house more flower beds had been planted and the fruit trees stood taller and fuller, and on the steep hillside behind, the rainforest had thickened. But the wide porch with the carved rockers remained just as the day I had left. Birds squawked from the courtyard cage; I wasn't close enough to tell what kind. Inez waited at the top of the stone steps, her arms crossed and her short, grey legs shoulder-width apart.

The ground felt as if it had turned to water underneath my feet. Inez didn't move, and I couldn't quite read her expression. She had never been a great talker, but as I got closer I could see that she was stunned. Only when I halted at the top of the steps, waiting for her to permit me inside, did she reach out and brush my hair behind my shoulder. Hers was grey with a few black tufts remaining, the ancient braid climbing down her back like a vine. I need never have doubted my visions of her; she would remain here until she died.

Inside, a flat-screen TV hung in place of the old set. Two maids, young women, were cleaning the windows. The house smelled like Pine Sol, tamales and dogs, the smells of my past. What I had failed to predict were the foreign mutts that collided with me at the threshold, a half dozen shaking, pawing dogs of all shapes and sizes; a tiny, slender one with a coat like a fox and blind eye licked my hand; others growled until Inez scolded and called them off, then told me to wait. How could I have failed to imagine something so simple and obvious—that the dogs of my youth, the graceful ridgebacks, Shaka and Zulu, and the adorable, tumbling mutts, Angel and Cocoa, would have passed away long ago? What else had I failed to prepare for, I worried as I drifted among the couches, my mouth turning dry. Inez's footsteps clacked down the hall. She had called my father on his cell phone, she said, and he was on his way.

"Is he at the fields?" I asked.

She shook her head, one hand kneading the armrest of his chair, the leather split and sunken. "No, he is down at the stable with the new horses. That's where he is most days."

"What did he say when you told him?" I asked, my heart thudding so loud, I felt sure she could hear it. "Did he seem angry?"

Inez opened her mouth to answer, but nothing came out. Someone slid the glass door open behind me and a moment later, Papi came striding forward.

His late-afternoon stubble had turned shades of salt-and-pepper, and the ridges had deepened along his forehead and eyes. But the same dark brown irises bore into mine; he wore the same face. I noted little else because an instant later, he was clasping my head, his rough fingers scratching my scalp, asking over and over again, "You're here?" He squeezed me in a hard, rocking hug, and I returned it, rubbing his back. Dust, sweat, and the odor of horses mixed with the remnants of his early morning shave. Not until his scent struck me did a lump tighten in my throat. Rivulets glistened down his cheeks, and from his shirt pocket he pulled out a bandanna—I couldn't believe it—an old purple paisley one now faded to lavender and a threadbare thinness. A hole gaped from the cloth's corner as he dabbed his eyes. More sunspots dotted his neck and hands than I remembered. He settled into his chair, and I sank onto the couch. "Why now, after all these years?" he asked.

An awkward pause arose before I could find words. "I hope it is okay that I stopped by. I didn't know if I should call first."

He crammed the bandanna back into his pocket, mouth quivering. "Look at you," he said. "You look wonderful. I had always hoped that one day, you would realize—and when you were ready, well, you would come back." He shook his head absently. Over his shoulder he called for Inez: "Make something special for dinner, will you? Whatever Mercedes would like."

"Oh, there's no need to trouble Inez. The driver probably needs to get back before then."

He waved me off, saying, "Don't be silly. We'll have an early dinner."

Inez asked if we'd like coffee or tea. "Nonsense, this is the most special of occasions," he said, and crossed the room to where the liquor and glasses were kept; he moved with the stiffness of a farmer who has labored for years. Otherwise, he appeared stronger than ever, and still handsome. I wondered if he had a novia—or a wife.

"You look well," I said.

"Do I?" he replied. Inez brought ice, lime, and tongs. I didn't recognize the brand of rum he poured—not Flor de Caña. He crushed the lime, whisked over the drinks. We toasted and sipped. The rum's heat expanded in my throat and chest, the lime refreshing but tart.

"No cigar?" I asked.

"No, no more of those. The doctor said it was compounding my stress, that they would kill me." He strolled over to the humidor, raised the lid.

When he dropped it, the inside made a hollow sound. "You know what I told him? 'Damn it, I didn't live this long to die from cigars.'"

A dog that appeared part Australian shepherd jumped onto my lap and sniffed, eager to get acquainted. Glossy horse magazines lay strewn where his *Cigar Aficionados* had once piled up. "Inez gave me the impression that you don't bother with the cane too much anymore," I said. Papi resumed his seat. "I prefer to let the men handle it." He peered into his drink, swirled its contents.

"Luis?"

"Luis is dead." He brought the glass to his lips, adding, "An accident, six—no, seven years ago. Tragic." By his fleeting gaze I knew not to ask any more about it.

"So how have you been spending your time? Inez mentioned horses."

"Horses, yes," he said, straightening up. "But not just any horses. Spanish beauties, direct from Juarez. Have you heard of them, the dancing horses of southern Spain?"

I shook my head. "But it sounds like you've found something you really enjoy," I said. "How has it gone with the displaced? The problem is worse, I've heard." I caught myself, about to say *since my return*. I wasn't sure yet how to divulge what had brought me back.

"Six million, some say—I don't really know. I haven't had anything to do with them for ages."

"You don't give them work?"

"Work, sure, but I don't let them make camp. I'm not interested in being a slum lord." He arose and gazed over the valley, raised his arms and parted them. "My only desire at this age is to create beauty. Would you like to see the horses? They are magnificent."

"Soon. Not yet."

"What about you?" He motioned to me with his drink. "Where have you been?"

"Here and there." I stroked the dog on my lap. "I just started a new position, actually. Working on human rights' cases, you could say." I thought of my job: the latest reports on operations to halt criminal gangs, the drug mules caught at airports, mostly teenagers.

"For who? The Red Cross?"

"No, another organization." I stared into my drink. "It's complicated. I'd rather not get into it."

"You always were such a bright girl. I'm sure they are lucky to have you." He passed by and touched the crown of my head. Then topped off his drink, asked if I'd like another.

I declined, already feeling the rum, and excused myself.

The downstairs bathroom felt like it belonged in another house—the tile and fixtures the same, the plush towels and décor different from what I remembered. I considered Papi's change in habits: the switch from his favorite rum, the empty humidor, the horses. So far, his life seemed much improved, his demeanor more relaxed and positive. Was this really the case? What might be lingering beneath the surface that I was missing? I fixed my hair and shawl, pleased with my choice to leave my embassy credentials at the hotel, although not so certain about omitting that I worked for the U.S. government. But I hoped to steer clear of career speculations. I was not about to sacrifice what I had come to ask in these precious few hours of reunion.

When I returned the dogs surrounded Papi, leaping and yelping over one another for his attention, and he ruffled the backs of a few and tossed them treats from a jar. "Are you ready to see the horses?" he asked.

"I suppose. Since when did you stop drinking Flor de Caña?"

His eyebrows furrowed. "Don't you like this?" he asked, lifting his glass. "It's Ron Centenario, the best rum in Costa Rica."

"I like it. Only you always said nothing could compare to Nicaraguan rum that had sat undisturbed for ten years, while the Sandinistas threw out everyone civilized. That it was the one good thing to come out of that war." I couldn't help grinning.

He smiled. "Yes, well," he said, and gestured to the liquor shelf, the various brands lined up. "In recent years I turned to Colombian rum, and now"—he raised the bottle of Ron Centenario, with the emblem of a horse's head, mane blowing back on the wind—"Costa Rican."

"But you drank Flor de Caña with Uncle Charlie," I said, insistent. "I remember."

He shrugged, peering over the rim as he raised it. "So what if I did?" He drained the glass, set it down with a thud, and headed outside, the sun halfway in its descent to the west.

A herd of grey-white horses pranced and circled in the paddock where the Paso Finos once swatted flies. Now the work horses occupied the pasture next to the alpacas, Papi pointed out as we crossed the lower yard. Stable boys led horses to and from stalls, overseen by Vincente, wiry and weathered as a coffee farmer at the market. He called, "Buenas, princesa," like I had been gone for a vacation instead of years. So Vincente was still here, Luis was not. I wondered about the jefes, those absent as well as the men passing by with feed sacks and saddles. Were the new faces former commanders of lethal private armies, ordering villages burned and women raped?

Papi leaned against the fence, voice swelling with pride as he described the sixteen mares and two stallions, pointed to those he had begun to breed and show throughout Latin America. The graceful footwork and impressive, stylized jumps performed by the horses, much like those of the famous Lipizzaner stallions, were battle tactics invented by Spanish monks during the Crusades, designed to protect the animal and rider by frightening—and possibly maiming or killing—the enemy. Papi waved over a slight man with a black goatee who approached, leading a mare, introducing him as Alejandro, a trainer from the riding school in Juarez; he spoke with an Andalusian accent. Papi joked, "This man is not only my horse trainer, but my secretary and personal priest," thumping him on the back.

"Priest?" I asked. "What do you mean?"

Alejandro feigned protest, and Papi said, "No, really. He counsels me on everything. Without him I would no longer be sane." The heaviness of his admission was undercut by the jovial banter between the two. It was obvious he and the Spaniard had become good friends.

After Alejandro led the horse away, I asked Papi if he had a woman in his life. "Oh, you know how it goes," he said. "Off and on. I have found that love only comes around a couple of times, if you're lucky. Like a comet, I'm afraid." He chuckled but it faded fast. "Such a deep love is truly rare. And that is the only love worth uprooting your life for."

I remained quiet, the real reason for being here prodding me. But before I could say something, he asked, "How about you? I noticed you don't have any rings on your fingers."

"Certain things have made that difficult, like my job." I backed away from the fence, adding, "I'd like to see the horses up close. They're so beautiful."

"Aren't they?" he said, beaming. He opened the gate, led us down the cool corridor of stalls. I asked how he became so consumed with them.

He petted a mare in the stall ahead. "I needed to do something after you left," he said. "After the first few months, when you refused my calls—well, I tried to keep busy. The nun would stop by. She encouraged me to give you space, after what you'd gone through. That eventually, you'd come around. But after six months, and then a year, I was barely leaving the house. The fields I left to the men. I never stopped thinking about the ugly business of clearing out the squatter camp." *Clearing out*—the phrase quickened my blood. Embassy workers had described the Colombian police launching into the slums with bulldozers and guns in "cleansing" operations during President Uribe's years. Babies had been thrown in the river and drowned.

He stroked the horse's nose and talked to her. "That was a dark year," he said. "I never stopped thinking about you."

"I wish things could have been different."

"They happened the way they happened," he said. "At least I knew you were safe."

"What do you mean?"

He straightened and his hands left the horse, hung heavy at his sides. "I wasn't surprised by your leaving, Mercedes. It was the way you left that nearly killed me. No phone calls, no emails. Cutting me out of your life. Do you have any idea what that does to someone?"

That's how I felt after you had Manuel murdered, I thought. But this died quickly, silently—his question a piercing echo of Gracia's and Emilio's. Indeed, how had I turned my back so ruthlessly on my loved ones? To completely sever ties with the past, all of one's youth—could anyone succeed in doing so without suffering cracks? If I got the answers I sought, who was I then?

He wrapped an arm around me, smoothed my hair. "But you're here, mi princesa. We're past all that now."

I pulled away. Nothing was past; Manuel was still dead and Papi still responsible. "I wish Colombia was past it," I said.

We continued walking the stalls, Papi greeting each horse as a friend. He spoke about how Colombia would wage her Holocaust until the rest of the world saw what went on—that as long as the problems remained invisible here, and in Mexico and Venezuela, the violence and injustice would continue. "But we don't even make the global news," he said. "I do the best I can to keep my distance."

A shiver ran up my spine, at his mention of the news. But if he had seen me on TV, he didn't let on. I asked, "What happened to Uncle Charlie?"

"He had his own solutions to fix things, but he was not such a good guy, sometimes," he said. "Carlito, what a crazy one. I miss him, though."

"And Sister Rosemary? Where is she now?"

"Oh, she's been gone a long time. After 2000 she moved south to a mission. Later we heard she got killed in the fighting, while helping refugees."

I pressed my forehead to the horse's nose near me, thinking of the sister drawing hearts in my notebook, sweeping the cash underneath her shawl. "I had to leave, but I didn't expect to stay away for so long," I said. I was trying to find the right words, and failing. Even after viewing the police evidence I had never envisioned the elapse of so many years before returning or seeing my father, without so much as a phone call. But that was the trouble. In my grief-stricken conviction of his guilt, I had never envisioned anything. I said, "I started school and was swamped with family. Learning English."

"I guess you learned," he said. "How is your mother?"

"She's fine. She lives in Israel."

"What's she doing there?"

I explained to him how Paula had been an Israeli citizen for a number of years now, and about her work, studying the psychological trauma of long-term conflict zones.

"Did she ever ask about me?" His face searched mine for an answer before I could speak.

"Sometimes," I said. "I told her about the farm, the dogs and alpacas. That you were doing well." I stopped short. None of this was true.

Dim clouds rumbled low overhead. He asked if I'd like to go riding before dinner. I gestured to my dress slacks and low-heeled work shoes coated in sawdust. "Maybe another time," I said. "You go."

He ordered the stable boys to saddle a mare, slender and high-spirited, but as soon as he swung into the saddle, she snapped into focus. Moments later, they were cantering around the paddock, Papi leaning back, confident, an expert horseman. They made an idyllic picture: the aging gentleman farmer in his cowboy hat and the Spanish mare, white mane flying, the fiery trees in bloom and dark mountains rising behind them. If only the reality of living here matched the picture, but it didn't, and I knew better than to fall for the illusion. Papi would never leave because he knew what was required of those who stayed; it was all he knew. Sometimes lies are what we tell ourselves in order to survive, a substitute for faith.

Soon after we left the stable the world blotted out to grey. Papi, the horse trainer, and I sat under the porch as the rains fell; Papi had waved for him to join us after he was caught crossing the yard in the downpour. It was after four o'clock, and dinnertime aromas escaped the door whenever Papi returned with ice and rum, which was often. Throughout my childhood he had been a light drinker, but I wasn't sure if that was still the case. He was the first to top off his own glass, hover with the bottle, and exclaim, "What, no more? We must celebrate!" Perhaps he was just a father ecstatic to have his daughter home after fifteen years. The speakers blasted gitano tracks that I had long forgotten but instantly recognized, and the rain and rum lulled me back to the hacienda's comforts. Manuel rose from the ashes, my ghost.

Out of limes, Papi slipped inside again. Alejandro and I sat opposite one another at the table where the jefes had played cards. A silver crucifix peeked from the gape in the horse trainer's button-down shirt and vest. I wondered if he really was religious, or if Papi had been joking. By his neat, tailored clothes and reserved demeanor, the Spaniard appeared a mannered, well-bred guest. I said, "He must do something else besides the horses. Does he go anywhere?"

The rain drummed harder and from inside, someone—Papi—cranked the music up. "He loves the horses," Alejandro answered. "I can't speak for his spirits before I arrived—I hear he was quite low. He takes care of those mares better than he does himself, although he is in good health. The doctor claims he has the strength of a man half his age. He could live to be one hundred, if he wants. But I don't know that he does."

"Why not?"

"After the horses, what then?" He grasped his glass with both hands; several rings, thick gold with square stones, rubies and emeralds, adorned his fingers. "Today is the happiest I have ever seen the man. Nothing can replace the human family. I know how much I miss mine."

"Has he ever confided in you what happened between us?" I asked.

"No," he said, shaking his head. "As much as he calls me his personal priest. We talk about many things. He is obsessed with God, so I offer what I can. He has told me about some of his past." Someone jostled the door—Papi. "Make no mistake," Alejandro said, lowering his voice, "your father has plenty of material comforts. But he is a lonely man."

Papi paraded toward us with a bowl of limes, which he then balanced on his head. He outstretched one hand like the Chiquita Banana lady and performed a little dance step, catching the bowl just as it began to slide off. He pronounced dinner to be ready but wouldn't let me pass, pulling me to salsa with him. "The princess is back, back again," he sang, and we were both smiling. Alejandro and I declined another drink, but Papi refilled his and crushed a handful of sliced lime on top.

Inez had made a spicy chorizo, yuca, and carrots. Alejandro dined at Papi's left where Luis had always sat, the Spaniard a marked improvement, sharing stories from Sevilla and the history of the famous dancing horses. For most of the dinner I listened, much as when I sat in the same place as a teenager. The sun dipped low in the west, the valley darkening. I asked Inez to make a plate of food for the driver and tell him I wouldn't be much longer. "What's going on?" Papi asked, holding up his hand. "You can't be leaving yet."

"I've got to get back soon," I said. "You didn't think I would stay the night, did you?"

"You'll come back tomorrow then."

I traced the pattern of the tablecloth. "I can't. I'm leaving to go back tomorrow."

He sat back abruptly, glanced from me to Alejandro as if we understood something that he didn't. "But why such a short visit?" Papi asked. "You fly home to surprise your father after fifteen years, and I think you'd want to stay at least a week."

"I came down here for my job, Papi. It happened to be a good opportunity to see you."

Alejandro suggested we have sherry, and excused himself to peruse the liquor collection. The maids murmured to one another while washing up, the plates clattering upon entering the dishwasher. We didn't have a dishwasher, growing up. I couldn't look at my father and stared at the flan Inez had set in front of me instead.

"What is this job, that you can't stay an extra couple of days? Can't you explain to your boss, in the U.S.?" Papi flipped a hand as his spoke, one knee crossed over the other. "I'm heading to Bogotá after this, actually."

"Even more reason to stay then."

"It's not so simple, okay?" I said. "I work for the United States government, conducting research. I'm assigned to the embassy. Same floor as the DEA."

He exhaled through his nostrils, long and sharp, and his eyes narrowed, darting over me. I hadn't witnessed this kind of fury, barely contained and poised to erupt, in years. My breathing turned shallow and tight.

"DEA?" he repeated. "So that's the real reason you've come here. To snoop." He froze, neck strained.

"Not at all. This visit was entirely on my own."

"You expect me to believe that?" he said, cold and even-toned. "Tell me, why should I? Several times I bring up your job. You had plenty of chances to explain. Instead you give grey answers. I thought you were working for some kind of refugee organization." He pushed back, leapt to his feet. A tide of purple-red crept up his tanned neck and face. "You lied."

"It's the truth."

"Who sent you? The driver outside, he's DEA, too?"

"I'm not an agent, I'm a researcher. I have my doctorate from UC-Berkeley." I recoiled too, and reached for my purse. "Isn't that what you wanted—for me to get the best education? Well, I did. I'm a scholar. You should see my awards. I've published a book, did you even know?" My hand shook as I grasped the purse strap. "This was a mistake, my coming here. I'm sorry for troubling you."

His hands gripped my shoulders. "Sit down. You're not going anywhere."

He steered me over to the living area, pressed me into a chair. Alejandro was holding a bottle of sherry; Papi lunged past him and flicked off the music. "I hope you don't mind leaving us," he said to Alejandro. "I'm afraid my daughter and I must settle a few things."

Alejandro's gaze fell. He replaced the sherry and slipped out without a word. Inez shut off the faucet, dried her hands, and left, the kitchen flashing to darkness.

"Stand up." Papi stepped close, his breath heavy with rum and chorizo. "What weapons do you have on you?" He whipped off the shawl, and I cried out, startled. "Well, that was smart. Sit." I was afraid he might pull a gun from the drawer by his chair—he used to keep one there—but he sank down in silence. When one of the dogs trotted up, he snapped his fingers and scolded her, and she scampered down the hall.

"I meant everything I said earlier," I said, my voice weak and wavering. I swallowed. My temples were starting to throb from the rum. "I've always wondered about you, if you were still down here. If you—" and I stopped.

"But not enough to pick up the phone or plan a trip," he said. "No, you waited until it was convenient—until they sent you, and you recognized something you wanted. I see you have fully become an American."

"I told you, I'm not an agent," I said, breathing hard. His glare was as bold and fixed as a portrait's. "My job has nothing to do with you."

"Doesn't it?" He clenched his drink, wiped the sweating glass with his bandanna. "Then why are you here?"

"I want to know the truth about Manuel's death. And why you kept me from my mother and grandparents."

His lips twitched, and for a moment I thought he might laugh. "Manuel's death? What do you mean?"

"I'd like to know how you were involved. I think I deserve to know. Don't you agree?"

"Is that what is so important to you, after all these years? Would it really make so much of a difference?"

"He bled to death in my arms," I said. Heat spread across my chest and cheeks. "Do you think I would forget?"

"No, you wouldn't forget," he said. "What I am more curious about is why you are so convinced that I had something to do with it. When you know as well as I do that his outspokenness made him a target. Do you know how many guerilla cells there are in Cali?"

"Actually, I do," I said, chin lifted. "And I also know how much you wanted me to get out of here to finish school. Although not enough to help me contact my mother or grandparents, or even let on that they had tried to reach me."

"I had my reasons—it wasn't safe for them to come, did anyone ever consider that?"

"That's just an excuse," I cried. "I could have met them for a visit in Costa Rica, or just talked on the phone. Never once did you mention they had tried to get in touch with me. Paula, you always described her as this fragile person. She's nothing like that."

"She abandoned you, and I was supposed to let her waltz back? No.

"And you think that because Manuel was in the way, I had him killed? You believe I could do that, rob a young man of a bright future?"

"Yes," I said, exhaling. "Especially after the conversation I heard you have with Luis."

"What conversation?"

I raked my palms against my thighs, said, "I heard you and Luis talking in the courtyard, several nights after the murder. You had arranged something—brought someone down, paid off a worker." My voice trailed. I had only ever described this aloud to a few people—Emilio, Asaf, and most recently, Gracia—only now it sounded vague, grasping.

"So you condemned me based on part of a conversation? Is that right?"

"Not just that. I learned things from Manuel and his brother, even before the murder. I saw evidence. That's why I began to take precautions, sneak around."

Papi held his glass near his lips, a low rumble of laughter escaping him. Smirking, he sipped. "Evidence, is that right? I'm curious to know what kind."

"Files, police reports. On several different occasions, I saw them."

"And it never occurred to you these documents may have been fabricated?" he countered. "That one or both of those narrow-minded brothers may have had reason to poison you against me, if not just to get you, an innocent, pretty young girl, into bed?"

I shook my head. "No, Manuel was incapable of that," I said, and after a pause, "Emilio wouldn't have stooped so low, either."

"You're so sure, are you? Well," he said, taking another swig, the ice rattling. "We all see things others do not."

"Fidel—the driver—what ever happened to him?"

"Fidel?" he said, and quickly lowered the glass. "Oh, yes, I remember him. That soldier from the Colombian Army. He barely stayed a year, ended up in Ecuador or Peru or someplace, I don't know. I thought he'd be more invested in the farm. A disappointment." He thumbed his chin, and his gaze sprung to meet mine. "Why is he important?"

"I just wondered. He used to help me see Manuel, if I came up with something to bribe him. It was the only way I could sneak around, without you finding out."

Papi leaned forward on his elbows in the semi-darkness, hung his head for a moment and when he raised it, the lamplight illuminated the creases in his face that had arisen in my absence. He said, "He was a grown man in my employment, with no family, desperate for a job. The first time he came to me and said you'd given him some trinket in exchange for keeping secrets about this new boyfriend, we had quite a laugh about it. Afterward, he asked me what I wanted him to do. I decided for him to keep up the ruse, let you think you were buying some kind of confidence. Teenagers will be defiant, no matter how parents restrict them. But that way I knew I could keep an eye on you. Did you really have no idea?"

I sat stunned, until I released a long held breath. "So all those times, you knew? Did you know I took cash, too?"

Papi lifted his hands, palms up, and shrugged. "Fidel would just put the money back," he said. "I knew everything."

Something began to boil inside me again, and I shifted, gripping the couch. "So then you knew," I said. "How can you sit there and expect me to believe you had nothing to do with it, when you knew about the letter?"

"Letter?" he stared at me quizzically. "What letter?"

"The letter. Manuel and I were planning on—" But I didn't finish. He hadn't known about the letter, didn't have a clue about the elopement. Fidel must have kept quiet in that instance, but why? Had he perhaps been remembering his own young love? I would never know, except what a mess

I had made of things. In a low voice, mostly to myself, I said, "So you really didn't know?"

Another rumble sounded from his throat. He drained his rum, shoved the glass aside, and arose. "You think I don't know what real evil is, Mercedes? That I don't know the ugliness of men's hearts?" He stood there, swaying, before squatting at my feet, planting both his hands on the arms of my chair, trapping me. Leaning closer, he said, "How dare you." His voice, low and grating, flickered with rage. "You think if I had wanted Manuel killed, I would have let him hang around for months? I tell you, if that was the case, he wouldn't have made it so far as the driveway after that first visit."

"What?" I said, and shrank in my seat.

He cocked his head. "Maybe I should leave you to speculate about what really happened. Why shouldn't I? What does it matter, from my end? You made your judgment about me, years ago. You didn't even give me, your father, a chance. When I did everything in my power to shield you. Then you show up here today, I welcome you home, and I find out this is your reason—and you demand that I tell you. Make some kind of confession."

A panicked, sinking feeling plummeted within me—an incredible sadness. "You can't do that. Let me leave here with these questions."

"You're right," he said, dropping his chin, "I won't." He leaned in closer, and his scent mixed with earth and animals filled the air between us. His eyes—wounded, defiant—bored into my soul. "I didn't kill Manuel."

I released a shaky breath, and he backed away, arose. The clock above the mantel ticked. "Yes, but what about all the others?" I said. "Do you feel anything for those those you had killed? You kept me from my mother and her whole family. That was cruel, don't you understand? You lied."

He wandered off, fists pinching his waist and boots scraping the tile.

"I wasn't about to take that risk, of them coming down here and taking you back," he said. "Not when you were all I had." He lifted his hands. "I did my best as your father, even though I am guilty of lies, yes, and murder. That's my cross to bear. But what does it matter? I lost you anyway," he said, after a long silence.

"Maybe we can make things right somehow," I said.

"After this, mi hija"—he reached into the old humidor, withdrew a cigar and lighter—"I really don't know."

My gaze fell to the coffee table strewn with magazines, the shelf of gitano CDs, back to Papi. The bitter odor of tobacco stung my eyes, now filling with tears.

He stood up and gestured for me to do the same. "Isn't your driver waiting?"

I arose, clutching my sides through the shawl. A panicked, sinking feeling plummeted through me—an incredible sadness. He gripped my elbow and led me toward the door, the mutts rising from the corner and trotting up, nails on tile.

"I thought you said you gave up cigars," I said in the doorway.

"I have." He inhaled, and the embers flared orange. "But I was keeping this for just such an occasion."

"I'll call, next time. Would that be okay?" I touched his shoulder.

He stepped back, held the door open widely between us. "It doesn't matter. Goodnight." I lingered for a moment, the heavy wooden door in my face. On the other side of the great windows, Papi poured another drink. When he lifted it to his lips, he caught my eye and turned his back.

The chorus of cicadas enveloped me as I trudged to the car, the sky brighter than any I'd seen in a long time. I had forgotten the stars were so many, and so bright. The car sped through the valley, the driver silent and the radio chattering politics. The stars blurred in my vision but never left my sight. Their light kept going. Never bending backward, it shined on and on through space.

CHAPTER TWENTY

In Bogotá I called into work Monday morning, told them I was following a hot lead, then phoned Gracia and asked her to set up my meeting with Emilio. "Do me a favor," I told her, "don't mention that I work for the U.S. embassy. Let him think I'm just seeking him out as an old friend. Because I have some questions."

"Sure," she said. "Just be aware that he's as attractive as ever. Charismatic. I run into him sometimes, and he always asks if I'm single."

"Actually, I know who you can tell him I'm working for." When I told her, she laughed so hard she needed to catch her breath. "Oh, Mercedes, I don't know what happened in Cali but you had better tell me soon."

I promised her that I would. Soon after, my phone lit up with a text from Emilio, expressing delight and giving instructions on where to meet. The following afternoon I passed through security at the investigative building—the wayward female still bereft after all these years, blissfully ignorant of the corruption-fraught DAS. A secretary instructed me to wait in a common area, then escorted me past agents' cubicles to a private corner office.

"Mercedes," Emilio said, arms extended. He grasped my hand with both of his, drew me in, and kissed both cheeks. "How wonderful to see you," he said. The scent on his collar and the ancient afternoons spent in the brothers' apartment rushed back.

"You look well." I let go of his grasp but didn't move, captivated—the encounter far more uncanny and valid than the fleeting image onscreen. So this was how Manuel might have appeared in his prime—the trim, filled-out physique and handsome face, a few strands of grey at the temples. The faint beginnings of crow's feet around the eyes.

"Please, sit down." Emilio resumed his seat. Behind him hung a giant map of Colombia with little red flags pinned to various locations, many to the east and south. "Gracia tells me you're working for Delta. That must be a wonderful way to see the world, I'd imagine."

"Yes, actually—I just got assigned this route." I said, sitting opposite. "Although I'm afraid I was still picturing you in a churchyard someplace." I smiled, hands folded in my lap. Told myself to breathe, play it cool.

He laughed, leaning back. "No, that ended for me long ago. I decided the year after Manuel's death, although I was having my doubts before then. Maybe those cold nights in the jungle, I don't know." He was smiling, one hand over the desk, turning a pen in somersaults. "Anyway, all that's behind us. Almost seems like another life, doesn't it?"

"There is another reason for my wanting to see you. Other than friendship."

"Oh?" He caught the pen, flicked it aside, and sat forward. "What's that? No trouble, I hope?"

I smiled back, smoothed my skirt. "Nothing like that. I'm wondering if you might be able to help fill in some missing pieces, about what exactly happened back then with the murder investigation. I remember certain things, of course, but I was so young, and it was such a terrible shock. I haven't thought about it for years, even coming back here, until just recently."

The smile fell from his face. "I've done my best to put it behind me too. But that loss is always there. Manuel, I always looked out for him, you know? My little brother." His eyes softened and met mine; he cleared his throat. "Next month it will be fifteen years. It seemed impossible he was gone. Still does."

"Yes. Everything changed after that, and I left so suddenly. I don't think I realized how fast."

"I did. It was quite a slap in the face. Although I probably needed to be slapped, I was so out of my mind." He gave me a small, knowing smile. "Anyway, all that's passed. Why haven't you come to see me until now?"

"Because I haven't been back."

"You haven't? What about your family?"

I shrugged. "I have no family here. Once I knew Papi was behind it, I made plans, very carefully, to leave. He didn't suspect at first—he thought I was away at a boarding school. Devious on my part, I admit. But no, I never spoke to him again."

Emilio idly tapped the pen against his palm. "Incredible," he said, staring off. "I had no idea."

"Nobody knew. I didn't tell anyone. Anyway, I keep thinking back to the day I met you at the cathedral, and you showed me the police file. How were you able to get it?"

He flung the pen onto the desk. "It's been so long, I don't know if I remember all the details," he said, and rubbed his temples. "I was questioned in the first twenty-four hours, not as a suspect, of course. But they asked if I knew of anyone specific who had it out for Manuel, or didn't like him. I named a few people, including your father, because Manuel mentioned all the time how Diego didn't like him. Before I left, I asked a detective I knew to please keep me informed on anything that turned up. So I went home, but all I kept thinking about was your father, how I just had a bad feeling about him. I called up the detective and told him I'd be really interested if anything turned up about Diego Martinez and my brother's murder. This was a detective I'd known from the government negotiations the Church was helping facilitate, so we had a rapport. He said sure, give him a day or two. Diego Martinez might be involved, after all, he said."

"You mentioned something over the phone," I said. "Remember? After the AUC had that broadcaster killed. Wasn't that when you said something about evidence?"

"Yes, but I didn't know anything, really. I wanted to get your attention, so you'd observe more closely what was going on at the hacienda—if something was indeed being covered up."

"Some priest you'd make."

He glared and appeared annoyed. "Anyway, the next time I called, the detective mentioned this file. He couldn't allow the original to go missing, so he'd photocopied the documents and swore me to secrecy—that it was just for my personal peace-of-mind, to know what had happened to my brother. He'd gotten to know us pretty well and considered it a favor. But he actually made me nervous, because he said if it ever was discovered that the file was leaked, I'd better watch out. So I thought long and hard about showing you, a sixteen-year-old girl. But I remember thinking, how could I not? She loved him too."

"There has only been one other person since, who has meant as much." My gaze dropped to my lap. "Thank you."

"That's pretty much it. You saw what was in the file. Your father paid off the police, the hit man walked away free. Manuel's murder goes unpunished." He rocked back, scratched behind his ear. "There's nothing more to tell."

I arose, strolled past him to the map. Red flags clustered the center and south, surrounding Cali. I said, "I'm not even sure if my father's still alive."

"Oh, he's alive. He doesn't leave his hacienda much, from what I've heard."

"Really? How do you know?"

"We keep track of who's around, the quiet ones too." He pressed his fingertips together. "At least I do."

"What if I went to see him? Maybe I could get him to confess the truth."

"Your father is far too smart a man to fall for that. Why don't you just forget it?"

"Because I can't." I paced. "I did, for a long time, but Gracia and I were talking the other night. Something doesn't add up. Maybe he won't admit anything, but maybe I could find out something that will settle it for me, in my own mind. Whoever he might be to you, he's my father." I paused over his desk, arms crossed. "And in other respects, a good one."

"Do you believe he's innocent?"

"I don't know. But isn't it worth finding out?"

"That file was all the proof I needed," Emilio said, pushing back his chair. "Do you really think he's going to welcome you back with open arms, after all this time?" He grunted and rose. "He would have faced a tough prison sentence if he hadn't helped bring down Escobar. You might not know it, but Diego got one hell of a sweet deal." We met in the middle of the room, inches apart. "If you're going to show up and confront him,

Mercedes, I'd be extremely cautious about how you do it." He touched my chin briefly, searching my face.

I stepped away. "Actually, I've just gotten back from Cali, and my father gave me a warm welcome. At least until I brought this up. So I have questions for you, and I want the truth."

The mask of charm fell from his face. He placed a hand on his hip and nodded, gestured toward my seat and sank into his. "My father didn't have anything to do with Manuel's murder," I said, standing behind the chair. With both hands I gripped its back. "He didn't even know of our elopement plans. So what is it you're not telling me?"

Emilio ran a hand through his hair, stuck his fist to his lips. A wedding band gleamed gold above his knuckles. His gaze darted but finally fixed on me. "I was hoping that wouldn't be the case," he said. "That there was a possibility he might have been aware of the arrangement, after all, been somehow complicit—"

"What are you talking about?"

He pressed his hands against his lips before he spoke, as if in prayer. "I admit that things got screwed up, Mercedes. I'm sorry I didn't tell you everything before, when you asked about the file. That was why I didn't want you to go see your father, but then I thought, well, maybe something new will come to light. I didn't know the full extent until years later, believe me."

On weak knees I lowered into the chair facing him. "What the hell are you talking about?"

"When I went to the police and asked about your father's possible connection to the case, I didn't realize what I was doing, how my request might be—misinterpreted. See, sometimes we had to give our police contacts payoffs if we wanted anything checked out. For La Maria Juventud, the negotiations, anything."

"You're kidding me," I said. "Manuel too?"

"No, not really Manuel. Mostly me. And I hated doing it, but when you become involved here you realize pretty quickly that this is how things work. If you don't play the game to a certain extent, you'll get nowhere. So once in a while, we bribed contacts for information. And I found out later that this detective treated my request about Manuel's killer the same way. Although I hadn't the faintest idea at the time." He looked up, pleading. "I swear."

I stared at him, stone-faced. "Go on."

He exhaled, lowered his hands. "When I shared the file with you linking your father to the murder, I believed it was entirely real. I had no idea this detective would have interpreted what I'd said as a request for false information, to link Diego Martinez to the case just to placate me, or get me off his back, who knows. But a few years after I joined the DAS, we busted a police ring charged with falsifying documents to make suspects appear guilty. I was heading the investigation, and when they brought the same detective in for questioning—you can imagine, I freaked out. I thought, that's it, my career's over. He admitted to falsifying the document, and I lost it. We were alone in the interrogation room. I told him that's not what I'd been asking for in my brother's case, for him to create a fake file. I hadn't paid him anything, either. But then I assured him I'd get his charges diminished, if not erased, if he kept quiet about the whole mess. And he did."

"You didn't pay him? You're sure about this?" I shook my head. "Why would he have done it then? Nobody fakes documents just to be nice."

"I don't know, Mercedes. I was a wreck after Manuel's death, out of my mind, but I'm positive I didn't pay him. No, it was a simple favor, a request. That's all, I'm sure of it." He ran a hand through his hair again, the thickness sticking out every which way.

"Anyway, nothing came of it, thank God. Although I did take the opportunity to ask him what had happened with the real suspect—they'd had the hit man in custody, remember, but something had spurred his release. So that's how I found out who was behind Manuel's murder. It was Carlos Castaño Gil who ordered the hit—in the actual police report, the suspect stated he was a subordinate in the AUC, one of the main assassins. Talk about real corruption. Because Castaño paid off the Cali police to release his hit man and close the case."

I sucked in my breath. "Where is he now?" I asked, recalling Papi's nostalgic remark. I hadn't studied Carlos Castaño Gil.

"Castaño's been dead for years. His brother worked to bring him down around 2004. This was 2007, when we busted the Cali department, so he was long gone by the time I knew the truth." He folded his hands, rested them on his knee. "I had no idea until today that you had cut off ties with Diego. I've been wondering if your father had known Castaño was behind the hit, after all—maybe Castaño had taken care of it for him, that sort of thing. But now I think we both can rest assured it was entirely Castaño's doing. The man was ruthless, a sociopath, and Manuel was far too much a threat to exposing the AUC atrocities. So Castaño had him followed, and that was it." Emilio sat back. "I'm sorry, Mercedes. But at least Castaño eventually paid the price."

We sat in silence except for the footsteps passing outside the door, the hum of printers and quiet office chatter. "But you didn't tell me this at first," I said slowly. "I came here and you lied, hoping my father still might have something to do with it." I was standing now, swaying, my voice shrill and melodramatic, but I didn't care. My life had ruptured, and the man who was partly to blame stared blankly at me with the eyes of my first lover; it was too much to bear. "Do you have any idea what it was like—fleeing this country behind my father's back, swearing never to speak to him again, believing he was a murderer? Then to finally have him welcome me home after all this time, only to leave with him shutting the door in my face?"

"I told you, I believed the file that detective gave me was real—"

"Why should I believe you? You have resources. You could have tracked me down in the U.S. when you found out about Castaño." I marched around the desk. He arose, our faces separated by inches, his cologne a too-strong musk. "But you didn't. Do you have any idea how this has affected my life, what it's cost me? You're just like all the other two-faced dogs down here."

His face and neck flushed red. "I told you, I knew nothing at first. How was I to guess you wouldn't speak to your father for the next decade? It might have helped if you hadn't completely deserted your friends, or told anyone what the hell was going on with you. But I guess I was too beneath you. I would never have measured up to Manuel, would I, Mercedes? Just good enough for a fuck."

I shoved him in the chest so that he stumbled awkwardly, taken off-guard, and I choked back a sob. He steadied himself and glared back at me, then grabbed the phone. The secretary answered via the speaker. "Señorita Martinez will need an escort out," he said, voice like steel. "Now, please."

He clapped down the receiver so hard it clattered. I stepped forward. "Why don't you just tell me, Emilio—how many files did you pay this Cali cop to invent, for your noble cause? Because we both know you didn't have any money. How much did you skim from the Church—a couple of hundred bucks? Did you really think you'd win me over, that I'd fall for you after Manuel? Then one day you'd get to be king of the hacienda, or what?"

He leaned over the desk on his wrists, jaw set, and stared straight ahead. The two security personnel appeared. I turned on my heel, my chin lifted. My cheeks were still burning as I pushed through the glass doors to the street.

A few hours later Gracia and I met at a cavernous costeno restaurant, probably opened by desplazados from the Chocó province. Such restaurants featuring Pacific fare were now popular in Bogotá, the tables packed. We ordered seafood, split a pitcher of borojó juice. Rustic paintings of beaches, fishing boats, and villagers adorned the walls. If only the sunny depictions were true. But in the years since the AUC had been forced to disband, neo-paras had arisen to replace them, and the desperation of the rural violence continued.

I had told her the entire twisted story and she listened wide-eyed. By the end, she was shaking her head. "So he lied about the bribes, to the very end," she said. "Unbelievable. I mean, Emilio was never the same after Manuel's death, but I didn't realize how he'd turned down this dark road because of it. I'd heard he ran into some trouble in his previous position—everyone did, just hoped it wasn't true, you know? So what do you think was really going on with La Maria Juventud? Manuel and Carlos, I wonder to what extent they knew—they were so young, it's possible their brother was just using them, too. I'm sure we'll never know."

I told her I wasn't sure, but it sounded like Emilio may have done the best he could as leader, until Manuel's death caused his unraveling. Gracia said she would have nothing to do with Emilio, after this, if he rang her up in Bogotá. "But I probably won't be here much longer," she said. "My father's getting worse every day. After all these years, my mother reconciled with him, moved back in—would you ever have imagined, after their big divorce? Me too, though. You probably don't remember, but I barely spoke to him during high school, I was so angry."

I stirred my juice, nodded. "I remember."

"Never in a million years did I think we'd be friends. But we're closer now in these last few months than we were our whole lives. He has no one else to take care of him. I'm heading down there in a few days. What about you? You must be reeling."

"I'm not sure," I said. I explained how I had requested the relocation to the embassy, and the approval and red tape had taken weeks; my boss would not look upon me favorably if I abandoned the assignment early, so soon after rehiring me that spring. I had a small cushion: the inheritance from my grandparents. "I know I shouldn't touch that," I said. "But I feel so shaken up, and—restless."

"Maybe you should travel," she said. "Sort things out. I would, if I had the means. It's always nice to come home, but after a while, I can't wait to get out of here." She winced and sipped her drink. "I feel so bad admitting that, but it's true. Just don't disappear on me this time."

"Pretty impossible after this, don't you think? Although I'm sorry it happened in the first place."

She shrugged it off. "We're in touch now. That's what's important."

"Do you ever wish you had stayed with Esteban? What do you think would have happened?"

"Oh, I'd be touring with him and some little company. Maybe we'd still be in love. But I would have been half-fulfilled with dance, I'm sure. Like I am now. You know the standards in the developing world—not up to par, from the American viewpoint. So fewer opportunities."

"You wouldn't have known what you were missing, though," I pointed out.

"No. But that would have been the real tragedy, wouldn't it?" She laughed. "Now I'm so worldly, I'm a snob. Oh, well. Maybe in light of things, we should be grateful that we were destined for other places."

"I didn't think about Manuel for so long," I said, fingering my napkin. "I've been dreaming about him lately. What do you think that means?"

"It means you really loved him."

"But I wonder if we would have stayed together if he hadn't died," I said. "Because I think I was starting to have a change of heart, about my future—or maybe I was just scared to death. I don't know."

"You would have stayed with him," she said. "Isn't that strange? In a way he had to die, for you to have the life you have now. You know?"

When I entered my apartment, the late afternoon shadows stretching across the floor, I peeled the photo of Manuel and me from the dresser mirror. I tucked the print in a journal, newly bought but blank. Then lifted my embassy badge from where I'd left it, in my jewelry box, empty. True to my flight attendant guise, I'd worn the earrings to see Emilio. But did my job really have nothing to do with my father, as I'd claimed? My mind swept back over the years to college, the conflict I'd felt when the time came to schedule courses for the next semester, how I'd cast aside my newfound interest in writing and literature in favor of Latin American studies and International Relations, trumped by a nagging pull to right the wrongs I was convinced Diego Martinez perpetuated. Wouldn't that have been what Manuel wanted?

How easily I had forgotten that what Manuel had wanted was a devoted wife—not for me to obtain an education.

Might I have had another calling entirely? Journeyed to a less familiar continent for my Fulbright, explored some other topic or field? Probably I would have never landed at the State Department. I would have chosen different lovers, and not endured three failed romances in my twenties, the last of which left me nearly as bereft as Manuel's loss. Or perhaps my youth spent in Cali would have sparked me to seek that path nonetheless. But if I'd had my father to consult with, and we had begun to be friends, I might have salvaged the relationship with Jeremy that made Bogotá a ready escape from the life he and I had shared in D.C. Perhaps things would have worked out had he and I not constantly fallen into arguments about how difficult I could be—distrustful of intimacy and secretive about my Colombian family. Not all of my choices, but certainly the ones that mattered the most, would have been very different had I not believed my father responsible for Manuel's murder, had I been open to giving him a second chance. Had I only been able and willing to see the world in shades of grey, rather than black and white.

I called my boss in D.C., told her I had some information about a corrupt investigator currently working for Colombian national intelligence. "We'll pass this along to our contacts there right away," she said. "That this had to do with your own past—that's just incredible. He should lose his job in the very least," she added. "The new Colombian intelligence doesn't mess around. And if he's gotten a pass before, managed to not get the axe when they cleaned house at the DAS, then he's a real snake. Excellent work." A pang struck me, hearing this, unable to shake the image of Emilio's chiseled face stiffening with shock as the Colombian agents swept into his office, stripped him of his laptop and badge and steered him out to the sidewalk. At least he'd never work in law enforcement again.

I had wanted to obtain an extended leave of absence. But my boss insisted that whether I chose to stay in Bogotá or return stateside, such a leave would be impossible; our research and reports were vital to counter-narcotics efforts, and she could not hold my position. So I quit. I didn't know whether or not I might pursue a government career again, once I regrouped; maybe I'd give journalism another try. But I could no longer remain in Bogotá; I needed to piece together my life, and who I really was. I made arrangements with my mother to occupy my grandparents' house in Florida, which had been on the market for months. I must have sounded rattled over Skype; my mother asked if I was all right. When I told her I wasn't, not really, she suggested I start a journal to sort out my story first, in the privacy of paper. It was something she'd encouraged me to do for years, after I shared some poems I'd written in Argentina.

"Will he ever want to see me again, after this?" I asked.

"I understand you're anxious about it, Mercedes. But you're just going to have to give it time, you know? Maybe try calling him in a few days, let him know you care. That you're not just going to disappear again. He may come around." She rubbed her arms, her eyes bright and steady on the screen. "The big question for you is, what do you do now?"

I saw again the door in my face, Papi's glare as he brought the glass to his lips, then turned away. "I'm going to make one more trip down to Cali before I head back," I said. "Gracia's going in a few days, I can stay with her. Maybe he'll see me."

"Maybe," she said. She tilted her head, squinted at the camera. "Are those pearls the ones your father gave you?"

"Yes. I always wondered if they belonged to you—maybe a wedding gift."

"Yes," she said. "When I left I wanted you to have something of us. I made him promise not to give them to you until you were old enough to appreciate them." She dropped her gaze. "Maybe after this you can understand better why I couldn't stay there, that I hadn't been capable of understanding the enormity of my choice in marrying him, and quitting school. But that's youth, isn't it?" The faintest smile played across her lips. "Leaving that marriage was the first real step I took toward adulthood—reclaiming myself. I knew despite his dealings, Diego would be a good father." She paused. "So lovely still, those earrings. And much prettier on you than if they were shut away in a box." She placed her hand over her mouth and her wedding band flashed, tarnished but luminous.

"What was your gift to him?" I asked.

"Oh, I doubt he has that anymore," she said. "I could barely afford anything, and I was so embarrassed when I gave it to him."

"What was it?"

"I'm embarrassed to even tell you," she said, shaking her head. "But it was a set of purple paisley handkerchiefs." She laughed. "I bought them at a cowboy store at Cali's downtown market, the day after we arrived. Your father was buying something at another stall, and I wandered into this store with leather boots and belts. I had only a little Colombian money, I couldn't even afford a belt—imagine! But I saw these handkerchiefs, so that's what I bought. Then your father found me and I pretended being interested in this ugly leather coat. Well, perhaps not ugly, but caballero gear was never my style." She raised her eyebrows at me knowingly, her earrings swaying against her neck. "By the time we left the shop he had bought me the coat."

"He wore a purple bandanna every day in the fields," I said. "Ever since I can remember."

Her smile faded. "You're kidding."

"He almost never left the house without one."

"Your father taught me how to dance the cumbia," she said looking off into the distance. "Do you know it?"

I nodded, picturing Gracia long ago at the Mirador, the valley and stars behind her. "I wasn't very good at it," she said. "Your father was. But that was why I picked out the handkerchiefs, I guess. You know in the cumbia, how the men—"

"I know. Please, can we not talk about this anymore?"

She pressed me on what I might do next. Would I search for a stateside job, something in the private sector, or another government position? Might I teach at a university, after all? With book publications I would make a competitive candidate. I had no idea, I told her, just hoped the rest of the trip might clear my head. But I kept thinking of Papi with his white horses and loyal men, heard the yearning in his voice when he'd inquired about my mother, if she had ever asked about him, and my response—a lie.

As I packed, I wept.

When the Avianca flight landed in Cali a few days later, I didn't call my father. Gracia's mother picked us up and we got settled in her apartment, yet not even then did I call. Alone, I took a cab downtown, asked the driver to drop me off at the Catedral de San Pedro. Down the avenue the stinking traffic honked. A wedding party descended the gleaming white steps, flocked by a dozen or so well-wishers, the bride in a short dress, the groom a suit, thick-waisted—an older couple. In one of the plaza's grassy triangles a teenage girl posed, the statue of Cayzedo, erect and mid-stride, behind her, the satin of her quinceañera gown glimmering a lustrous emerald; the photographer leaped up to sweep a loose strand of hair from her glossy face and she blinked, hard and fast, in the sun. Where the Juan Valdez impersonator had once stood a young man fervently strummed a guitar; a young woman, head wrapped in a bright scarf, sang along. A trio of backpackers, frumpy and sunburnt, had stopped in front of them; one stood filming on her phone for a few moments before plodding away—they were speaking German or perhaps Swiss; I couldn't tell.

Sugar and bubbling oil wafted from a vendor's cart. I joined the line. Gangly school girls tugged knee-length skirts, the boys jostling into them, laughing, their mouths open and crooked. Olbeas, I had never much liked, the thin wafers topped with dulce de leche too sweet for me. But I found what I wanted and ordered, gratefully took the paper and fork, carried it over to a bench. Grease scorched my fingers through the wax. I knew how it would taste before I bit into it, the corncake salty and sweet, arepa cooling in my lap. I dug in my purse, shoved aside my phone. I would call my father, but not yet. The photo was gone, slipped away. I grasped the journal, the cover grainy and pages sleek, and began to write.

ACKNOWLEDGMENTS

I would like to express my gratitude to the following: Vermont College of Fine Arts, where this novel began, and my teachers there, Douglas Glover, Xu Xi, Robin Hemley, and Domenic Stansberry. To the Corporation of Yaddo, the Ragdale Foundation, the Virginia Center for the Creative Arts, and the Writers' Colony at Dairy Hollow for their invaluable gift of time and space. To Mary Jane Arner and Tony Broy, for hosting me at their lovely homes at different stages in the drafting process. To early readers Lauren O'Regan and Robert Eversz, whose feedback I returned to again and again. To Sanford J. Greenburger Associates and my agent, Matthew Bialer, for his enthusiastic belief in the project from day one, and his assistant, Lindsay Ribar. To the team at Curbside Splendor Publishing, especially Victor David Giron, Naomi Huffman, Gretchen Kalwinski, Jacob Knabb, Catherine Eves, and Alban Fischer, for their vision, commitment, and editorial expertise. To Philip F. Deaver, Susan Lilley, and the late Jeanne Leiby, for their friendship and guidance. To my parents, as always, for their generous and steadfast support. And lastly, to Boris Fishman, whose keen insight at the witching hour opened my eyes as to how to make this a more fully realized work.

This is a work of fiction brought alive by the juncture of research and imagination. I am indebted to the following texts: *Revolutionary Social Change in Colombia: The Origin and Direction of the FARC-EP*, by James J. Brittain;

Blood and Capital: the Paramilitarization of Colombia, by Jasmin Hristov; *Beyond Bogotá: Diary of a Drug War Journalist in Colombia*, by Garry Leech; *Bandits, Peasants, and Politics: The Case of "La Violencia" in Colombia*, by Gonzalo Sánchez and Donny Meertens; *The Dispossessed: Chronicles of the Desterrados of Colombia* by Alfredo Molano, and *America's Other War: Terrorizing Colombia*, by Doug Stokes.

VANESSA BLAKESLEE's debut short story collection, *Train Shots*, is the winner of the 2014 IPPY Gold Medal in Short Fiction and long-listed for the 2014 Frank O'Connor International Short Story Award. Vanessa's writing has appeared in *The Southern Review*, *Green Mountains Review*, *Paris Review Daily*, *The Globe and Mail*, *Kenyon Review Online*, and *Bustle* among many others. Finalist for the 2014 Sherwood Anderson Foundation Fiction Award, she has also been awarded grants and residencies from Yaddo, the Virginia Center for the Creative Arts, The Banff Centre, Ledig House, the Ragdale Foundation, and in 2013 received the Individual Artist Fellowship in Literature from the Florida Division of Cultural Affairs. Born and raised in northeastern Pennsylvania, she is a longtime resident of Maitland, Florida.